Praise fo

"A perfectly paced, compulsive Cold War thriller."

— Alan Bardos, author of *The Assassins*

"A gripping slow-burn of a story about a community of immigrants with a shared ancestry of persecution in Eastern Europe . . . Kalns takes the reader on a heart-pounding ride that teaches us dark truths. In these times, especially, this book feels essential."

— Kate Evans, author of *Call It Wonder* and co-author of *Revolutionary Kiss*

"A spellbinding tale of murder and dark intrigue . . ."

— The Prairies Book Review

"Sure to enthrall spy novel lovers, East European culture mavens, and students of the Cold War alike."

— Wolf Bahren, author of *Source of Deceit* and *Agents of Suzharia*

"A beautifully written historical novel with a perplexing mystery and startling discovery. A must-read for all those who enjoy reading through the past."

— The Independent Book Review

FriesenPress

One Printers Way
Altona, MB R0G 0B0
Canada

www.friesenpress.com

Copyright © 2023 by Matejs Kalns
First Edition — 2023

BALTIC SHADOWS is a work of fiction. All incidents and dialogue
and all characters found within are products of the author's
imagination and are not to be construed as real. Any resemblance to
any persons living or dead is entirely coincidental. Where real-life
historical or public figures appear, the situations, incidents, and
dialogues are not intended to change the entirely fictional nature of
the work.

Cover design by: Estratosphera Designs
Map design by: Brian Oliveira
Author photograph: Austin VanDeVen

ISBN
978-1-03-915810-8 (Hardcover)
978-1-03-915809-2 (Paperback)
978-1-03-915811-5 (eBook)

1. Fiction, Mystery & Detective, International Mystery & Crime

Distributed to the trade by The Ingram Book Company

Also by Matejs Kalns:

Beasts of the Night

Baltic Shadows

A NOVEL

Matejs Kalns

For Alfons

Leningrad

S.R.

Pskov

N S.S.R.

Daugava

R.

UNION OF SOVIET
SOCIALIST REPUBLICS
(U.S.S.R.)

Volga

Moscow ◉

Smolensk

Minsk
◉

BYELORUSSIAN S.S.R.

Chernobyl

UKRAINIAN S.S.R.

During the Second World War, Europe was set alight. Empires warred across the continent, while smaller nations struggled to assert their independence, often proclaiming their neutrality in vain.

In June of 1940, the Soviet Union annexed the Baltic States of Estonia, Latvia and Lithuania, and unleashed a campaign of terror across their newly acquired colonies. In Latvia, this brutality culminated on the night of June 13th-14th, 1941, whereby 34,000 men, women and children were deported to labour camps in Siberia.

A week later, Nazi Germany invaded the Soviet Union, and Latvian sovereignty changed hands once again. Swastikas flew high above the capital city of Rīga, fascism reigned supreme, and the local Jewish population suffered immeasurably at the hands of a new racial ideology, tens of thousands perishing in the country's forests, prison camps, and ghettos.

In the autumn of 1944, with Hitler's war all but lost, Red Army forces pushed west into the Baltic States once more. Many Latvians knew all too well what fate awaited them at the hands of the NKVD—the Soviet secret police—and fled westward toward the Baltic Sea. It is estimated that two hundred thousand found refuge in the displaced persons camps of Europe, many eventually settling abroad as new immigrants in the United States, Australia, and Canada.

Vibrant communities flourished in exile, rich in culture and tradition. Succeeding generations were steeped in the belief that once Latvia was liberated from Communist rule, they would return to their ancestral homeland, and begin their lives anew. And while across the ocean Eastern Europe fell into darkness, few would have predicted that Latvia would remain occupied for nearly half a century.

BALTIC SHADOWS

PROLOGUE

IN A DIMLY LIT JAZZ LOUNGE, DRIFTS OF BLUE SMOKE CLUNG TO the ceiling, and bottles glimmered faintly behind a long, oaken bar. On stage, a chanteuse in black velvet sung a soulful melody whilst clutching a steel-grille microphone, accompanied by a single piano helmed by a mustachioed gentleman with a most delicate touch on the keys.

A sparse crowd, on such an evening—midweek, and a late hour. A smattering of applause rattled around the room as the duo concluded their latest number with nods of thanks to a grateful, if dwindling audience.

And at the far end of the bar, located conveniently close to the service entrance, stood a couple engaged in a rather strained conversation, should anyone have bothered to take notice.

"I'm only saying," said the man, pausing to light his partner's cigarette, "that there is talk. I have ears, don't I?"

The woman did not speak.

"There are rumblings, in certain circles, that operations such as yours are no longer . . . let us say, *viable*. That such approaches are outdated. They take too long to bear fruit."

The man paused for a moment, awaiting a reaction, and finding none.

"You know very well how the tide is shifting in Moscow, the new way of thinking. The mood is turbulent of late, and patience is waning. On the one hand, there are those who wish to see results, immediate results. They have no time for subtlety. And yet, others believe that such tradecraft is redundant, even misguided. The emphasis on everything military now, of course, with satellites, micro-cameras, all sorts of modern gadgetry . . ."

The woman remained silent, a bit of theatre as she studied the crimson smudge of lipstick on the butt of her cigarette.

"Come now, I'm not here as a representative."

"Aren't you?" she replied.

"I thought you would care to know. That you'd be interested in which way the wind blows these days."

The bartender slid a martini glass across the bar top, the vodka crystalline with three olives punctured by a toothpick.

"Indulge me, if you will"—the man propped an elbow against the bar rail—"how are things progressing?"

"Exactly as intended, so long as no one interferes."

"It is not *we* who mean to interfere . . ."

The woman scoffed. "You give the Latvians too much credit."

"Perhaps you don't give them enough. There are two sides to every ruble. Who's to say they don't have their own fox in our henhouse?"

"They know nothing," she said curtly. "They are paranoid, most certainly, a fear of everything Russian, but that is all."

"Not everyone back home sees it that way."

"Nor are they *meant* to see. Perhaps they need reminding that it is my job to operate in the darkness."

The man smiled thinly at the remark. "I'm only saying, you've been here for some time now. People can become . . . complacent."

The woman turned her head, dismissive, and took a drag of her cigarette. Above the service door, the 'exit' sign cast a pale red glow upon her cheek.

"It's only natural," he continued. "Once in a while, it's good to remind ourselves that we're not the only ones playing at this game. It keeps us sharp." The man sighed, his expression softening. "I've known you since you were a little girl, Galina. I'm only looking out for you."

"And the company you keep, they believe I need looking out for?"

"As I said, the Directorate only believes in results."

"Do you know what I believe?"

"Mm . . ."

"I believe that old men who eat caviar and weekend on the Crimea would do well to remember their place."

The man grinned.

"The seats of power have made them soft. At times it seems they've forgotten that the war is not over, that there are those of us who remain in the trenches, sacrificing our sweat and blood for the cause."

"A matter of perspective, I suppose."

She pulled gently on her cigarette, allowing the smoke tendrils to drift from her nostrils. "Still, if it's a demonstration they're after, the timing is . . . favourable."

"You have something planned?"

She glared at him, dismissing the question, then tapped her cigarette above an ashtray. "Moscow," she sighed, "they bicker like old widows, don't you find?"

The man grinned once more.

"Patience is a virtue, comrade," she said.

"Not in Moscow."

"Well I suppose it's a good thing I'm not in Moscow, isn't it? Perhaps when you return you can remind them of the fact." She reached for her drink, sliding an olive from the toothpick with her front teeth.

"We fly out tomorrow morning. Tread carefully, Galina. Our families go back a long way, and I can't help but feel I owe it to them to watch over you. Much as I am able . . ."

Tilting her head with indifference, she sipped her martini, then pushed it back across the bar. "Tell them to leave me to my work." And with that, she ground her cigarette into the ashtray, pushed open the back door, and slipped away into the night air.

I.

AUTUMN
1986

ONE

Toronto, Canada

IT WAS ONE OF LIFE'S MANY GREAT IRONIES THAT LATVIA, A NATION whose history consisted almost invariably of serfdom and subjugation, should boast of women with such a flare for corporal punishment. For there was not a boy, or man, whose backside hadn't felt the keen sting of feminal discipline when good manners went unheeded, or when flippant tongues wagged a little too freely. Sisters, wives, mothers, and grandmothers—*vecmāmiņas*, in the native vernacular—were crossed at one's own peril, the homestead ruled by a firm hand and, if need be, by all manner of household utensil.

A slipper. A cane. In the summertime, *žagari*—thin bundles of green branches that whistled frightfully through the air. Winter brush was far too brittle, and therefore of little use. A spatula. A broom. Heaven help you if you deserved the belt.

And yet there was always as much love and tenderness as there was regimen—the hidings were *never* without cause—as the women served effectively as vanguards of the culture, ensuring the continuity of tradition for a nation that had always struggled on the greater diplomatic stage. On the shores of the Baltic Sea, a humble state of only two million, forever caught in the crossroads of empires that waged war along the bloodlands of Eastern Europe. An unfortunate victim of geography, an unwilling subject to the whims of foreign capitals with colonial agendas.

Hitler and Stalin had once signed a secret pact that carved up Europe like a black forest cake, sealing the tragic fate of millions prior to the outbreak of war. And while the negotiations took place in Moscow, had someone dispatched a *vecmāmiņa* with a rolling pin, the history of Europe might have turned out rather different.

And so it came to pass that on a frosty evening in late autumn, Gustavs Ziediņš himself suffered a familiar fate at the hands of a wooden spoon. The reprimand was swift and delivered with precision: a blur of wood carving the air, the hollow rap across his knuckles, then the frantic waving of fingers to dull the imminent sting.

"Those are for the guests!" scolded the women in unison—the spoon already returned to the pot, engulfed in steam.

It had been a foolish attempt. Even in his youth, Gustavs had never been quite fast enough, and now, in his forty-first year, age certainly hadn't improved his agility. In keeping with tradition, he paid the price for his poor sleight of hand, a punishment meted out since ancient times to every boy—and man—to have ever wandered into a kitchen feeling a tad peckish.

Yet how could he resist? The aroma alone was practically entrapment. Freshly baked *pīrāgi* bursting at the seams, stuffed with smoky bacon, savoury onion, a hint of warm pepper and mustard seed—a crust of golden brown, still warm from the oven. Food for the gods.

"Out, out!" said Omīte.

"Out with you!" echoed Irina.

"Alright, I'm going, I'm—wait. Here, this one's smiling at me."

A clever tactic. A smiling *pīrāgs*—a bun which had split in the oven—was, of course, fair game. Such a blemish could never be presented to the guests; reputations were at stake, after all. The faintly singed, the slightly misshapen, the abominations mashed together by a niece or nephew who had "helped" with preparations, all promising candidates for sampling as—

"None of them are smiling! And keep your grubby fingers to yourself," Omīte replied. This time another spoon whipped against his pants, an audible smack as it connected firmly with his buttock—the strike of a marksman. The wooden spoon, longish and thick, was the weapon of choice for most grandmothers. Both a sword and shield to defend the realm, a tradition passed down over time, used as often to sauté cabbage and stir fragrant *zupas* as it was to hasten wandering hands into swift retreat.

"And take this platter," said Irina, thrusting forth a silver tray stacked with open-faced sandwiches, "you can have some afterwards if there's any—*ej!* Are you listening? Afterwards. Take these as well," she added, planting a stack of serviettes in his free hand. "Now shoo, listen to your grandmother."

Suitably chastised, Gustavs, having been assigned the role of head-waiter *and* maître d' for the evening, set out to make another tour of the house, latecomers still arriving by the back door in droves.

It was a lavish affair with everyone dressed in their very finest. The mesdames arrived with fur coats and fresh perms amidst veritable waves of saccharine perfume, accompanied as always by their gentlemen—suit jackets and mustaches, clouds of musty smoke mingling with the ever present *Brut*. While cars lined the twilit street outside, dusted by the light snowfall of a late autumn flurry, inside the atmosphere was warm and convivial, a celebration of life. Or, rather—three lives.

It had been well over thirty-five years since the women, each with little more than a single, battered valise, boarded the steamship *Aquitania* bound for Halifax. Closer to forty-five years since the week they'd first met: makeshift teachers in makeshift classrooms, residents all of the displaced persons camp in Lübeck, on the eastern border of British occupied Germany. But as of Wednesday, only three nights prior, the last of them had finally joined the others in passing that momentous milestone—entering, with grace and humility, their 80th year.

Among the matriarchs was Mrs. Mārtinsone, the renowned pianist, who in her day had struck fear into many a young person who had sat, invariably against their will, before her ancient Bösendorfer to practice their scales. Gustavs had long forgotten her first name, though never the tawny wooden ruler that served as her preferred instrument of critique.

Then there was Ms. Rudzīte, another first name long forgotten, though much better known to the community, rather affectionately, as *Lapsene*—Wasp.

The moniker stemmed from an incident long ago in Rīga whereby a young Dutch seaman had allegedly gotten a little handsy with the teenaged Ms. Rudzīte. When he refused to take no for an answer, dispatching with any pretense of civility, the young sailor was met with such an exacting slap across the face which, according to legend, spun his cap halfway around his head. As he fled the tavern, all sniffles and wounded pride, someone noted that the red welt on his cheek resembled a bee sting. Perhaps, even the bite of a hornet. And so the following day, and for sixty-one years thereafter, well—*Lapsene.*

And finally, Rasma Laiveniece, or simply Omīte, which is how Gustavs chose to refer to his great-aunt. It had been nearly three years since she had moved in with him, and while it was mutually agreed that the soirée was rather unnecessary, (Omīte despised being the center of attention), it *would* be rather nice to see old friends again and have all the little grandchildren whirring about like bumblebees. After all, the house had been quiet for far too long.

In the living room smoke hovered in the air, the antique décor enhanced by arrangements of roses and carnations, dahlias and cala lilies, sprouting forth from crystal vases, mason jars and, when they had completely run out of containers, two soda bottles and a milk carton. Naturally, it would have been unthinkable to attend a celebration without an exquisite bouquet. The atmosphere was jubilant, a vibrant hum that dipped and swelled throughout the room. Now and again a rogue guffaw rumbled over the crowd; a high-pitched cackle accompanied the clutching of pearls. Somewhere lost among the merriment, a symphony played on the radio.

Gustavs weaved his way through friends and familiar faces, while the *maizītes*—open faced sandwiches of smoked salmon, dill, and a thin slice of lemon—were eagerly plucked from the tray, serviettes a mere formality.

Further on, down in the basement, brewed a different mood from the main floor. Mostly men beneath the low ceiling, huddled, drinking scotch and tending bar, the talk of politics in hushed tones accompanied by a healthy dose of churlish humor safely hidden from the wives and well-mannered crowd upstairs.

Behind the bar, Paulis Zutis—an old classmate from Latvian school—diligently mashed sugar cubes and bitters with a wooden muddler. Already several sheets to the wind—judging by the sheen on his brow and the flush in his cheeks—he was nearing the punchline of some joke about a warthog and a farmer's daughter. His inner circle erupted in laughter—*and then the hairy snout!*— the *maizītes* were devoured, and they all drank a celebratory shot of some very old cognac because, well, Paulis was pouring.

Around the corner, the artists and the athletes. Eriks and Līze, the volleyball enthusiasts, fit and reserved and always with an anecdote about *that* tournament with the Lithuanians, they were sat across from Aija the jeweler and Viktors the oil painter. An intimate little affair by the wood burning stove, the foursome's reposeful manner suiting Gustavs just fine as his platter had been picked right down to the doily.

Taking the long way back to the kitchen, he passed by the downstairs guestroom, occupied by children of all ages watching an animated version of Robin Hood on the old console television. Seated front and center on the carpeted floor, he spotted one of his fellow waiters: Kārlis, aged nine, with his own personal platter of *maizītes*—German salami with a pickle garnish. When he saw Gustavs in the doorway he tucked his head and gave a bashful little smile, a twinkle of mischief in his eyes.

From the back door a gust of wind brought a drift of snowflakes into the foyer, the latest guests shuddering and stomping their boots in the threshold.

"Oh my, are we late? I'm sorry, so sorry, the traffic, my goodness—"

"Let me in already," grumbled the man. "God, this weather, it's as if we never left that damned mountain . . ."

"The roads were fine, a sprinkle, nothing more, and then suddenly caught in a snow globe—Gustav! How are you my dear, you look wonderful!"

Dagnija Barons, bundled in rabbit fur and a white woolen shawl, kissed him on either cheek, her skin cool to the touch. Shedding her coat, she revealed a fitted crimson dress—snug and suggestive—with silver bangles and a matching necklace. Somewhere in her late forties, full figured and butter blonde, she was especially fond of Gustavs—or perhaps not, he never could quite tell. She was both coquettish and bourgeois, at times a rather unnerving combination, not that Mr. Barons ever seemed to mind.

Imants Barons, dishevelled yet distinguished, silver hair and matching beard, had for many years chaired the Latvian National Federation of Canada, the LNAK, a position of no minor importance which commanded a considerable amount of gravitas within the community. A non-profit organization committed to the preservation of Latvian culture and the reestablishment of an independent Latvia, it worked in tandem with other Baltic liberation movements, at times with impressive global reach. Providing assistance to new immigrants, establishing ties with the dissident underground abroad, writing and courting and relentlessly harrying politicians to support their noble cause; the LNAK had no shortage of ambitious goals.

While of no actual relation to his namesake, the famed folklorist Krišjānis Barons, Imants had been known to insinuate otherwise after a few brandies, styling himself much in the same fashion—recently growing out his beard and sporting some new wire-rimmed spectacles. Barons had come under some scrutiny of late for his increasingly lavish lifestyle which, some were rumored to say, was a by-product of his partner's rather expensive tastes— their most recent jaunt to France only the latest example.

"Magical, just magical!" Dagnija gushed, regaling those nearby with tales of the anniversary ski trip to Savoy: the *pistes*, the sights, the charming towns of Courchevel, and my goodness, the pastries! Imants, being nearly twenty years her senior, was more partial to the comforts of the *après-ski*—namely hot tubs and gin—yet it was a trip to remember, with candlelight dinners and culinary delights each and every day.

"I, for one, am glad to be back," Imants said, receiving a playful smack on his shoulder. "The comforts of home, you know. And of course, one can only tolerate the French for so long . . . "

"Come now, Imant, don't be such a brute."

"Rasmiņa! There you are, *daudz laimes!* Your forty-fifth, was it?"

Eventually, with much prompting and prodding, the guests were herded into the living room for the requisite toast. Champagne flutes in hand, they sat anywhere there was space—on armrests, on handrails, children cozily settled in mama's lap. Gustavs stood amongst the gentlemen in the back, and at one point spotted young Kārlis, his furlough apparently cut short. With pouty lips and sunken shoulders, he slowly circled the room with a tray of champagne glasses, dragging his feet in a principled act of defiance.

The ladies of the hour were seated on a small divan, encircled by the crowd and Paulis, now well and truly lubricated, gave a sentimental and surprisingly heartfelt speech. Everyone raised their glasses to the triumvirate and followed with, as tradition dictated, a rousing rendition of *Daudz Baltu Dieniņu,* a few members of the old guard piping up toward the end with obscure verses—lyrics evidently known only to themselves—with the song eventually tapering off into murmurs and laughter, and concluding with enthusiastic cheers and applause.

The dinner spread that followed was of typical Latvian fare, rich and hearty and utterly carnivorous, mounded dishes artfully arranged across the dining table and buffet. Salmon of every inclination—hot smoked, cold smoked, citrus cured with capers, shallow poached with shredded egg. Sweet herring in vinegar, salted herring in cream, minced pork *kotletes* with wild mushroom gravy, sheets of succulent ham with a devilish mustard. There was rustic potato salad with carrots and dill, savory beet *rasols* with apple and veal, baskets of sourdough and rye bread, and the customary mound of golden *pīrāgi*.

Afterwards, in the parlor, as coffee and tea were served, Gustavs set about assembling a projection screen and loading some dusty slides into the carousel tray. The guests were treated to yet another banquet of delights: a freshly laid table of rhubarb squares, apple bread and, in the center, the obligatory *klingeris*: a braided sweet bread with dried fruits and saffron.

Dessert plates in hand, the lights were dimmed and the crowd chose their vantage points for the slideshow, Gustavs working the corded remote. A beam of light illuminated dust motes suspended in the air, and then—a flash. Germany. 1947. The guests of honor, a lifetime ago, standing before a pitched-roof barracks in Lübeck.

The carousel turned, clicked and flashed once more. Tuxedos and ball gowns at the Royal York Hotel. *What year was that?* someone whispered from the back.

Flash. The song and dance festival, Mrs. Rudzīte in mid-polka.

Flash. Mrs. Mārtinsone, elegant as always, at a concert recital, utterly engaged before a mirror-polished Steinway.

Flash. A wedding—*now who was that again?*—while off center, Mrs. Laiveniece, the bridesmaid with a glowing smile, a flowing dress and a playful wink for the camera.

As the hour grew late, Gustavs found himself by the bar with the waning basement crowd. Only a handful still remained, Viktors just then being reluctantly dragged away by his wife, and Imants having excused himself for some fresh air. Paulis continued to hold court, an arm around someone's nephew, breathing whisky-soaked advice to the grinning teenage boy. Ever the entertainer, the more Paulis drank, the more he reveled in the spotlight.

"Right, now see here—there's a Latvian rifleman, an honorable *strēlnieks* and he's hunkered down in a foxhole. The poor boy's been separated from his battalion and finds himself in quite the predicament. What to do? Should he leave, in hopes of rejoining his fellow combatants? Should he stay, holding position?" Paulis sighed, a dramatic shake of the head, "What to do, what to do . . .

"Just then—footsteps. No, boot steps! Moving at speed, advancing on his position! He pokes his head up and looks West, and there he is—the German. Sprinting at full speed, a maniacal look in his eyes, shouting all sorts of nonsense about *lebensraum* and sauerkraut and the Kaiser's grand mustache."

The boy giggled with anticipation and took a swig of his beer. Gustavs wondered if his mother knew he was hiding down here with these ne'er-do-wells.

"But then, from behind, oh god—what's that? The sound, too familiar . . . an advance from the East! The rifleman spins around only to see a Red Army soldier in full gallop toward him, a hateful snarl on his face. 'Down with the capitalists! Workers unite! Lenin promises free borscht for all!' he shouts.

"Mm, well, quite the quagmire for our young hero. The German bearing down on him to his left, the Russian in full sprint to his right. The rifleman picks up his weapon, works the bolt action, wipes the sweat from his brow. He takes a deep breath, sets himself, and takes aim . . . but who does he shoot first?"

The men fell silent. The boy shrugged. Paulis casually rattled the ice in his glass and downed the rest of his drink. Then, taking the boy by the shoulders, they locked eyes. "The German of course," Paulis said with a wry smile. "Business before pleasure."

Excusing himself to the restroom, Gustavs could still hear the chuckles fading behind him, the young man being treated to a lifetime of "wisdom" and questionable insights, the tutelage of the besotted an inevitability at this time of night. Rinsing his hands, he caught a glimpse of himself in the mirror, his gaze lingering. Steady on his feet, with a warm and welcome glow from the Courvoisier, he paused to take inventory.

Tired, but then, it had been a long day. Well, not that long. *Getting older then*, he thought to himself, turning his chin. Women, they said, had a preference for the tall, dark and handsome, and he considered this for a time. He'd never been tall, not really, a shade under six feet but an acceptable height; a height that never interfered with a woman's choice of footwear. A thick head of hair, dark locks that sprouted wildly and tumbled across his forehead, just a whisper of grey here and there if one were to squint. Dark brows, a touch of stubble. So, dark? Somewhat tall, somewhat dark.

He removed his black rimmed glasses, thick rectangles, placing them on the countertop. Tired eyes, but their colour had never changed. A tranquil shade of light blue, "like the shallow waters off the coast of Hvar," as he'd once been told. He couldn't recall her name, wasn't entirely sure he'd ever known it, but learned that Hvar was a small resort town somewhere in southern Yugoslavia, a dreamy little place of golden sun and crystal sea. The less he said the better that night, so many years ago. She seemed to gaze right through him to a different time—a different time, with a different man.

Not so bad, all in all. Certainly not at this age. Always the quiet type in school—the bookworm, the academic—and now, in a rather unexpected sort of way, at an age where—

A scream. Then, silence throughout the house.

Was that . . .

Another. Longer, undeniable this time, a visceral sound that pierced the air and made him gasp for breath. Gustavs snatched his glasses and shot out of the bathroom. Down the hall, trailing behind a patter of quickening footsteps and anxious voices.

The back door was already open as he trotted uncertainly toward it, dark silhouettes gathered in a huddle outside. It took him a moment to realize that he was standing in the snow with his socks, such was the commotion, the pain in the cries that split the night air. A woman lay crumpled on the ground, trembling, two men on either side appeared to be consoling her. Later he realized they were holding her arms to restrain her, and that she wasn't trembling, but struggling, reaching out toward something in the shadows.

It was Dagnija Barons. With an outstretched arm she seemed to grasp at the air, fingers splayed out toward the distant hedges and birch trees that lined the property. Gustavs turned his attention to where the small crowd was staring, toward a darkened mound obscured beneath the bare tree branches. Before him, the snow was freshly disturbed by footsteps that had trudged an uncertain path. Without thinking, he began to move toward it, drawn to it, as muffled shouts of caution were carried off by a passing breeze. When he noticed the blood, the sheer amount of it, it stopped him in his tracks. He moved no closer. Swaths of black ink had melted the snow, violent slashes left and right that scythed the fresh blanket of white powder.

He was close enough to see—to recognize the coat, the circle-framed glasses—but it was the beard that held his gaze, stained a bright red in contrast to the rest of the dark tableau. Imants Barons lay twisted on the ground, his right arm pinned beneath his torso, scarf unraveled, loosely coiled about his head.

Gustavs stood, frozen in place, feet numb beneath the ankle. For a moment he watched the snowflakes spiral, drifting gently down, a picture of winter serenity that melted into the old man's blood, soaking the cold earth. The night was still and silent, but for a gentle wind, and the sorrowful whimpers of an autumn widow.

TWO

Monday morning came like any other. A low, grey sky, imposing and bleak, sidewalks damp with freshly melted snow, and as Gustavs walked his usual route through High Park—the sprawling greenspace of Toronto's West End—he was struck by how swiftly it had all come to pass.

The ambulance arrived not long before the police, and both parties did their best to ensure a certain dignity to the affair. The paramedics went to great lengths to explain what had happened, the sober science behind the admittedly traumatic nature of the incident, and the two constables asked some routine questions, seemingly more out of procedure than any inquisitive agenda. They took some names and some telephone numbers, spoke with quiet assuredness, and, at least in Gustavs' mind, remained thereafter more as grief counselors than investigators.

The more senior of the paramedics, a gaunt man with a bald scalp, cautioned that while nothing was conclusive, they suspected the cause of death to be acute blood loss stemming from, more than likely, a ruptured esophagus. Ruptured varices, in his estimation, as if that were to mean something.

It was all rather confusing at first, with more than a couple of guests raising vocal objections, but when the subject of alcohol was broached a mollifying silence fell over the group. It was no great secret that Imants was a heavy drinker, which in itself was quite a conservative assessment. His health had been in steady decline for many years, though even in his youth he was far from a prime physical specimen.

"I feel as though I should say something," began Paulis, shifting his weight uncomfortably. "This won't be easy for some of you to hear . . ."

"Please don't," said Dagnija.

Viktors spoke up as well, with an eye to Paulis. "I think, perhaps, some of us have an obligation, at this time." Then, to Dagnija, "To better help our understanding . . . such as it may be."

Dagnija seemed to regain her composure, wiping her nose with a handkerchief and giving an abrupt little sniffle as if to defy her emotions. She looked to the two men. "So, you knew."

Paulis, for once, was at a loss for words and stared rather sheepishly at the floor, while Viktors gave a slow nod of acknowledgment.

"Well," she began, a final swipe with the kerchief, "I suppose there's no need for any secrecy now . . ." Reluctantly, she waded into the topic, guarded even amongst this intimate circle, contributing some personal matters—inevitabilities that Imants had insisted on keeping private amongst themselves, and only the closest of friends.

Imants' deteriorating health stemmed from alcoholic hepatitis, a diagnosis he'd received not long before their trip to France. The summer months had been particularly poor, giving rise to seemingly every manner of health complication. By August, he had fallen ill with a strangely timed flu which grew steadily worse until he found a splash of red in his vomit.

"I was the one who noticed, of course—Imants claimed it was the beets. Beets! For heaven's sake . . ."

He'd gone in for some bloodwork, some further tests, and then others still, and by the end of the "experiments," as he called them, despised the clinic and its staff as much as the diagnosis. The entire ordeal concluded with both denial and a stubborn refusal to change any aspect of his lifestyle. He'd had a good run thus far, and would be damned if he were to live out the rest of his days eating stewed prunes and porridge.

"Stubborn as an ox, my Imants," she'd said. "He didn't want anyone knowing he was ill. He didn't want to be treated differently." Dagnija was thoughtful for a time, clutching a mug of chamomile tea. "We'd never fought like that before, when he got the diagnosis. But even then, it was obvious, there'd be no convincing him. He would do as he pleased, just as he'd always done. Those of you that knew him best will understand, I'm sure." A few solemn faces nodded throughout the room. "And I honoured his wishes, that we would keep it to ourselves. Well, *mostly*, to ourselves." She acknowledged Paulis and Viktors once more, who bowed their heads. On the divan in the far corner, Aija, the jeweler, crossed herself and softly kissed the golden crucifix that hung on her necklace.

Gustavs had hardly slept that night, or the better part of the weekend, for that matter, and had decided to wake early, allowing himself enough time for a slight detour before work. Reaching the south end of the park, the bare-branched canopy giving way to urban sprawl, he emerged onto the Queensway and headed east, a cold wind from the lake rising to meet him.

His mood had turned decidedly foul, no longer just the sedate detachment stemming from the weekend's tragedy, but now accompanied by a shameful feeling of self-loathing. Imants, a dear friend to the family, a pillar of the community, lost to them not thirty-six hours before and already Gustavs warred with intrusive, self-serving worriment. Questions would once again be asked, there was no doubt, it was only a matter of time: "But who will take up the mantle now?" and "What the board needs is fresh blood, new leadership—a great loss, indeed, of that there is no question—but a chance for a new beginning." "Gustav, we know you've always had your reservations, but given such unfortunate circumstances . . ."

He admonished himself for the sentiment. But then, after a period of contemplation, considered that maybe it was only human nature, and in this fashion placated the demons, at least for the time being. It was moments like these when he missed Anna the most, desperate for the wise, soothing insight she could always provide.

Just north of the lake, on the south side of King Street West, stood the massive bronze sculpture, a greyish block cleaved nearly in two as if struck by a divine bolt of lightning. Beneath the jagged divide was one simple word with spacious lettering: K A T Y N. A monument built to honour the thousands of Polish officers—prisoners all—who met their fate in Soviet prisons near Smolensk. Men executed *en masse* in 1940 by the NKVD and buried in mass graves in the pine forests of Katyn. Two wreaths were balanced against the base of the structure, one wrapped in faded ribbon—the red and white of the Polish flag—and a pillar candle stood encased by a glass cylinder, the wick long since extinguished, drowned in a small puddle.

He brought no flowers today, only rarely now, on birthdays, anniversaries—celebratory, or otherwise. There was a time he'd come every day, sitting for hours, talking to her, persuading himself to move forward yet never quite finding the will. But now, rather inevitably, with the passage of time he came less frequently, and in the past year had more or less come to terms with the fact that there was no shame in a certain amount of healing, making relative peace with the fading of his guilt.

At first, it had enraged him, that anybody would dare to disturb the flowers he'd laid—withered and wind-blown in time, naturally, but how dare they, nonetheless. Perhaps the imagery was simply too graphic—the subtle lean of the telephone pole, blue paint scraped across its base, a wooden giant that now stood with an enduring injury. Then, later on, some nonsense about his improvised shrine being a distraction to other motorists; complaints from local commuters and oversensitive dog walkers.

So now, the Katyn memorial—just a little ways down the street, a quiet spot where he could still see the intersection where on one rainy night, four years before, the course of his life had been irreparably altered. A thunderstorm in September, a stale yellow light, and an off-duty security guard with the breath of a distillery. Painless, they had told him, and given the angle it was doubtful she even saw the car approaching. And though the images he conjured constricted his throat and welled his eyes with tears, in time he found a measure of comfort in the thought. His darling Anna. Here one moment, and at peace in the next.

No one dared to remove his flowers from the memorial, no matter how they wilted and cracked. At times they would get lost amongst the other bouquets—on Easter and Christmas, especially—*babushkas* with humped backs giving warm smiles as they tidied the arrangements on Catholic holidays. And on days when it was too cold, or too wet for them to risk the walk, he took up the mantle himself with a bit of housekeeping.

Gustavs sat for a time—stolid and reflective—then stood and

straightened the wreath that had been blown askew. He collected a few stray leaves and twigs, tossing them aside into the nearby shrubbery, managed to light the candle with the third match, and eventually, set about on his way.

A lifetime ago, in the years that followed the war, Roncesvalles Avenue—a stretch of city street running just east of High Park—became a hub for European refugees, particularly from those countries whose borders had been effectively erased. Nations not quite lost, not yet, but fading at an alarming rate into the long shadows cast by the Iron Curtain. Decades later, the neighborhood remained decidedly Polish, with a smattering of Ukrainians, Balts, the odd pocket of Germans—a community of immigrants with a shared ancestry of persecution in Eastern Europe; a history of blood, displacement, and loss. The ethnic makeup of the busy thoroughfare was clear to see, the names of shops, eateries, and local businesses all written in foreign scripts—letters bisected with curious slashes, vowels with umlauts and consonants with tails, the occasional Cyrillic scroll obscuring the contents of a particular storefront or a jar of preserves. And just a short ways past St. Casimir's Church, on the east side of the avenue—the Parkdale English Academy, whose doorbell jingled as Gustavs breezed through the threshold and into the foyer.

He greeted Kasia at the reception desk—his secretary's young niece looking up from her homework to give him a broad smile, all braces and gapped teeth—and proceeded up the steps to the second-floor office where Renata, the lifeblood of the academy, clacked away on her typewriter.

Gustavs had never taken notice of the building until Anna had begun volunteering on Friday evenings, and then on Sunday mornings as well, and eventually, several times per week. The school, part of a government subsidized initiative aimed at integrating refugees and new immigrants, had made considerable strides in recent years. Initially nothing more than a couple of classrooms—chalkboards without chalk, windows without blinds and the stale, lingering scent of fryer grease—it had flourished into a respectable, if humble resource center for new Canadians.

He'd first volunteered at Anna's behest, the academy struggling with a lack of staff during the recession, and completed odd jobs; procuring supplies, dabbling in accounting, even teaching the occasional class. After all, he certainly had the time. Having ignored the counsel of friends and professors alike, he had completed his doctorate in English literature and now possessed an unenviable ability to recite Chaucer in his sleep, along with an equally unenviable lack of a salary. Tenured positions at universities were few and far between, and seemingly occupied by contemporaries of Chaucer himself—dusty, bespectacled men with woolen vests and translucent hair—men who may well have accompanied the pilgrims on their procession to Canterbury.

Gustavs began to teach classes more regularly, eventually signing on full-time as an instructor, and later helped with expanding the curriculum on offer—business English and exam preparation—thereby receiving a promotion of sorts to "program coordinator." By the time the school doubled its teaching staff to four, he was a "senior" program coordinator, whatever that meant, and they were able to hire a nanny for childcare and launch a specialized career coaching seminar for job seekers.

After Anna's passing the school was in shambles for a period of time—not that he knew much about it, the months spent either in a restless slumber or a waking daze. Gustavs retreated from the world with indifference, preferring solitude to the painful reminders of his wife's charm and alacrity not only at the academy, but at seemingly every community event—social, political, or otherwise.

Eventually, when he rejoined the living, Gustavs found himself with the peculiar title of academy "Director." He was informed, rather matter-of-factly by the board—apparently a new management team had been created—that there was simply no one better suited to the role, himself having worked in nearly every capacity within the academy, from mopping floors to training instructors. Given his credentials, experience, and intimate knowledge of day-to-day affairs, he was both a logical and highly desirable choice. Gustavs agreed with only one condition: that Renata be promoted as well, as despite the praise of this new managerial committee, in truth, he would be utterly lost without her.

"Good morning Renata, good morning—how was your weekend?"

"Good morning Gustav," she replied, a polite, tight-lipped smile. "It was pleasant, thank you. And yours? How was the party?"

"Busy," he said, having already decided to forego the grim details for the time being, "but I believe the guests of honour enjoyed themselves."

"A successful party, then."

Not exactly. "I'd say so, yes. It's too bad you couldn't make it." The words felt particularly incongruous, what with funeral arrangements being presently made.

"Next time, perhaps," she replied, eyes already cast to the papers strewn across her desk, slender fingers nimbly moving across the type keys.

Renata looked as she always did, a stiff, erect posture, rose-rimmed glasses, and frizzy brown hair pulled back into a practical bun. In her fifties, with a sharp chin and yellowing, coffee-stained teeth, she held the academy together by balancing accounts, managing the payroll, hiring, firing, community outreach and heaven only knew what else. A tireless worker who shunned technology of nearly any kind—the telephone in the office was still regarded with derision two years on, startling her each time without fail. She was neat, organized, and took great pride in her role, allowing Gustavs to continue teaching as he preferred, so long as he signed this and certified that, and every once in a while, permitted her a half day on a Friday of her choosing.

"I took the liberty of interviewing Mr. Raul this morning," she said, not looking up from her ever-clacking typewriter.

"I thought that was on the 14th?"

The typewriter stopped. "Today is the 14th."

"Right. Of course." Gustavs nodded, clearing his throat. "How did he do?"

"An impressive resume, which we knew. He was professional. Agreeable."

"And how do we feel about him . . . ?"

She hesitated. "Well, a little too suave if you ask me," she said, primly smoothing her dress. "But, otherwise, I can see him being a good fit here, I suppose. He meets all the qualifications." Then, almost ruefully, added, "Exceeds them, if I'm being completely honest."

"Excellent. I suppose we should arrange for a follow-up interview then, let him know he has the position," Gustavs replied, removing his coat. For a moment he met her eyes, taking note of an almost patronizing expression upon her face. *And the point of that would be . . . ?*

"Unless, of course, you think there's no need."

Renata shrugged.

"Do we have an offer letter ready?"

"We do."

"And . . . he's signed it."

"He has."

"Ah."

She smiled. "I hope that's alright."

Gustavs made a cross in the air with two fingers. "I give him my blessing. He's one of us now."

Renata clucked her tongue at the blaspheme. "Also, if you don't mind, I was hoping to leave a half hour early today—Kasia has ballet, my sister asked if I could drive her."

"Of course, of course—you know you don't need to ask."

He poured himself a cup of coffee and rounded his desk, his eye catching a note he'd left for himself the week before. "Oh, before I forget, Elise has some relatives arriving from Chicago, she asked if—"

"It's already done, I've given her the week off and made arrangements for her classes."

"You didn't cancel them, did you?"

"Heavens, no," she said, mildly insulted. "They'll have a substitute."

"Who?"

"You."

"Oh."

"They lined up with your regular classes, although Wednesday you'll have a longer afternoon. Nothing you can't handle, I'm sure."

"I appreciate your vote of confidence." He leafed through his lesson planner and scanned the accompanying scribbles in the margins. Noting the time, he tapped his jacket pocket, and, upon feeling it empty, opened a desk drawer, then another just below.

"Renata, did you get any more of the"—he patted another pocket—"you know . . ."

"The chalk?"

"Yes. The chalk."

"In the classroom."

His lips parted once more, but before he could speak—

"The coloured chalk. Yes. Blue and red. As you asked."

"Renata, what would I do without you?"

"Likely forget your shoes if you ask me." A rare wisecrack from his stoic secretary.

Suddenly, the phone rang. Renata's hand flapped to her chest in alarm, her eyes pinching shut. She took a deep breath, and when she looked up, glared at Gustavs from across the room, slowly reaching for the receiver as it rattled in its cradle. Gustavs swiftly gathered his teaching materials, balancing papers along with his cup of coffee.

"Parkdale English Academy," said Renata, a tone unmistakably meant for Gustavs.

He turned the doorknob awkwardly with his free hand, doing his utmost to hide his smirk, all too aware of Renata's lingering gaze as he slipped through the door.

THREE

THE FUNERAL WAS HELD ON SUNDAY, CONVENIENT FOR ALL TO attend, and beneath the wide expanse of a cloudless blue sky, the turnout was something to behold. Young and old gathered in the Latvian quarter of York Cemetery, members of the community filing in amongst the rows of tombstones engraved with familiar names of the old country. *Bērziņš*—birch, *Upītis*—stream, *Vanags*—hawk, *Ozols*—oak. Surnames inspired by the fields they had sowed, the woodlands they once foraged, others reflective of Germanic and Slavic influence, legacies of foreign masters served. The ancient cultural traces of paganism, serfdom and folklore remained, still evident in the modern world.

Gustavs stood on the perimeter of the crowd, Omīte having momentarily taken a walk to lay some roses and light a candle at her mother's grave. The Barons' burial plot was located, rather appropriately, beneath an aging birch grove—the trees withered, their skin split, black seams opening to curling sheets of white bark—where the community pastor delivered his eulogy.

Amongst the crowd of familiar faces, Gustavs spotted Viktors. At times a bit of a recluse, more comfortable with palettes and paintbrushes than people, he was a remarkably kind and sensitive soul. He shook the hands of grieving family members, whispering heartfelt words of consolation, bent down to kiss the shrouded Dagnija on both cheeks, then slowly, respectful of the decorum, made his way back down the gravel road before finally sidling up to Gustavs. Viktors nodded a greeting, but did so with a tilt of the head, glancing over Gustavs' shoulder. "Incoming, on your left."

Gustavs turned to greet Valdis Roze wearing the doleful, firm-lipped smile of the funeral procession. A heavyset man, the Honorary Consul for Latvia wore a suit jacket a size too big, his tie already loosened beneath a flaccid neck and drooping jowls.

Some words were exchanged between the three men; generic euphemisms, words of wisdom, expressions of sympathy followed by moments of silent reflection and navel gazing. And then, inevitably, with the natural ease of a seasoned politician, Valdis steered the conversation where he had always intended.

" . . . And such a leader. A guiding light for the community, you might say. Certainly he had his opponents, of course, a man in his position, well—it comes with the territory." A passing breeze was apparently unwelcome and prompted the big man to produce a small comb, smoothing down the remaining strands of slick white hair that remained on his head.

"Though he always knew how to steady the ship, especially in times of crisis. You recall the 'better dead than red' days, the division in the community, all of that." He chuckled softly. "Who was that opera singer they brought over, with the awful hair, the one who would only sing Wagner?"

Viktors shook his head and gave a subtle shrug.

"Everyone thought she was a spy," Valdis continued. "Goodness, the paranoia of that time. It came from nowhere, inexplicable and thick as buttermilk, dividing friends, even families . . ." He sighed. "Imants was the only one who seemed to be able to unite the community. I don't know who else could have weathered the storm. Remarkable, truly."

"A great loss," Gustavs conceded.

"Tell me Gustav, how are you these days? We don't see you very often at the *Centrs*," he said, referring to the Latvian Community Center in the east of the city. "A man with your intellect, your *temperament*, we could really use you. You know how us Latvians can get, put three of us in a room and we come out with four opinions. Still, we're making some great strides, a lot of influence now in Ottawa. Bending the right ears. More political clout, as Imants liked to say. I'm not sure what your days currently—"

"I appreciate the sentiment, Val, I do, but politics," Gustavs shook his head, "it's never really been my thing. I hope you understand."

"Well, no, not *that* sort of politics. Listening to us windbags go on and on—no, the word itself hardly reflects our mandate at all. In fact—oh, are they . . ."—he glanced toward the casket where a crowd of men were gathering—"I'm sorry gentlemen, if you'll excuse me a moment, duty calls," he said, hustling over to join the assembly. At the front of the procession, an elderly fellow distributed leaflets to the swelling crowd.

Gustavs had noted the thin sash beneath Valdis' suit jacket, the tri-colour strip of orange, silver and blue of Fraternity Tervetia— one of countless, century-old brotherhoods. Bastions of tradition whose founding members had taught rural farmers and country bumpkins the social etiquette of the big city, showing young boys how to properly conduct themselves as gentlemen. They hosted impassioned literary evenings, fencing tournaments, opulent galas with contemporary sororities—customs of a different time, portraits of civilized society in Rīga.

The men—doffing their caps, heads held high—began to sing

a solemn chorus of farewell to their departed brother, and Gustavs couldn't help but notice that there were more than a few grey heads amongst the choir—the fraternity, much like his own, shrinking ever fewer in number with each passing year. Once the closing notes had been sung, the mourners took turns laying a final stem upon the casket and sifting handfuls of sand overtop, whispering their traditional parting words: *vieglas smiltis*. Let the earth be gentle.

It was then that a rather customary drama began to unfold involving the gravediggers; a routine affair that had, in recent years, become part and parcel of seemingly every Latvian funeral. In keeping with tradition, the Latvian representative would invite the male mourners to fill in the grave themselves, and the gravediggers, in turn, would stare in utter confusion and disbelief. Gustavs observed the proceedings from afar.

You mean to do what? No, that's not permitted, I'm sorry. You've . . . done this before? Well, yes that's fine, but it will take you all day. But of course it will. How many men? Impossible. What do you mean you brought shovels?

In fairness, on this occasion the season did raise the odds in the gravediggers' favor, however the earth was only cold and reasonably dry and, thankfully, not yet frozen solid. Shedding their suit jackets, the men began to dig in teams, trading four shovels between them, systematically working away at the mound of earth as the casket of polished oak slowly disappeared from view. Gustavs had a good sweat along his back and dirt smeared across his neatly buffed shoes when a familiar face appeared by his side.

"Well you certainly shovel like an academic, we'll be here all night at this rate," said the man.

Gustavs smiled at his old friend Tomass. "Typical, always waiting around 'til the work is mostly done."

Tomass grinned, then jutted his chin toward the road. Gustavs followed his gaze to where the gravediggers leant against a backhoe smoking cigarettes. The elder man had clearly observed the tradition before, while his younger apprentice simply stared in bemusement.

Tomass Ozoliņš was tall, broad-shouldered, a strapping man with a wild mane of blonde hair and a thick chevron mustache. The pair had been best friends since childhood, though Gustavs saw far less of him these days, as might have been expected. The handsome oaf had managed, one fateful summer's eve, to get Māra Zīle pregnant, who in the ensuing years bore him three angelic little girls. Tomass, the former volleyball star and devil-may-care lothario was now a husband and father, and had moved an hour north to Barrie, all but ensuring his effective disappearance from the face of the earth. Gustavs spotted Māra in the crowd and gave her a wave, her limbs entangled with golden-haired children of varying sizes.

The two men chatted awhile, covering the essential topics with an efficacy known only to childhood friends, as they scooped and scraped at the diminishing mound. When they passed off their shovels to the next men, Tomass brushed his sweaty hair back from his face and stood, hands on his hips, chest heaving like some Baltic Adonis. Gustavs noticed a doe-eyed brunette in the crowd, thoroughly engrossed in the display. She blinked, then lowered her head, brow twitching in self-reprimand. *You're at a funeral, for goodness sake.*

As the service drew to a close, the crowd began to disperse, piling into vehicles bound for the Latvian Center across town and the reception to follow. Omīte was chatting with a few of her girlfriends beneath a bare linden tree, the women nearly identical with stooped backs, wooden canes and silken kerchiefs knotted beneath their chins.

"I've always wondered about this crooked part here," said Tomass.

"Hm?"

"This part, it's always crooked." Gustavs turned to see his friend pointing to an impressive grey tombstone in the shape of a cross, the monument standing nearly ten feet tall.

"It's Russian Orthodox."

Tomass crossed his arms, studying the memorial.

"See, they have three levels—the top, where they inscribed 'INRI,' Jesus of Nazareth, the standard middle section here and then this lower tilted, or *crooked* level as you said, represents the footrest, essentially. Just a different style."

"Russian Orthodox . . ."

"This is Olga Romanov's tombstone, you never noticed this?"

Tomass shrugged indifferently, then scoffed. "Why would I notice some Soviet tombstone?"

"What?"

"What do you mean, *what*?"

"Romanov, Tom. Olga *Romanov*. They called her 'the last Grand Duchess of Imperial Russia.' Her entire family was murdered before there even was—" He shook his head and sighed.

" . . . Still Russian."

"You know it's been so long I forgot what it's like talking to you."

"History was never my best subject."

"Did you have a *best* subject?"

Tomass grinned. "Female anatomy?"

Gustavs shook his head, "I guess fatherhood hasn't changed a thing, has it?"

As they waited for Omīte, up ahead, by a distant bend in the road, two men emerged from a black Ford Crown Victoria, one of the last remaining vehicles in the cemetery. They approached from quite a distance, moving at a casual pace. Gustavs didn't recognize either of them.

"Gentlemen," the one on the left said, "my condolences. I'm Detective De Rossi, this is Detective Horowitz. You boys have a minute?"

Gustavs was uneasy for a moment, then said, "Yes, of course, officers. What can we help you with?"

De Rossi was about Gustavs' height, a thick physique, and significantly older than his partner. He was rather tired-looking, Gustavs thought, and wore a navy, pin-striped suit with a tie loosely knotted beneath an open collar. His salt and pepper hair was slicked back over his head, with small, clever eyes, pinkish and burrowed above heavy smoker's pouches. He looked like he hadn't shaved in days.

"No reason to be alarmed, just some due diligence, you guys know how it is." He shrugged, nonchalant. "Following up on a few things."

"About Imants?" Tomass asked.

De Rossi nodded. "How well did you know the deceased?"

"Most of our lives, really," Gustavs answered. "I mean, we all knew him."

"Quite the fella in your community."

"You could say that."

"Was the head of that, ahh," he snapped his fingers at his partner, "the LNK . . ."

"The Latvian National Federation of Canada," Horowitz said. Horowitz couldn't have been more of a contrast to his partner. Hair neatly parted and pomaded, shirt tucked, shoes polished. He had youthful, rosy cheeks on his cleanly shaven face, and wore a rather feminine set of steel-framed glasses.

"That's the one. The big cheese. *Il Duce*, right?"

"Imants was president for some time, that's right," said Gustavs.

"I heard you're next in line," De Rossi said, a sudden change in tone, eyes searching for a reaction.

"That's not—no."

"Who told you that?" Tomass interjected.

De Rossi shrugged, removing a pack of cigarettes from his jacket pocket. "As a detective, I make a lot of new friends." He flicked the top of his zippo lighter, a cloud of smoke drifting into the air. "I'm a people person."

"Our community likes to gossip sometimes," said Tomass.

"I'm not one for politics, detective."

"Mm. I must have misheard. You know the family?"

"We all do. We're not a very big community," said Gustavs. "It's not a stretch to say that everyone kind of knows everyone."

De Rossi turned to his partner. "What was the name of the widow?"

"Dagnija," Gustavs replied.

"A fine-looking woman," said De Rossi. "Real fine. Are you single?"

"Not exactly."

"And what does that mean?"

"I'm a widower."

"My condolences. He have any enemies?"

"Imants? Do we need to answer that?" said Tomass.

"You don't need to answer anything"—De Rossi shrugged casually—"we're just having a friendly chat here, right?"

Horowitz pulled out a small notepad and a pen.

"Imants was very well liked. And respected," said Gustavs.

"What do you do, Mr. Ziedins. Am I saying that right?"

Gustavs didn't bother correcting him. "I work at the Parkdale English Academy."

"You work?"

"I'm the Director."

"And where's that—the academy."

"On Roncy, just across from St. Casimir's. Can I ask what all this is about?"

A mood settled over De Rossi, his demeanour changing as he shifted his weight. Then, he inclined his head toward his partner, whispering a few quiet words.

"It's just that, we've already spoken to the police," Gustavs said.

"That's right," Tomass added.

Horowitz nodded his acquiescence to his partner, closed his notepad, gave a curt nod to both Gustavs and Tomass— "Gentlemen"—and turned back down the road.

"He's a good kid, this one," De Rossi continued, gesturing toward his colleague. "Of course, I can't tell him that, not yet, anyhow. Gotta keep him sharp, on his toes." De Rossi snapped his fingers a couple of times. "He's better than most of the new breed. So many focused now on documenting every little action rather than asking the right questions. How can you properly interview someone with your head down, scratching away with a pencil." He shrugged dramatically. "You can't. You'll miss all the cues. The subtleties. Most of them, they're hired now with all sorts of fancy degrees, all this special training"—he splayed his hands—"but no *instincts*. And that's what you need. You need instincts, and you have to work at them, too. Train them, sharpen them. This isn't the classroom, after all—things work a little differently out here in the real world. You can't read about it in a textbook."

He took a pull of his cigarette and exhaled forcefully. "I swear, some of them watch a few Dirty Harry movies and think they know something about the job—that is, if they didn't sign on just to get themselves a pistol, you know what I mean? It's partly why I'm out here speaking with you fine gentlemen today. It's these young upstarts that botched the initial investigation, so here we are following up. Crossing our tees, so to speak . . ."

"I'm sorry—investigation?" said Gustavs.

De Rossi waved this away. "I shouldn't use that word. What I mean is, from what I've heard—from the initial reports—it looks like my colleagues from last week spent more time comforting the women than asking any relevant questions. We still don't even have a complete picture of who was at the party."

"I gave my statement to them that night."

"I know you did. Let's just say I'm not thrilled with the way things were conducted. But, that's no fault of yours, of course."

Gustavs adjusted his glasses. "Am I missing something? The paramedics said, and the coroner confirmed that—"

"I know what they said, and they weren't wrong. I've seen Mr. Barons' medical history." De Rossi whistled. "A lot of mileage there. The man really wasn't in the best of health. Makes you consider your own habits"—for a moment, his gaze drifted out toward the treeline, then returned. "I'm just here," he sniffed, "tying up some loose ends, you could say."

Gustavs considered this for a time, contemplative, then tugged at a thread. "At someone's request?"

This seemed to throw the detective off for a moment, a slight hesitation, and he conceded a single nod. "Sometimes, events like these . . ." He searched for the words. "Tragedies. Accidents. Call them what you like—they can be traumatic for certain individuals. You were there, I'm sure you can understand that. You know, the *optics*. He didn't exactly slip away peacefully in his bed. It's not supernatural, what happened, always just boils down to simple science. But, visually. Those images. They stay with you." He shrugged sympathetically. "You know how many parents tell me their kid couldn't have done it? Assault. Murder. Suicide. The mind is a funny thing. For some, this sort of stuff, it just doesn't sit right"—he tapped his temple—"up here, you know? They need finality."

"Finality."

"Take my card," he said, fishing around in his jacket pocket. "I know you gave your report to Officer Reilly last week, but if you remember something else. Anything you might want to, oh, I dunno, get off your chest. Mr. Ozolins, right? Here, take one as well." De Rossi stared at Tomass, squinting as a plume of smoke drifted into his eyes. "I'm a good listener."

Gustavs examined the card. "Homicide?"

"Nothing to worry about, cross my heart. Just tying up some loose ends. Finality, that's all."

Arriving home after the reception, Gustavs loosened his tie and put on the kettle as Omīte gathered tea cups and a fresh pot of honey. On the kitchen table, a bouquet of chrysanthemums from Renata, along with a note of birthday blessings in familiar cursive scroll.

"Yes, Gustav, when you get to my age it's just one funeral after another," Omīte said, stirring her mug. "We used to go out, you know—parties, balls, getting up to all sorts of mischief. Now my social calendar is dictated by the dead. I swear it, every time that phone rings, I think, 'well, who is it this time?' I half expect it to be Death on the line, telling me it's my turn."

"Don't talk like that, Omīte."

Swiftly, she changed the subject. "Oh, and Aivars! I couldn't believe my eyes. Truly, does the man have no shame?"

"They were on the board together for years, weren't they?"

"That's not the point, Gustav. Alright, fine, Imants—I'll grant him this one, but the rest? What about Biruta Jansone, just this past summer. I don't think I ever heard the two of them exchange a kind word. Not once. And Ingrīda Cīrule! Ingrīda practically forbade her husband from associating with him, you know."

The target of Omīte's most recent indictment was none other than Aivars Šteiners, a rather garrulous fellow from the old guard—opinionated, vain, emphatically obese—and, much to Omīte's irritation, a rather *too* frequent attendee of community funerals.

"Everybody knows, we all talk. Always first in line, plate piled high with *desas* and *rasols*, and then again with the cakes." She clucked her tongue. "He only comes for the food, we all know it. No matter who it is, as if they had been the very best of friends."

Poor Aivars had unwittingly gained quite a reputation among certain members of the formidable *Dāmu Komitēja*—the Ladies Auxiliary Committee—which was no trifling matter. Formed during the postwar years as a charitable branch of the church, the committee was composed of spirited, indefatigable women who governed their households much as they did the community. They raised money for Latvian exiles still struggling in European camps, organized fundraisers for the congregation. They prepared sumptuous Easter brunches and hearty Christmas dinners, planned concerts and recitals and bazaars and literary evenings. There were roughly thirty members in all, though the late pastor Čops had famously once said that he considered all women in the congregation as an extension of the committee. Active in nearly every aspect of community life, they wielded considerable influence accordingly. Tireless, benevolent, meticulous and determined, God help you if you ever crossed them, though He would be wise to side with the women.

"Shameless, I mean it. Make note Gustav, if I so much as come down with a sniffle, that vulture will be circling above our roof looking for pickled herring."

Gustavs could only shake his head—it was better to just let it pass, there would be no changing her mind in such a mood.

Omīte had moved in not long after Anna's passing, an arrangement that neither had considered until Paulis, thoroughly soused as usual, made an off-hand remark over Christmas. Widowed nearly ten years before, it was becoming increasingly clear, despite her vehement denial, that she required the slightest, only the *very* slightest touch of assistance around the house. There were doctor's appointments, household repairs, the treacherous walkway that needed salting in the winter. As the years wore on, the once routine chores had begun to present their various challenges.

And, as always, there was the rather delicate topic of the driver's license. Long since expired, much like the prescription glasses, but what did that matter? "Anywhere I need to go, it's hardly a ten minute drive, stop overreacting," Omīte would say. "Who is going to give me a ticket, I'm old!" Though she too was eventually forced to swallow her pride—in truth, there was little to be said following the episode with the hedges. A beautiful young shrub, newly planted by the end of the driveway and promptly dragged half a kilometer down the center of the boulevard trailing a wake of black soil. This impromptu bit of landscaping seemed to finally humble Omīte enough to at least consider certain changes in lifestyle, although any long term resolutions remained rather complicated—her eldest daughter living in Calgary; her younger son in California.

Gustavs, for his part, now lived alone in a three-bedroom house, a widower without children, a backyard left untended and a kitchen all but abandoned, with the exception of the microwave. After some discussion, it was decided that the guest room along with the entire east wing of the house would be converted into a makeshift apartment complete with a separate bathroom and sitting room. It was a perfectly agreeable arrangement for the two of them, and soon the pair found an unexpected, but rather reassuring comfort in looking out for one another.

Gustavs observed his great-aunt as she sat at the kitchen table, already peeling potatoes for supper, unable to sit still for even a moment. She looked exactly as she always did, a side portrait, an image strangely unaltered from childhood. Hunched over a weathered cutting board, she worked with restful concentration. Her hair was a soft cloud of limp, grey curls that hovered above thick, smudged glasses. Behind the frames, a set of warm, rheumy eyes, a pale shade of green, mouth forever set in a drooping frown that stretched down to her chin, where the odd wiry silver hair, almost imperceptible, tickled you upon a goodnight kiss.

As always, she worked with her small paring knife, the tool an ancient relic now, perhaps not unlike herself. It was no more than a few inches long, the steel mottled and whetted paper thin, sharpened over time into more of a pencil than a blade and set in a cracked, wooden handle. It had traveled with her from Latvia, of course, during the flight in 1944, and now traveled in her cardigan pocket, forever on hand to dice a radish or snip a loose thread.

For a time, he simply watched her—a faint smile creasing her cheek as she listened to the classical melodies forever playing on the radio; age-spotted fingers already pruned from the potato skins.

And then, out of nowhere, "And what did that Jew want at the cemetery. Him and his chubby friend?"

Gustavs nearly coughed into his teacup. "What?"

"I saw him walking back to his car, you were all talking. The skinny one with the glasses."

"It's nothing Omīte, and please don't say that."

"Say what?"

"You know exactly what . . ."

"That he's a Jew? What's so wrong with that?"

"Nothing is *wrong* with it, but you don't know that, and it's hardly relevant anyway."

Omīte scoffed. "*Bah,* so sensitive, your generation. I don't understand you. If he was black, I would call him black. If he was Chinese, I call him Chinese. I don't see what all the fuss is about. He's a Jew, I call him a Jew."

Gustavs sighed, rolling his eyes in defeat. "How could you possibly know he's Jewish?"

"I saw him! For heaven's sake . . ." She began to cube a potato on the cutting board. "What was his name?"

"He was a policeman, actually."

"His name, Gustav. What was his name?"

Gustavs huffed. Said nothing.

Omīte put down the latest potato, waiting patiently.

" . . . Horowitz, but that's hardly the point here."

Omīte shrugged with a sort of indifferent triumph, returning to the task at hand.

Gustavs pulled up a chair, and began chopping carrots for a salad. They sat in silence for awhile, the ebb and flow of frenzied strings over the hollow taps of wooden cutting boards.

After a time, Omīte put down her knife rather theatrically. "Well if you're going to sulk about it . . ."

It took him a moment. "Oh, no, it's not that . . ."

She eyed him uncertainly, wiping her hands with a towel. "What then?"

Gustavs sighed. "Just the funeral, I suppose. It just feels, so very strange. So foreign. I don't know. And those policemen . . ."

"What did they ask?"

"Nothing much. Routine things. I don't know what to make of them."

"Be mindful of your emotions, Gustav. We are all still healing from this."

"I know. It's just that, I feel as if . . . as if we're all just circling the drain or something. I can't put my finger on it . . . *ah*, I don't know."

Omīte began digging out the eyes of a potato. "Those that are closest to us, when they leave, they take a part of us with them. That feeling of hollowness. It heals, in time, but not always entirely." She looked up, "We know this better than most, Gustav."

He nodded in agreement. "Maybe."

The melody on the radio had changed, a spirited piece that caught his ear.

"Who is this?" he asked.

"*Ah*, Mendelssohn. His overture to *A Midsummer Night's Dream*."

"I thought it sounded familiar."

A smile arced across Omīte's face as the crescendo swelled with the freefalling notes of the famous composition.

"That would be *Felix* Mendelssohn."

"Mm."

He scraped the carrots carefully into a bowl. " . . . Jewish, no?"
"Oh hush, Gustav."

FOUR

Rīga, Latvian Soviet Socialist Republic (LSSR)

ON A FOGGY, LATE AUTUMN MORNING, ON THE WESTERN CORNER of Lenin Street and Engels Street, stood an impressively regal building in the art nouveau style, a structure rather at odds with its bleak surroundings. A classical rose in a garden of socialist thorns.

Perhaps a bit worse for wear these days, its decorous façade was begrimed with urban soot, its elegant arches chipped and crumbling from decades of neglect, balustrades weathered and water-stained. Like a film star in her twilight years, perhaps lacking the spritely zeal of her youth, but aging gracefully, all subtlety and *savoir-vivre*. A quiet allure about the starlet now, a certain sophistication achieved only through the passage of time, a wisdom bestowed upon her by the very years she silently rued.

And the building had reason to rue those years, for they had hardly been kind. She no longer housed chic apartments and flower shops, but jail cells and interrogation rooms. There was no polished mahogany, no luxurious sleeping quarters, but rather earthen floors of muck and filth, wires and bars to intimidate the perpetually surveilled. In a courtyard of stagnant puddles, trucks had idled, conspicuously loud, masking the gunshots that echoed from Nagant revolvers. There were cries in the night, hungry bellies during the day, and verses of folk songs surreptitiously carved into the walls—small acts of defiance for whomever might be unfortunate enough to read them.

And in a sixth-floor window—one of few without bars—a small desk lamp cast the silhouette of a man, pensively smoking a cigarette. The man looked out over the main thoroughfare, all but deserted in the early dawn hours, observing a solitary woman dressed in rags pushing a stroller. As she approached the building from the north, she crossed the street, seemingly for no other purpose than to avoid passing by the doors of what locals had long ago dubbed the *Stūra Māja*. The Corner House.

The man sighed, giving the very slightest shake of the head. Superstitious fools, he thought. What a silly little land this was.

Arkady Vassilyevich Zharkov, 1st Deputy Chairman of the KGB in the LSSR, Order of the Red Star, was a slight man in his fifties. He had thinning brown hair, neatly parted to one side, with steel framed spectacles perched on a slender nose, and angular features that gave him a distinctively elfish appearance—pointed ears, a sharp chin, thin colourless lips. And while his age was evident in his sallow cheeks and stooped shoulders, an ankle that bothered him increasingly with each passing year—some miscellaneous shrapnel, enduring mementos from Voronezh—the pitiless intensity behind his dark eyes had never wavered.

Zharkov checked his watch, then brushed some ash from the lapels of his overcoat.

It was not an epiphany, he concluded. Epiphanies appeared from nowhere, falling like raindrops from a clear blue sky. No, this was something different altogether. The culmination of a logical course of events. Undeniable. An inevitability.

And therefore, only a singular course of action to be taken. One that *must* be taken, he resolved. For the collective good. Acts of individualism could be disregarded if they were honorable, patriotic duties for the glory of the Union. Did Comrade Lenin not take it upon himself to call for proletarian revolution? Did he not, on his own, draft and deliver his impassioned speeches for the benefit of the working classes? And Comrade Stalin, were it not for his leadership, we might well be goose-stepping along Red Square this very day, speaking *deutsche*! No, what did this great man do? Mobilized our resources, our oppressed citizenry. Held the conspirators, the saboteurs accountable. Harnessed the blood and sweat of the Russian people, of the workers. With heavy industry and sheer force of will, we were victorious and continue ever onwards with our relentless march toward socialism!

Zharkov exhaled twin plumes of smoke from his nose, stubbing out his cigarette in a gold-plated ashtray.

And yet, here he stood, banished to a city crawling with the very vermin they sought to exterminate. It *was* banishment. Exile. Why should he think otherwise? Betrayed by these modern age thinkers, neo-liberals with their grand ideas. *Glasnost.* Hah! A bourgeois intellectual's notion of progress. When your boot is planted firmly upon the neck of your enemy, do you simply release him? Of course not!

Zharkov struggled to contain his frustrations. What was happening to this once-progressive state? He should have been praised for what he divulged about his colleagues. Arseni, that pissant, with his collections of Western books and magazines. Research? He had almost laughed when he heard the riposte! The little shit should do his research in Siberia, five years in a coal mine would teach him exactly what he needed to know. And Grigori, the rat himself. This capitalist ideologue, extolling the virtues of liberalism, democratization. The man should be taken to the Lubyanka and shot. It wasn't so long ago that this would have been exactly the way his *tolerance* would have been rewarded.

And now, Riga. Nothing but dissidents and fascist sympathizers, speaking in foreign tongues and listening to Western radio. And to think we should reward such insults with leniency. Free speech? For what purpose—to allow them to besmirch our great history, to poison the minds of our young?

No. No, this would not do at all. And he would see to it himself. Of course he would, for that was his *duty*. For the greater good. For the Union. For the people.

Zharkov circled the large desk—stacks of manila folders and various telephones—some with Soviet insignia, the direct lines to Moscow. He picked up a receiver.

"Find Vadim. I want him here as soon as possible." He hung up, then checked his watch once more.

Zharkov walked down the hall, carefully descended a flight of stairs and stepped forward into a little room with beige walls and a tessellated floor, a simple wooden desk with a paper and pen, and a singular chair. In the far corner stood a man, barefoot and utterly disheveled, gently swaying on his heels. He had red welts around his cheeks, dark rings beneath his eyes. With a trembling hand he clutched his pants to keep them from falling. To Zharkov's right stood an officer, hands folded in front, holding a long, black truncheon. The room was warm and stuffy, and smelled heavily of sweat and ammonia.

Zharkov glanced at the folder in his hands, licked his finger, turned some pages, then handed the file to the officer.

"I wouldn't usually involve myself in a situation where . . ."

Zharkov paused, then tilted his head. "Vasili, is this man dribbling on my floor?"

The officer turned his head, looking beyond the desk to the puddle that had formed at the prisoner's feet.

"I believe so, Comrade Chairman," he said, supressing a grin. "I don't believe he's aware."

Zharkov turned to the officer, holding his attention, and prompted him with the most diffident of shrugs. "So make him aware."

The officer stepped forward and swung the truncheon, a blur of ebony that thudded against the prisoner's thigh. The man collapsed to his knees, clutching his leg, then gasping for air.

"Clean up this mess at once," said Zharkov.

The prisoner, jolted back into consciousness, fixated his eyes on the new man in the room.

"Go on. Clean it up."

The man looked at his surroundings, dazed, then tried to speak. He whispered through chapped lips: "I can't."

"Can't? You can't?" Zharkov turned a half-step. "Vasili, he can't."

The blow from the truncheon made a sickening sound as it struck the man on the back, causing him to seize and collapse onto the floor. Slowly, he gathered himself, removed his shirt, and began to sop up the puddle in which he knelt.

"There we are, excellent! You see, Vasili? All that is ever required is the proper motivation. Well done, young man. At first, reluctant, and now, instead of being wasteful this man uses his own clothing, his own resources for the collective good. We shall make a party member of you yet."

"Minister of Textiles, perhaps."

"Hah! Well said, Vasili. Well said, indeed." Zharkov took a few steps forward and faced a portrait of Felix Dzerzhinsky on the wall, the founder of the Cheka looking rather aloof in his cap and bristling goatee. Beside him, in an identical wooden frame was Lenin, beady eyes and a broad forehead, looking to the future. Zharkov raised his chin in salute.

"Your name is Aleksandrs, correct? Go on, take a seat. Yes, it's alright. Vasili, fetch me a chair as well, would you?"

Aleksandrs crawled a couple of paces before hoisting himself onto the chair. It was obvious that he had not slept, nor even sat, for days.

"Why, may I ask, do you insist on using this Germanic spelling? You Letts, you all claim to be your own people and yet, *Aleksandrs*. Why not Alexander, spelt properly, with an 'x'? There are a great many Alexanders from whom you could draw inspiration. Pushkin, of course. Or Suvorov, our great general. Alexander the Great! Not Russian, mind you, yet what a legacy. But no, here you choose to spell your name like a Kaiser."

Vasili returned with an upholstered chair, sliding it behind Zharkov's knees.

"*Spasibo*, Vasili."

Zharkov faced Aleksandrs across the table, removing his spectacles and a handkerchief from his pocket, polishing the lenses. "Normally I would not be so candid but, given our unique circumstances"—he replaced his glasses—"I am faced with quite a dilemma, Aleksandr—may I call you Aleksandr?"

The prisoner did not respond.

"I do not hold any sympathy for foreign agents such as yourself. Saboteurs, bringing with you your imperialist ideologies, perverting the minds of the hardworking peoples of this land, seeking to undermine the socialist movement for your own ends. Still—and this is very important for you to understand, Aleksandr—I also, am partly to blame. *We* are to blame. Who am I to be so aggrieved when infection festers in an unattended wound? To take issue with a worm for burrowing in a rotting apple? This is the natural order of things, is it not?"

Zharkov winced as he stood, slightly favouring his right foot, and returned to the portraits of Lenin and Dzerzhinsky. "You see, these great men, they did not wage these internal battles with themselves as I do. They were far too busy building something great, something historic. A better future for all of us. They held deviants, spies accountable for their actions. But now, much as it pains me to say it"—he lowered his voice, the seemingly avuncular interrogator now rueful and ponderous—"much as I *should* not say it, the party, the leadership of our great Union . . ." He trailed off with a sigh.

When he looked back to Aleksandrs, the tone of the room shifted. Zharkov was not overly fond of the expression on his captive's face, a face which had regained some of its colour, and now looked upon him with fatigued revulsion.

A shadow settled across the stern features of the deputy chairman. "I was twelve when I first went to war. Have you ever been to war, Aleksandr? No, I thought not. We were but children, all of us when we volunteered, but it didn't take long for us to become men. In Voronezh I met a Ukrainian man, Kostya—Kostya from Kiev, we called him. And I must say, he had the most ingenious methods of extracting information if someone was, well, *reluctant* to converse with us."

Aleksandrs tried to swallow some dry saliva, and looked away.

"There are various techniques as you may well imagine, each with their own benefits, but Kostya's preferred method of persuasion was truly something to behold. You are bound, of course, without the use of your limbs, and he would place an open cage over your torso, say"—Zharkov extended his hands a foot apart—"about so. And at the other end of the cage there is a little door with a latch. Can you guess what the door is for, Aleksandr? No? That's alright, I'll tell you. Kostya would place a rat inside the cage. A filthy, blackish thing, starved from the long winter. And then, he would light a flame."

Zharkov paused for a moment, watching as Aleksandrs began to shift in his seat, his breathing unsteady.

"You're a clever boy, Aleksandr, what do you think happens next? Mm? The rat panics. It darts around the cage, hissing, squealing, the little fellow is terrified, and can you blame him? That long tail of his, it's never quite far enough from the heat. Clever creatures, rats, not so unlike yourself—it doesn't take them long to grasp their surroundings. Metal grating everywhere, seemingly in all directions. All . . . but one. They realize there's a way out, only one way to get as far from the fire as possible." Zharkov leaned forward, folding his hands onto the table. "And so they burrow, Aleksandr." He bared his teeth with their gold fillings, gnawing his bottom lip. "They burrow."

Aleksandrs struggled to maintain his composure, though now he shuddered uncontrollably. A single tear rolled the length of his cheek, betraying him.

"Do you know what I remember most from that day? It wasn't the man, or his crimes, his pleas for help. It wasn't the sound of fabric being torn by those little claws, the sound of what was torn thereafter. No, no. It was the squealing of the rat. That high-pitched, feverish squeal. I'll never forget it."

Zharkov removed a lighter from his pocket, reached for the

blank paper on the desk, held it aloft and set it on fire. Aleksandrs looked from the paper to his interrogator and back again, the page curling with orange flame, and in moments reduced to flakes of black ash.

Zharkov stood. "You are a foreign dissident, Aleksandr. A trespasser. A Western agent seeking to undermine the integrity of the Union of Soviet Socialist Republics. I do not need your confession. I do not need you to list your fellow conspirators. I will find them. I will find your family, your loved ones, your friends." Aleksandrs hung his head and silently wept. "This passport you have used, whether genuine or falsified, is of no matter. There is no one coming to assist you. There is no one that knows you are here. You will answer to me for your crimes against the state."

Aleksandrs looked up, eyes wet and swollen, and simply stared at Zharkov, a last act of defiance.

"Vasili . . ."

Aleksandrs glanced furtively at the man rounding the desk, moving behind him, then pinched his eyes shut and began to whisper a prayer.

"Look at you. Groveling like a dog at my boot. Your God has abandoned you, Aleksandr."

With a single movement, Vasili slid the truncheon beneath Aleksandrs' chin, wedging the far end into the crook of his arm and lifting his prisoner into the air. Aleksandrs sputtered and gasped, shackled hands fumbling at his throat.

Zharkov leant across the table. "This is where your prayers will get you . . ."

Vasili wrenched the truncheon further as Aleksandrs' eyes bulged, but he no longer made a sound, bare feet twitching beneath him across the cold tile.

"*Ak dievs, ak dievs*," Zharkov parroted. "Comrade Gorbachev is your God now, and I am the angel of death."

FIVE

Toronto, Canada

THE ROOM WAS HUMBLE YET COZY, AND PLAINLY FURNISHED; A BED, a small dresser, an armchair and *écritoire*, a rather large bookcase, a nightstand with a lamp and a fabric-bound book of *dainas*—poems. Musty history texts were scattered about on any surface that might hold them. Outside, a cruel winter had arrived, leaving frost roses in the corners of windowpanes and, every now and again, blowing with a fierce, howling wind, as if to remind the world of its presence. Down the hall, someone, likely a granddaughter or grandson, all spiffy for the occasion, plinked away on an out-of-tune piano. At first, a festive melody Gustavs couldn't quite recall, but then, "Oh Tannenbaum." The Latvian retirement home, *Kristus Dārzs,* was full of lights and song and warm holiday cheer.

Gustavs set out three small glasses and unscrewed the lid of his thermos just as the toilet flushed and, a moment later, Alberts Riekstiņš shuffled out of the washroom with his walker. Already dressed in his best chestnut suit—a vest, no jacket—freshly shaven, his shaggy yellowing hair combed neatly into place. He caught sight of the glasses and smiled broadly, a flicker of conspiracy in his hooded eyes.

"You're a saint Gustav, I don't care what the others say about you."

Gustavs grinned and produced a package of tinfoil, unwrapping it to reveal thick slices of smoked boar and boiled fava beans.

"Come on, while it's still warm." Gustavs poured two glasses of mulled wine and hovered the steaming thermos above the third. "You think she'd like some tonight?"

"I think she would."

Gustavs poured, and the two men lifted their beverages, a silent toast to the empty chair.

"Well," Alberts began, "as they say, 'never eat on an empty stomach.'" The pair clinked glasses and drank.

"My that's good. That's better than I remember."

"Some extra cloves, this time. And a splash of brandy."

Alberts winked, savoured another sip, then pinched a fatty slice of pork and tucked it into his mouth. "So you think he was joking?"

"Who?"

"Tomass. About Olga Romanov."

"Oh," he chuckled. "No, sadly, I don't think he was."

Alberts sighed. "I wasn't the best history teacher, I can admit that much. Still, to think she was a communist . . ."

Gustavs clucked his tongue. "Excuses? It's a poor man who blames his tools."

"Hah! Tools, no. This tool, perhaps. A little duller than the rest. But shiny at least, nice to look at."

"At least he has that."

"Mm," Alberts smiled, a nostalgic look in his eyes, rubbing his palms against his pants. "You were good boys, though. I couldn't tell you that at the time. Reminded me of myself once or twice, back in the day. What *do* you remember from my classes?"

Gustavs smirked. " . . . The Romanovs?"

Alberts harrumphed. "Of course. Not paying attention as usual. Too busy chasing my daughter around." He conceded a knowing smile.

Gustavs recalled a certain Friday evening at the Latvian heritage school where, at the roguish age of sixteen, he had poked his head into Anna's history class, intent on passing her a note. A careless first step, a creak of the floorboards, and out of nowhere, Mr. Riekstiņš' personal copy of *Nineteen Eighty-Four* flew across the room and crashed against the doorframe. Riekstiņš roared, Anna blushed and Gustavs fled down the hall to a chorus of snickering.

"Poor Olga," Alberts said. "They chased that poor woman to the ends of the earth. As if her family's fate weren't enough. She died practically penniless here in Toronto."

"Is it true that we were involved?"

Alberts spoke through a mouthful of mashed beans, "We? Involved?"

"The Romanovs. That it was us. The executioners."

"No. No it wasn't, but the rumors persist, nonetheless."

"They say the shooters were Latvian, from what I've read."

"And in its own way, that is also true. They were certainly *called* Latvians."

Gustavs gave a slight headshake. "I don't follow."

"Well, first you must understand that we had a fearsome reputation at the time. The *strēlnieki*—our riflemen, were instrumental in the Bolshevik seizure of power. Lenin's *landsknechts*, I've heard them called. Mercenaries. It's been argued that Lenin would never have succeeded were it not for the Latvian regiments, to whom he promised freedom, independence, all those utopian dreams at the beginning. Anyhow, within Russia we were often referred to as *Letts*, a vague terminology which in turn has caused a great many vague inferences among historians. The term *Latvian* was used increasingly to refer to anyone who wasn't Russian, or Russian speaking, so you had many Latvian guards or soldiers who might well have been German, Austro-Hungarian, what have you. The question of ethnicity was secondary."

"So the executioners . . ."

"Referred to as Latvian at the time, and therefore, often in history books. But no, mostly Russian. We were there, of course, guarding the Ipatiev house, and if memory serves there was one amongst the, what was it," Alberts scratched his head, "eight or nine shooters I believe. Celms. Yes, Celms was his name. Come to think of it, the Romanovs' head footman was Latvian as well, Trūps, executed alongside the entire family that very night."

Gustavs sighed dramatically. "You know, this might be the most dreadful conversation I've ever had on Christmas Eve."

Alberts guffawed and nearly spilt his wine. "It was you who asked! Twenty years after class is dismissed and finally I can teach you some proper history." He took another sip of wine. "Enough! No more of this—goodness, is that the time?"

"I'll get your jacket, eat some more, it'll be a long while before dinner."

Gustavs collected the requisite items: jacket, coat, scarf, mittens, flat cap and cane. As always, he took a moment to admire the photograph of his late wife, a picture framed in driftwood on a shelf by the door. An intimate portrait on their wedding day, candid, a streak of sunshine illuminating her face as she laughed.

Alberts, now properly bundled, tugged his cap, cleared his throat and thumped his cane twice upon the floor, as if testing its durability. "Thank you for picking me up, Gustav."

"Of course."

"How do I look?"

"Dashing."

"Well, some things never change, do they? We're off."

On the southeast corner of Jarvis and Carlton Street, a church tower built in the neo-gothic style rose high above the city, its old copper steeple, a faded pastel green, vanishing into the black of night. A light snowfall had begun, thick flakes twirling as they drifted gently down, melting upon the pavement. Inside, a jolly crowd, the congregation of St. Andrew's greeting one another with heartfelt embraces, pink cheeks and watery eyes, everyone thawing from the cold. Organ music played in the background as worshippers put away their coats, greeted old friends and loved ones and leafed through the Christmas bulletin.

Gustavs took his seat in the usual pew with his family: his mother Lūcija and older brother Oskars, recently arrived from Florida and its more temperate climate; Omīte's two children, Uldis and Mirdza along with their two little rascals; Alberts, his other two daughters, their husbands and *their* daughters, and the relations continued round to seemingly fill the entire row. Smiles and nods of greeting to familiar faces in the crowd, old and young, recognizable from a lifetime of community events—dance troupes, boy scouts, summer camps, and song festivals alike.

Omīte sat with the choir in the balcony as she had for thirty years, the collection plate went round to gather donations for aid in Latvia, and when the lights dimmed for the final hymn of the evening, Gustavs' mother produced a handkerchief to dab at the odd tear, the organ lulling everyone into memories of yuletides past, and bittersweet remembrances of loved ones who would join them no longer.

Back home, a night of tradition. A crackling fireplace and a candlelit tree, dogs and children running amuck while the adults drank mulled wine and prepared a feast. In keeping with familial custom, someone had started the fire with the flue still closed, fumigating the living room with a cloud of blue smoke as Gustavs marched round opening windows. After stoking a few logs, he caught sight of two little tykes, heads buried beneath the lowest spruce branches, rustling amongst the wrapped packages, little bottoms wiggling in the air, one of which he gave a light boot with his slipper. "We were only looking!" they squealed, and ran sniggering into the kitchen.

A meal of glistening ham, scalloped potatoes and rich mushroom salad was accompanied by homemade rhubarb wine and savoured to the last bite, much to the aggravation of the young ones who squirmed impatiently in their chairs. Afterwards, by the candlelight of the Christmas tree, the children recited poems for elders with proud smiles, the necessary performances before a single ribbon could be tugged. Ieva, Gustavs' niece, plucked a lovely little piece on her *kokle*—a morning star engraved into the face of the wooden instrument, its strings quivering at the touch of her nimble fingers.

At long last, the gifts were distributed, and soon thereafter bows and tissue and sheets of wrapping paper blanketed the floor. The children busied themselves with their new toys as the adults picked at gingerbread cookies and indulged in various *digestifs*, the evening slowly drifting toward the midnight hour. Classical carols played softly on the radio while the dogs nestled themselves by the fireplace, the hearth no longer crackling with bright flame but casting an ambient orange glow, embers flickering in the darkness.

Over the next few days, the social events of the season took their toll, and by New Year's Eve, Gustavs—overfed and over-fraternized—was thoroughly exhausted. The Latvian Center was hosting a ball—a sophisticated evening of champagne and dancing—and the Ziediņš clan, with all its various branchlets, was rather keen on attending. The only impediment seemed to be the two schnauzers, which presented Gustavs with a perfect opportunity to volunteer his services.

Would he mind? Not at all. But truly? Yes, truly. And he would walk them, feed them? Happily. Gustavs played the role of benevolent dog-sitter with sincerity, secretly elated to have finally contrived a quiet evening to himself.

Omīte was of a similar inclination, and preferred to remain home with two of her favourite holiday pastimes; the first, her pre-ferred *kirschwasser*, a potent German cherry brandy which, by her second glass, led inevitably to her second pastime—the irresistible silver screen charms of one Cary Grant.

Gustavs, meanwhile, took up position in his favourite armchair with a pipe, a tin of Turkish tobacco, a cognac, and a battered copy of *The Count of Monte Cristo* while the schnauzers curled about his slippers and chased hares in their sleep. For a time, he puffed contentedly and read of the extraordinary adventures of Edmond Dantés, dozed off at some point and awoke with only minutes to midnight. He found Omīte similarly napping on the couch and shook her gently awake to inquire about champagne, to which she brusquely replied that she was only resting her eyes and to make sure the bottle was properly chilled.

In Omīte's sunroom, they toasted the new year and all that 1987 would bring, gazing through the window onto the blanket of snow that lay undisturbed across the yard, little caps of white piled atop fence posts in the distance. He refilled their glasses and they sat for a long while, cozy and warm looking out into the cold, and Gustavs did his best to ignore thoughts of what had transpired only a few short weeks before, on a similarly serene, moonlit eve.

II.

WINTER
1987

SIX

Renata was in a mood, a frightening mood. She sat as she usually did, her posture completely rigid, striking her typewriter fiercely as if she meant to snap the keys. Her eyes were narrowed behind her glasses, lips pinched together, faint creases webbing the corners of her mouth. Gustavs bided his time behind his desk, tense, his mind wheeling through the previous week's 'to-do' list and any pertinent items he might have missed. He leafed through some assignments and waited for an opening which finally came in the form of a curt, singular sigh from across the room.

"Is everything alright?" he asked in a most obsequious tone.

The typewriter stopped clacking, and Renata closed her eyes and exhaled through her nose, folding her hands primly in her lap.

"Ah, I'm sorry Gustav, it's just, Kasia's father . . ."

Gustavs breathed a sigh of relief. "Oh?" he said. *Worried? Who was worried?* He removed his glasses thoughtfully, a man without a care in the world.

"Andrzej was supposed to take her to ballet this afternoon and has now been held up with, well, heaven knows what. *Work*, he says. Work, my foot. As if this man has worked a single day in his life. Excuse me, Gustav, but I'm not afraid to say it: in this world there are men of character, and then, there are just men. My brother-in-law is very much the latter."

A clever little witticism, and one that tempted Gustav into a smile, though he knew better than to risk that.

"Is it the usual class?"

She nodded, peering over her glasses at a desk calendar. "As if I don't have my own responsibilities . . ."

"I can take her if you like, I don't mind."

Renata seemed genuinely surprised by the offer. "I couldn't ask that of you."

"You're not, I'm offering. I have my car with me today, anyhow."

"You're sure?" she said, hesitantly.

"Of course. Kasia is practically *my* niece, the amount of time she spends here. I can finish marking these tomorrow."

"That would be terribly kind of you, Gustav."

"Not at all," he said, rising to grab his coat. "I take it she knows the way?"

As they set out in Gustavs' old Berkshire Green Volvo, Kasia proved an excellent navigator, regaling him with tales of famous ballerinas and punctuating her stories with "right!" and "left!" She found them a spot along College Street where he parked and proceeded to walk with her a while to the studio. Kasia was telling him about her recent outing to see the Nutcracker, when she suddenly called out "Madame!" and took off sprinting down the sidewalk. She stopped in front of what appeared to be a small bear smoking a cigarette in an alcove, a diminutive beast covered in thick fur that knelt down to the beaming young girl and pinched her cheek.

When he caught up, he overheard the bear saying, "You have your slippers this time?" Kasia nodded exuberantly and half-turned to show her backpack. "Good girl, now, up you go." Slender fingers emerged from the coat sleeve and smacked Kasia's bottom as she whipped open the door and bounded up the staircase without so much as a wave goodbye.

The bear was not, as it turned out, a bear, but a beauty. The woman was short in stature and wore a large, brimless fur hat, her chestnut hair spilling over the front of a velvety fur coat that hung well past her knees. She had sharp features: a small, pointed nose, pronounced, rosy cheekbones and stared at him intensely through pale brown eyes that matched her shade of lipstick, a colour that reminded Gustavs of creamed cocoa. She blew a cloud of smoke and warm breath into the air.

"Your daughter is quite the talent," she said, a somewhat husky voice, her accent heavily Slavic.

"Sorry? Oh, oh no, she's not—I mean, I'm not . . ."

"Your niece, perhaps."

"We're not related, I'm just helping out my friend. Not my *friend*—she works for me. She's, well . . ."

"You're a jittery one, aren't you? Are you always like this?"

Gustavs cleared his throat. "No, no I'm not. Gustavs," he said, extending a gloved hand, trying not to flush.

The woman waited for just a moment, surely toying with him, then tucked the cigarette between her lips and reciprocated with a firm handshake.

"Tatyana." Then, almost as an afterthought, "Ivanova."

"Is this your studio?" he asked, craning his neck upwards.

"My husband's, technically, on paper. But yes, my own."

He nodded.

"Ah, you're from the school then, am I correct? The English school?"

"That's right."

"A teacher?"

"I suppose so, more or less. Director, officially."

"Ooh," she intoned. "The *boss* man."

"Not exactly. We're just a language academy. Quite boring, really."

"Did you study to become a teacher?"

"No. English literature, actually"—he silently cursed himself, then decided to make light of it—"even more exciting than teaching, I know."

"Ah, a professor, then, perhaps. Are you a poet?"

"Just an admirer."

"And do you read any *other* literature?"

"Such as . . ."

She took a long drag of her cigarette. "Russian."

"Some."

She hummed, reflective. "Everyone knows Tolstoy, of course. Dostoevsky. But Akhmatova, Bulgakov, *Chekhov* . . . Pushkin!"— she clicked her tongue and gave him a sly wink—"this is essential reading, professor, if you are truly a lover of literature."

"I'll have to look into those." A fierce wind cut through him and he coughed into a raised fist. "And you, did you study ballet?"

"All my life."

"Professionally, or . . . just a passion?"

"I danced with the Kirov."

Gustavs nodded slowly, prompting an impish smile from Tatyana, a singular dimple creasing her cheek.

"Professionally," she said.

Gustavs rocked on his heels, glancing back down the street. "Well . . ."

"Kasia has a knack for it, you know. A *naturelle*." She looked him up and down for a moment, appraising eyes behind dark lashes. "You should come see her. We have a recital next month."

"Oh. Well, I suppose I could look at my calendar," he said, reaching into his coat.

"The 12th."

Leafing through his pocketbook, he said, "As I'm sure you're aware, the life of a teacher can be very busy—so many opulent galas to attend, but, I think I could fit it in."

"Mm," she replied, head tilted ever so slightly now, studious eyes upon him. "7 p.m."—she straightened her posture—"don't be late."

"Will there be a dress code in effect?"

"Of course."

Gustavs waited for the rest of her response until he realized that he had received it.

"*Ahem*, I should . . . get going, your class must be starting soon."

Tatyana's expression had shifted, looking past him now and into the street. In his periphery, he noted an approaching shadow, and then another, flanking him on either side. While it took him a moment, he soon recognized the two detectives from the funeral.

"Gustav, Happy New Year," said De Rossi, his partner Horowitz adding a nod of greeting.

Gustavs said nothing, looking back and forth at the pair of them. De Rossi gave a quick nod of acknowledgment to Tatyana.

"We have a few questions for you, we were hoping you could join us for a brief chat," said Horowitz.

"Questions about what?" said Gustavs.

"Last autumn," said De Rossi.

"It won't take more than a few minutes."

Gustavs hesitated and glanced furtively at Tatyana. Her cigarette glowed in the air as she propped her elbow in her palm, eyeing the new interlocutors with suspicion.

"Alright," he said finally, and began to move toward the black Crown Vic, parked off to one side. De Rossi opened the back door, and Gustavs turned back to look at Tatyana, words failing him.

"So boring, you teachers," she said, a pinched smirk on her face.

"This isn't—it's not what it looks like."

Tatyana said nothing, raising a brow. *Oh?*

"Watch your head," said De Rossi. Gustavs ducked down and sank into the backseat of the car, flinching as the door slammed.

SEVEN

GUSTAVS WAS ESCORTED TO A CRAMPED LITTLE ROOM WITHOUT windows. The walls were concrete block, painted an anemic shade of yellow, and in the center of the room was a rectangular steel table bolted to the linoleum floor. While he waited, he noticed that his seat was also fixed to the ground—cold steel, padded with a grimy, flaccid cushion. A pungent, chemical odor of disinfectant lingered in the air.

It wasn't long before Horowitz returned with a manila file folder and lined pad of paper in hand. "Mr. Ziedins, it's important that you understand this is completely voluntary," he began. "You're not under any obligation to stay, we just had a few clarifying questions about Mr. Barons' unfortunate passing last year. We were hoping you might shed some light on the events."

De Rossi entered shortly thereafter with a box of donuts and a coffee, which he placed on the table. Horowitz flipped a sheet of paper and began scribbling on the pad.

"In the event that you—"

"What can you tell us about Maxim Fyodorov?" interrupted De Rossi.

Gustavs looked to the older detective, who appeared a study in contrasts. His suit was perfectly tailored, yet wrinkled, as though he might have bunched up the jacket and used it as a pillow the evening before. A crisp Windsor knot sat well beneath an open collar, while his features were strained and gaunt. His eyes were dark, and appeared to be encircled by a faint bruising.

"Pardon?"

"*Doctor* Maxim Fyodorov."

"I've never heard of him." He took a sip of the coffee, lukewarm and burnt.

"He was Mr. Barons' physician."

Gustavs looked from one officer to the other, then shrugged his shoulders. "Alright?"

"We have some concerns regarding his credentials," said Horowitz. "We were wondering if you knew anything about him, his practice."

Gustavs made a face and shook his head.

There was something about the older detective that gnawed at him, chafing a particular nerve. He had never been one to seek out confrontation, but he couldn't help the swell of indignation that rose with each of De Rossi's brusque comments. Perhaps it was simply an innate character trait of the Baltic peoples, a ritual distaste for authority, given that such parties had usually been unwelcome foreign occupants. Centuries of servitude and repression, and now a visceral reflex against men in uniform. Gustavs gently pushed the coffee cup away and leaned back in his chair.

"His name is Maxim *Fyodorov*," said De Rossi, enunciating each syllable. "What does that tell you?"

Gustavs shrugged again. "That he plays hockey for the Soviet Olympic team?" He looked to Horowitz. "Is there anything else I can do for you gentlemen? I don't see how I'm going to be of any help with, whatever this is."

"We've been informed that—"

"We've been informed that you put the Barons' in contact with a Russian doctor whose paperwork isn't exactly as tidy as it should be," said De Rossi.

Gustavs furrowed his brow.

"Got your attention now, have we?"

Horowitz shot his partner a cutting glance, though De Rossi didn't notice; his gaze still fixated upon Gustavs, watching every movement, hanging on every word.

"We're just following up on a lead, that's all," Horowitz counselled.

"I don't understand."

"Think, Gustav."

"What's the matter with his paperwork?"

"It's just a tip at the moment," said Horowitz. "Also, and I'm sure you can understand, there are certain elements of this equation that we can't reveal to the general public." His expression softened. "Reasons of confidentiality."

Gustavs thought it over for a moment. "Most people in our community go to the same doctor. At least, many, I should say. An older Latvian fellow, he lives in the west end, out toward Etobicoke." He paused, then recalled something—a casual chat, the most innocuous of conversations. He wondered why it didn't come to him sooner, but then, why would it?

"Actually, there is something. This must have been, well, over a year ago at least. Imants mentioned something about family physicians. Like I said, most of us just go to Elmārs—Elmārs Krūmiņš, he's a GP—but the Barons' live out in Don Mills. Elmārs is really out of the way for them, on the other side of the city . . ." He adjusted his glasses up the bridge of his nose. "I think I suggested they try someone more local, someone in the area, simply for the convenience." He nodded to himself, "That's right, it was winter, the roads were especially bad, his wife doesn't drive and Imants' eyesight, well . . ."

Horowitz asked him to spell Krūmiņš' surname, then looked over at his partner who gave a reluctant nod, seemingly in agreement.

"Anyone else you know use this guy?" asked De Rossi.

"Krūmiņš?"

"Fyodorov."

"I wouldn't know. I never *suggested* him—whoever *he* is, I just said it would make more sense to find someone in the neighborhood. Which, of course, it did."

Horowitz removed a string-tie envelope from the file, unwound it, and produced a photograph, laying it on the table. The photo was a grainy black and white print, taken covertly from across the street without the subject's knowledge. A man sat in a restaurant booth by the window drinking coffee and reading a newspaper.

"You recognize him?"

Gustavs leaned in. "Kind of hard to tell from the distance."

"So that's a 'no'," De Rossi grumbled.

"No."

Horowitz removed another photograph and laid it beside the first: a woman at a train station wearing a trench coat and shawl, holding a large handbag. A brunette, likely in her thirties, apprehension etched across her face, troubled eyes peering down the track.

"What about her?"

Gustavs shook his head. "Neither, sorry." Then, "Should I be concerned?"

"No, no," Horowitz replied, scribbling something else on his notepad. "Thank you, Mr. Ziedins. I hope you understand this is just some information-gathering on our part. Sometimes we get a

phone call, a letter, obviously it's our duty to follow up on things."
He shrugged his shoulders sympathetically. "You know, most of
the time, detective work is just us chasing our own tails. Hence,"
he gestured to the photographs.

Gustavs nodded. "I don't suppose you could tell me more about
this tip?"

De Rossi pulled out his chair and took a seat, propping his
elbows on the table, making his presence known.

"Unfortunately," Horowitz continued, "we can't reveal that sort
of information. These things are usually done anonymously for
a reason."

Gustavs looked between the two men, awaiting something more.

"We think he may have been poisoned," said De Rossi.

Horowitz stopped writing and turned to face his partner, clearly
caught off guard. De Rossi pushed the box of donuts across the
table. "Boston cream?"

Gustavs said nothing, speechless, as Horowitz capped his pen
and placed it neatly on the table.

"What . . ." Gustavs began, "is that true?"

"Not exactly," Horowitz replied, his tone cold and bureaucratic.
"There is no evidence to suggest anything of the sort."

"Then why are—"

"Sometimes we have to follow up on information we receive,
no matter how *absurd* it may seem," Horowitz replied, a derisory
glance at his partner. De Rossi slid a cigarette from his pack and
brought it to his lips, never breaking eye contact with Gustavs.

"What the hell are you guys playing at?"

"There's no cause for any concern, Mr. Ziedins, that I can say
with certainty. I'll admit, not an ideal way to end a conversation,
but I think that's all we need for today. Thank you for coming in,

your cooperation is appreciated, and I apologize for causing you any undue anxiety. I can assure you, there's nothing to worry about."

Gustavs looked to De Rossi. "It certainly didn't sound like that."

De Rossi lit his cigarette and peered at Gustavs through whorls of grey.

Horowitz adopted a more sympathetic tone. "From what I understand, Mr. Barons was highly respected within the Latvian community, and very much loved as well." Softly, he added, "The mind is a very delicate thing. When faced with tragedy, or trauma, some people . . . they have a very difficult time letting go."

Gustavs wasn't quite certain what to make of the pair of them. Horowitz—fresh faced and unfaltering, but holding something back? And if so, to what end? Or perhaps, all of it simply a matter of investigative routine; the simplest explanation, and the most rational. De Rossi was a different story altogether. Like some kind of pit bull that enjoyed playing mind games. And if the intention here was to provoke a reaction, he certainly wasn't about to give the man the satisfaction.

And so, Gustavs stood, buttoned his coat without a word, and began to move toward the door.

After a few steps, De Rossi called out: "Charlotte Lazdina."

Gustavs stopped, holding the door ajar and looked over his shoulder.

"You know her?" De Rossi asked.

"I know a lot of people, detective," he replied, and let the door slip through his fingers.

It was dark when Gustavs returned home. The lights were on in the kitchen, and from Omīte's living room he could hear the familiar sounds of the Golden Girls—poor Blanche being chastised, yet again, for her libertine ways.

A vaguely familiar voice giggled along with the television set, and he found Irina, their Ukrainian neighbour, seated on the couch alongside his great-aunt.

"Ah, at last, he returns. Come join us," said Omīte. "There's some beet soup on the stove and Irina brought cabbage rolls, it's the Ukrainian New Year."

"Oh, I should probably be going," said Irina, shifting in her seat. "I've got an early start tomorrow."

"Nonsense, Gustavs hasn't seen you since my birthday."

Irina smiled demurely and glanced away. No longer the sous-chef ordering him around with platters of hors d'oeuvres; the clock had struck midnight, transforming her once more into the bashful neighbor girl from across the way.

Irina was just the sort of young woman to inspire all manner of quaint maternal maxims—the girl who was "raised well" and would make a "suitable wife." She had wavy bangs, sparkling blue eyes, and a bright, almost moonstruck smile forever teetering on the brink of laughter. Sweet, with a sort of youthful naiveté, for some reason she often reminded Gustavs of the cartoon Bambi.

"It's been a while, that's true. How have you been, Irina?"

"Oh, wonderful, yes. Keeping busy. We had a great celebration last weekend for *Malanka*—hopefully a sign of good things to come this year."

"Pancakes and polka?"

Irina smiled. "Of course. "

"Though hopefully not in that order. Never wise to skip and dance with a bellyful of jam."

"Oh, no! Of course not," she said, her hand nervously darting around her collarbone. "And yourself? Any resolutions for the new year?"

Gustavs exhaled. "I hadn't really thought about it. I don't bother with them much. I'll usually have them broken by now anyway . . ."

"Or maybe no bad habits," she said, then flushed suddenly at the implication.

"You can stop smoking that pipe, for one," Omīte chimed in.

Gustavs shrugged and looked to Irina for support. "I like to have a puff from time to time."

"So does a chimney," said Omīte. "Now, get yourself a plate already."

"No, no, take your time," said Irina. "I need to be on my way, truly. I'm sorry, Rasmiņa"—she rose, then bent down to kiss Omīte on both cheeks—"we'll do this again soon, I promise. You both enjoy your evening."

After Irina had left, Gustavs settled in behind his bureau with a newspaper and a bowl of soup, spooning in a hefty dollop of sour cream and stirring the dark beets into swirls of bright pink. It wasn't long before Omīte came shuffling around the corner, wrapped in a thick, crocheted afghan.

"So?" she intoned.

Gustavs had a mouthful of beets.

Omīte's eyes darted back toward the front door, her thinly painted brows twitching.

Gustavs sighed. "Not for me, Omīte."

"Why on earth not?" she demanded.

"We've had this conversation before."

"She's a lovely girl!"

"Of course she is. She's just, it's not . . ." He searched for the words. "A match."

"I'm starting to worry about you, Gustav. Lately I feel there's an odor in the air, and it's not just your awful pipe. You're starting to smell like an old bachelor."

Gustavs chuckled.

Omīte's expression turned decidedly sour. "You're not seeing one of those . . . you know, one of those *darker* girls again, are you?"

"Oh for God's sake." He let his spoon clang against the rim of the bowl.

"What?"

"How could—you don't mean Isabelle?"

Omīte raised her brow in defense. "You can't expect me to remember all their names."

"Names—as if it were a procession. Who have you met other than Isabelle? And she was from Madrid, if you'll recall."

"She looked like she was from one of those harems," Omīte mumbled.

"Harems? What harems! She was *Spanish*, not some sultan's concubine!"

"I'm only *saying* . . . don't get so defensive. You need a nice girl, Gustav. One of your own people, someone who understands you. Understands your history, your heritage. It's time. What's so wrong with Irina? At your age you can't afford to be so choosy."

"Your vote of confidence is appreciated."

"Where else do you think you'll find a nice girl like her?"

"Surely they have others down at the Ottoman palace. Dancing nude in the fountains . . ."

"Don't take that tone with me—I say this for your own benefit. It's not good to mix blood you know, it's not healthy for the child."

"Jesus Christ."

"Gustav!"

There was a momentary détente, Omīte standing with lips pursed, shaking her head. Gustavs removed his glasses.

"I really hope you don't speak like this outside of the house. Bad enough that I have to hear it."

"Speak to who? I'm old! I can say what I like. It's one of the few privileges that comes at my age."

"You can't say things like that Omīte, really."

"*Ahh,*" she swatted this away, and slowly trudged back toward the kitchen, muttering to herself. "Good stock, she is . . . comes to visit, brings us cabbage roles . . . those beautiful eyes . . . and still, his *highness* does not approve . . ."

Gustavs ate, famished, but struggled to focus his mind—the newspaper serving as mere décor, overlaying his desk. Like old vinyl, forever skipping on a record player, he could only replay his earlier encounter with the detectives. It was De Rossi and his needling that made him truly uneasy.

Charlotte Laz-*dee*-na was, in fact, Šarlote Lazdiņa, though those who knew her best simply called her Lotte. Gustavs, for his part, had barely given her a second thought in years. They were little more than children when they'd first met, a lifetime ago in *ģimnāzija*—the Latvian high school held on Friday evenings. Quirky and kind and irresistibly charming, she was a couple of years older than him which, as a bespectacled young boy at the tender age of fourteen, effectively made her a goddess amongst mere mortals. And yet, in a most extraordinary twist of fate, the goddess had apparently seemed to notice Gustavs as well, this lowly being who worshipped her from afar. More than that, she had even taken to casting him the odd flirtatious glance or two between classes and during assemblies—glances that hardly went unnoticed, or unremarked, around the school.

Soon there were rumors being whispered and notes passed between confidantes, until one fateful autumn weekend when Paulis Zutis—the life of the party, even then—decided to host a getaway at his family cottage on Lake Simcoe, about an hour north of the city. At one point on an otherwise damp and dreary Saturday afternoon, Lotte took Gustavs discreetly by the hand and the pair broke off from the crowd and absconded down a path that led into the forest. The enveloping foliage was painted in vivid shades of sepia and marigold, the air heavily scented by woodsmoke and wet earth. All the while Gustavs' heart raced with wild anticipation, pins and needles prickling his limbs.

It was a predictably awkward affair, and hardly the romantic setting he had envisioned, though nothing could ever tarnish the memory of that afternoon. Her mouth was unexpectedly cool, tasting of beer and the cigarettes they had smoked earlier. And there, on a damp carpet of fallen leaves, he fumbled like the schoolboy he was with a bulky sweater and the cursed wire contraption beneath, pinching and pulling until it yielded to his will, cupping at the warm flesh beneath. Her hands were rough and cold, but only at first.

Gustavs may have left down that path a boy, but he emerged from the forest a man, a colossus in his own right. He no longer walked but strode, tall and strapping and basking in the giggles and blushes that came from Lotte's girlfriends. He soared on high for two magnificent weeks until, in true Icarian fashion, he abruptly fell from the heavens and plunged headfirst into an ocean of all-consuming melancholy. In the end, it was those very same whispers that betrayed him, murmuring in the halls that Lotte had made a pass at Tomass—his good friend and already a budding

Casanova—and that the pair had gone to the cinema to see West Side Story, amongst other extracurricular activities.

Tomass was apologetic but wouldn't deny a thing, leading to the first and only fight the two best friends ever had; Gustavs catching his new adversary square in the jaw with a tidy right hook. Tomass accepted his punishment gracefully, refusing to fight back, and instead ended up walking his inconsolable friend to the corner store for a bag of frozen peas, a sprained finger only adding insult to injury.

It wasn't long before Tomass himself felt the keen sting of Lotte's changeable affections. They had both heard the chatter that their mercurial beauty had always carried a torch for a much older boy—apparently some volleyball star from Michigan. Lotte and this American heartthrob had allegedly been star-crossed lovers for some time, quarrelling on and off again for several years—a romance that, if those damned rumors were to be believed, had been rekindled in earnest.

Gustavs leaned back in his chair, a nostalgic smile for the weighty emotions of his adolescence. One would be hard-pressed, even now, to find someone with any unkind words for Lotte Lazdiņa. The pair had always remained on good terms as there was never any malice in her actions; she was simply a beguiling free-spirit that seemed to cast her spell on most everyone she met—man or woman, young or old. He recalled one summer's eve at *Jāņi*, the annual summer solstice festival where she, like all the unwed girls, wore the traditional *vaiņags*—a garland of field daisies upon her head. With her cascading blonde hair, full cheeks and golden halo of fresh blooms, she looked the very essence of Latvian beauty. In another life she could have very well been the inspiration for Milda—the famous copper maiden that held her three stars aloft on the *Brīvības Piemineklis*— the Independence Monument, in Rīga.

After completing a degree in journalism, Lotte had become increasingly active in the Latvian community's politics—vocal and frequently critical of LNAK and what she labeled as an "antiquated" and "worryingly pacifist" approach toward the restoration of independence. At least, so he had heard. Gustavs didn't have much patience for diplomacy to begin with, but when Latvians began to point fingers at each other rather than at Moscow, he found himself increasingly cut adrift from his social circles, and very much by his own hand. Now, years later, with this strange convergence of circumstances—Lotte, Imants, the insinuations made by Valdis Roze at the funeral—it seemed the community, or rather its politics, weren't entirely finished with him.

For as long as he could remember, there was always talk of how involved the KGB were in the daily lives of the Latvian diaspora. Tales of those who were particularly outspoken being followed home by shadows that flickered in the twilight. Breathy telephone calls at three in the morning that played on the mind. Perhaps most distressing of all, insinuations of collaborators, those who would betray their own community from the inside. Imants had once confided that he woke one morning to find a dead raccoon gutted and splayed across the hood of his Buick.

But, then again, Latvians were also particularly fond of a good story. Hopefully, De Rossi was too. If there was any truth in what the detective had suggested, Gustavs was wary to uncover his role in an increasingly unpredictable, and rather disturbing narrative.

EIGHT

"WHY THIS SUDDEN INTEREST IN PUSHKIN?" ASKED ALBERTS, hunched over and skimming an arthritic finger along a row of books.

"No reason," Gustavs replied. "Expanding my horizons."

"Surely you've read some of his work before."

Gustavs shrugged. "Russian authors weren't exactly encouraged in school."

His father-in-law turned with a disapproving glare. "I certainly hope you're not referring to your literature teacher. Mrs. Miķelsone was a dear friend you know."

"I'm only joking. It's been a long time since I sat in her class."

"That it has," Alberts replied, turning his attention back to various rickety towers of assorted texts, some resembling Pisa more than others.

Alberts' desk was, as usual, littered with stationary. Envelopes, stamps, hand-written letters and press releases, communiqués to ministers and media outlets, all part and parcel of the old man's unrelenting work on behalf of the LNAK. Amongst the usual clutter, Gustavs' eye was drawn to an open journal scribbled with names and biographical information, seemingly historical figures from the turn of the century.

"Ah, here we are," said Alberts. "I won't subject you to Godunov, but his collected works, mainly the poetry, is quite good." He removed a red hardcover from a wobbling column as if it were a game of Jenga, and handed it to Gustavs.

"I have my work cut out for me," Gustavs replied, leafing through the book. "Speaking of, what's all this—Alksnis, Pēterss. Catherine the 1st?"

"Ah yes, our last conversation got me to thinking"—Alberts lowered himself into his chair with a groan—"Celms and the Romanovs, all that. I thought I might compile a list of famous, or rather overlooked Latvians, perhaps even work toward another book one day." He coughed something phlegmy from his throat. "If I still have the time, of course," he added with a grimace.

"Don't talk like that. Alksnis I recognize, head of the Soviet air force for a time . . . ?"

"Correct. Glad to see you didn't sleep through *all* of my lectures."

"Catherine of Russia?"

"There's some speculation there—Lithuanian, most likely, at least in part. But she was raised in Alūksne for most of her childhood."

"No kidding."

Alberts gave a proud nod, he himself having been born in the same small town in the country's North-East. "The first woman to rule Russia. It's likely we went to the same church."

"I don't recognize this Pēterss."

"Ah, yes. This fellow was a rather recent discovery and, I must admit, he may very well be the most interesting character of them all. A most colourful life. You know, he was born—"

"Hold that thought." Gustavs reached down into a burlap tote bag he'd brought along and removed two glasses, a knife, a bottle of *melnais balzāms*—a famously bitter botanical liqueur—and a fat link of kielbasa sausage.

"You're a saint, an absolute saint."

"Someone has to look after you. You're wasting away here."

"Gustav, if you wouldn't mind—push that dresser in front of the door, will you? There's a new nurse on this shift and she patrols the halls like the bloody Gestapo."

Gustavs did as he was instructed and then distributed the contraband between them on the nightstand. They clinked glasses and Alberts took a sip of *balzāms*, licking his lips with satisfaction. "Nectar of the gods, that is."

"Gods today, demons tomorrow. *Prozīt.*"

"Now, listen to this. Jēkabs Pēterss. Records first take note of this lunatic—for there is no other word, in Liepāja in 1907. Evidently stirred by the revolution a couple of years before, he gets himself arrested for the attempted murder of a factory director. He's eventually acquitted, but not before the Tsarist police remove his fingernails during the interrogation. He decides he's had enough of Europe for the time being—evidently not a fan of Russian manicures—and moves to London where, upon joining a group of gangsters, ends up involved in what the Brits refer to as the "Siege of Sidney Street." Initially a robbery gone bad—it seems the jeweler had other ideas; they have a shootout on the streets of London in broad daylight with the local constabulary.

"Anyway, the then-Home Secretary Churchill brings in the military to quash the whole affair, a building catches fire, several officers are killed and Pēterss ends up being arrested. The man seems to have horseshoes to spare, as he's acquitted due to a lack of evidence and scurries off back to Russia, just in time for the Bolshevik coup. Right in the thick of it, is Pēterss, so much so that he ends up as deputy head of the Cheka and, listen to this—when Dzerzhinsky takes a leave of absence for a few months in 1918, he becomes the interim head of the entire bloody organization. He's drawing up execution lists from phone books."

"I've never even heard of this man."

"Eventually they put him in charge of Tashkent, and, while in Uzbekistan, he bumps into an old gangster friend from London. This fellow, incidentally, has been ordered by Lenin himself to oversee operations in Persia. So the pair of them set out by train through the bloody desert—at one point driving a vehicle borrowed from Trotsky—and end up being ceremoniously greeted by a cavalcade of horses as ordered by the Shah."

"Sounds like a film. What happened to him?"

Alberts shrugged. "Not so ceremonious, in the end. Few escaped Stalin's paranoia in the thirties. Arrested and shot in '38 alongside most other Latvians. Alksnis included. Not that he didn't deserve it, of course. A ruthless man. There are still rumors that he might have been Peter the Painter, a sort of mythical figure from London's criminal underworld that was never caught."

"The legend lives on."

Alberts took another sip of *balzāms* and studied his guest through hooded eyes. "Am I boring you, Gustav? You seem distracted."

"Do I? I'm sorry. It's been a strange week."

Alberts lifted his glass. "Come on then, out with it."

Gustavs hesitated, scratching at the fabric of his armrest.

"That strange?"

"I wasn't going to say anything, but it's been eating at me. It might sound a little . . ."

"While I'm young, Gustav."

"Well, it's about Imants. I was approached by a couple of

police detectives and, they said—*hinted* that . . . that he may have been poisoned."

Alberts replaced his glass on the table and folded his hands in his lap.

"One of them said he was just following up on a tip, that they have to follow all leads no matter how absurd. Which is true, of course, to a point. The other guy, well, he's a piece of work, that one."

Alberts was silent for a time, hands clasped, rubbing his thumbs against one another. "Poisoned?"

"They didn't say much else. I couldn't get a read on them, if they were just trying to make me uncomfortable, see if I'd get nervous and tell them something. As if I had something to tell!"

"It seems they succeeded, at least in part."

Gustavs returned his attention to the armrest, picking at it with a fingernail.

"I suppose, if we take a moment to follow this line of reasoning, the first question to ask would be, who would stand to gain from something like this?"

"Apparently me."

"They said this?"

"Implied as much. Last year, at the funeral. They think I'm going to be the next president of LNAK."

"So they've been asking around."

"They're detectives, after all."

"The heir apparent . . ."

Gustavs rolled his eyes. "I still don't understand why. You would think they'd look to someone with at least a bit of experience. Someone more active in the community."

"Don't forget, you *were* rather active before. My Anniņa used to drag you round to all sorts of events, and, if I recall, you quite enjoyed them. A real social butterfly, you were. Had a knack for it, too. I had many a conversation with people remarking about my soft-spoken son-in-law." After a momentary pause, Alberts took a breath and made a face, a slight wince, as if being careful not to offend. "It does all sound a bit . . . fantastical, don't you think?"

Gustavs nodded. "It does. Still, when you're sitting in one of those damn interrogation rooms . . ."

"Well, are you genuinely concerned?"

"Of course I am."

Alberts shook his head. "You misunderstand. What I'm asking is this: Are you concerned that what they are saying is true, or are you concerned about the consequences, the ramifications, if it were true?"

Gustavs gazed toward the window, contemplative, and after a time said, "It does sound a bit far-fetched, don't you think?"

"Yes . . . and also no. The Russians, they have a vested interest in sewing discord within our community. In all communities. The regime is no longer ruled by the iron fist. The hammer has rusted and the sickle is dull. Stalin's cult of personality is long dead, Gorbachev himself is calling for liberal reforms and the return of history. Real history, mind, not the revisionist pish they print in their textbooks now." Alberts sighed. "Still, in another sense, this makes them more dangerous than ever. They risk losing their empire."

"What does this have to do with us?"

"Don't underestimate our influence, Gustav. Nationalism is on the rise throughout the Soviet republics, there are writings on self-determination widely circulated in *samizdat*, other Western literature smuggled in by exiles and dissidents. And that is us,

Gustav, make no mistake. The work we do is crucial in supporting the underground movement in Rīga. Yes, we make donations as we always have—smuggle in money, goods, what have you—but we provide intellectual support as well to the budding intelligentsia abroad. Moscow perceives us as a great threat, and they do have an eye for it. We support every movement that seeks to undermine their authority, and we have the liberty and financial capital to do so. And perhaps, more importantly than any of that, we have a desire, a burning desire deep in our very bones."

"And you think they're capable of doing something like this?"

"Capable?"—Alberts' brow shot up—"most certainly. Without question. But, do I think they did it?" He held Gustavs' attention for a moment. "No. I do not."

"No?"

"Purely from the perspective of risk versus reward, I don't see what they would stand to gain. Imants was a colossus in our community but over the years his health had deteriorated, he wasn't the thorn in their side that he used to be. I would argue that there are many others, far more outspoken critics who might be targeted. Bigger fish to fry, as it were. They have their hands full with their own people—Sakharov, Brodsky, Solzhenitsyn, Orlov, Alexeyeva. And only thereafter do they look to their satellites, the exile communities, and we are far from the only ones. The Poles with the weight of Catholicism behind them. There are always rumblings in Prague. Never mind the Romanians, Ceausescu himself seems to prove a perennial nuisance for the Politburo. And then, there are the Americans. All things considered, why bother with Imants?"

"Does the name Fyodorov mean anything to you?"

Alberts drew a palm back over his head, smoothing his shaggy hair. "Should it?"

"Imants' doctor."

"Well, I wouldn't say I'm paranoid, but I do tend to avoid Russian doctors if I can. Dentists, especially. As a boy our local dentist was from Pskov—a damned sadist, he was."

"You think I'm getting carried away with this."

Alberts opened his palm. "What I think . . . what I think is that, from a policing perspective, it's their duty to examine a particular situation from every angle, no matter how obscure, no matter how outlandish the claims may seem. Things are missed all the time— cold cases, for example, evidence overlooked. I would say that most of their job consists of digging into every nook and cranny, asking discomforting questions. You said it was a tip they received? We have more than our fair share of loons in the community, you know this. Just because it smacks of something from a Hollywood film doesn't mean it's not deserving of some inquiry. Or," he shrugged, "perhaps they were simply trying to rattle your chain."

"Consider it rattled."

Alberts' cough returned and he cleared his throat. "Now, I have a small favor to ask, if you don't mind."

"Of course."

"Would you leave these glasses with me until your next visit?" He ran his thumb across the intricate, frosted embossing. "They're quite lovely."

Gustavs regarded his father-in-law for a moment. "Just what are you up to?"

"And the rest of the *balzāms*, if you wouldn't mind."

Gustavs crossed his arms and pitched a brow.

"It's been a while since any of us have had the good stuff, you know." Alberts picked up the bottle and gave it a very unconvincing examination.

"Any of who, exactly?"

"The residents! Who . . ."

"A particular resident, perhaps?"

Alberts replaced the bottle and huffed. "For goodness sake, if you *must* know, there's a Mrs. Jansone, Agnese Jansone from down the hall, you might remember her daughter—"

"Ahh"—Gustavs rose from his seat—"so this was the reason for the special *balzāms* request. Well, well, I know when my company is no longer required."

"Don't be so dramatic, just the other day she was mentioning how she missed it. The recipe dates back to the 18th century you know, and the herbs, they have medicinal properties."

"Do they now?"

"Of course!"

"Alright, Casanova," he said, reaching for his coat.

"I'm only old, you know, I'm not dead."

"Just don't get yourself into trouble, alright? Shall I grease the nurse's palm on the way out so she looks the other way?"

"Don't be absurd," said Alberts. Then, after some hesitation, "But, do let me know if she's still out there, will you?" A genuine look of concern flickered across his face. "Agnese is just down the hall, yet every time I visit I feel as if I'm making a dash into West Germany."

NINE

THE DOORS OF THE LOCAL ELEMENTARY SCHOOL AUDITORIUM clanged shut, Gustavs wincing at the sound. Looking out past the audience toward the stage, he noticed more than a few heads had turned—pursed lips and astringent glances directed at the inconsiderate latecomer. He moved swiftly, and rather self-consciously down the center aisle until he spotted Renata, motioning to a vacant chair.

"Sorry," he whispered, seating himself and brushing the snow from his coat.

Renata put a finger to her lips. "It's just starting."

The auditorium was small but filled to capacity. Parents looked on—nervous and excited, bulky video cameras perched on the odd shoulder and pointed in the direction of the stage where, before a verdant tableau of pine trees and shrubbery, a small grouping of fairies came skipping out from the underbrush and into the spotlight. They were little more than toddlers, prompting adoring murmurs from the crowd, and with emerald tutus and sparkling tiaras they scurried about the stage scattering flower petals and pausing for the occasional, rather wobbly plié.

Soon, another set of woodland creatures appeared, a few years older than the fairies, performing a charming *pas de quatre* from one side of the forest to the other, until they were harried off stage by Kasia and her winged nymphs, the eldest trio of girls dazzling with pirouettes *en pointe*, and leaping through the air to a chorus of applause.

Gustavs was mesmerized by the performance, though hardly by the ensemble of pixies and sprites. Every now and again, a solitary dancer would emerge from the shadows, gliding seamlessly amongst the performers to steady a young pupil's *arabesque*, or rescue an especially ponderous fairy—less concerned with choreography than with the sucking of her own thumb. Tatyana floated in the background as a pagan goddess, draped in ribbons of green silk overlaying her black leotard, a humble crown of ivy resting atop her head. Her paces were fluid and precise, her footfalls like velvet.

Gustavs was entranced. The ballet seemed to come so naturally to Tatyana, her figure muscular yet lithe, shoulders pulled tautly to reveal a sinewy back that flexed with every graceful motion as she shepherded her students amongst the *mise en scène*. She faded into the background as much as she was able, ensuring the spotlight remained invariably upon her students, and took center stage only briefly during a final repertoire with the eldest dancers—the forest maiden's climactic *fouetté*, a whirling blur of elegance.

As the performance concluded, Tatyana gathered her troupe at the front of the stage; curtsies and waves for the audience, who in turned showered the dancers with prolonged cheers and applause. One of Kasia's trio of winged nymphs was handed a microphone and narrated a brief tale to the crowd. Evidently, the "Forest Mother" was required to dance a final piece with her "King," lest she be cursed to return to the depths of the woodland and spend eternity in tragic solitude. The performers took to shielding their eyes, peering out into the crowd in hopes of identifying a worthy nobleman. A giddy murmur rippled through the crowd, accompanied by a fair amount of elbow-prodding from wives and mothers; the roaming eyes of their male counterparts looking in every direction but the stage. It was all delightfully amusing to Gustavs until Kasia suddenly bounded off stage, skipped down the aisle and grabbed him rather firmly by the arm. He had hardly begun his protest before the crowd started shouting encouragements and Renata all but shoved him forward onto his feet.

In the next moment, Gustavs found himself standing before a crowded auditorium, dry-mouthed, feeling the warmth of the stage lights upon his face which, he knew for certain, had turned a mortifying shade of harvest tomato. He shifted his weight nervously while the winged nymph continued speaking into the microphone, though he heard nothing more than muffled tones over the rush of blood in his ears. Tatyana appeared at his side, kohl-rimmed eyes and ruby lips, and demonstrated a basic plié with a playful little grin.

Gustavs stood, confounded for a moment, until he was prompted to replicate the movement along with the other fairies. Angling his feet and bending his knees, he gave a dramatic flourish with his hand and felt relief wash over him as the audience tittered and clapped. Tatyana then lifted her heels, rising into demi-pointe, a position matched once more by the fairies and their budding guest star, the latter with a slightly stiff and unorthodox technique. Now the Forest Mother scowled, placing her hands on her hips and looking out into the audience with a dramatic shake of the head. *Well, this won't do at all now will it?*

She faced Gustavs once more, winked, and proceeded to leap into the air, fluttering her feet in an effortless *entrechat*, sending a roar of laughter through the crowd.

"Give me your hand," she whispered. "Higher."

Gustavs held her fingertips aloft as she ascended *en pointe* and proceeded to spin before him like a dervish. Lowering herself, she pressed up against his chest, the scent of warm sweat and perfume lingering between them. "And . . ." she prompted, a subtle glance to the floor. Gustavs chivalrously obliged, cradling the small of her back and carefully dipping her, Tatyana sweeping her free hand through the air and extending a rigid, porcelain leg to the rafters.

It was over in the briefest of moments; the audience applauding the finale and the nymphs encouraging Gustavs to take his bow. He managed a meek wave and required little prompting to disappear from the stage at the earliest opportunity, trotting quickly past the curtains and away from the spotlight.

The auditorium had mostly emptied by the time Kasia re-emerged alongside her mother, and was accompanied by two friends, their parents and Tatyana trailing in behind. Renata presented her niece with a bouquet of carnations, with the ladies congratulating their ballerinas on a wonderful performance, as well as the headmistress who had toiled over the production. There was even a brief nod to Gustavs and his impromptu repertoire.

The group wrapped themselves in scarves and toques and woolen mittens before bracing the cold outside, a frosty evening beneath an expansive black sky. As they bid their farewells and dispersed into the night, Tatyana sheltered a flame, lighting her cigarette. From beneath her brimless *shapka* she gave him a wry smile, blowing a puff of smoke. "Your plié could use some work."

"I'm surprised my knees didn't crack," he replied, stifling a shiver.

"Mine crack all the time. Are you this way?"

He nodded, and they fell in together, a casual pace as the cold air nipped at their cheeks.

"I took your advice, by the way," he said.

"Oh?"

"Literature. I've been reading some Pushkin."

"And?"

"Not bad."

"Not bad?"

"Alright, it's quite good."

"I told you," she said with a cheeky grin. "Let's see. I doubt you would begin with a novel. Too ambitious. Perhaps a short story to get a feel for his style. Mm . . . still, I would say, some poems?"

Gustavs smiled. "A collection of his poems, yes. How did you know?"

"Much like our dear Pushkin, you're quite easy to read, Professor. Do you have a favourite?"

He considered this for a moment. "I enjoy 'The Flower,' maybe for its simplicity. It reminds me of my childhood. And 'Winter Morning,' although I can't help but feel that there's something lost in the translation. That the English doesn't quite do it justice."

"Exactly right. A beautiful love letter, still, but a cheap imitation of the original Russian."

"He died quite young, I believe."

"*Da*. In a duel. Quite a scandal involving his wife and a charming French officer."

"Do French officers come any other way?"

"I suppose not. Georges d'Anthés was his name. He married Pushkin's sister-in-law but, the rumors persisted. Natalia Pushkina was quite the beauty, they say. So, Pushkin challenged d'Anthés. Pistols at dawn."

"Naturally."

"It turns out our beloved poet was a much better writer than a marksman." She drew on her cigarette. "Nobody does drama quite like us Russians."

He chuckled. "May I ask where you're from, exactly?"

"You may," she smiled. "I'm from everywhere, really. My parents were in a camp in the east when I was born, but we moved back to Tselinograd soon after—my mother was Kazakh. In truth, I spent most of my childhood in Chelyabinsk, and then left for Leningrad when I was, oh, about nine."

"By yourself?"

"By myself."

"And then Canada."

"Not exactly, no." She slowed her pace. "This is me," she said, stopping before a pastel-grey Mercedes.

"Well"—he succumbed to an irrepressible shiver—"I'll wait until it starts. Your car, I mean."

"It will." She laughed softly. "It's funny how you Canadians believe you have bad winters. When I was a girl, my aunt would always remind us when playing outside: 'Don't forget to rub your face,' she would say. To keep the blood flowing when it was minus forty, you know. Frostbite. My nose would stay red for hours afterward, not from the cold, but from the mittens." She smiled at the memory, putting the cigarette to her lips.

"Do you really use sledgehammers over there to help start your cars?"

Tatyana nodded. "Sometimes."

"And this works?"

"Obviously," she said, as if this required no further explanation. Then, "It's only physics. The vibration, it warms the engine just enough."

By now Gustavs was having a difficult time containing the chatter of his teeth, his body rigid as winter embraced him. Tatyana appeared to take some pleasure in watching him squirm and shift his weight, herself completely at ease enveloped in layers of fur.

"So, are you going to tell me what happened with those policemen?"

"Oh, yes . . . that."

"Yes, *that.*"

"A misunderstanding. They weren't after me, I'm not in trouble or anything. They had some questions about a friend of mine who passed away. It's complicated. A conversation for another time."

Tatyana eyed him inquisitively. "Another time? Will we be seeing each other again?"

Gustavs faltered. "I only meant . . ."

"You're not asking me on a date, are you Professor?"

He smiled ruefully, shaking his head and turning his attention to the frozen ground. "I wouldn't presume to ask a married woman out on a date, no. That would be . . . inappropriate."

Tatyana kept her penetrating gaze on him for a time, and when their eyes met once more she gave him a curious little smile, as if he had just given himself away. Gustavs cleared his throat, adjusted his glasses.

"Perhaps an English lesson, then."

"English . . ."

"You are a teacher, correct? And with my accent . . ."

Gustavs wasn't entirely sure what to say.

"I'm going away for a few weeks. With any luck it will be spring by the time I'm back. You'll have likely tired of Pushkin by then and will need further education in the Russian classics. Yes?"

"Sure."

"You're not very eloquent for a student of literature, you know."

"Sorry."

"Mm . . ." She blew a final cloud of smoke into the air and crushed the butt beneath her boot. Then, she extended a dainty hand from a furry sleeve. "Mr. Ziediņš."

"Mrs. Ivanova."

TEN

Rīga, Latvian Soviet Socialist Republic (LSSR)

ARKADY ZHARKOV SLAMMED THE TELEPHONE RECEIVER BACK into its cradle. For a moment he simply stood, then lifted the receiver once more and brought it crashing down again, and again, and a third time as well, the bell ringing with every violent motion, while a small marble bust of Marx rattled precariously close to the edge of the desk. After taking a breath he adjusted his coat, brushed his lapels, and sat down. Removing a cigarette from a silver case, he lit it with a *snick* from his lighter, then rose once again in a fury.

"*Blyadt!*" he shouted, pacing toward the window with a laboured stride, favouring his right leg. "Despicable, treasonous . . . of all the attacks we have faced throughout our history, here we stand, undermined by our own flesh and blood. Our own kin! Imbeciles. Disgraceful. Tell me, Vadim Sergeyevich, is it I who is suffering from dementia? From a bout of insanity? Speak your mind, comrade! Don't be concerned, the Center appears to encourage such liberal principles—embrace your individualism and to hell with the common good!"

On the far side of the office, the room was already darkened by twilight—the pallid winter sun swallowed up by the city's perennial grey, its light filtered by windowpanes dappled with grime. A bronze plated moulding of a hammer and sickle was mounted on the wall, casting a faint shadow and obscuring the man who stood beneath; a hunched figure, dark and squat and silent. In the dim light, his features were accentuated: the prominent, sloping forehead that descended to a broad, singular brow—black and dense and growing faintly across the considerable bulk of his nose. He had a large mouth and thick lips that never fully closed, a sort of slack gape that one might attribute to a catfish. Forever stooped, his shoulders pressed up by his fleshy ears, he stared vacantly through a thicket of dark bristles across the room.

"Nonsense, utter nonsense. And of the worst kind, for it comes from men in positions of influence—our leaders, the very vanguards of socialism. Misha Gorbachev and his deviationists, they seek to rewrite our glorious history and pervert it with Western falsehoods. These numbers they tout, these repressions, so-called, by great Stalin—I ask you, where do these figures come from? They're fantastical, exaggerated, without a single shred of legitimacy. One million, fifty million, what's next, one hundred million? Nothing more than fabrications, numbers pulled from thin air, I tell you, floating down from a fog of imperialist propaganda!

"Tell me, Vadim Sergeyevich, when our father's fought, side by side in the Great Patriotic War, who could have weathered the fascist storm if not great Stalin? Who industrialized our lands? Who restored the glory of our armed forces? Who was it that ensured our great union prospered as we crushed our enemies underfoot? We should look back at our history in awe and revel at our achievements! Did you know that even now, at this very moment, there are those who march the streets of Moscow, of Leningrad, collecting signatures? Signatures, to serve as witness to past crimes, to make records. Can you believe such a thing? Crimes? Crimes! We served as soldiers when we were nothing more than boys, you and I, do they think it was easy? It was war! A time when bold men needed to make bold decisions for the good of the people! The way they speak now about Comrade Stalin, these ingrates . . . send them off to Magadan I say, the lot of them!"

Zharkov marched back across the office, ash trailing a cigarette that went unsmoked. "Misha and his little ferret Yakovlev. Is it any wonder that they espouse such perverse capitalist ideals? How much time did they spend together in the West, rubbing shoulders with class traitors and the bourgeois before returning to Moscow, bringing with them these infectious philosophies? Yakovlev," he snorted, "forever bending the ear of the General Secretary, contaminating his mind with this . . . this filth. The man advocates for non-intervention within our own territories, our own lands! Can you believe such talk is tolerated? The man should be sent away for re-education. When the rats run amuck, do you simply shut the door and pretend not to see? Hah, what a concept! The man would risk the demise of the state and deliver it straight into the greedy hands of the imperialists. One could be forgiven for thinking he might prefer it. He is a saboteur amongst us in the politburo, and likely not the only one to have succumbed to such backwards thinking. A wolf in the chicken coop."

Zharkov paused to take a draw of his cigarette, realized abruptly that it had gone out and crushed it into an ashtray. He sat down, lit another, and inhaled deeply, composing himself.

"I have given this a great deal of thought, Vadim Sergeyevich," he said with a measured tone. "It is important work and it needs to be done. Our enemies are emboldened, you see. It would be foolish to underestimate them. They swarm like locusts over these

lands, seeking to infect the minds of the hardworking Soviet
man and woman. It is our duty, you understand. There are those
who work day and night, here in this very city, to undermine the
regime, but"—he raised a finger—"they are not alone in this aim.
Increasingly they are aided by foreign governments, communities
of exiles, ideological centers that promote misinformation as rou-
tinely as they draw breath.

"I speak to you now because you have been a close confidante
for many years, Vadim Sergeyevich. We have bled together, you
and I—our blood still stains the earth in Voronezh, and I believe
you are of a similar mind." Zharkov sighed heavily, tapping his
cigarette above the ashtray as his subordinate gave an almost
imperceptible nod.

"The Center can no longer be depended upon. Ever since
my . . . my *banishment* to this rathole, it is difficult to tell in which
direction the winds blow over Moscow. I am no longer privy to
such discussions. Though I must admit, Riga has given me fresh
perspective. A certain distance. And what I do see, it worries me
greatly. Even here, now, the poison that is regularly circulated
in *samizdat*, it is not only printed here underground, beneath
our very noses, but smuggled in from abroad. These western
spies they send, like vermin, crawling around in the cellars of
this city, they slip in and out with ease as we fumble about in
the darkness. Our *dezhurnye*, they accomplish nothing. They
are meant to report on the activities of these tour groups, report
irregularities, recruit and seduce agents of foreign influence and
potential sympathizers." He scoffed. "More often than not they
are as corrupt and immoral as the very infiltrators themselves.
Weak, and tempted by flesh and capital, seduced by the lascivious
excesses of the West.

"No, no this can no longer be tolerated, lest we become accomplices ourselves. We are patriots, you and I, are we not? This is our duty. Let the pages of history pass judgment."

Zharkov rose and returned to the window, staring down past the tram wires into the grey slush that mounded along the curbs of Lenin street. A black Lada drove past, slashing its way through the leaden snow.

"I have a job for you, Vadim Sergeyevich . . ."

III.

SPRING

1987

ELEVEN

THE CHANGING OF THE SEASON USHERED IN A FAMILIAR DRAMA that played out across the landscape, the welcome birth of spring and its battle with a recalcitrant winter frost. At midday the sun shone brightly, stirring virgin buds into bloom, while snowbells and crocuses poked their heads out from pale carpets of matted grass.

And yet winter, harried away over a series of weeks, still clung to its former glory like an old tyrant, yearning for the days when it triumphed over the land. Stubborn in the face of melting snows and sun showers, the earth itself remained cold, hard and unforgiving, loath to thaw and yield its last vestiges of influence. And while the sky stretched out endlessly, cloudless and blue, a fierce and blustery wind would still cut through to the bone, winter's chill defiant to the last.

For Gustavs, on a crisp morning in late April, the season meant only one thing: bees. Historically, the Latvians, to say nothing of their East European neighbours, harbored something of an obsession with the spirited pollinators. Honey was an ancient remedy for a variety of ailments, with the honeybee herself playing a central role in many a poem or folk song—the diligent worker, invaluable for the nation's harvest; a nation of *zemnieki*—quite literally, people of the land.

Raised on a small farm near Cēsis, Omīte had cared for dozens of hives, another half dozen in Milton before her husband's passing and, not long after she moved in with Gustavs, made it clear that she had every intention of continuing with her childhood hobby. The topic of bylaws and regulations surrounding urban apiculture was raised only once, promptly dismissed by Omīte as "bureaucratic hogwash," although, as it turned out, she was keenly aware of the impediments and particularly shrewd in the construction of her new apiary.

She first met with their westerly neighbour, Olga Kovalenko—Irina's mother—who was gifted with a small pot of honey from Omīte's reserve supply in the cold cellar. Olga required little convincing. As a young girl in the Crimea, her neighbours tended to numerous colonies and she had fond memories of sucking on pieces of sweet honeycomb, neatly cut and parceled from the sticky wooden frames.

Mrs. Petrauskas, to the south, was apprehensive at first, though she too agreed to the plan after some persuasion. Birute Petrauskas was a consummate homebody—timid, anxious and especially well-mannered. She was also exceptionally frugal, though Omīte had other words to describe such economy, and was tired of paying the "extortionist" prices they charged for honey at the local farmer's market.

No one knew the neighbours to the southwest who would have completed their little quartet; they kept to themselves and rarely seemed to be home, and so the plan moved duly ahead.

With the committee assembled and sworn to secrecy, Gustavs began by prying apart several planks of wood at the intersection of their picket fences, creating a communal piece of land large enough to sustain three hives. Several evergreens provided a natural camouflage, with newly planted forsythias further obscuring the colonies from any prying eyes. Omīte, as the self-appointed capo of this clandestine network, was more than happy to tend to the bees, with Olga lending a helping hand whenever her health would allow, while Birute, visibly thrilled at the conspiracy of it all, remained primarily as a silent partner.

After a few months, the operation hit a snag when their heretofore absentee neighbour began to grumble about a peculiar, and rather immutable hum in their backyard. Olga plead ignorance and then snubbed the woman outright, after which she confronted Birute, who promptly arrived at Gustavs' doorstep thoroughly distraught, as if convinced that they all might be arrested and bundled off to a labour camp. Omīte called a meeting of the bosses to steady their nerves, and calmly explained that she would see to the matter.

The following morning, Omīte approached their querulous neighbour with a fresh pot of honey, neatly wrapped and adorned with curling red ribbon, and offered her—a Mrs. Eleanor Johnston—what Omīte referred to in heavily accented English as "a piece of the action." Having disappeared for some time, Gustavs eventually poked his head over the fence to spot Omīte seated on the back porch with Mrs. Johnston sipping tea—sweetened with honey, of course—having successfully bribed their prickly neighbour like some kind of prohibition era bootlegger. From then on the operation moved smoothly, and on the first of every month, Gustavs left a humble jar of golden nectar—tied off with a little red bow—on Mrs. Johnston's doorstep.

Three years on, Gustavs spent his Saturday morning doing some routine spring maintenance—pressing an ear to the hives and listening for activity, lifting the cover boards to visually inspect the clusters, removing entrance blocks as the bees prepared for flight. From the backdoor, he heard Omīte call his name. A telephone call.

Gustavs picked up the receiver and stretched out the curling red cord.

"Hello?"

"Hello Gustav . . ."

A woman's voice, soft and vaguely familiar, awaiting recognition. It took him a moment, but when it came to him, he was certain.

"Hello Lotte."

A faint chuckle from the other end. "Very good. For a moment, I wondered."

"You sound the same."

"Goodness, it's been so long. I mean, I know it hasn't, not *really*, but it feels that way, doesn't it?"

"Time waits for no man . . . or woman."

"*Oof*, and don't I know it." She sighed nostalgically into the receiver. "I had the most wonderful memory the other day. That road trip we took to Cincinnati, with Anna and Paulis. Do you remember? We must have eaten our weight in Cheetos."

"The two of you had a heated debate about Robert Redford and Paul Newman."

She laughed. "We did! Honestly Gustav, how do you remember such things? I was always a sucker for the Sundance Kid, that dimpled smile!"

"He was no competition for Cool Hand Luke."

"No, I suppose he wasn't." A mournful silence lingered for a time, but her words were tender. "Ah, Gustav, I miss her dearly."

" . . . So do I."

"I was hoping we might catch up. Are you free this week?"

"Sure. I don't have any classes after four from Wednesday onward"—he reached for a pen and pad—"I don't think I have your new number, I can call to confirm."

"Oh, I don't have a telephone, how about Thursday?"

It took Gustavs a moment. "Alright, let's say, Thursday at five? You're still at—"

"Let's meet downtown at one of our old haunts. Meet me in front of Mars, on Bathurst Street. You remember? I haven't had one of their shakes in years."

"Sure thing."

"Five o'clock then. I'm looking forward to it."

On a fine, temperate afternoon beneath an overcast sky, just off the corner of College and Bathurst Street, Gustavs stood with a bouquet of freesias, observing a homeless man trying his luck with the coin return slot of a newspaper box. Unsuccessful, the man dragged a fingerless glove beneath his nose and snorted, mumbling something to no one in particular, before shuffling rather aimlessly into oncoming traffic. A taxi rolled carefully to a stop to avoid striking him. While the driver laid on the horn and threw his hands in the air, the rear window of the cab descended.

"Well, hello there," Lotte called, flittering her fingers, golden hair swirling in the breeze.

Gustavs smiled, then made a speculative gesture with his thumb toward the restaurant.

Lotte curled her lip, "I've had a change of heart. Hop in."

The old friends greeted each other affectionately, kisses on both cheeks as the taxi merged back into traffic, the driver still muttering to himself about the city's entitled pedestrians.

For Gustavs, a weighty bout of nostalgia, for she smelled exactly the same—warm and woodsy, a comforting memory of a simpler time. And while he would have recognized her anywhere, life had left its mark. In a pastel blue turtleneck and woolen beret, she was as stylish as ever—the top matching her eyes, cornflower blue; dangling amber earrings matching her cap.

And yet, there was something amiss, something not as easily attributed to the passing of years. There were shadowed contours beneath her eyes, unevenly masked with concealer. Her cheeks, no longer rosy and plump but drawn, colourless like her lips. Her blonde hair cascaded about her shoulders, though the colour was faded now—split ends, a few strands of grey. She had always been slim, but now, as he stole a glance at her figure, that wasn't the word that came to mind. Not slender, not lean. A natural beauty, as she'd always been, but—thin.

"Gustav, I can't believe this," she said, grasping his wrists, looking from eye to eye. "You haven't aged a day. You look exactly the same."

"So do you."

"Please," she waved a hand, "ever the flatterer. You'll have to tell me your secret."

"I stay away from all the politics. Less stress."

Lotte laughed, a look of cynicism flashing across her face. "You're more right than you know," she said, taking a deep inhale from the bouquet.

They caught up for a time, exchanging the customary pleasantries. They touched on family and loved ones, branched out to friends and acquaintances, then work, life, and eventually drifting into reminiscence of their youth.

They had entered a residential neighborhood—Gustavs hadn't been paying much attention—when Lotte tapped the driver on the shoulder and said, "Just up here is fine, by the fence." The driver appeared uncertain until a twenty was pressed into his shoulder, the cab rolling promptly to a stop.

Gustavs didn't recognize the street and followed Lotte along a narrow footpath, flanked on either side by a chain-link fence that led between twin red-brick homes into a park. He was asking idle questions about her freelance work—an article she had written for *Latvija Amerikā*, one of the community's weekly papers—when she stopped momentarily to glance up at him, lamenting the fact that so much time had passed. She linked her arm with his and they set out across a small clearing.

It was subtle and fleeting, but she had—he was certain of it— glanced just over his shoulder, as if looking for someone. As if she half-expected to spot a face in the distance, one that she didn't particularly wish to see.

Lotte pivoted to a childhood memory of eating saltwater taffy in the park with her mother, and they emerged into a side alley behind a row of parked cars, before turning left down a leafy boulevard. Gustavs recognized the familiar home just ahead of them, unchanged by the years, as Lotte made an offhand remark about the tonic of spring weather.

Once inside, Lotte put on the kettle and apologized for the clowder of felines that hopped off ledges and chairs to greet him, mewing and purring and slipping about Gustavs' ankles. "Make yourself at home," she said, jutting her chin toward the living room, "I'll be just a moment."

Gustavs entered a veritable library—dimly lit, musty and replete with stacks of books, magazines and newspapers. The curtains, crocheted white cotton, were drawn, with slivers of sunlight streaming in through the patterned loops of fabric. The walls were wood-paneled, and on the near side hung a framed piece of embroidery—three golden stars arcing atop a red castle, the coat of arms for the city of Aizpute. Across the room, just above an antique piano, was an oil painting of a farmstead: cattle grazing before a sweeping forest of silver birch, a dilapidated barn on the distant horizon.

He seated himself on the couch and cast an eye over the coffee table: piles of old Latvian newspapers—*Laiks* and *Latvija Amerikā*; the scribbled, dog-eared notepads of a seasoned journalist; a copy of *TIME* magazine, the April edition featuring a black-eyed U.S. marine and the 'Spy Scandals' ongoing at the American embassy in Moscow. In the center of the table was a marble chess set, deftly poised in middle-game, and beside it, a brown, ceramic ashtray—empty, but for a half-smoked marijuana cigarette delicately balanced on its ashen tip.

A kettle whistled in the kitchen, and Lotte strode back into the room with a pot of linden flower tea. She set down some cups and saucers, along with a handful of *gotiņas*, the little fudge candies of their childhood, brown cows pictured on the yellow wax paper wrappings. "I don't take sugar with my tea, just a little sweetness on the side," she said. After pouring, she produced a small bottle of cognac, wiggled her brow mischievously, prompting a chuckle from Gustavs, and set it on the table.

"Whose turn is it?" he asked, staring at the board.

"Black," she replied, taking a seat on the opposing divan.

"You play against yourself?"

"No, it's . . . it's Aleksandrs' turn."

How could he have forgotten the name? The volleyball star from Michigan, that old romantic rival from his adolescence.

"Of course, sorry—I'm somewhat out of the loop."

"Hah," she waved her hand about, "I love that about you. Our community loves to gossip, I swear it sustains the older women—the elixir of youth." She smiled. "We were all a bit silly back in those days, impetuous, but it's been a few years now. What can I say? He's the love of my life. He's . . . well, he's partly the reason I wanted to meet."

Gustavs sipped his tea, the steam momentarily fogging his glasses. "Is that what the whole show was about?"

Lotte said nothing, merely assessing him.

"The cab, the sideways glances, the detour through the park. I've been to your house, Lotte, it hasn't been *that* long."

She pinched her lips into a shy smile and ran her fingers back through her hair. "Ah, Gustav, you're a breath of fresh air. And I desperately need it."

"Is everything alright?"

"Yes, yes, it's fine. And it's lovely to see you again, truly, this is long overdue, but I'm afraid I haven't been completely forthright. I do have a sort of, favour, I may need to ask of you. It might not come to anything in the end, but . . ."

He glanced at the bottle of cognac. "On second thought . . ."

She splashed an inch into either cup. A scratching sound came from the back door, and Lotte rose to let in yet another cat—a nimble Abyssinian with a butterscotch coat, brushing between her calves before disappearing into the hall.

"I know you've never been one for politics, Gustav, but how much do you know of what goes on?"

"Are we speaking locally or, in the greater sense?"

"Both, I suppose. I know it's never been an interest of yours, despite your, well"—she returned to her seat—"suitability, let's say. There would be practically unanimous agreement, you'd be an excellent figurehead, and I believe that opinion holds true on either side of the divide in our opinionated community. Honestly, I've always thought you were above that sort of thing. The egos, the hidden agendas, the backstabbing, all that. I always figured your time would come later, afterwards."

"You're starting to lose me now . . ."

A shadow passed over her face, a certain gravity settling in her expression. "I've always trusted you, Gustav. It should go without saying. You're a good man, and we've always had a certain . . . bond, you could say. An understanding. It's hard to put into words, but, you would agree?"

He nodded. "I think I would."

"This conversation is between you and I, Gustav. And only, you and I."

He glanced at the marijuana cigarette in the ashtray, Lotte's eyes following, her expression breaking into a rueful smile. "It only helps with the nerves," she said.

Rising from the couch, she clasped her hands together and began to pace. "Let me provide some context. You know very well that for the past decade or so—longer, in fact, there's been a sort of fission within the community. The *LNAK* and the *Daugavas Vanagi*—the old guard, you could say, has been at odds with organizations such as *LATS* and the comparatively new political thinking. The old guard believes that we should continue to push for independence, stitching up political contacts, raising awareness. Pressing for international acknowledgment that the Baltic states remain under illegal occupation. The new wave agrees, of course, however it's in their methods that the divisions arise.

"As you're probably aware, Imants' LNAK has always been suspicious of any contact with those behind the Iron Curtain, even, and especially Latvians. And they do have a point—how can we trust anyone? Soviet sympathizers, KGB plants, these writers, artists, intellectuals that are granted Western visas—who's to say they don't have their own agendas? Agendas forced upon them. The new wave, however, for them these artist types are exactly the sort of contacts they wish to cultivate, and empower. The dissident underground, the new, forward-thinking intelligentsia—there's a belief that we must do everything to support the movement for independence from *within*. The Trojans built an impressive stallion either way, but hardly as effective if left outside the walls.

"Both sides have valid points, of course, and that is essentially the basis for the schism. The organizations, *Daugavas Vanagi* as opposed to *LATS*, then the schools, *Sestdienas skola* versus *Valodiņa*, the summer camps, the social circles, onward it goes. We're united in preserving our culture and in seeking independence, but our approaches differ considerably. Unfortunately, the very nature of the problem breeds suspicion and mistrust. It doesn't help that with Latvians, there can be no compromise. For all our prejudices against the Soviets, here we are with our own committees, endlessly squabbling with one another. It's as intolerable as it is disheartening."

"Are you asking me to pick a side?"

"No. Just the opposite, in fact."

Lotte crossed her arms and took a breath. The room was silent but for the steady creak of the hardwood floor.

"There is a third group. A separate movement. Small, tightly knit. We don't have a name. We believe not only that these divisions are extremely counterproductive, but beyond that, there are actions that must be taken—actions that cannot rest on the whims of old men drinking coffee and eating *sviestmaizītes*."

It was subtle, but her pace began to quicken as she moved about the room, a slow crescendo in a voice full of conviction. She gestured while making her points, no longer speaking to him alone but rather preaching to a phantom audience. He noted the fire in her eyes now, a different woman before him—spirited and determined.

"The time is now, Gustav. Now or never. Gorbachev will be our greatest opportunity, mark my words. He has opened the door only a sliver, and we have managed to wedge our boot across the threshold, but we cannot rely merely on good fortune. It is up to us now. Up to us to heave our backs against the door and break it down once and for all.

"Russia needs a strongman, you see. They have always gravitated toward men of power while deriding the democratic—the weak, as they see them. Lenin. Stalin. And then, what legacy does old Khruschev hold? His denunciations at the 20th Party Congress, the mass release of prisoners, the Krushchev Thaw. Hm? So they turned to Brezhnev and the return of repressions, then Andropov, the KGB chairman. The Kremlin is more divided than ever thanks to their new General Secretary—the old *apparatchiks* have no time for his *demokratizatsiya*. They yearn for the return of a hardline ruler. For the glory days of old. Gorbachev's neoliberal policies of *glasnost* and *perestroika* went up in smoke last year with the Chernobyl reactor."

A Siamese leapt up onto the armrest of the divan, its dark paws contrasting against its light fur, as if having recently tread across a pile of soot. Lotte absentmindedly stroked the length of its figure as she passed.

"We've made great progress, but we must push harder than ever now. A couple of years ago I was in Copenhagen for the tribunal, do you remember? The trial against our occupation. To hear the

panel of judges conclude, for all the world to hear that the subjugation of Baltic lands constitutes a clear violation of human rights—
ah, Gustav, I can't express what we all felt that day in the city
square. Just as last year, the Chautauqua Conference in Jūrmala.
To have the American delegation declare the 1940 elections a farce,
and doing so within the Soviet Union, on their side of the wall!
They passed out lapel pins with our flag, our *real* flag, and no one
stopped them."

She placed a palm against her forehead, then slid it down
against her cheek, turning to face him for the first time in a long
while. "Goodness, look at me go," she said, chuckling softly.

"It's alright. I do pay attention to what's happening, of course,
only from a distance. I could never stand the bickering, you know,
everyone arguing amongst themselves. We're not great in number,
and yet in every meeting, blaming one another, finger-pointing.
And that's if we weren't too busy rehashing national tragedies.
Occupied by Poles and Swedes, Germans, Russians, deported here,
murdered there, my God, *we know*. It became as though every
time we'd meet it was some morbid remembrance. Always looking
backwards, and never forward." He shrugged. "It grated on me.
Anyway, I haven't ventured over to Denmark, but . . . you were
saying, something about a third movement?"

"Mm, yes." She circled the divan and sat down, taking a sip of
her tea. "You're familiar with Helsinki-86?"

Gustavs gave a subtle tilt of the head. "Somewhat."

"They founded the group in Liepāja last year. Grantiņš,
Bitenieks, Bariss, among others. Ordinary individuals—beekeep-
ers, jewelry makers—an organization based on the Accords of '75,
openly anti-communist, committed to the preservation of human
rights. Aleksandrs had been working with them for quite a while,

behind the scenes, so to speak. We both have. We traveled frequently. There is a major demonstration planned for June, to commemorate the deportations of 1941. A peaceful yet open defiance against the regime.

"You see, Gustav, it's all well and good to keep our fight in the public eye—in the newspapers, on television, in the speeches of foreign dignitaries. But it's behind the scenes where much of the struggle plays out. In the backrooms, and in the shadows. The movement in Rīga needs our support, and Moscow obviously does not take kindly to any outside influence. There's a reason every Latvian granted a visa is accompanied by KGB escorts, if they aren't KGB themselves.

"They listen to everything. The state remains under constant surveillance, informers everywhere, and the arrests are as arbitrary as they've ever been. It's a far cry from the purges of the '30's, but, the psychological ramifications of living under such a system . . ." She searched for the words, left the thought unfinished. "It's not only those who actively seek to undermine the system that are at risk, it is those who are thought, who are perceived, who are believed on nothing more than a *whim* to be less than completely loyal to the state. The authorities operate with impunity across the land, and without an appropriate response we are doomed to failure. Newspaper editorials and charitable contributions be damned."

Lotte let out a heavy sigh. The sun had shifted, and through the curtains a shaft of light illuminated the side of her face. For a moment, her expression appeared rather fragile, the revolutionary zeal having faded, and Gustavs noted a faint shimmer in her eyes.

"Aleksandrs is in Rīga, a routine trip, if you can call that sort of thing routine. I haven't heard from him in a little while." She swallowed, and took an unsteady breath. "There's a system," she continued, clearing her throat. "We obtain certain items, smuggle them in if need be along with the usual—fabrics, feminine products, money, of course. In exchange, we retrieve certain information as well. Documents. Recordings. Photographs. Things the Russians don't want seen in the light of day. And it goes much deeper than that. Aleksandrs was retrieving a rather important package this time, and"—she rubbed her palms nervously across her knees, then clasped her hands together—"well, I shouldn't let my imagination get the better of me."

She reached for the cigarette in the ashtray, tapped it a couple of times with a finger, produced a lighter from her pocket and then a flame. A grey fog billowed and hung in the air before she blew a stream of dank fumes through its midst, the smoke churning like a roiling cloud.

Gustavs adjusted his glasses. "What exactly was"—she offered the thin cigarette, which he dismissed with two fingers—"what was he looking for? You make it all sound rather ominous."

Lotte took another thoughtful drag, inhaling deeply, then nibbled at her bottom lip. She raised her eyes, studying him, eventually finding what she sought.

"We think there's someone in the community, Gustav." She left the words suspended in the air, drifting with the wisps of smoke.

"Someone."

"An outsider."

"One of . . ."

"One of theirs."

Gustavs leaned back in his seat. "You're sure of this?"

A subtle lilt of the head. *No.*

"Aleks . . ."

"Was going to confirm."

Gustavs took a moment. "Lotte," he began, searching for the words, "I want you to know that I'm not making light of this, but . . ." He jutted his chin at the cigarette in her hands.

"As I said, for the nerves." Her face was stone now, no time for levity. She wasn't about to entertain any insinuations of conspiracy or paranoia. "Gustav, we think . . . we think it has to do with Imants."

Gustavs said nothing.

"We think he may have been poisoned."

His gaze shifted, the wheels cycling in his mind. After a moment, he said, "It was you. The detectives."

She nodded.

"You told them they should look into it."

Another nod.

"You know they brought me in for questioning."

"You're not the only one."

"And you . . . you believe this?"

She blew a plume of smoke and extinguished the cigarette along the edge of the bowl. "Sometimes I don't know what to believe, Gustav. I don't *want* to believe it, but, we've suspected something like this for a while now. And by that I mean an outsider, of course, a presence. To what extent, we don't know. Certainly no one anticipated something so utterly blatant, so dreadful. We were trying to make sense of it, piecing the clues together and having a horrid time if I'm being completely honest. There comes a time when you start to believe the paranoia, and you can't separate reality from . . ."

Gustavs furrowed his brow. "I don't think they have any evidence. The police, I mean."

"No, not that I know of. They can only do so much with a tip. We were going to provide them with something more substantial."

"Through Aleks."

"Through our contacts. Yes."

Gustavs puffed out his cheeks. "This is . . ." He had a look of bewilderment painted across his face.

"Not what you expected, I know."

For a time they simply sat, consumed by their own thoughts while from somewhere in the house, the steady tick of a clock underscored the silence.

"Well," Gustavs said, "I suppose for starters, let's assume we can trust Aleks."

It was an offhand remark, the words partially muffled as he rubbed his chin, yet Lotte gave him a hard look. He met her stare.

"Look, you're the one who called me. You brought this up, whatever *this* is. If you believe there's a . . . for goodness sake, what do they call them, moles? A mole?" He scoffed, incredulous. "If that's what you truly believe, then what's the first rule? No one is above suspicion, right? Not you, not me, not Aleks. Taking offense shouldn't be your first instinct here, it should be considering every angle."

Lotte seemed to relax as he spoke, subdued, her eyes clouding over in acquiescence, slightly disconcerted that this was, in fact, just the sort of insight she'd been hoping for. "I suppose you're right," she said, almost in spite of herself.

"So, assuming Aleks is fine, what about this third party, the contact?"

"I'll save us some time, Gustav. Our group is small, insulated, incredibly cautious. Patriotic, above all. The same cannot be said for the community here, all the more so for Rīga. There are too many variables at play."

"When was Aleks supposed to come home?"

"The timelines are never definitive. We keep schedules irregular, often unknown to members themselves until the last minute. No patterns. Still, it's been far too long now, I feel." She crossed her legs. "And . . . this is where I have something to ask of you."

"You said you *may* have something to ask of me. That it might not come to anything at all."

"That part is true."

"Why do I get the sense that I should be concerned here? If I'm taking you at your word, Lotte, I have to admit I'm already a little uncomfortable with this entire conversation."

She exhaled. "I understand, and I hope you can appreciate how important, how significant this is. It's not only for me, for us, but for all of them. We're talking about something far greater than ourselves. We're talking about freedom, Gustav. About *independence*."

He nodded along, the patient skeptic.

"In any event, this would be more of an alternative arrangement. A precaution we feel is necessary, on the off chance that the situation should present itself. Always wise to prepare for all scenarios."

She was building toward something, and so Gustavs remained silent, the clock forever making its presence known.

"We may need you to acquire the package."

" . . . The package."

"We need the information, Gustav, it is absolutely vital. And if Aleks continues to be delayed . . ."

He hesitated. "You said Aleks is in Rīga."

"Yes."

"Jesus Christ, Lotte," said Gustavs, rising to his feet, not sure whether to pace or simply stand. Hands on hips, he opted for the latter.

Lotte spoke calmly. "We may—*may* need someone who can meet our contact and retrieve whatever documents they have for us. And if such a situation were to arise, it has to be someone above suspicion. Someone completely disconnected."

"And you think that's me."

"It's *exactly* you, Gustav. You've shunned involvement with the *LNAK*, or any political groups for that matter. You attend the odd social function, sure, but you're hardly perceived as someone in the know, someone who makes waves. You speak the language fluently, yet have never traveled to Latvija. No one knows about you, Gustav. You have the perfect cover. Just any other tourist, visiting relatives. And, most importantly, I know I can trust you."

"And you're telling me there's no one else? Why can't you go?"

She shook her head. "I would prefer it, but it's impossible now, for something like this. To say we're under surveillance is"—she swept her hand, dismissive—"everyone is under some sort of surveillance, but I've been too many times. One of our sources informed us that they almost certainly have dossiers on us now."

"Dossiers. Who, the KGB?"

She nodded.

"How could you possibly know that?" he said brusquely.

"One of my sources, as I said. The travel guides, the ones that work for Intourist—they're all KGB. Guides in name only. They spend most of their time gathering intelligence on what questions the tourists ask—who they speak to, what they want to see. They're nothing more than an extension of the security apparat. There's a young girl, one of ours, she's good at getting close to them, the male guides. They can be careless with their words . . . in the right setting."

It was Gustavs' turn to pace now. "Let me see if I've got this: You want me to travel to the Eastern bloc, to Rīga, pretending to, what—visit relatives I don't have, under continual surveillance, and then somehow acquire documents which, let me guess, aren't exactly the type of papers you want to be caught carrying across a border . . ."

"*If* you were to go, and it's a big 'if,' I assure you—everything would be arranged. You would have specific directions. You'd meet a contact. They would provide you with, yes, likely some documents, some papers to—"

"—To what, *smuggle* out? Do you realize what you're asking me?"

"Yes. I do."

He returned to his seat, collapsing into the cushion with a heaving sigh. "This is insane," he whispered to himself.

"I know."

"You know? And what if I get searched, if something happens?"

"We're very cautious, Gustav."

"I'm sure that you are. But I'm asking, what if"—he leaned forward—"what if something *happens*?"

He could see the conflict in her eyes, dancing for a moment, searching for a tempering response. "I suppose they'd want me to tell you they have contingencies in place."

"Contingencies," he said flatly, "at Soviet exit control, you have contingencies."

She cast her eyes downward and back again. "We need your help, Gustav."

"You need Roger Moore is who you need."

She forced a grim smile at the attempted levity. Then a tempest of emotions clouded her face—pity, gratitude, affection. She held his attention and placed a hand slowly, dramatically, onto the tea pot, then wrapped the fingers of the other around the bottle of cognac. Her head tilted one way, then the other. An offering.

"This has happened before," she said, pouring another inch of cognac into either tea cup, "delays like this. Not with Aleks, but with others, and it's always worked out. The difficulty, more often than not, is with communications. The precautions are time consuming."

"I can't give you an answer, Lotte," he said, cutting her off. "Not the one you want. Not now."

"I understand."

They sat in silence for a time, Lotte retreating in a way, stroking the Siamese as it audibly purred in her lap, while Gustavs nursed his drink, contemplative.

It was a strange mood that descended upon him now, a peculiar sense of conflict that he hadn't expected to hold his attention. He wondered what Anna would have said. The situation was almost comical, in spite of itself. A subject he could never raise with his family, the concept alone enough to send them into conniptions. And yet, when he thought of his father, of the few memories he still held—increasingly blurred with age, fragments of childhood—he could still clearly sense the passion, hear the unwavering allegiance in his words. The devotion to a country lost, stolen, abandoned. He wondered what Omīte would say.

Theirs had always been a different sort of patriotism, Gustavs had thought, the Baltics as a whole. A fervent nationalism, inherent, instinctive, yet wholly separate from the militant connotations that now accompanied such ideology. The dangers of *nationalism*: tribal affiliations that served as fertile breeding ground for the spread of separatism, fascism. The ethnic conflicts that violently disfigured society, dividing regions, families, dissolving entire nations from within. The imperialist ambitions of empires in faraway lands, ever expanding, never satiated.

It had never seemed this way to Gustavs, nor among his peers, his community, his *tauta*—the collective national culture. Theirs was a loyalty rooted in perseverance, in resistance, in the preservation of an identity—unique, and fragile. Their nationalism had always been the safeguarding of a heritage forever threatened by Vikings and Tsars, by vast marauding armies that swept across their plains and forests as unwelcome as a winter frost. A heritage tormented once more by a familiar spectre from the East. A populace ensnared, a language repressed, a nation subjugated only to be snuffed out like a flame, absorbed into the unforgiving blackness of Marxism.

His thoughts drifted back to Lotte's proposal. He had no intention of going along with it, whatever *it* was. Madness. What else to call it? Dangerous, irresponsible, highly illegal—certainly viewed as such by foreign authorities with a frightening prerogative. Orwell's nightmares come to life.

And yet, there was something unusual about the notion, about the request. It stirred a sort of innate morality; an ember, long dormant, but forever glowing amongst the ash. From another perspective, was it not, almost, irresponsible to decline? To cower behind a life of comforts, of freedoms, of rhetoric, when in truth, it was little more than chance that separated the fate of his family from the fate of others. Nothing more than a slice of fortune for the Ziediņš family, so many years ago when Europe was aflame.

Strange, he thought, to be so far removed, to never have laid eyes on a parcel of land and yet feel such a sense of, what—duty? Steeped in the culture since childhood, citizenship granted by birthright even in exile, and now, decades on, some part of him was drawn to the request, as if having to atone for the sins of those who fled. To repay a debt.

It had little to do with Lotte, thankfully; their youthful indiscretions providing him with enough immunity to her charms, potent as they remained. Still, he felt a pull, a peculiar tug where his conscience warned him, yet countenanced this strange, aberrant impulse.

"So . . . is this turning out as you'd envisioned it?" he finally asked.

She gave him a warm smile. "I'm not sure. I figured you'd be upset, maybe angry. But then I could never picture you angry. Always so stoic. Calm."

He shrugged. "No sense in getting upset."

She smiled again. "Rational."

"What happens now?"

"Nothing. Not really. It was only meant to be a conversation."

"Something for me to mull over."

She nodded. "Though, there is one thing. Just, on the off-chance, while you're mulling . . ."

"A contingency?" he smirked, surprising himself.

"Yes. Just so."

He leaned back, interlaced his fingers in his lap. "Well?"

She downed the last of her cognac. "Is your passport still valid?"

TWELVE

Slouched over a cluttered pile of language assignments, Gustavs—bleary-eyed with head in hand—nursed a steaming mug of coffee, a remedy for the residual effects of a late night, a restless sleep, and the cognac that accompanied the evening's perturbations. Renata scribbled the latest figures in her expense book, the scratching of lead on paper the only sound in the office. If she had noticed—*of course she had noticed*—she graciously said nothing, yet did rise to put on a second pot, effectively confirming the matter.

Gustavs stared at the latest tests to grade—common idioms and expressions—though despite his best efforts, found his thoughts drifting relentlessly, an undertow pulling him beneath the current, and back to Lotte.

A soft knock on the door. Gustavs glanced up to find Kasia standing in the threshold, her perennial smile beaming at him, perhaps even brighter than usual. In her hands she held a small, cream-coloured envelope.

"Hello, Kasia, how are you?"

"Good morning Gustav," she smiled.

"That's Mr. Ziediņš, Kasia."

"Oh, it's alright," he replied.

The young girl was fidgeting in the doorway now, unable to stand still. "I, erm . . . here," she said, skipping forward and handing him the envelope. Then, unable to contain herself, "It's from Madame."

"Oh, right. Of course. Thank you, Kasia."

He could feel Renata's eyes from across the room as he withdrew a single note:

> *Gustav,*
> *I meant to write sooner but fate, it seems, had other plans. Regardless, I'm long overdue for an English lesson, and we surely must continue your education in Russian classics. Are you free this Friday evening? I considered leaving my telephone number, however, I couldn't disappoint Kasia. She seems quite excited to be playing the role of messenger.*
>
> > *Yours,*
> >
> > *T.*

Gustavs glanced up at the young teen, practically vibrating before him now, face flushed pink and wringing her hands in anticipation.

"Was there anything else, Kasia?" Renata inquired, a lightly scolding tone.

Gustavs smiled. "Tell Madame . . ." He leaned back, exhaling. "Tell Madame six o'clock, at the Revue cinema on Roncesvalles. Can you do that?"

Kasia was glowing. "Six o'clock. Revue cinema. Roncesvalles."

He gave her a wink, and she proceeded to spin on her heel and scamper back toward the door.

"Oh, Kasia, one more thing"—he reached into his briefcase and removed a large manila envelope—"I almost forgot. Could you keep this at the front desk with you. There's a Mr. Braun to collect it later today. He may not come until after you've left for ballet, but . . ."

Kasia nodded happily, accepting the package and disappearing just as quickly through the doorway.

Renata had been carefully observing the interaction, watchful eyes flickering above her perched glasses. A palpable silence filled the room. Gustavs cleared his throat, discovering a newfound pre-occupation with the paperwork before him.

"And here I thought it was Kasia who had invited you to the performance, all along."

Gustavs glanced up, taking a sip of his coffee. "Tatyana was very generous with her praise. She said Kasia was a real talent."

"Mm-hmm?"

He swallowed. "And you know I've always been a great supporter of the arts."

Renata pressed her lips into a taut, angular line. "You were certainly supporting something on stage . . ."

"Yes, well. One has to play the role." He opened his mouth to say something further, and decided instead on another sip of coffee.

The evening was unseasonably warm—humid, following a brief shower, and with hardly a breeze, and beneath the glowing lights of the Revue cinema marquee, Gustavs paced to pass the time. His mind still whirred with all the implications of what Lotte had said, palms clammy from thoughts of Russian border guards with *karakul* hats, interrogation rooms with singular, flickering lightbulbs. He conjured an image of himself, shaven head, sallow cheeks, dressed in moth-eaten rags with black and white stripes. *Enough now, enough.*

For the occasion he had worn his best jacket overtop of an open collar, paired with some jeans—an ensemble fraught with indecision, lengthy moments spent staring nervously into a mirror, turning this way, then that; smoothing here, brushing there. The note was clear enough—a date, surely, yet the more he turned it over in his mind, the words began to take on a different meaning. Overdressed? No, surely not. Surely?

"You know," came a familiar voice from behind him, "according to *Cosmopolitan*, dinner and a movie is very outdated."

He turned around, nodding along.

"Old fashioned," Tatyana continued.

"Well, if it's in *Cosmo*," he replied, yielding to the sage wisdom.

"I don't usually read it. I was at the dentist. Paulina Porizkova was on the cover."

"Russian?"

"Czech. Russian legs." She flashed her impish smile, the same dimple creasing her cheek.

"But no," he said, pivoting. "I just figured this would be a convenient place to meet. Unless," he jutted a thumb at a wall of movie posters, "*Lethal Weapon* or *Beverly Hills Cop*."

"I don't understand this genre. They're police movies, yes? But also, comedies?"

"More or less."

She made a face.

"What is it?"

"They would never make such films in Russia."

"No?"

She shrugged. "In Leningrad, there is nothing funny about police."

Gustavs acknowledged this with an involuntary smile, then motioned with his head. "Hungry?"

"Always."

They walked south along Roncesvalles, a leisurely pace mingling among families, grocery shoppers, the cheerful, carefree smiles of happy hour. Tatyana was stunning alongside him, and he was grateful for the stroll, easier now not to stare. She wore a white blouse, tucked into a pair of grey checkered pants with black ankle boots, a voguish outfit revealing a timeless, dancer's figure. Her long, brown hair flowed over her shoulders, and he caught a faint scent of the familiar perfume—orange blossom?—as they brushed past a giddy young couple with ice cream cones.

"I feel as though I owe you an apology," she began.

"For?"

"We agreed to see each other before and, since then, well, it's been some time."

"I'm sure you have your reasons."

"I do. But that's not the point. I'm not one of those women. Changeable. Floating along in whichever direction the wind blows."

He looked at her, then nodded, acknowledging the sudden shift in mood. "Alright."

"Alright." She glanced up, waiting to meet his eye. "I'm getting a divorce."

"Oh," he said, caught off guard. "I'm sorry." Then, after a moment, "I hope it's not . . . that I'm not—"

"Not what, responsible?" She chuckled. "You think your dancing was that good?"

"I didn't mean it like that," he said, relieved.

"I'm only kidding. A long time coming. And a longer story."

"I have time."

She sighed. "We might as well, I suppose. Anyway, it's important to me that you know that. A married woman shouldn't go on long walks with strange gentlemen. I could only wonder what you'd make of it, what you thought."

"I wasn't really sure myself, to be honest."

"But still you came."

"I suppose I did."

"Mm."

" . . . Difficult not to."

She met his eyes once more, only this time a flicker of vulnerability, a shy smile.

"Here we are," said Gustavs, pushing open the front door of Līdums Delicatessen, a dense fragrance of cured meats wafting across the threshold to greet them.

Tatyana hummed with delight, taking in the aroma—smoke and spice, sharp peppercorns and charred wood.

"They have a smokehouse in the back," he said, leading her through the store, wondering how many *pīrāgi* to buy.

They drifted alongside an assortment of salads in the refrigerated glass display—potato, mushroom, herring, radish, and then past an ambrosial selection of cakes and tortes—raspberry, cottage cheese, chocolate, and cherry.

"When I was a boy, I would come here every day after school, we—"

"*Bozhe moy!*" Tatyana exclaimed. "Lingonberries!" She plucked a jar from a shelf, scrutinizing the label. "I've been looking everywhere for these. Gustav, what is this magical place?" she said, grinning.

"My home away from home. Savory or sweet?"

"Savory. Then sweet."

"We'll grab some Alexander *kūkas* as well."

"I'll have to make some *blini* to repay you," she replied, reaching for another jar.

"*Blini?*"

"Russian pancakes. We stuff them with minced beef, mushrooms, fry them in butter." She put her hand to her chest, "Like heaven."

Gustavs nodded. "We do the same. *Pildītas pankūkas.*"

"I never asked," she said, turning to him. "You have a Nordic face, but I can't place it." She examined him like a specimen. "Scandinavian?"

He shook his head.

"Ziediņš?"

"Ziediņš."

Her lips moved silently, scrutinizing the letters.

"Polish?"

"Latvian."

"Ah, a *Latysh*. Like Baryshnikov."

He chuckled. "And I think we can agree that's where the comparisons end. Born in Rīga but to Russian parents, if I recall."

"You know what Solzhenitsyn said about your people?"

"I don't think so."

"About the revolution. That he likes the Estonians and the Lithuanians, but your lot . . ."

"Yes?"

"'I don't like the Latvians,'" her voice deep and theatrical, "'when all is said and done, they started it all.'"

"You know your history."

"I know my dissidents," she countered.

Outside, they crossed the busy thoroughfare for some coffee, then headed further west, passing through an old neighborhood of red-brick homes and mature maples. A decision was made that, with the weather having cleared, it was far too perfect an evening to spend cooped up indoors, and so they made their way into High Park, clutching paper bags full of bacon buns and raspberry cakes.

"By the way," Gustavs said, sidestepping a puddle, "the Kirov? Very impressive."

"Ohh," she said with a smile, her mouth still full. "So you know it now?"

"Certainly. I mean, there may have been some confusion. Here we still refer to it as the Mariinsky ballet company."

"No you don't."

A smile crept from the corner of his mouth. "No, we don't."

She eyed him curiously, taking another bite of a *pīrāgs*. "I'm picturing you leafing through an encyclopedia . . ."

"That's exactly what I did."

"No," she chuckled.

"Oh yes. Founded in 1860, named for the wife of the Tsar, Empress Maria Alexandrovna—"

Tatyana burst out laughing, raising a hand to cover her mouth.

"I told you. I had to redeem myself, for goodness sake. It's only the most famous theatre in Europe."

She drew a finger beneath her eyes, glistening now. "The professor reading an encyclopedia. I should have known."

"I'm the one who should have known. What was it like?"

"The company?" She took a few paces in silence, a dreamy look of nostalgia on her face. "For a time, it was magnificent. What would you like to know?"

"Everything."

"Hah. I doubt that very much."

"When did you, I mean, may I ask *how* did you . . . ?"

"Come over?"

He nodded.

Tatyana sighed. "The accent always gives me away."

"Your English is excellent."

"I defected, of course."

Gustavs nodded, puzzled.

"We don't all make headlines. Only Misha, Rudolph. Not me, a lowly *coryphée*."

Gustavs shook his head.

"Part of the dance troupe but one of the background dancers, you could say. Not the lead. The prima."

"Background," he parroted, a question in his tone. "I thought you were quite good the other night."

"The recital?" She chuckled. "You're very sweet."

"I've never been to the ballet."

Tatyana looked incredulous. "Never? Well, we'll have to do something about that, now won't we . . ."

Not far off the path, they came upon a bench shaded by an ancient ash tree. Sipping their coffees, the pair chatted idly about the famous park for a few minutes, before Gustavs returned to the subject of ballet, and, more pointedly, to Tatyana's defection.

" . . . I was actually born the same year they renamed it the Vaganova academy, in her honour. I've been dancing ever since I can remember." She draped a leg over her knee, and leant against the backrest with a sigh. "I did a lot of folk dancing when I was a child. We all did. Put on little plays, dreadful stories about socialism, every performance carrying a deeper message about the worker's state. Not a second thought for the art itself. Even as a girl I found it tedious. Still—performing, dancing—it was like being on a different planet. I loved every minute of it.

"I joined the academy when I was nine, after my audition. It was the proudest moment of my young life. We trained, six days a week, I can't remember how many hours. Endless hours. With strained ankles and bruised toes—feet so swollen we couldn't fit them into our slippers. Technique, academics, French lessons, of course I loved the classes on Russian literature. Then rehearsals, perhaps a performance. And then more training, after hours, perfecting every technique you struggled with, so, perfecting *everything*.

"More than anything, I was known for my style of performance, my finesse. I was never all that strong, but I could float with ease. Neither could I jump particularly high, but I could pirouette on a ruble. From an early age, too. Unfortunately, there's only so much you can do with a natural talent. We're not as teachable, as easy to mold."

"What do you mean?"

"Better to be a blank canvass—flexible, athletic. Absorb every detail and allow yourself to be sculpted into the ideal performer. But with me, it was different. I was born with my talent but could never develop it the way some had hoped. The way that *I*, had hoped. It was a difficult truth to accept. After a time, my body simply wouldn't cooperate." She glanced down at her foot. "My achilles. At first, only inflammation. Then, a partial tear. And then my ankle, of course, compensating for the tendon. And on it went. Like dominoes. Injuries are common, naturally, but mine, well, there was nothing to be done. Genetic, they said. Inherited. So, no more daydreams of Esmeralda and her tambourine, the light and dark of Odette and Odile." She sighed heavily, looking off into the distance. "I cried for weeks."

"I'm sorry."

She came to, waving a hand in dismissal. "I took my time and, with commitment, graduated. I should have been ecstatic. A contract with the Kirov"—eyes widening in disbelief—"my goodness, who would have thought? But I knew I would always be, what is this expression . . . 'playing second fiddle.'"

She smiled once more at a memory. "I loved the academy, the dormitories with my friends. I was never competitive the way the rest were, despite my ambitions, and I think that's why so many of the girls warmed to me. It's ruthless, you know, the competition. But then, every summer, I would return home to Chelyabinsk. Back to the countryside, as far from any culture as you could imagine. I might as well have been on the moon.

"My uncle, forever writing his poetry, blind and deaf to the world around him. And my aunt, the perfect Communist. She kept a red corner, a little vigil for Lenin—a candle and a small portrait. Her treasured Little Octobrist pin. All my friends had joined the Young Pioneers, or the Komsomol. God, how I hated it there. I spent most of my days lost in my uncles' books, the banned novels he kept hidden beneath the floorboards, even hidden from my aunt. I suppose he had no choice in that. At least we shared that much.

"I longed to be back in Leningrad. Longed for it every minute of every day. But eventually even Leningrad wasn't enough, the more I heard about the West from the other dancers, those who had toured abroad. And not just the West—everywhere. Paris, London. The Caribbean. China! It all seemed so magical, places of real colour and light. Fairy tales."

She brushed something from her thigh, speaking slowly now. "Looking back, I think I had known for a long time. Somewhere"— she twiddled her fingers behind her head—"subconsciously maybe, I had made up my mind years before. It was as if I had been leaving a trail of breadcrumbs my entire life, and only then rediscovering the path out of the forest. Truly, it was only a question of when, and how.

"Our company wasn't touring at the time, and so I convinced some teachers of mine to provide me with references for the Bolshoi. I could expand my repertoire, immerse myself in a slightly different style of dance. A fresh start, in a way. I was still a very good dancer, and they were sympathetic, in their own way, after all my injuries. A change of scenery might be best. I danced with the Bolshoi for three years, before the tour in '79. We were in Hamilton, a few dates in Canada before we moved on to America."

In front of them a young mother passed pushing a pram, while a toddler gawked in wonder, a toothless grin on his cherubin face. He giggled happily, drool streaming down his chin. Tatyana cooed at him, wiggling her fingers adoringly.

"Oh, what a handsome little fellow . . ."

"You have children?"

She shook her head. "No, you?"

"No."

She took a breath. "I'm not boring you with my story, am I?"

"Not at all. You were in Hamilton . . ."

"That's right, yes. Well, that night in the hotel, in the lobby bar, some of the girls and I decided we'd get our handler especially drunk. A pathetic little man, insecure as could be, he loved himself almost as much as his authority."

"Your handler. A bodyguard?"

"Something like that. After Boris defected in '74—well, no, that's not true, we always had security men watching over us. Not for our protection, but to make sure we didn't embarrass the Party by leaving. Luckily for me, no one really pays much attention to a *coryphée* with an injury-plagued career. Still, I've never been so frightened in my life.

"We had ourselves a little party. Practically drowned the man in vodka. Janus, was his name. Pathetic, as I said, and always with an eye for us dancers. Always leering when he thought we couldn't see. Handsy when he drank, which, on that night, worked in my favour. The more he drank, the more we flirted. The other girls eventually went to bed, and Janus sent his colleague away, but I stayed a while with him, letting his hands wander a bit. There was a lot of luck that night, when I think back. The bar was full, lots of rich business-men. Or, maybe even poor businessmen, but rich to me, I suppose, at the time. What did I know? I put on quite the show. Joking and laughing, flipping my hair. I was terribly drunk, too. I can remember Janus singing folk songs, some of the men buying us drinks.

"I was looking for anyone that night, making eyes at every man I could but, in the end, it was Pierre who came to my rescue. Janus was in a state, half asleep on the rail. I whispered, likely slurred, and with my terrible English who knows how he understood. I begged him for help. That I was afraid, that I needed to escape—right there, right then. He was kind, Pierre was. And handsome." She let out a breathy laugh. "You know, I thought he was French, with his accent. It's how we communicated, my French better than my English. And I suppose he was, in the end, only French-Canadian. And here I thought he'd whisk me away to Paris!"

She shifted in her seat. "We agreed to meet by the restroom, close enough to the back entrance. In the end, it was hardly secretive at all. Janus was face down at the bar, unresponsive. I hid in Pierre's apart-ment for a few days while he made the arrangements, helping me apply for asylum. The company moved on and no one made a peep, which surprised me. I didn't hear a thing, nothing in the newspapers, nothing at all. But, the more I thought about it, it made complete sense. I was a nobody, and it would have been an embarrassment. Yet another. It wasn't long before Sasha in New York. Then Valentina and Leonid in Los Angeles. They stole the headlines, you could say.

"And there you have it. We married, shortly after, Pierre and I. He was a good man, a kind man. And he helped me in my moment of need. I guess you could say that I felt I owed him that much. It was never a marriage based on love but, on mutual need, I suppose. Perhaps less so for Pierre. I was a plaything for him, a broken toy in need of repair. It made him feel, oh, honourable, I suppose. Chivalrous. He *was* rich, as it turned out, and after a few years he was bored. There are younger ballerinas now. Younger models. He's often away on business trips." She sighed. "I'm not certain if I blame him. We tried, in the end. But the marriage was always based on, I don't know what you'd call it. Not love, anyway. Something like it, perhaps . . . something like it."

Tatyana smiled to herself, then looked up at him. "Nobody knows this about me," she said quietly.

Gustavs acknowledged the moment. "Thank you for telling me."

She was studying his face once again, trying to read behind the glasses. "And now that I've told you my story . . ."

"I'm an open book."

"You're not married?"

"No."

"I find this very hard to believe. Those baby blue eyes of yours."

His gaze lingered on the dimple creasing her cheek. "I was. Married. It's been," he exhaled, "almost five years now."

Tatyana said nothing, her eyes asking the question.

"Car accident. It was, *he* was drunk. Instantaneous, they said. For both of them."

She placed a hand over top of his.

"I miss her, still. Greatly. But, it's different now. It's been so long. There's almost—guilt, that I can't picture her face any longer. I mean, I can, but they're all photographs. They're all just pictures I have, they're not *really* her . . ."

She gripped his hand softly now, rubbing her thumb across his knuckles. "Tell me about her."

He smiled to himself. "Anna was . . . very sweet, very generous. One of the kindest souls I have ever known." He chuckled. "And opinionated, my goodness, so opinionated. Once she was set on something, that was it. There was no sense in trying to talk her out of it." He sighed. "Always so bloody *stubborn*," he said with a laugh.

They were silent for a time, drifting through reverie. The air was still muggy when dusk descended, a darkness cascading through the treetops, enveloping their surroundings in heavy shadow. In the distance, a chorus of instruments had begun to play, a melody floating along on a passing breeze.

"Is it a concert?" Tatyana asked.

"I'm not sure. Let's go see."

They walked north through the park, the music growing steadily louder, a bouncy melody of piano and accordion with warbling feminine vocals. Eventually, they came across an eclectic crowd in a small clearing amongst the trees, dancing and lazing in equal measure, smoking and drinking wine from paper cups as a radio played nearby.

"Ahh," Tatyana said, stopping to observe the group as the music swelled, "Edith Piaf."

There were maybe twenty of them, Bohemian types enjoying a sultry spring evening, blankets and pillows strewn about the grass, transporting themselves back in time through drink and the timeless voice of a beloved chanteuse. The air was warm and fragrant, smoke mingling with springtime in bloom.

There came a pause between melodies. For a moment, only the chatter of the crowd, before the music started once again, the whimsy of a clarinet playing a slow, soulful harmony with a violin.

"I know this song," he said.

"Sidney Bechet," she replied, reaching for his hand. "*Si tu vois ma mère.*"

Couples paired off as the music played, languid and slow, a delicate vocal arrangement accompanying the instruments: "*Quand je pense à toi . . . aussitôt je vois . . .*"

Tatyana led them into the midst of the crowd before circling to face him, reaching up and slowly draping her arms around his neck. They moved as one to the soulful melody without speaking a word, though Tatyana kept her eyes on him, forever searching for something, it seemed. At one point she took his cheek in her palm, a most intimate gesture, before lowering her head and resting it upon his chest.

And on a balmy spring evening, they danced. The musical notes of a bygone era moving them together, stirring them song after song beneath a clear, starlit sky.

Renata let out a weary sigh as she approached the window, twisting the blinds shut. She switched off the coffee machine, draped her jacket over her arm, swung her purse over her shoulder. After a final, cursory glance around the office she flicked off the lights and proceeded downstairs, fishing around in her handbag for a set of keys. She had already moved behind the front desk when she noticed the man seated in the foyer across from her. The academy was rather dim in the soft evening light, though she wasn't startled as much as she was confused. A man whom she hadn't heard enter—no jangling of bells in the doorway, no echo of boots on the floor. He was, until that very moment, simply another piece of furniture, materializing before her very eyes.

"Oh, I'm sorry," she said. "I didn't hear you come in." Renata shuffled a couple of steps uncertainly, adjusting her glasses.

"Quite alright, I haven't been waiting long." The man rose from his seat, placing a palm against his chest. "My apologies if I startled you."

"Not at all. However, we're closing just now. Is there something I can do for you?"

"Perfectly alright. My name is Mr. Braun. I've only stopped in to retrieve a package."

"Ah yes, of course. If you'll just give me a moment"—she glanced about the reception desk, lifting a few loose papers—"I know Kasia had it . . . ah, here we are."

Renata came around the bureau and handed the envelope across, the man bowing ever so slightly in appreciation. A little closer now, the light illuminated the man's complexion for the first time, and for some reason, the first thought that came to Renata's mind was, simply—beige. A man of various competing shades of brown completing a rather drab tableau. Hair, a light brown, parted to one side, perhaps not quite thinning but, thin, nonetheless. An unremarkable brown coat, worn but not entirely threadbare. He held a scuffed briefcase that matched his scuffed shoes which matched a face that was, well, how else to describe it? Beige. A dull, featureless sort of face that was, when put together, somehow less than the sum of its parts. As he smiled at her, graciously accepting the package, she realized that he might very well have been the most ordinary man she had ever seen.

"Lovely. Thank you, Miss?"

"Pawelski."

"Pawelski. Ah, in that case, allow me to say, *dziękuję.*"

"*Proszę,*" she replied.

Mr. Braun bowed his head once more, the faintest wisp of a smile, and motioned with an open hand toward the door. *After you.*

Renata moved past him to turn off the lights, plunging the academy into darkness, and pushed open the front door, the bell ringing rather loudly in the silence of the evening. She allowed Mr. Braun to pass, then turned to lock up, giving the handle a firm yank. From behind her, a flurry of tiny paws skuttled across the sidewalk, and she looked down to find a Boston terrier sniffing inquisitively at her ankles. An elderly man smiled, then tugged at the leash.

Mr. Braun was nowhere to be seen.

The old man and his companion continued on their way, while in the distance, a streetcar glided along the center of the road, sparks briefly flickering from the trolley poll. For a moment, Renata looked around, in search of the beige man who had seemingly vanished as suddenly as he had appeared. But soon, she too was overcome by the warm embrace of the spring air. A long day, and now a rather quiet evening, she thought to herself. *Just perfect.* She adjusted her purse strap, and began the long walk home.

THIRTEEN

On the final weekend in June, the city of Rīga was all but deserted. Citizens departed their urban homes for the countryside, dispersing to family cabins and back wood retreats, while across the ocean, the diaspora community of Toronto flocked to the respective nature preserves of Sidrabene, Saulaine and Tērvete. The festive tradition of *Jāņi*—the pagan midsummer celebration, had no place in the city. It called for forests and fields and starlit skies; roaring bonfires in the virgin wilderness.

Gustavs arrived in Sidrabene in the late afternoon, the grounds already flooded with crowds—tents spotting the landscape, couples wearing wildflower garlands and oakleaf wreaths, folk songs in the air. Sidrabene, named for a famous castle in what was once ancient Semigallia, was an oasis on the city's outskirts, tucked away amongst farmer's fields and nestled in the broad shadow of the Niagara Escarpment. Acres upon acres of land with humble woodland cottages, expansive meadows, a placid winding river. A place of camaraderie for the community to escape the urban grime and the blistering summer heat.

"Gustav!" shouted a male voice. "*Ej!* Over here!" Paulis Zutis waved enthusiastically at the edge of a crowd that had gathered by an old wooden stage. There must have been several hundred people, all drinking and merrily singing songs as they awaited the performance.

"Look who made it!" Paulis exclaimed, wrapping an arm lovingly around Gustavs' collar, eyes already glassy and peregrine. "Here—*ej!* Oh!" he hollered, trying to attract the attention of a young woman carrying a tray of beer.

"No hurry," Gustavs said, wriggling himself free and proceeding to greet the rest of the group—handshakes and kisses, loving embraces. Viktors was there with his wife Lidija, a modest display of paintings set up by their campsite across the field. Aija was there as well, surely with her own jewelry exhibit somewhere nearby. He greeted some former schoolmates from Latvian school, and over their shoulders spotted all the old, familiar faces—the community, his extended family. Everywhere there were nods and smiles of kinsfolk with uncertain first names. Closer to the stage, he could see Tomass, towering above the crowd with his golden mane of hair, though Māra and the children were nowhere to be seen.

From a set of mounted speakers, the crackling of static gave way to the plucking of strings, a *kokle* playing an ancestral folk melody. Two columns of dancers emerged at either side of the stage—a slow polka, skipping in time to music accompanied by the emotive voice of a single soprano. They were fully garbed in traditional dress: women with intricately embroidered linen blouses and bejeweled fabric crowns, hand-woven shawls pinned with ancient silver brooches. The men were stalwart—black top hats and knee-high leather boots, woolen waistcoats and striking belts fashioned from bronze. The varied colours and designs on stage reflected the different regions of the old country, while in their hands, the dancers shook their *trīdekšņi*, jangling wood and brass instruments matching the rhythm of the song. Some of the snow-capped elders seated in the front row clapped along to the beat.

A young woman with golden braids passed with a tray of *Jāņu siers*—festive cheese with caraway seeds—while a brunette in a linen cap distributed cups of beer. Gustavs chatted awhile with Lidija as others drifted amongst their little entourage, brief hellos and festive greetings, until Otto Blaževičs sidled up beside him, offering his hand.

"*Nu nu,* Gustav, what news from your neck of the woods?"

Gustavs smiled and accepted the politician's disconcertingly limp handshake, like gripping a wet trout.

"Not much to report, I'm afraid. How are you, Otto?"

"Oh just fine, yes. I suppose no news is good news! Rasma is well? Behaving herself?"

"Best as she can."

"Hardly a ringing endorsement," he said, a wink and a teasing nudge to Gustavs' ribs.

Gustavs couldn't recall ever seeing Otto Blaževičs, the career schmoozer, wearing anything but a suit. He was considerably dressed down on the day, certainly by his standards—a striped shirt with a rakishly open collar, a paisley orange tie knotted just beneath. A rather pale complexion, he had a pockmarked face and greyish hair, wildly unkempt, forever at odds with the ministerial persona he so diligently cultivated.

"Say, I was speaking to Valdi the other day—Roze, he mentioned that he'd spoken with you. An interest in a new role perhaps, drafting press releases if I'm not mistaken?"

Gustavs raised a brow.

Otto hesitated. "Given your command of both languages. *The Star. The Globe and Mail,* writing articles . . ."

Gustavs underscored his prior response by taking a sip of beer—crisp and bitter—while Otto chuckled to relieve the tension.

"Hm, maybe old Valdi is getting ahead of himself again . . ."

"It's fine. Last I spoke to him was at Imants' funeral, but there was hardly any talk of a role. Not from me, anyhow." He forced an empathetic smile.

Otto raised a hand, lips curling into a sheepish grin. "Already forgotten."

"Have you heard anything more about the demonstrations?" Aija interjected.

Otto shook his head. "The same as last week, I'm afraid."

"I've heard they're making arrests, calling some of the men up for military service," she said.

"I've not heard anything definitive. The same rumors, of course, but"—he gave a shrug—"only rumors, as far as I can say."

Aija gave a nod of acquiescence.

"I just don't know about all of that," added Lidija. "I don't want to use the word *foolish*, but, I can't help but feel—"

"Hardly foolish, a peaceful demonstration. How else to do it?" replied Otto.

"What's this?" asked Gustavs.

"Last week," Otto said. "On the 14th, crowds of thousands gathered at the *piemineklis* in Rīga, honoring those deported under Stalin. It was Helsinki-86, among others, organizing it. They broadcasted the event on Radio Free Europe, then by word of mouth. A *peaceful* protest"—he glanced at Lidija, emphasizing the point—"the first of its kind against the Soviets. A risk, of course, I'll admit that much—"

"A huge risk," Lidija stressed.

"Yes, but a worthy one. A statement to Moscow. This is our

history, real history. It will not be forgotten. You might wish it so, but we remember."

As others joined the conversation, Gustavs' thoughts turned to Lotte and to Aleksandrs' role with the new liberation movement. Her vague references about his involvement, and now the uncertainty of his whereabouts. Lidija was right. A huge risk. And a risk for how many now? Thousands, apparently. Openly defying the regime in the streets, provoking authorities that had no qualms about snatching people in the night, disappearing them into the bowels of Russia.

As he listened half-heartedly to Otto's pontificating—the man with an audience, in his element now—Gustavs couldn't help but think of Lotte pacing in her living room, railing against these very men, these very discussions. What was it that she'd said? *Endless squabbling.* Politicians meeting for coffee and cakes, while in Rīga, young men and women risked everything on the cobbled streets. Nowhere to hide, once exposed. Nowhere to run, the decrepit foreign gatekeepers obstinate for over forty years.

" . . . And so we come full circle, then. Why not? Why not hold our own demonstration? In solidarity. To keep Latvija, to keep all the Baltic states in the forefront of people's minds. Remind the world that we are not so far away, so easily dismissed."

"Come now, Otto," said Viktors. "This is a completely separate issue. We could march in the streets for days without getting so much as a ticket. You cannot compare our efforts, the risk involved."

"I'm not saying—"

"They shouldn't be so bold," added Lidija, keeping on her point, "it's far too dangerous, even now. We've seen how they respond. Just ask the Czechs, the Hungarians. For heaven's sake, the Afghans."

Otto swatted this aside. "You're talking about ancient history now, Lidij, please. Gorbachev would never march into Rīga the way they did in Budapest, in Prague. He relishes his image in the West, his 'socialism with a human face,' all of that."

"They're playing a dangerous game over there," said Viktors, shaking his head.

"Someone has to," said Gustavs, almost to himself.

A silence fell over the group, looking to him, a queer moment of disbelief. Gustavs felt the eyes, the attention, and so, shrugged. "It's all well and good to exchange words, but sooner or later . . . words lose their meaning. Not every window of opportunity remains open indefinitely. I think it's very brave, what they're doing. I wonder if any of us would have the same courage."

Aija was smiling at him, as were the others, and Otto put a hand on his shoulder. "Could it be?" he said, smirking. "Gustavs Ziediņš, taking a stand?"

"Oh leave him be, Otto."

"The man speaks at last!"

"Alright, alright." Gustavs shook this off, accepting some affectionate ribbing from old friends.

The performers on stage were well into a lively number—the women twirling like teetotums, colourful skirts hooping with every turn, the men proudly stomping about with arms raised high. Beyond the frizzle of Otto's coiffure, Gustavs' eyes were drawn to Tomass once more, this time speaking animatedly with Dagnija Barons. He politely excused himself, weaving his way through the crowd toward the front of the stage, and was received with open arms and air kisses from Dagnija, and a hearty embrace from his old friend.

"Where's Māra and the kids?"

"At home! Thank God . . ." said Tomass.

"A lion released back into the wild," teased Dagnija.

"Ah, that explains it."

"What—I don't deserve a break?" said Tomass. "And speaking of release, it's been a while since we've spent a *Jāņi* together"—tapping his cup against Gustavs'—"and I'm here every year," he added pointedly.

"Well, I suppose that's fair."

Tomass grinned with the slow blink of a lush. "It's nice to see you out." Then, to Dagnija, "Both of you."

Dagnija smiled, looking more like her old self—butter blonde curls and just the slightest brush of maquillage. She squinted into the setting sun, the wrinkles on her forehead like fine silken threads, betraying her age, but only just.

They watched the performance for a time, admiring the show of tradition against the festive backdrop. The stage was painted to resemble a wood garner, the sloping roof buttressed by beams covered in leafy foliage—linden and birch—with thistles and thorns to repel the evil spirits of old.

"Gustav, do you have a moment . . ." Dagnija said, leaning in, her voice low. "Maybe"—she turned from the stage, away from the crowd—"a walk?"

The crowd broke into applause as the performers bowed, and Tomass, pinching his fingers against his lips, whistled piercingly.

"Of course," Gustavs said, trying to read her expression.

Tomass downed the rest of his beer, then waved across the way at some former volleyball teammates, allowing Gustavs and Dagnija to slip away down a gravel path past some cottages. They stopped on a couple of occasions—an elderly pair from the church choir, inevitably pressing them to join their ranks, and further along, one of Dagnija's old flames, an awkward fellow who stumbled over his words, evidently still carrying an everlasting torch. It seemed a time-honoured solstice tradition, never walking more than ten paces without bumping into an old friend or acquaintance.

"I feel so silly," Dagnija said, once they were alone again on the path. "I didn't mean to sound so mysterious."

"Not at all. Something wrong?"

"Not really. Well, I don't know . . . I wanted to speak to you about Imants." She rubbed the back of her neck, a sort of nervous tic. "Those detectives. At the funeral. Do you remember?"

"Sure."

"They came and they spoke to me. Initially, I mean, after everything. But, then again. This was, oh, a few months ago now."

"I know. Me too. Some others as well, apparently."

She nodded along. "They said some things, Gustav. They told me not to speak about it, not to anyone. It was about our doctor."

"Fyodorov."

"They told you," she said.

"In a roundabout way."

"Yes. Well, what they said—I mean, what they *implied*. What am I supposed to think? And not only that, then they had these questions. Why him? Why a *Russian* doctor? As if this is some crime now, simply to *be* Russian. What do I know about him . . ." She huffed, an indignant sound. "What do I know—as if these were social visits. I knew how to look for jaundice in my husband's urine. I know the symptoms of liver failure, that is what I know, for heaven's sake."

"I'm sorry, Dag. For all of it." Again, he thought of Lotte, of her theories. Imploring the detectives to help. How much would they have revealed to a dead man's widow?

"What else did they ask you?"

"Mostly they wanted to know about Doctor Fyodorov."

"Did they show you any pictures?"

"Pictures? Of what?"

He shook his head. "Nothing, just, thinking out loud . . ."

"I know they're only doing their jobs, and that's fine. It's not as if"—they passed a younger couple, the woman heavily pregnant, exchanging greetings—"yes, I'm, well now I've completely forgotten what I was saying."

"It's alright."

"Regardless, that's not what I wanted to speak to you about."

He looked to her, prompting.

"It's that officer."

"Which?"

"The Italian."

"De Rossi."

She nodded.

"What is it?"

She stopped to face him, the two of them alone now on the gravel road, obscured among the pines. Below the embankment to their right, a thin stream flowed silently past a mound of dried riverbed.

"I don't like him, Gustav. The way he is, with me."

Gustavs crossed his arms.

"He asks me questions . . ."

"Such as?"

"Personal questions, Gustav. Things that have no relevance to, well, to anything. The younger one, I feel fine with him, I believe he's trying to help." She shook her head, scoffing once again. "Help. With what I'm not really sure, but, I'm a good judge of character. He's a good egg, that one. But this De Rossi, the way he looks at me . . ." Her face changed, as if seeing phantoms in the pine trees.

"We ladies, from an early age—you wouldn't understand, but we're used to this sort of thing. The attention. How to, deflect it. Ignore it outright. Dismiss a man's advances with only a look." She smiled just then, a puckish flicker in her eyes. "Call it a survival skill. It's not always bad, of course, the attention. What woman doesn't like to be noticed on occasion. But sometimes, with some men, the attention is . . . of a different sort." The shadow returned to her face. "Some of them . . . oh, I don't know . . ."

Gustavs thought back to the funeral, so long ago now. What was it De Rossi had said then? *How well do you know her? A fine-looking woman.* Something more? Something he had forgotten?

"I don't think you should speak to him anymore, Dagnija."

"He calls, Gustav."

"Calls?"

"Calls the house. At night. Sometimes, I think he's been drinking."

"Have you told anyone?"

"Tell who? His partner? Other police? I live alone now, Gustav. I don't know what to do. I'll admit, it's been better of late. Maybe the dumb ox finally got the hint. But I don't know for certain. The man makes my skin crawl."

"I haven't heard from either of them in a while. Listen, if he bothers you again, insist on speaking to Horowitz and no one else. And then call me right after. If it happens again, I'll take care of it."

"I'm sorry to bring this up to you, like this."

"Oh come on . . ."

"Thank you for understanding." She sighed, exhaling a deep breath of relief. "I feel better already," she said, somewhat robotically.

"How are you, Dagnija? I mean, really."

She searched his face for a moment, her lips firming into a patronizing half-smile. "Old, Gustav. Old, and alone." She anticipated the reaction, cutting him off. "Don't. It's alright, really, it is. You, on the other hand, are only *young* and alone." She cupped his hand between both of hers, patting it a couple of times. "Don't end up like me. Imants loved you like a son. As do I." Now the smile was genuine. "Come now, let's get back. We've left Tomass unsupervised."

Darkness had fallen across the grounds, yet the festivities had only just begun. Across the fields campfires flickered and cast their shadows, illuminating silhouettes, the distant flames dancing like fireflies in the night sky. The fires would burn through the night, minded by those who still held fast to the old traditions—staying awake until dawn for good fortune in the coming year.

Gustavs walked alone by the riverside, replaying the conversation with Dagnija, thinking his way through niggling doubts and feelings of impotence. *If it happens again, I'll take care of it.* Was that so? He reprimanded himself for a time, though eventually concluded that it was the right thing to say even if, in truth, there was little substance to the bravado. He was well-intentioned, which seemed to reassure her in the moment, and perhaps that was what mattered most.

He slowly made his way back from the floodplain to the *kafejnīca*—the little café where Omīte and the *Dāmu Komitēja* would be awaiting their chauffeurs. As the gravel crunched beneath his feet, he was drawn to some giggling beyond a thicket to his left, catching a glimpse of two shadows at the base of a tree, shadows drunk with young love. He smiled to himself, at yet another solstice superstition. The old saying, *"ielīst krūmos"*—quite literally, to sneak into the bushes. More good fortune for these two, it seemed, in the year to come.

Whether it was the songs, the outdoors, the scent of wood smoke drifting through the still air, he couldn't tell. But it moved him, that evening. The atmosphere conjured something within him, something long dormant. It couldn't be defined, or easily categorized—just a feeling. A deep and inherent love, an affection for a culture which had always been there, and would always remain, despite his gradual drift over the years. He didn't care to question the how or the why of this separation, the gradual divide that had grown between himself, his life and the traditions with which he was raised. It didn't matter. What mattered was only the moment, enveloped in the tender night air and the melodies of his childhood, returning to a place where he was forever welcome, and forever at home.

FOURTEEN

ON A COOL, DAMP MORNING, THE AIR STILL HEAVY WITH THE scent of rainfall, Lotte Lazdiņa sat on an old, wooden bench not far from the mucky banks of Grenadier Pond. She sat primly: back straight, knees together, hands folded neatly in her lap, watching a family of sparrows dart in and out of the treetops, and the bullrushes that swayed gently in the breeze.

To her right, an empty fabric tote bag with floral print, and the contents formerly therein: a set of Zeiss binoculars with a brown leather case, charcoal sketching pencils, a cartridge paper sketchbook, a silver thermos with black tea, a liverwurst sandwich on rye—tidily wrapped in wax paper—a handkerchief, and a tattered old copy of Peterson's *Field Guide to Birds*.

With a slight tilt of her wrist, she glanced subtly at the time. *Not quite.*

Now she turned her attention to the guidebook, an ancient, weathered thing, the spine clutching at the musty yellow pages. She could hardly stand the sight of the book as a girl—her father obsessively flipping through its contents, forever wandering around in the backyard, gazing into the evergreens. But it felt like so much more than a book now. A living, breathing thing—she could still feel his presence whenever she turned the pages, carefully, delicately.

She checked her watch again and noted that familiar sensation in her chest—slightly taut, matching the quickening of her pulse. *Even after all this time.*

Lotte replaced the book and picked up the binoculars, removing the caps, and scanned the treeline first to the east, then skimming the waters back west. She took a deep breath of the fresh, morning air, casting a surreptitious glance left and right. Then, she raised the binoculars once more, and squinted.

She looked across the water. Past the weeping willows that hung, forever melancholy. Beyond the forested embankment with its thick web of leaves and branches and found, there, amidst the wood panel siding on the second floor of the house, a small window with French shutters. She steadied her breath, blinked, lost the window for a moment, and found it again just as the shutters were pushed open. She felt the rush of blood pulsating in her hands, the window so far away the slightest tremor shook the image out of focus.

Lotte exhaled slowly, focusing on the grainy movement of a stocky, silver-haired woman who leaned her upper body out over the ledge. She had thick arms and an enormous bosom—her squat figure filling the window frame—and proceeded to beat a small grey doormat with a broom handle. After a few moments, she drew the mat inside.

Lotte held her breath. *Too long? No. The shutters, still open.*

The woman reappeared. A different mat in her hand now— dark, crimson red, on this occasion—and she smacked it violently for a time, before disappearing once again.

Lotte exhaled. The entire affair took no more than twenty seconds, before the woman emerged a final time. She reached out toward the shutters and, in the briefest of moments, paused to look out over the pond, a proud, indomitable expression, before the shutters were closed.

Lotte returned the binoculars to their leather case, snapping the clasps shut, and retrieved her breakfast. She unscrewed the cap of her thermos, pouring a steaming cup of black tea, then patiently unfolded the wax paper in her lap, lifting a small triangle of black rye. She looked at one corner, then the other, and took a small bite from the middle.

That evening, Lotte took the tram home, but not before stopping off at the liquor store to purchase a bottle of wine—a full-bodied *Barolo Gattera*—wrapped in a brown paper bag. She got on at Bathurst Street, taking the 501 streetcar west along Queen for several blocks. When she got off, she drifted amongst the bustling crowd for a time, before spotting an opening in traffic and swiftly hopped across the street to where another tram had momentarily stopped along its eastbound route. She waited until the doors were closing, ensuring she was the last passenger aboard, and flashed the driver her transfer ticket along with an enchanting smile. The driver, a sweaty man with a walrus mustache, shifted in his seat to watch her down the aisle, and for this received a remonstrative clucking from a prickly old woman in the front seat.

Dufferin. Ossington. Bathurst. As the tram stopped at Spadina, several more passengers stepped aboard, the last of which—a rather unremarkable, middle-aged fellow—took his time moving to the back of the carriage. He carried with him a beige leather valise that matched his beige overcoat and drifted through the crowd virtually unnoticed; a non-person that floated about like a phantom, one that could have hardly spooked a mouse. In the crook of his arm, he cradled a brown paper bag.

Lotte shifted aside toward the window, and the man promptly

sat down in the vacated seat. He unbuttoned his coat and placed his bag between them.

"A chill in the air today," he said, a soft voice.

"Not so chilly where I'm from."

They sat in silence as the tram glided through the streets, the odd spark above as they crossed an intersection, passengers steadying themselves on their feet when the carriage halted abruptly.

Jarvis. Sherbourne. Parliament. At last they passed over the Don River, and the tram slowed before Broadview Avenue. Without another word, the man reached for his paper bag, rose from his seat, and floated the length of the aisle before stepping down to the street. Lotte watched through the finger-smudged window as the tram glided forward once more, and the man faded anonymously into the cobbled streets and brick tenements of Leslieville.

Back home, the house was unwelcoming—cold, shrouded in darkness. Lotte flicked on the lights and moved to the kitchen where she put on the kettle, and then her reading glasses. From the cutlery drawer she removed a paring knife, and from the cupboard above, an artisanal clay bowl, handmade and fired in Ventspils, a white fishing boat intricately etched along the bottom in the sgraffito style. There was a faint scratching at the back door, and she moved to let in the Abyssinian—"Come now, Pūka, there we are"—which slipped lovingly between her feet, purring softly in greeting, before trotting off toward the bedroom.

Lotte placed a cigarette between her lips and bent down to light it off the stovetop, inhaling deeply. Then, she removed the bottle of *Barolo Gattera* from the paper bag, followed by the envelope—postage from Vancouver, signed as always in the elegantly indecipherable cursive of "Aunt Ophelia." For a moment, she winced, the smoke drifting into her eyes.

Slipping the knife beneath the sealed flap, she flicked her wrist and unfolded the envelope's only contents: a single piece of off-white stationery, which she held out above the kettle. She angled the paper above the spout, and waited patiently, the steam slowly building before churning out thick rolling billows beneath the page.

And then, after a long moment—an apparition. In the blank spaces amongst the fanciful scrawl of Ophelia's correspondence, the message appeared—short and concise, block print carefully penned—faint letters summoned from the page. The message, as always, was brief; the language cold, bureaucratic.

Her jaw tightened. She drew on the cigarette, deeply, inhaling all she could in that instant, unable to take her eyes off the page. For a time, she chewed her bottom lip, turning the words over in her head, until at last she moved the kettle aside, and lowered the letter onto the glowing burner. The near corner curled black before catching fire, and she angled the page, encouraging the licks of flame, before dropping it into the clay bowl. She watched the message smolder before her, tending to the blackening drifts with the tip of the knife, and watched silently as the fishing boat was lost beneath a coating of grey ash.

IV.

SUMMER
1987

FIFTEEN

THE ROYAL YORK HOTEL WAS A JEWEL IN THE HEART OF THE CITY. A regal limestone chateau, complete with Romanesque arches and a pitched copper roof that rose twenty-eight stories above Union train station. In addition to its regular stream of illustrious guests, through its opulent halls had passed kings and queens, dukes and duchesses. The expansive lobby was as luxuriant as one might expect: crystal chandeliers, ornate wood-carved ceilings, and a grand, sweeping staircase at the top of which stood Gustavs Ziediņš—dapper in suit and tie—leaning against the railing, perusing a newspaper.

While he waited for Tatyana, apparently running late, he read intently about the former Gestapo chief Klaus Barbie, recently convicted of crimes against humanity in Lyon, and sentenced to life imprisonment. Hardly a severe penalty, given the harrowing accounts, and hardly an appropriate topic for the evening, he thought, turning the page. Here was a clever little cartoon: President Reagan, huffing and puffing like a fairy tale wolf, blowing down the Berlin Wall as communist piggies scattered in every direction.

When Tatyana finally appeared, it seemed to Gustavs a scene from a film. As if a spotlight had descended, following her across the lobby while patrons—men and women alike—tried not to stare. Even the desk clerk stole a furtive glance. She glided across the floor, elegant and unhurried, a slimming black dress with an open back and plunging décolletage, an ensemble made all the more stunning by her rather modest bust and svelte physique. The dress was enhanced by crystal drop earrings and a matching necklace that shimmered in the soft light.

"I think we missed our reservations," he said.

"I know. Forgive me?" She added a rueful smile to the question, not that she required any response.

"I will. By the bar?"

"You read my mind."

The famed Library Bar was rather busy that Friday evening, so they pulled up two stools and ingratiated themselves to the barman.

It was undeniable now, the sheer magnetism between them; a palpable current of energy whenever they locked eyes, when their fingers touched, when she playfully drew the top of her foot along the length of his calve.

It had been a slow, patient courtship, adding to the sense of ceremony. At first, little more than a meeting of chance, a nervous flutter of emotion. This was followed by stolen conversations here and there, walks in the park, and then, just the other week, a film, or at least, *most* of a film—an evening cut short by a power outage, of all things, disrupting the mood. The world working against them, it seemed. But not tonight. An evening of luxury. Tatyana had insisted, acquiring tickets for the ballet—a performance of Masada—followed by a night for themselves while her soon to be ex-husband was away in Cincinnati.

She insisted on *zakuski*—cold hors d'oeuvres with colder vodka—and they dined like royalty. Exquisite Sevruga caviar, glistening black pearls in a crystal bowl, served with crème fraiche and accompanied by shaved egg and crostini. Tatyana took her time with the vodka selection, asking for the barman's recommendation and then dismissing it just as quickly. "The Finns do a fine job," she said, "but I have a weakness for Żubrówka."

Among stacks of old books illuminated by a wall of prismatic bottles, they relished their meal, sitting close and conspiratorial, lost in their own private world. And so, Gustavs took the opportunity to study this striking young woman, as if for the first time, exploring all her captivating imperfections. The hidden warmth to be found behind those dark, inscrutable eyes; the sultry mouth, revealing a few small, slightly jagged bottom teeth whenever she laughed. He ran the pad of his thumb over the twin moles on the side of her neck—little fang marks just below her left ear.

"You found my secret," she said.

"I always thought you were a bit pale."

"I performed there once, in Romania. *Bukharest.*"

"Did you . . ."

She leaned in, whispering by his ear: "There was a Count, a mysterious man in the front row."

"Strange characters in those faraway lands. One hears stories."

"One hears legends of bats that flutter in the night." She drew a fingernail the length of his neck, from jawline to collar."

"Should I be worried?"

She pulled back, that sly, single-dimpled smile. "Maybe a little."

He never expected it, not really. They checked in at the front desk, and once upstairs he shut the door, stepped politely aside, except that Tatyana didn't move. And so he shuffled once more, only to have her counter, moving against him. She reached up, brushing past his collar, and pulled him down, guiding him toward her mouth. After a moment, she took him by the hand, leading him toward the bed where she sat him down. She held his gaze as she loosened his tie, his collar, undid the buttons of his shirt. When he reached up to help her she took hold of his wrist, kissed it, then pushed it aside. She knelt, untying his laces, removing one shoe, and then the other. And when she stood, positioning herself between his legs, she ran a hand through his hair, tilting her head, as if fascinated by the dark locks that slipped between her fingers. When she undid his belt, his eyes drifted down until she caught him, pinching his chin and lifting it upwards, a scolding glance and a schoolteacher's shake of the head. She made sure he looked straight ahead, hypnotized by those dark, smoky eyes as she worked at his buckle, the clasp, and then the rest.

Was that the time? The ballet! Only the briefest of pauses following the briefest of affairs—perhaps more brief than Gustavs might have intended—before another flurry of activity: the matting of hair, the smoothing of creases, the re-zipping of a delicate, yet stubborn dress. They were nearly out the door before a final hurried search party for an earring.

The O'Keefe Center was only a couple of blocks east, on the south side of Front Street, and they breezed through the concourse and into their seats just as the orchestra tuned to pitch, the notes swelling in tandem and filling the concert hall. As the house lights dimmed the pair exchanged subtle, knowing glances, faces still flushed from the dash across town, and found themselves grinning absurdly at the stage as the curtain rose. Tatyana smoothed her dress more than once, as if to assuage the suspicions of the audience.

It was an impassioned performance, the choreography appropriately set to Rachmaninoff, retelling the tragic Jewish tale of the Roman siege of Masada, and the hundreds that chose to end their lives rather than risk capture by the legions. Veronica Tennant was a delight to watch, Tatyana rapt by the performance, and Gustavs couldn't help a smile whenever her leg would twitch beside him as if she were onstage herself, leaping into the air.

After the performance, the air outside was warm and still. A busy Friday night downtown, humming with life. They held hands as they walked in silence back to the hotel, through the lobby and up the stairs, returning to their room without a single word.

They took their time. The embraces softer now, the movements slow, purposeful. Along Tatyana's back, the stubborn zipper was encountered once again, more amenable this time, lowered inch by inch until the satin slipped from her bare shoulders. The hem of her dress, by contrast, lifted, bunched into his palms and teased the length of her thighs, and further still, revealing the embroidered lace beneath.

A sensual duet, Gustavs studying her figure like an exquisite canvass, while Tatyana teased her role, nibbling gently at his ear, arching her back just so, melting into positions and smirking playfully whenever she caught that enchanted look in his eye.

She remained with him throughout, until the very end, until she let herself go, drifting off somewhere he could not follow. Somewhere he could only observe as she closed her eyes, bottom lip pierced between her teeth, until her mouth widened, and widened still. And then, a look, a portrait forever etched into the most private recesses of his memory.

A shaft of pale streetlight filtered through the curtains, illuminating a cloud of smoke that hovered, suspended in the air as Tatyana stood, naked, by the mahogany dresser. Her head was tilted, cradling the telephone receiver by her shoulder, her right hand holding a cigarette by her waist while she examined a menu. Gustavs lay in bed, sheets tangled about his feet as he watched her. Her long hair, tousled by her shoulder blades, nearly black in the ambient light. Further down, that firm cleft, descending elegantly from her lower back. The muscular calves and calloused heels. When she shifted her weight, her bottom shifted with it—perfectly comfortable in her own skin, at ease from years on the stage, or, maybe, more than happy to tease him a little with a view. Perhaps, Gustavs thought, a bit of both.

A late night banquet for the pair of them, so extravagant that Gustavs felt a little guilty about the expense, though Tatyana would hear nothing of it. So then, Lobster Newburg—decadent chunks of shellfish marinated in a cognac cream sauce, and as an accompaniment, so as not to be *too* bourgeois—French fries. Though these too had been decadently fried in duck fat. And to drink? Champagne. *What else?* A frosted bottle atop a mound of crushed ice.

"No wonder you didn't fit in, the way you eat," he said, stretched out across the bed. "Your aristocratic tastes must have been frowned upon."

Tatyana sat cross-legged, a sheet wrapped across her bust, smiling. "No, not really. I'm a peasant girl at heart. A good cabbage stew will do me just fine on most days. With a slice of black rye. This, well, this is a luxury we never had. A luxury no one had, not that I knew. It was the stuff of fairy tales. So every once in a while, I treat myself, and I savour it." She smiled again, sucking some duck grease from her index finger, her thumb.

"A rare treat for me, on an English teacher's salary."

"And mine." She shrugged. "I consider it payment."

"Payment?"

She nodded. "Our broken vows, Pierre and I. Our marriage, from the beginning, it had very poor foundations. And I share responsibility for that, of course. Difficult to work on such a marriage. Like building on sand. Still, I was always faithful. Always."

"But not Pierre."

She licked her lips for a moment, a thoughtful look in her eyes. "How do I smell, my dear Professor?"

" . . . Is that a trick question?"

"*Nyet.*"

"Heaven."

"I will pretend you never said this."

"For the best, I think. What I meant was—"

"I know what you meant. But, you know, don't you? And I, you. It is part of our intimacy. So, when a man, your husband, for instance, returns home late from work, and there's a fragrance . . . I'm no fool. I'm not a vengeful person, you must know that about me. But everything has a cost."

"Lobster and champagne, in this case."

She pitched a brow. "Why not?"

Gustavs acknowledged this with a single nod.

"But," she said, skewering a piece of lobster, "truly, I could live on cabbage rolls and borscht. This is only for special occasions where I can pretend I'm Anna Pavlova."

"A ballerina, I'm guessing."

"*The* ballerina. One of them, anyway, from before the revolution."

Gustavs took a sip of champagne, sparkling and dry. "What was it like?"

She took a moment. "Russia?"

He nodded. "All of it, just . . . life."

"Life in our great socialist utopia."

"Yes."

She sighed. "You really want to know, don't you . . ."

He nodded, and she in turn motioned to the champagne bottle, Gustavs dutifully refilling her glass. She took a sip and leaned back against the headboard.

"Grey. This is the word that comes to my mind. Only grey." She was still for a time, her mind sifting through the years, eyes flickering.

He said nothing, letting her remain there, wherever she was, observing her as she drifted between memories. Then, a shadow swept across her face, darkening her features.

"I remember when they took my father. In a *voronok*, of course, as always. Black Mariahs, I've heard them called."

Gustavs shook his head.

"The black vans that would come. They would appear in the night, and you, or your neighbour, your friend, you would just, disappear. We lived in fear of these machines." She shook her head. "*Nyet*, not fear—paranoia. Like this. There was never any, how can I say, justice. No charges. At least, not real ones. Your name simply appeared on a list, somewhere, drawn up by *apparatchiks*. Endless lists, in my country. And then"—she blew a puff of air from her lips—"gone. Prison, the camps, the Lubyanka. Who knows? Just, gone.

"I hid in the closet when they came, the second time that they came for my father. He was a poet as well, like my uncle. Was very fond of French poetry in particular. French philosophers. He even spoke French. Took too much of an interest, apparently, in these poisonous ideas. I heard that, at first, they threatened him with the *psikhushka*—the psychiatric hospital. It's where they send you for re-education, to cure you of your illness. You see, we lived in Lenin's great utopia, and therefore, if you weren't pleased about it, there must have been something wrong with you. If you disagreed with the party line on anything, anything at all, you were a threat, and this had to be fixed. I suppose he called their bluff, they never took him to the hospital. Only another work camp. We never found out who told them, but in a land of *stuckachi* . . ."

"Informers."

"Informers, yes. Everywhere. Always. They weren't all of them, you know, henchmen? They didn't want to work for the Chekists, the security services, but . . ." She sighed. "It's like this: Maybe one night you're out, drinking some vodka with friends, and, you say something you shouldn't. Nothing serious, even—a joke, maybe, about Khrushchev's underpants. As we say, even the walls have ears. So then, later that week, someone, maybe a stranger, he needs a favour. And if you don't feel like doing the favour, well, you're reminded of your, hmm, your *anti-Soviet* sentiments. Maybe you don't even remember making the joke—but, here you are, about to be labeled as an enemy of the people if you do not cooperate. And the favour? Maybe just to listen, to listen about which of *your* friends makes the jokes next time. The silly joke you don't remember. And in this way, they know everything. They are everywhere, because they are your own people." She paused, taking a slow sip of champagne. "Now I've lost my thinking . . ."

"You said your father, he was a poet."

"Ah, yes. My father. We'd been released only a few years before, you know. I was born in that camp, somewhere out in the East. In Solzhenitsyn's Archipelago, as he calls it. I was eight the second time they came for my father. A much harsher sentence, this time. Kolyma. I remember hiding in the closet, the light underneath the door, the long shadows of their boots. Heavy boots. Mud on the floor. It felt like such a long time, but it was minutes. Only minutes. My mother crying, hysterical. Pleading with them. This sound she made . . .

"I remember thinking, never before so loud, and after, never so quiet. She never recovered, my mother. When I was born, at least we were together, in the camp. We were a family, we had each other. But she was nothing without him. An eggshell with no yoke. We sent care packages for a while, close to a year, until one day when a letter was returned. 'The prisoner has no more need,' it said. It was as close to a death certificate as we could get, more than most would receive. My mother, she would sit by the fire, all day, and every night. I would make sure she stayed warm, go to market and buy us food, chop wood—well, as much as I was able. The only time she left the house was for vodka. We had such little money then. I can't remember how long before she sent me to live with my aunt and uncle in Chelyabinsk. I never saw her again.

"I was, oh, maybe thirteen when they told me. When I read the letter from our old neighbour. She had drank herself blind, my sweet mother." Tatyana picked at the bedcover with a single fingernail, absentmindedly scratching at the thread. "*Moonshine*," she emphasized the word, "I think you call it, but, different, in Russia. As a girl I didn't think anything of it. I didn't know. Alcohol, it's only something that smells terrible to a child. And vodka, it costs money. When she ran out, she would make her own. Insect repellant. Brake fluid. The mechanic, I remember, he was frequently around. A certain . . . exchange. We didn't have a car."

Gustavs took her hand.

"I always dreamt of getting away. I think my father did as well, in his own way, in his books, in his dreams about Paris. I was his daughter, certainly. Always curious about the outside world, always wanting more. As beautiful as it was in Leningrad—the frozen Neva, winding through the city; the Hermitage, of course. Sometimes, in the spring, we would practice our routines in the palace square, and after school some of the local children would join us, pretending to be ballerinas." She gave a faint, sober smile. "But I always knew what I wanted. I wanted more, to get out of that bleak, that grey prison. There is no living there, not really. Only surviving."

She looked him over, studying his face as she liked to do, a bemused expression tightening her lips. "Why do I tell you these things?"

"I don't know. Why do you?"

"You asked."

"You don't strike me as someone who does what she's told."

"Oh no?"

A slow turn of the head. *No.*

She grinned, then ran her fingers through his hair. "I could say it's those baby blue eyes . . ."

"But it isn't."

"No, it isn't."

"What then?"

She chuckled. "*Lyubov' zla, polyubish' i kozla.*"

Gustavs knotted his brow.

"It means, 'love is evil, you may fall in love with a goat.'"

"A goat."

"But such a *handsome* goat."

"Well, in that case . . ."

She smiled, cupping his cheek for a moment. When she leaned over to kiss him, he pulled her close. Pulled her across the bed, embracing her, the sheets twisting and tangling as they paid them no mind. They snickered when the neglected silver tray clattered onto the carpeted floor, while the bucket of champagne remained, sweating upon the nightstand.

SIXTEEN

GUSTAVS RAPPED A SINGLE KNUCKLE ON THE DOOR, ALREADY OPEN a crack, through which he could see Alberts seated in his armchair. A nurse tended to a sling, tidily wrapped around the old man's shoulder.

"What's all this?" Gustavs asked, entering the room.

"Ah, my favourite son-in-law. Yes, come in, come in."

Gustavs balanced a tray of coffee and bagged croissants, motioning with his free hand. "What happened?"

"Oh, this—nothing. Old age," Alberts replied.

"Nothing?" said the nurse, crossing her arms and looking to Gustavs. Her expression had all the levity of a Franciscan nun.

Alberts waved this away and harrumphed.

"I hope that's fresh fruit in your bag," said the nurse in a stern, querulous tone. "His cholesterol levels . . ."

"Just plain croissants. Low in fat."

"Mm-hmm." She eyed him uncertainly, then made a rather strange, pinched face, as if having mistakenly sucked a slice of lemon, though too proud to admit it was a bit tart. Turning back to Alberts, she said, "I'll be back later to change the dressing," and promptly left the room.

"There's a dressing, too?"

"Oh please," Alberts said, waiting just long enough to hear foot-steps down the hall. "Pay no attention to her."

"That's the one?"

Alberts grimaced. "Nurse Ratched in the flesh."

"Come on, she wasn't *that* bad."

Alberts harrumphed again. "Likely worked for the Stasi before coming here. I should ask for her reference papers. Now, tell me those aren't actually plain croissants."

"What do you take me for?" Gustavs said, handing the old man a coffee and laying the paper bag on the table. "Chocolate filled with marzipan. Now, what on earth"—pointing to a wrap of gauze along Albert's forearm—"are you alright?"

"Come now, I'm fine, just an accident, that's all." He looked to the paper bag, which Gustavs dramatically pushed a few more inches out of reach.

"For goodness sake—I fell! Alright? An accident, as I said."

"Fell where?"

"The shower." Alberts shrugged.

"The shower?"

"Mm"—he took a sip of coffee—"that's good." Then, examin-ing the paper cup, "Where is this from?"

"Are those stitches?"

"Unnecessary, I said. You know how they are with their precautions."

"Albert . . ."

He huffed, putting his drink aside. "Christ, are you here to torment me? You're no better than that bloody prison guard out there with her clipboard." He sighed once more. "Alright, alright. If you insist on involving yourself in my business, I was only vis-iting Agnese, down the hall there and, well . . ." Alberts shifted uncomfortably in his seat. "In the heat of the moment, I . . ."

Gustavs waited.

"The mattress, it . . . well, the covers, really. I misjudged"—he mimed some sort of mess with his hands—"you know . . ."

"Did you fall off the bed?"

"I did not *fall,* for goodness sake! Why does everyone keep saying that? I slipped, alright? There. For the last time—an accident. End of discussion."

Gustavs tried. Truly, he did. Lips pressed together, face taut. But when Alberts glanced up and met his eye, he couldn't help it any longer. At first, only a snicker; not even. More of a snort. Alberts grumbled as Gustavs covered his mouth with his palm, trying to halt the mounting convulsions. But when he saw the old man's trembling chin, it was all over. A moment later, the pair of them were laughing like schoolchildren, breathless and gasping for air, tears dampening their cheeks.

"How did"—Gustavs struggled between breaths—". . . the stitches?"

Alberts retrieved a handkerchief from his pocket, dabbing the corners of his eyes, wiping his face. "It all happened so fast. I placed my hand on the mattress to steady myself, except the mattress was no longer there, nothing but a woolen blanket, and then—*whoosh.* Straight down." He blew his nose into the handkerchief. "Her daughter had come on the weekend and left some flowers. Peonies in a nice crystal vase, she left them on the nightstand. Apparently I brought them along with me on the way down."

Gustavs stifled a few final chuckles. "Truly, are you alright?"

"Oh fine, something sprained up here"—he winced—"I don't know. The cut is nothing, I've had worse. Though I gave the nurses quite a show."

"I can imagine."

"Poor girls. Sadly it wasn't that she-devil on duty, I would've gladly shown *her* my backside. A couple of the younger ones, goodness, they couldn't have been more than teenagers. Likely scarred for life . . ."

"I'm sure they're professionals."

"They bloody well are now."

Gustavs smiled. "And the romance . . . ?"

"Gone. For the time being, at least. Snuffed out like a candle."

"I suppose all good things must come to an end."

"Ah, never mind all of that. What news from the outside world?" He jutted his chin toward the paper bag, which Gustavs dutifully opened for him.

"Actually, on the topic of romance . . ."

Alberts' eyes widened at first, then narrowed. "No. Could it be?"

Gustavs shrugged. "It's strange. I feel . . ." He let out a long exhalation. "I don't know how to feel, really. Guilty"—nodding slowly to himself—"yes, guilty."

"It's only natural," Alberts replied, soft spoken now. "To a certain degree."

"I suppose so."

"It's been almost five years, Gustav. You didn't have children. Seeing as how Anna was my own flesh and blood, I feel relatively confident that I can speak for her." He leaned in. "She wouldn't wish you to be alone." Then, with a shrug, "She wouldn't wish you to remarry within six months either, but . . ."

Gustavs smiled. "I know. It just feels, so very foreign."

"Always the philosopher, my Anniņa." Gustavs could see that he meant to say something more but, all of a sudden, Alberts was overcome with emotion, looking to the ceiling, blinking away his misty eyes. When he recovered, he said, "Wherever she is, I know she wants nothing but your happiness."

"I hope so."

"Trust me." They sat in silence for a moment, before Alberts raised his hand. "You're a good man, Gustav"—with two fingers, he made the sign of the cross—"you've grieved long enough." Alberts smiled warmly, and winked. He took a bite of the croissant and made a deep, soulful sound of appreciation. Then, he chuckled. "Look at you now, I know this face. Daydreaming already, are we? Come on then, let's hear it. Where is she from?"

"What a question. Russian, can you believe it?"

"Ahh, fallen for their Slavic charms, have we?"

"Difficult not to."

"Indeed. You know, I knew a Russian girl myself, once upon a time."

"I'm sure. A charmer since the bassinette."

Alberts gave him a cheeky smile. "What can I say? Olga, her name was. Goodness, I couldn't have been more than, what, thirteen, fourteen? Every summer I would visit my aunt and uncle in Ludza, out in Latgale. They had their own farm, not far from the border. There was an Orthodox church in the city, the priest was from, oh I can't remember, Opochka perhaps, somewhere across the way. One summer, his eldest niece came to stay with them."

"His niece?"

"Well, yes."

"The priest . . ." Gustavs shook his head.

"What? She was an absolute beauty. We would sneak around—behind the haylofts, down by this quiet little stream not far down the road. I never could tell what she was thinking. We could barely understand one another. Her Russian and my Latvian. Just expressions, mostly." He shook his head, puffing his cheeks. "No words were needed," he said, smiling from ear to ear. "Young, innocent love," he added with a chuckle. "So, what is her name, this sweet-heart of yours?"

"Tatyana. God only knows what Omīte will say, the rest of the community."

"Oh *pish*, let them talk. Philistines. As if we're to condemn every Russian on earth for being birthed a few hours to the East."

"You know how it is. The politics."

"And what are *her* politics?"

"She fled. Defected."

"Hah! Well, there you are. You just never mind about all that Gustav, all of that talk. A woman who flees from the Soviets, we should embrace her as one of our own. And let me tell you some-thing else about these *politics*, my boy. Half our bloody country were socialists in the beginning. Card carrying Communists singing *La Marseillaise*. Let us not forget that, either. Nobody knew, of course, the dangers of Marxism, back then. No one could have predicted the terror that was to come. But, at the time, to many of us—*zemnieki*, farmers—it didn't sound like such a bad idea." He nodded, as if considering the weight of this point. "Take it from an old professor, to move forward as a nation we must acknowledge our past, the good *and* the ugly. We cannot pick and choose. Otherwise we're no better than our revisionist comrades in Moscow, *apparatchiks* rewriting history books and inventing truths. Political views, they're very personal, don't ever forget this. Usually one can find their origins quite close to the heart."

"You can't deny there are many with very heartfelt views about the Russians."

"And many wiser who would counter that they have heartfelt views about the Soviets and their bureaucrats, and not necessarily the people themselves. In fact, perhaps old Volodya, old Lenin is the best example of this. The pure Marxist, the founder, the revolutionary."

"Another lesson."

"How else to repay you for the croissants? Ask yourself, why did the man do what he did?"

Gustavs shrugged. "He was tired of the oppression, the rule of the monarchs, the inequality—"

"Yes, yes, this we know, the bread and butter. But, what did I say—more personal."

Gustavs took a moment. "His brother."

"That's right. Alexander. Their plot to assassinate the Tsar is foiled by the Okhrana, the boy is put on trial and executed. Quite personal, no?"

Gustavs nodded.

"But further still, where does this, this *hatred* for mankind come from? His policies during the Red Terror, to eliminate vast segments of the population, not by race—as it was with the Nazis—but by class. The intelligentsia, the *kulaks*, quite literally anyone who opposed his ideas."

Gustavs waited, taking a sip of coffee.

"When Alexander was arrested, their mother, Maria Alexandrovna, took a horse and wagon two hundred kilometers, *by herself*, to appeal his sentence. Lenin, only seventeen at the time, went around his hometown of Simbirsk banging doors, asking anyone and everyone for help. Keep in mind, they came from a good neighbourhood—he's knocking on the doors of doctors, lawyers, civil servants—these are the middle classes, the same as his family. And what happens? They slam their doors in his face. They refuse to help him. Alexander is executed, and these same people, those that would come over for croquet tournaments and play chess, they now shun Lenin and the Ulyanov family."

Alberts leaned back in his seat. "Throughout his life, Lenin would refer to his mother as 'a saint,' a woman whose hair was said to have gone completely gray the very same day of the execution. It wasn't long before they sold their house in Simbirsk and moved. And do you think he ever forgot what those people did? These well-to-do folk and their insult to his mother, his brother, his entire family? There is always something more beneath the surface of one's politics. It should go without saying. But the Red Terror against these perceived oppressive classes—well, it doesn't get any more personal than that."

SEVENTEEN

GUSTAVS ARRIVED HOME TO AN EMPTY HOUSE. HE FOUND OMĪTE in the backyard, tending to her rosebushes, Irina alongside huddled over a bushel of grasses and brush. To their right—the vegetable garden, lush and full and immaculately weeded, no chicken wire or fencing to be found. Evidently, there was no need. Omīte kept her little harvest plot so pristine that even the rabbits, squirrels, and all manner of woodland creatures seemed to forgo their customary plundering simply out of respect.

"I see you two have been busy," he said.

Irina beamed and tucked a loose strand of hair behind her ear.

"Ah, Gustav, it's good that you're home," Omīte said, crouched on a little footstool. Her hands were blackened, arms covered in red knicks from the thorns.

"Yes?"

"Lotte has been calling for hours."

Gustavs made a face.

"I've put the phone by the window. I've left it open, though she said she'd call again around five."

"Did you get her number?"

"She only said she would call back."

"Alright. Well, the garden looks terrific," he added, though

Omīte was already back to pruning dead stems. Irina's mood had also shifted, it seemed, now busying herself amongst the shrubbery with a trowel.

Once inside, Gustavs poured himself a tall glass of buttermilk and waited by the phone, uneasy about Lotte's apparent urgency. What could she possibly want? It wasn't good, whatever it was, and Gustavs found himself reflecting on their meeting at her home, wishing it had never happened. Wishing he hadn't picked up the telephone the first time, never mind waiting for this call now. He tried to force the thoughts from his mind, stonewalling the ruminations with any manner of distraction. He fidgeted with his glasses while gazing out the kitchen window, the cobalt sky deep and vast, though in the distance, creeping shadows of thunder-cloud threatened heavy rain.

It wasn't long before the telephone rang.

"Hello?"

"Gustav. It's me."

"Is something wrong?"

"I need to see you. Tonight, if possible."

He hesitated. "Sure. I don't see why not."

"Tell me, do you remember Elmārs Zandbergs?"

Gustavs snorted, almost sentimental. "I haven't thought about him in years."

"He was caught smoking, that time. Do you remember? By Mrs. Gulbis."

"Of course. How could I forget—"

"Don't say it. Meet me there. Inside. Seven o'clock."

He took a moment, then glanced at his watch. "Okay. Seven." Then, he added, "Lotte, are you sure everything is alright?"

"Everything is fine. Not to worry. I'll see you soon."

The rain was steady, streaming down and pattering the roof of the car; a hollow, tinny sound. Across the street Gustavs could make out the hazy outline of the church, barely lit by the faint, nebulous glow of streetlamps. He glanced in the backseat and grabbed an old newspaper, which he folded in half and held over his head, emerging into the deluge. He dashed across the empty street, shoes splashing in puddles as curbside rivulets flowed past, and entered on the north side, the heavy, wooden doors clanging shut behind him, echoing throughout the foyer.

The air was musty and damp as he shook himself off and wiped the fog from his glasses, proceeding along the creaking floor of the vestibule and emerging into the main hall. The office was empty, and the kitchen doors were closed across the way, his footsteps the only sound in the great, empty gallery.

"Cuckoo," sang Lotte, off to his left in the cloakroom.

They exchanged air kisses, and he took a seat next to her in a partitioned space with empty coatracks, obscured from the entrance.

"You know, I had a thought on the way here," he said.

"Did you?"

"A few. They weren't pleasant. And neither is"—he made a circular gesture with an index finger—"whatever this is."

Lotte wore a dark raincoat, her hood still up, blonde hair tangled and matted down across her front. "I'm sorry, Gustav." The apology seemed genuine, though her eyes looked tired, encircled in shadow.

"This can't possibly be what I think it is."

Lotte reached into her coat, removing a large manila envelope.

"And just what the hell is that?"

"Your documents. Passport. Visa. Business cards. Everything

you need." She lowered her gaze sympathetically, then spoke slowly: "I would not ask, if there were no need. Honestly."

Gustavs caught himself before blaspheming in the church hall. "What—what happened to all the hypotheticals, Lotte?"

"Don't be naïve, Gustav," she said, her tone suddenly cold and pragmatic. A different Lotte now. Though once she saw the change in his demeanor—Gustavs stunned into silence—she pivoted once more. "Listen to me, please. You know I wouldn't put you in harm's way. I need you now, and I need you to appreciate how important this is."

Gustavs looked upon her face as if for the first time. Looked into the eyes of an entirely different woman. No longer the trusted, old friend, but a handler now. And a skilled one, at that.

"If it's so important, then you can go yourself."

"It's too dangerous. They know—"

"Oh, well," Gustavs scoffed, "in that case . . ."

"They know too much about me, about us. No one knows you, Gustav, as I've said. That's why it *must* be you."

"What about Aleks?"

Lotte swallowed, looking to the floor. "He's . . . not coming back." Gustavs said nothing, and Lotte recovered after an unsteady breath. "He's been arrested, we think. And if they're onto him, they might well be onto more than that. We can't be certain, and that's the problem."

Just then, the sound of shuffling footsteps echoed throughout the hall and an elderly woman, the caretaker, poked her head around the partition. She had frizzy white hair tucked away beneath a kerchief, and wore glasses as thick as a stained glass window.

"I thought I heard something," she said. "What are you two doing hiding back here?"

Lotte transitioned into a new character with disconcerting ease. "Mrs. Briede! I hope we didn't startle you. Gustavs and I were just discussing the readings for this Sunday. I was in the neighbourhood and I thought, well, what better place to meet?"

"Oh, lovely!" she said, clasping her hands together. "Can't be caught out in the rain on a night like this. Take all the time you need. Would you like some coffee and *kriņģelis*? There's some left over from the committee meeting."

"That's alright Mrs. Brie—"

"I'll get you some," she said—a rhetorical question, apparently—and promptly shuffled back toward the kitchen. Soon there was another female voice, and the sound of dishware clinking in the sink.

Lotte swiftly returned to the subject at hand, a woman accustomed to shedding personas as needed.

"As I was saying, I can't go. Believe me, I wish I could. Which leaves me—leaves us, in a delicate position. We're rather exposed at the moment. If they're onto Aleks, then perhaps there's something more. We need to know."

"Is that meant to be reassuring?"

"It's meant to be convincing."

He removed his glasses, pinching the bridge of his nose. "This is insane. You do hear yourself, don't you? I can't do this. I just can't."

"Yes, Gustav. You can. Your flight leaves Monday."

"Jesus—"

"—You have the rest of the week to make any personal arrangements you may need. Everything else, is in this envelope." She paused to take a breath. "We've known each other a long time. I trust you like no other."

She extended the parcel between them as Gustavs replaced

his glasses, staring at her. The moment seemed to last an eternity. Finally, he let out a sigh of exasperation, and reached across.

"Once you're there, you'll meet with our contact. As of Wednesday, every morning. Same time, same rendezvous point. Directions and times are—hey, are you listening?"

Gustavs nodded half-heartedly, and Lotte placed a hand on his forearm. "Read what I've written down. Memorize it, then burn the paper. In your fireplace would be best. Do it tonight. Understood?"

He nodded once more.

"Follow the directions *exactly*. It won't work otherwise, she won't respond."

"She?"

"You will be on a routine business trip to Finland. And while you're out that way, you've decided to spend a few days visiting relatives in Rīga. Tourism like this is quite frequent nowadays. Nothing could be simpler." She leaned in. "Take what information they give you, including the package. They'll help you, you can trust them. I'll pick you up from the airport when you land. That's it."

"That's it," he said, acerbically.

She glanced at her watch. "I can't stay, and we won't have any contact until you return. If you have any questions, now is the time."

Gustavs said nothing.

"I'm aware of what I'm asking. I am. And while you have your doubts, I'll ask you to consider what this all means. *Why* we're doing this. We have a debt to repay, Gustav. We all do."

She patted his forearm twice for good measure, and stood, leaving Gustavs seated and staring at the envelope in his hands. From the edge of the partition she looked back with the same tender blue eyes, a smile she knew would have the desired effect, tugging at his emotions like a marionette.

"Do you trust me?" she asked.

He considered this for a moment. " . . . Sometimes."

She smiled contritely. "Then this is one of those times."

Once Lotte had left, Gustavs sat for a long while in silence. For a brief moment he thought she had returned when Mrs. Briede turned the corner with a tray of coffee and sweets.

"Oh? Where did she disappear to?"

"I'm sorry, Mrs. Briede—Lotte had to run, you know how she is . . ."

"Oh, do I ever"—she carefully laid the tray on a wooden bench, chuckling to herself—"I've known Lotte since she was just a child. You know, her family and mine, we come from the same parish. Rudbārži. Do you know it? Near Skrunda."

He shook his head. "Sorry, no."

"We were all schoolmates, you see, her family, when we were children. Then, when the war came, we left together, both of our families and, oh—oh yes, the Liepiņi as well. All three families in the same convoy of wagons."

"Is that so . . ."

"Mmhmm. We even took the same fishing boat to Gotland as the troops were moving in. Or so we had heard. Goodness me, there must have been three times as many as that boat should've carried. Packed like little sprats in a can. I remember I could reach out and touch the water, we were sitting so deep. Oh, yes. We waited three days and nights for that boat. It wasn't always safe, you know, with the patrols. But, we made it, in the end."

Gustavs didn't say anything, finding himself strangely invested in the story.

"Your aunt was on that boat as well, you know. Rasma. I didn't know her at the time, just another face in the crowd, I suppose. But

I believe she told me that, once." She smiled to herself. "Funny, the way memory works, isn't it?"

He nodded. "Kristaps Liepiņš is a good friend of mine."

For a moment, Mrs. Briede was confused.

"You mentioned the Liepiņš family . . ."

"Oh right, no—a different family, I'm afraid. So many Liepiņi out there. We were separated once we got to the coast. There were only so many boats, you see, only so much room. Fishing trawlers, you know. Not meant for, well . . . dozens. Certain families had to wait. I remember my father drawing straws . . ." Mrs. Briede's eyes were suddenly moist, and she drew a sharp intake of breath. "We sang the national anthem as we rowed away from the shore . . ."

Gustavs wasn't sure what to say, but Mrs. Briede recovered in an instant. A woman with a lifetime of memories, wise in her old age, and rather adept at keeping certain events neatly compartmentalized and tucked away.

"Anyhow, look at me go on. When you're finished with this, just leave the tray. I'll pack it away later."

"Thank you, Mrs. Briede."

"Oh for heaven's sake, Gustav—Tamāra. I feel old enough as it is." She smiled, deep wrinkles creasing her mouth, and was up again in an instant, shuffling back across the floor, leaving him alone with his thoughts in the empty church hall.

EIGHTEEN

Gustavs spent much of the week in a daze, the weather suitably reflecting his mood—cloud cover that never truly broke into rain, merely a perpetual drizzle from an overcast sky. During the day, he moved half-heartedly through his lessons, his evenings spent in his armchair beneath a halo of pipe smoke, a glass of cognac in hand, mind spinning relentlessly late into the night, the damp air creeping in from the windows.

On Friday afternoon, he stopped by the ballet studio to pick up Tatyana, who, despite the gloomy weather, looked every inch the Bohemian beauty. She wore a cream linen dress with a simple side braid in her hair, and carried a mason jar filled with wildflowers. Gustavs gave her a knowing smile as he turned the wheel, pulling away from the curb.

"Did you expect me to come empty handed?" she asked.

"Of course not. What's in the bag?"

"Never you mind what's in the bag," she said, lighting a cigarette from the car lighter.

Gustavs conceded with a weighty nod. "They're nice," he said after a time.

"I should hope so. Took me all morning."

"You picked them?"

Tatyana was almost offended. "Of course."

Omīte was in the kitchen, hunched over a sizzling cast-iron pan, stirring the contents with a wooden spoon. The air was warm and fragrant with the scent of onions and garlic frying in butter.

She had been reluctant, at first, when Gustavs raised the prospect of dinner, and quick to make snide remarks about his new Russian *duņa*—the old Latvian slang for a churlish peasant woman. "With a hairy chin and that awful red Russian hair-dye . . ."

He took it in stride, and it was well worth it in the end, as he relished the transformation upon her face when Tatyana entered the kitchen.

At first, there was a moment of confusion; Omīte's old eyes appraising her new guest from behind the smudged lenses. Gustavs watched the wheels slowly turn, until she noticed the wildflowers.

"*Nu!* Look at these!"—she examined the jar—"you must have picked these yourself."

Tatyana smiled. "I had a bit of luck with the weather and thought, why not?"

"Mm, that's right—a good week for it, just wet enough out there." She inhaled deeply from the petals. "Oh! Then I'm sure you'll appreciate these as well, come, come . . ."

Omīte lead Tatyana over to the near counter where she lifted a cheese cloth, revealing a glass bowl of freshly foraged mushrooms.

"Oh, the little beauties!" Tatyana exclaimed, cupping her hands over her mouth. "Did you . . . ?"

"No, no—I have a friend, at the Estonian store." She leaned in close, the two women putting their heads together as Omīte whispered. "She always puts some aside for me, you know." Omīte smiled proudly, the smile of a woman with influence. "My knees, I'm too old now to go . . . we say, *sēņot*, in Latvian."

Tatyana nodded. *"Khodit's za gribami,"* she replied, "for us. When I was a girl, my mother would take me. Deep into the birch forests we would go, all day filling our baskets, after the rain . . ."

Omīte brought her palm to her chest and sighed. "I can smell it now, the birch trees, the wet earth . . ."

And after that, Gustavs was, at best, little aside from décor. The ladies talked amongst themselves as if old friends that had simply lost touch over the years, with Tatyana lending a hand preparing the meal. The mushrooms were sautéed in butter, the pork seasoned and pan-fried, the gravy simmered as the crepes were wrapped and tucked, neat little pockets sizzling on the stovetop. At one point, while discussing the Hermitage, Omīte appeared to remember that Gustavs was still in the room, and directed him to bring them two vodka martinis with a dill pickle, just like in Warsaw. *Whatever that meant.*

The trio savoured their meal, especially Tatyana, who, despite her usual inscrutability, praised the chef with a sincerity he had rarely seen, speaking of how it brought back memories of her childhood in the Urals. For dessert, Gustavs opened a jar of Omīte's preserved pears in sweet syrup, while Tatyana presented her host with a bottle of black currant schnapps. Gustavs dutifully poured three glasses and refilled them in short order, while Omīte closed her eyes, head gently swaying to the melody on the radio.

"Gustav?" Omīte prompted.

He listened for a time, then shook his head. "This one . . ." Another brief wiggle of his chin.

Omīte looked to her guest. "My dear?"

"Prokofiev," Tatyana said with a smile.

Which led, somewhat predictably, into a prolonged debate about the greatest epochs of classical music, with Omīte steadfastly defending the Baroque Era—Handel and Bach alone, for heaven's sake—while Tatyana respectfully presented her case for the Romantic period—Chopin, Brahms, and, of course, the greatest of all time, P.I. Tchaikovsky.

Tatyana insisted on clearing dishes, all but pinning Omīte down in her chair by way of persuasion, and while she lathered plates in the kitchen, Omīte patted Gustavs on the hand, her wide smile revealing the single gold crown of her molar.

"I like her," she said.

He smiled back. "I know."

Gustavs turned off of Lawrence Avenue onto a quiet residential side street, slowing by the curbside.

"This is perfect, yes," Tatyana said.

"You sure I can't walk you home?" His eyes scanned the streetlamps and the shadowed front yards below.

"I need to stretch my legs. Walk off those delicious *blini*."

"*Pankūkas*."

She leaned over to kiss him. And then kissed him once more.

"*Do vstrechi*."

"Oh yes," he replied, a stern expression. "Of course."

She smiled, brushing the hair from his forehead, a seemingly incorrigible habit of late. "See you."

Gustavs watched her disappear down the street, never looking back, her silhouette gradually fading beneath the umbra cast by a stretch of oak trees.

He was glad to be alone. A lovely evening, he thought; he couldn't have imagined it any better, but hardly the best timing. His mind now forever fixated on the conversation with Lotte, always drawn back to that evening, the same gnawing thoughts never far from his consciousness. And how could they be?

That envelope. That bloody envelope. A plane ticket in two days time. Business cards. American dollars and Finnish marks. Lists of inventory. Catalogues of every type of vodka imaginable with prices, volumes, shipping information. A passport, *his* passport, now with several Finnish entry stamps, despite him never having been to Helsinki. His hands turned clammy at the mere thought and he drew a palm across his forehead, rubbing his brow.

Back on Lawrence Avenue, he spotted the neon glow of a bar sign. As good a place as any, he thought, then pulled over, crossed the street and descended some narrow concrete steps, entering the basement pub through a small door.

An intimate if grubby place—dark, with darker corners, the air stale with yeast and old smoke. The barman dragged a wet cloth along the grain and nodded a greeting as Gustavs settled himself onto a stool. An ancient jukebox played U2.

To his right, at the end of the bar, stood a pair of gnomes—stocky men with whisky noses and heavy eyelids, propped up against one another and murmuring confidentially. Behind them, alone in a booth sat a middle-aged woman with ratty hair, sipping her glass of merlot. As she fiddled with her pearl necklace, she stared vacantly at an oil painting on the wall—a shrewd red fox slinking its way along the roof of a henhouse, the golden frame marred with streaks of black and red graffiti.

The barman pulled Gustavs a frothy pint, and as he took a sip, he heard the front door open. A man entered, clomping down the stairs and sighing heavily as he manoeuvred himself onto the adjacent stool. Gustavs looked up, and into the beady, bloodshot eyes of Detective Angelo De Rossi. The detective placed a cigarette in his mouth, clearly relishing the moment, then motioned wordlessly for a pint of his own.

"Following me now?" Gustavs said, looking straight ahead.

"Me? No."

"So, what is this then?"

"Don't flatter yourself"—De Rossi coughed into his fist—"it's my local watering hole."

"Is it now . . ."

De Rossi lit his cigarette with a zippo lighter, inhaled, then met Gustavs' eyes. "What do *you* think?"

"What the hell do you want De Rossi?"

"I just wanna talk, Gus. We're in a bar, aren't we? I'm a social guy."

"Well I'm not. So cut the shit."

De Rossi seemed to concede with a nod of sorts, then acknowledged his pint and swallowed a couple of gulps. "Never one for foreplay, are you?" He grunted, ashing his cigarette into a glass tray. "How's your Russian lady friend feel about that?"

Gustavs stared straight ahead.

"A beautiful woman, truly, you'll get no debate from me there." De Rossi nodded approvingly. "Quite something, though, to be playing so far out of your league. Must be hard to keep up, no? I mean, I suppose I just don't know what she sees in you—you certainly don't have any money, we know that. Still, it's always the knockouts that are the crazy ones, am I right?"

Gustavs pushed back his stool and rose, removing his wallet.

"It got me to thinking, you know, about our doctor friend. You remember him?" He cocked his head to look up at Gustavs. "Yeah, that's about the same face you made the last time. Well, seems he's in the wind. You wouldn't happen to know anything about that, would you?"

"What I know is this: It's been almost a year since you started this little campaign against me. And still, here you are, asking the same dumb questions without any answers. You homicide guys sure move quick. Does your partner know you're here?"

"Who, Dan?" He chuckled. "No, no, it's past ol' Danny boy's bedtime. Now will you sit back down already, you're making everyone nervous."

Gustavs remained where he stood.

"Christ, so temperamental. Still, since I'm such a decent guy, I'll let you in on a little secret, my friend—"

"I'm not your friend."

De Rossi opened his palms, the cigarette dangling from his mouth. "It's a figure of speech, for Christ's sake." He sighed. "As I was saying, me and Danny, well, we're not really on the same page these days. You see, for matters that need not concern you, there's certain aspects of the investigation—and I do mean *investigation*, this time—how'd they put it . . ." He scratched at his chin. "Aspects that I'm not privy to, at the moment."

"That must hurt."

"It does, you know. I'm not made of stone. But, here's the thing." He shifted in his seat to get a better look at Gustavs. "In my experience, this sort of thing only happens when you start sniffing around the right places. Sticking your beak where it doesn't belong."

"Maybe you should just take the hint."

De Rossi narrowed his eyes, pointing at him with his cigarette. "And that's exactly why you're not police. You see, the thing is, sticking my beak where it doesn't belong? That's my entire job description. It's what I do. The answers aren't on the surface, my friend. You gotta get right down there in the dirt and the grime, sift through all the nasty stuff. Ask the uncomfortable questions that people like yourself would never ask. For instance"—he took a heavy drag—"I might ask you, did you know your pal Tomass Ozolins is half-Russian? His mother, Svetlana, born in Kalingrad . . . Kalinograd, some such place, anyhow. Hm? I'll take that as a 'no.' So your best friend is half an Ivan, then there's this Doctor, and now, this little ballerina, too. I mean, what is it with you and these Russians? Thought your people fuckin' hated 'em?"

"Excuse me," Gustavs waved to the barman. "This man will be paying for my drink." The barman was indifferent, and Gustavs began walking toward the door. De Rossi grabbed at his arm, and Gustavs snatched it away. "You stay the hell away from her. You stay the hell away from all of us."

De Rossi smiled wearily, the pouches beneath his eyes shifting as he winced from the smoke.

"You keep harassing us like this, I'll report you to your superiors and have you suspended."

De Rossi chuckled, then coughed into his fist. "You see a badge on me now, kid?"

Gustavs wasn't quite sure what to say, and turned, uncertain, toward the door.

"I got all the time in the world for you now, Gus," De Rossi called as the door swung open. "All the time in the world."

When Lotte woke, she had a chill. Curled into a ball on the divan, bare feet exposed beyond the quilt, she shuddered. At first, utter confusion. Then, drearily, she began taking inventory of her surroundings, soothed by the familiar comforts of home.

She let out a labored sigh, her emotions having finally caught up with her, and this time she had surrendered herself completely.

Still, she had managed to keep her wits, done what needed to be done, pressed on despite the turmoil within. No message that morning, at the park, but she went diligently as always, making notes, completing her checks. And then, as soon as she stepped foot in the house, the wave that had been cresting for days finally broke and crashed, enveloping her, pulling her beneath.

Aleksandrs. Her dearest Aleks. She couldn't help but consider all the possibilities, all the horrific scenarios. They would have to be entertained sooner or later, that much she knew—it was only possible to hold back the tempest for so long. The uncertainty was torture, and the torture—whatever form it would take—was the only certainty she had. Snatched, somewhere in the night. Gagged, cloaked, thrust into the cold metal of a black van.

Her thoughts pivoted to the fates of so many of her countrymen and women, all who had suffered similar tragedies in the years, the decades gone by. The dead-eyed bureaucrats of some KGB troika, delivering verdicts, passing judgment before great red banners emblazoned with the hammer and sickle. The innocent, blindfolded, thrust up against posts. Rusty drains set in concrete, collecting rivulets of blood in the basement of the Lubyanka. Cattle cars, fetid and rife with disease, rattling forever eastward toward a barren, frozen tundra. And once there—a life of imprisonment, slaves to be worked to death in the sprawling camps, if not succumbing first to the elements, to malnutrition, to the boundless cruelty of Siberia.

Enough. Enough, now. She refused to let her imagination wander any further. She had permitted herself a moment—collapsed onto the divan, shivered and wept, wept until tears streamed down her face and soaked the cushion, and then fallen into an exhausted, dreamless sleep. Slept like the dead until, whatever time it was now. Enough.

Lotte rose, wrapping the old quilt around her shoulders and passed the mirror in the hall, pausing as she noted the mascara smeared beneath her eyes, her hair the wild mane of a lioness. *Goodness, what a fright.* She sniffled, smoothed down the blonde locks with her palm.

It was already dark out, and so she flicked on the kitchen light, put on the kettle, put a cigarette to her lips and bent down to light it from the glowing element. From the backdoor, the familiar scratching and a mournful *meow*—Pūka, desperate to return and join the family. She opened the backdoor a crack, letting in nothing more than a gust of wind.

And then she felt it. Some part of her, the tingle of her subconscious. Not merely the foreign shadow that loomed on the back porch, but the dark presence that accompanied it. No ordinary shadow. Instinctively, she pushed the door further open, and gasped, rooted to the spot.

The faint light caught the edges of the man's profile, a silhouette that stood, silent, imposing its will. His right hand released Pūka, who landed softly on the ground, trotting casually past Lotte's calves. In the man's left hand, the outline of cold, gray steel, the angles sharp and menacing as they melded into his palm.

She was trembling now, and resented the reaction, clenching her fists by her side. The light from the doorway cast a glow across the man's face, and she willed herself to look at him. She could barely make out his features, only the thick brow that occulted his eyes, the broad mouth that hung open, gaping like a fish out of water. He said nothing. Only stared, impassive, his thick neck craned to one side.

The man raised his arm. Lotte swallowed, squeezing her eyes shut, her pulse racing, the blood pounding in her ears. She heard nothing but the sound of her thunderous heartbeat.

And then, trembling in the cool night air, she found her strength. Opening her eyes, she willed herself back into the moment, forcing herself back to the present. Slowly, she raised her head, looking up, past the cold barrel of steel, and met his gaze. She clenched her tremulous fists, digging her fingernails into her palms and drew her shoulders back. Drawing deep upon the well, she looked straight ahead, staring past the heavy brow into vacant, shadowed pockets. She would not look away. She gritted her molars, raised her chin, and stared in defiance.

A flash of light, but no sound. The flare seemed to linger for a moment, before brightening into blazing rays of sunshine. And then, from the unknown, conjured from the inexplicable depths— a fleeting memory: Sunrays warming her cheeks on the beach, children laughing, crystal waters lapping at her ankles as she curled her bare toes into the soft, wet sand.

NINETEEN

They sat at the kitchen table, silent and solemn. The radio was off, for the first time in ages, it seemed. Omīte had seen to that. So now, only the faint *tick* of the living room clock. Outside, the occasional rustle of leaves in the treetops, an errant shriek from one of the children playing across the street in the park. But at the kitchen table, only silence.

It was Paulis Zutis that had called. Gustavs thought he hadn't heard him properly. And when it finally did register, he said nothing, remaining that way for so long that Paulis asked if he was still on the line.

He was. Paulis was still talking as Gustavs replaced the receiver into its cradle, Omīte no longer stirring her broth, having noted the look upon his face. She inquired several times before he responded, and when he spoke, she asked him not to whisper. Eventually, they found themselves at the table, Gustavs staring into the flakes of beeswax that drifted in his tea, two bowls of cold chicken bouillon between them.

The words felt foreign on his tongue, as if reciting the obituary of some stranger in the Globe and Mail. Surely not someone he knew, someone he loved, part of his community, practically family. Omīte had bowed her head when he told her, felt for the gold chain beneath her blouse, its small crucifix never far from her heart. She crossed herself with bony fingers that faintly trembled.

And then, he told her everything. Not out of intention, nor, strangely, out of any desire to contextualize the heartbreaking news. The words simply came, streaming out, falling from his lips and breaking the awful, deafening silence of the home. He sat, staring past his knees at the floor, not exactly speaking to Omīte, but telling her all the same. About Imants, the peculiar circumstances surrounding his death, and the detectives. About Lotte re-entering his life, and the queer little favour, almost laughable in its absurdity that now, inconceivably, had turned into a terrifying, material reality. The conspiracy. The paranoia. The envelope. The plane ticket . . . the plane ticket for *tomorrow*.

Gustavs spoke for a long while, rising only once to stomp over to the buffet, snatch the telephone and tear it from the wall, the cord snapping like a whip and putting an end to the incessant ringing.

After a time, his consciousness out in the open, he wondered how his great-aunt would react. She didn't speak a word as he recounted everything, only sat still, her face forever set in that drooping scowl, watching him from behind those thick, smudged lenses, hands folded neatly in her lap. Yet as she watched him, he could tell that she was elsewhere. Her mind having already absorbed every element of the equation, and now working away at the problem. And in that moment, he began to sense the change in her. As if there were an aura, emanating outwards, symbolic of the transformation taking place.

It was no longer Omīte that sat across from him. No longer the old woman, forever puttering around in the kitchen, smoothing the same stretch of parquet flooring with her slippers. A matriarch, venerated and wise, but undeniably in the twilight of her years;

savvy and resilient, but also increasingly gruff, obstinate—a cynicism galvanized by age. A sageness manacled by the confines of the constricted world in which she lived.

No longer Omīte, this face before him. This was the look of Rasma, now. Rasma, thirty-eight years old, and in flight. The woman who fled with her daughter and so many other thousands as Russian soldiers broke through stalwart defences, traversed detonated bridges, commandeered farmsteads—marching, burning, raping, and killing. Rasma, who left it all behind—her home, her belongings, her beloved dog, Pērkons—taking only one suitcase, and with her child slept in open fields at night, subsisting on whatever they could find, fleeing the mayhem of yet another war that ravaged the fields and towns of her country. Rasma, the survivor.

After a long while, she finally moved for her spoon, stirring her soup. "Well, it's settled then," she said matter-of-factly, and carefully raised the spoon to her lips. "You'll go."

Gustavs could only stare, a certain nonchalance etched across Omīte's face as if she were simply remarking on the weather. Spurred by his silence, she continued.

"You must, Gustav. You understand that."

To say that it had been an emotional week was almost farcical, and Gustavs, hardly a wordsmith at the best of times, had exhausted himself of all conversation. Perhaps, when considered from a certain perspective, Omīte was right. Then again, perhaps she was senile. He couldn't make up his mind at the moment, nor did he care to try. What on earth had happened this past year? A quiet, peaceful existence of coffee, books, and English lessons. Where had his life gone?

Omīte took another mouthful of cold soup, tapped the spoon neatly on the rim of the bowl, and set it down with a sigh.

"Let me show you something," she said. And with that, she rose, hobbled along unsteadily and stopped at the threshold of the living room. "Come, Gustav. Indulge an old woman."

Omīte led him into her room—pale, jade curtains matching the well trodden rug—a space he recognized but never ventured. On the far wall, she opened a closet revealing waves of gowns and a sable coat from the great ballroom days of old, ensembles that hung in retirement above stacks of shoeboxes and a cedar chest. The closet smelled faintly of mothballs and the floral notes of Rochas' *Femme*. On a shelf above—woolen blankets, mittens and scarves, a brown cloche bucket hat with a bow, a rosewood jewelry box and a battered old suitcase wedged into one corner.

"Fetch that for me, would you?"

Gustavs obliged, carefully laying the suitcase on the bed. It was an ancient and fragile thing, its handle taped into place, the tarnished bronze latches whinging as they sprang open at the touch of her fingertips. At first, she only stood—gazing down upon the valise as if greeting an old friend, then ran her palm across its surface, feeling the knicks and scratches that marred the old leather.

Gustav could sense the emotion when she finally lifted the lid. The case was lined with a thin fabric—a faded pattern of vines and rose petals—and the contents were few. A small collection of letters and envelopes, handkerchiefs with embroidered edges, gilded wood picture frames without pictures, and a pair of black leather boots in dire need of a polish. The letters were handwritten on thick pulp paper and posted, some of them, to cities that no longer existed on maps of Europe. The air had turned decidedly stale, as if no life had existed in the dark suitcase for decades which, in a matter of speaking, was true.

As they stood, Gustavs noted the rhythmic change in Omīte's

breathing, and realized that her eyes had swelled with tears. She reached into the suitcase for one of the handkerchiefs, slowly pressing it up beneath her glasses, closing her eyes and cherishing the touch of the fabric.

She recovered rather quickly, he thought, for in the next moment she had produced her paring knife from her cardigan and examined the edges of the inner lining. Then, she pinched the blade between thumb and forefinger, and began to work at the stitching, nicking the threads apart. When she had made her way across the breadth of the case, the lining wilted open like a pocket. Reaching carefully inside, she grabbed a handful of dark red fabric, and slid the package out from its hiding place. She clutched the mound of cloth to her face, inhaling deeply.

When Gustavs glimpsed the narrow strip of white—more of a peaked yellow now, sullied from the years and the journey—he knew exactly what Omīte was holding. She laid the flag down on the bedspread, and together they unfurled the layers of pleats until it covered the entire bed. The flag was old, even for its time, even before the decades it had spent hidden away in the false compartment. Two thick, maroon swaths, cutting horizontally across, separated only by a thin belt of white in the middle.

"You know its story," Omīte said, not exactly a question, but rather seeking confirmation.

Gustavs nodded. There were many stories, of course, but they all shared a similar theme. An origin story shrouded in myth and folklore, it was the tale of a famed Latvian battle in the 13th century and a wounded chieftain, speared clean through by an enemy sword and laid down to rest on a white sheet, soaking the fabric with his blood. When they removed him, only a thin strip remained dry, just beneath where his body had lain. As legend would have it, the

Latvian forebearers stormed back into the fray using the bloody sheet as a banner, ultimately victorious.

The faded flag on the bed before them kept this history, and then some. Frayed edges carefully restitched. Burn marks and small tears throughout, the maroon fabric smeared in one corner with dirt.

Omīte sat down on the edge of the bed, patting a corner of the fabric. "This was Emīls' flag," she said, wistfully.

He paused, aware of the moment's fragility. "Emīls . . ."

She looked up at him, a tender smile now, and patted the bedspread, inviting him to sit. "No, he's not someone you would know. Somehow . . . and God help me, I don't know where the years have gone . . . but somehow, I think I may be the only one left who did." She sighed. "Your great-uncle knew him, Konrāds."

"Your husband."

"Yes." She turned her head. "Do you have any memory of him?"

"Some."

"You were so young then, before he became ill. As were we, all those years ago." She took a breath. "They were best friends, the pair of them, he and Emīls. Inseparable. He was such a deep soul, Emīls was, even-tempered, calm. It made me crazy at the time, I was only nineteen when we met. An impulsive girl. And my dear Konrāds, he wasn't always the man I married. He used to drink, become, oh I don't know—sloppy. Boorish. Don't misunderstand, my husband and I had many good years together, many. I don't regret a moment. But back then, we were so young, so full of life and passion." She looked back to Gustavs. "Hard to imagine your Omīte as a young girl, hm?"—she nudged him—"pursued by strapping men in uniform."

"Not at all," he replied.

She stepped back in time once more, old memories casting long shadows across her face. "I loved them both, in my own way. Your uncle and I, we were always fighting back then. Hot and cold, as they say. And whenever it got really bad, despite my guilt, I found myself running to Emīls. Straight into his arms. He was always so *calm*. It was otherworldly. I always picture him with the same serene expression, sitting by the bank of a still pond, staring deep into the water.

"My goodness, one time the pair of them got into it, I thought your uncle was going to kill him, out by the woodpile. But Emīls held his own, skinny as he was. I remember standing there, shouting like a fool for them to stop. They did, eventually, exhausted, covered in dirt and red welts. I felt so guilty." She permitted herself a little grin. "So silly, looking back now . . . young love."

Then, she turned her attention to the flag, and her mood changed. "They came for him, that night, in June of 1940. Your uncle and I were already married then, Mirdza was our first, just a little girl at the time. No one knew Emīls was visiting me that night. No one outside our circle, and still they came. Three men, just after nightfall. Emīls had already left by the time they arrived—he was part of the *Robežsargu* brigade, the border guard, and had been summoned to Masļenki.

"We hid at the edge of the forest. We thought Andris had already left—he was a simple boy from town, he helped us around the homestead from time to time—but they found him out back still fiddling with a wagon wheel by the light of a fire. They interrogated him right there, I could see him clearly through the trees. He didn't know a thing, poor Andris. But to be certain, they cut off his ear. I remember Mirdza biting down on my finger as I held my hand across her mouth to keep her quiet. I almost smothered her.

And Andris . . . I had never before heard a man make such a sound.

"It didn't matter, in the end. That night they attacked the border post where Emīls was stationed. There was a shootout, they said it was hard to see in the early morning fog. Many died, more were captured. They set the guardhouse on fire. It was a provocation, the next day the Russians invaded. Colonel Bolšteins had been ordered not to resist, that they should not fight back. He took his own life not a week later, unable to bear the shame of it. The indignity of being so complacent. Emīls had idolized the colonel."

Omīte fell silent, twisting the thin gold wedding band on her finger.

"And . . . Emīls?"

She let out a deep sigh. "Nobody knows, really. Someone saw him shot, apparently, falling into the Ludza river. After that—captured, maybe, it's hard to say. The fog was thick, the smoke, even thicker. There are numbers now, of this Masļenki incident as they call it, but who believes them. My Emīls simply disappeared from our lives, like so many others. It became common, after that, when the occupation began. People would simply vanish, and the worst pain was knowing that there would never be any closure."

She ran her hand across the flag once more. "He is Mirdza's father," she said, then looked at Gustavs for a reaction. "I think, in some way, Konrāds always knew, and made his peace with it. We had Uldis, afterwards, and he is our own. And though it seemed like the weight of the world was on my shoulders then, I believe, in some way, even Konrāds was glad. I had lost my first love, and he, his best friend. And with Mirdza, a part of him remained with us."

Omīte turned to him and grasped his hand, her face suddenly stern. "I tell you this for a reason, Gustav. I never pushed you, when others did. To join the cause. And I had every right. We've always been close, you and I, in our own way. I never said anything. *Anything.* But I'm saying it now.

"This will continue. They will not stop. They will not yield an inch. All of this, what you've told me—Imants, Lotte, this boy, Aleksandrs, this may all come as a shock to you and your generation, but not to mine. Not to those of us who were there, and the few of us who remain. We know very well what they're capable of, and they're about as subtle as a kick from a mule."

Gustavs removed his glasses, kneading his forehead. "I'm in over my head here, Omīte."

"So stand up straight and make yourself tall. Lotte wouldn't have asked this of you if she didn't think you were capable. And she needs you now. Who knows how important this information will prove to be?"

Gustavs replaced his glasses and looked to his great-aunt, her shoulders back with an unflinching gaze, determination personified. "What's it like, over there?" he asked.

Omīte considered the question, then looked to the flag once more. "This flag has not seen the light of day in forty-three years. Not since I wrapped it around myself the night we left. I stitched it into the lining while on a horse-drawn cart as we left Ludza behind, the city where I had spent my entire life." She took a breath, her tone darkening. "No one in our closest circle, and I mean *no one*, Gustav, knew that Emīls was visiting me that night in June. Back then, Mirdza was still our secret. And I thank the great goddess Māra that she has my features. Yet still, they came for him. Someone knew, and someone told them where to find him. These informants, this system of *stukachi*, it is the very foundation of their strength. It is the very reason there is so much distrust within our own community, and it works to their advantage. If Lotte believed there is someone within our circle, her death all but proves it. And it will be like this in Rīga, only so much more so. This is how they work, Gustav. Like spiders, forever lurking in dark, dusty corners. Most of the time you will hardly take notice, but they are always there, spinning their webs, waiting." She took a deep breath, then patted his hand. "You've got a good head on your shoulders, my boy. You're clever, more clever than you think. Keep your head down, and your wits about you. Bring home what she asked. We all have our role to play when fate knocks on our door. It knocked on mine many years ago, and it's come calling for you now."

The hour was late, and Gustavs packed an old valise by lamplight. An old valise which hadn't been used since his honeymoon; inside was a singular, creased business card for a taxicab in Toulouse. He filled the case with some clothes and essential toiletries, and did so in a peculiar, detached trance, his mind at odds with his actions— one man folding an undershirt, another drifting through rosy memories of a young, aspiring journalist. He gathered his belongings with an eye on the clock, and an ear to the front door—visions of that bloodhound De Rossi and his homicide squad storming in and rampaging through the foyer at any moment.

And yet, despite his ruminations, no one ever came. And so he set about tying off loose ends, first by telephoning Renata to ensure his classes would be covered in the following days. A man answered, catching Gustavs completely off guard, and for a moment he faltered and squinted at the scribbled numbers in his address book. Once on the line, Renata's responses were brusque and to the point, as always. If she was irritated by the late call, she hid it well, and he knew he would have to explain everything upon his return. Mostly everything.

He telephoned the Kovalenko household, Olga passing the receiver to Irina. While she was pleased to check in on Omīte during his absence, she struggled to hide her disappointment. How long would he be away? Not long, he said. And where, exactly? Visiting some relatives, out of town. Irina's voice wavered on the line: "Well, I very much look forward to seeing you, when you return."

At long last he telephoned Tatyana and briefly considered lying, mostly because no rational person would ever believe the truth. Eventually, he thought better of it, which was just as well—he struggled to find the will just as he struggled to fabricate any sort of reasonable explanation. Still, it wasn't as if he was taking a day trip to the seaside. So then, what to say? He could barely wrap his mind around the week's events himself. All the while, the two men dwelled within him: one making telephone calls, dutifully counting pairs of socks, while the other stood confounded, wondering what on earth the first fool was doing.

In the end, he muddled through the conversation, vague responses and feigned insouciance. Something about relatives in Rīga, which he supposed, was at least somewhat true. It was enough to let her know that he couldn't quite say, though eventually found himself desperately wishing he could tell her everything.

Tatyana didn't press—sensed it, certainly, but knew not to ask, not to force him into a corner. Rather, she too offered to check up on Omīte while he was away; she would stop by Tuesday and Thursday when she didn't have an evening class. Gracious, yet still curt in her way, forever the loveliest of enigmas. For a time there was a strained silence that lingered over the line, some crackling static, and Gustavs could picture her curling the phone cord between her fingers. He was relieved when, during the final awkward farewell, she insisted on having the last word. "Hurry back to me, Gustav."

He would.

V.

AUTUMN

1987

TWENTY

Northern Vidzeme,
Latvian Soviet Socialist Republic (LSSR)

IN THE THICK FOG OF THE BALTIC HINTERLAND, THE GENTLE rhythm of a rail carriage lulled its occupants to sleep, the train rattling its way through forests of birch and sweeping fields of rye. Aboard the overnight passage from Tallinn to Minsk—complete, as a matter of course, with a brief stopover in Rīga—those who resisted the invitation of sleep could glimpse the countryside through sullied windowpanes: vast, and dark, with silhouettes of crumbling farmsteads illuminated by a sliver of crescent moon.

Gustavs didn't wake—not exactly, but rather stirred, opening grainy eyes to a dimly lit cabin. Across from him, a *babushka* with gapped teeth smiled at him, then returned to feeding her granddaughter segments of mandarin, the peels in her lap scenting the air with citrus. The young girl eyed him warily, face nestled into her baba's woolen sweater.

The trip had been decidedly uneventful, but for the prickling of nerves that accompanied each new leg of the journey. Gustavs had barely slept on the flight, but by the time they touched down in Helsinki he had exhausted himself, his mind whirring at a pace that rivaled the engine turbines. He hailed a cab down to the pier, where seabirds cawed and circled high above the grey waters of the harbour. The briny fragrance of sea water was a tonic, the air cool and damp upon his face, refreshing after the long flight.

Once aboard the ferry, he made his way to the bow, watching the white caps churn before him in the vast, open water. For the first time since he'd departed, he thought about a journey other than his own. He considered the flight of all the tens of thousands who had tested fate in the same waters decades before, not in ferries but in humble fishing craft, fleeing war and all of its accompanying, unforgiving chaos.

Disembarking in Tallinn, he held his breath in the customs queue. The border official was a severe-looking man in his uniform and cap, with high Cossack cheekbones and a thin red mouth, like the gash of a Soviet sickle. The man said nothing, so neither did Gustavs, who, keeping his eyes on the floor, sensed the official relishing the display of supplication.

Minutes later, a bespectacled vodka merchant emerged into the night air, clammy hands gripping a valise, eyes searching for a taxi. He found a rust-coloured Skoda parked nearby, and knocked on the window, waking the disgruntled chauffeur. He paid the man American dollars to drop him at the train station, and, for a handsome tip, asked him to scribble the name of the Latvian capital in Cyrillic on the back of a five ruble note.

Gustavs finally dozed at some point, for when he woke it was dawn, the sky a deep indigo blue as the train slowed into the station. The *babushka* gave him a final courteous smile as she ushered her ward out the door, with Gustavs following in tow, exhausted and in desperate need of a wash and a bed.

The Hotel Latvija was a fifteen-minute walk across town, and Gustavs was eager to stretch his legs and, at long last, take in the sights and sounds of the fabled city. Rīga may have been occupied, but for the first time in his life, he would be stepping foot in the land of his ancestors. He would embrace the charms of the quaint medieval trading port whose stories filled childhood nursery rhymes and volumes of poetry. Whose cobbled lanes, church spires and red-tiled rooftops inspired charcoal vignettes and oil on canvass, the historic skyline forever the artist's muse.

Gustavs' nostalgic sentiments about the old Hanseatic capital were effectively dashed as soon as he stepped out into the grey cityscape, the air heavy with the fug of diesel fumes. He took a moment to absorb his surroundings, craning his neck at the towering block letters above the station: *Centrāla Stacija*—mirrored by what he assumed was the same in bold, imposing Cyrillic. Gathering himself, accepting that he had finally landed on the foreign moon of the USSR, he winced as a bus trundled past belching clouds of black exhaust. Then, he crossed the street, and began heading eastward into the heart of the city.

The streets and structures seemed a paradox of the region's history. One could catch glimpses, here and there, of a prosperous past, a bustling metropolis frequented by German land barons and merchant guilds. An affluence that had been halted, stifled by the advent of communism, and left to wither at the hands of dereliction and neglect. The impressive *Jugendstil* architecture was barely visible beneath the ubiquitous grime of modern industry, elegant façades a somber reminder of what had once been. Presently, his eyes drifted over broken glass and weathered brickwork. Glancing down an empty lane, Gustavs caught sight of a crumbling stone balcony, a relic that appeared to struggle with the weight of a few clay pots beset by wilted vines.

The bleak atmosphere seemed to permeate the very soul of the city, a solemnity reflected in the faces of passersby. They shuffled about with sullen expressions, eyes rarely looking up from the cobblestones, and then only to cast a furrowed brow at Gustavs' peculiar fashion. The locals themselves appeared dressed uniformly in muted shades of harvest beige and leaden grey. Everyone seemed to be speaking Russian, the sound foreign and guttural to Gustavs' ears—nothing like that which Tatyana spoke—and any Latvian he heard was in hushed tones, as if use of the language itself were an act of resistance. As he walked, he passed a store that was named, rather aptly, *Gaļa*. Meat. Straight, and to the point, as was the long queue of women who stood patiently, almost wordlessly, along the sidewalk, hoping there would be something left to purchase.

After a time, the boulevard opened before him, revealing a small courtyard to his right where, just beyond, sprawling gardens and greenspace extended all the way to the banks of the city canal. He took a moment to appreciate the soaring white columns of the National Opera House, its grand classical design a symbol of an aristocratic past that still stood, defiant, seemingly thumbing its nose at the boorish imposition of socialist mediocrity.

As he moved through the city, the nerves that had accompanied him for the duration of the journey now seemed to give way, not dissipating so much as evolving. He became aware of a certain mood that had settled over him, stooping his shoulders, a tightness in the belly. Gustavs had been raised much as anyone in his diaspora community, forever carrying a knowledge of the occupation—born with it, it seemed—but this was something altogether different. Impossible, of course, to comprehend the full weight of it, but now there was certainly a profound sense of the burden. A strange emotion, a feeling of kinship with those who spoke in whispers and averted their eyes.

A certain *esprit de corps* with the numerous faces that streamed past, expressions drawn and acquiescent. It was rather unexpected for Gustavs, who had hardly lost sight of what, and who he was—alone in Rīga, so terrified he was practically numb, a man without a clue embarking on this most monumental of fool's errands. Yet it was certainly there, this raw sentiment. It was undeniable, and it festered like an untended wound.

Gustavs passed a flower kiosk where a group of surly youths in jean jackets were smoking cigarettes, then made a right onto Lenin street, formerly Alexanderstrasse, and, going back further still, *Brīvības Iela*. Freedom Street. He slowed and then came to a halt, much to the annoyance of an old man who shouldered him aside with a grunt, muttering along on his way.

Not a hundred yards before him, in the center of the wide thoroughfare, stood Milda on high, cradling her three stars for all to see—the Freedom Monument stretching upwards into the overcast sky. Milda didn't appear as she did in pictures, in paintings; no longer venerated as she once might have been, at least not publicly. No one acknowledged her as they passed, or looked on in admiration as he did. There were no wreaths, no roses laid at her feet. Instead, the copper woman stood alone, stoic as always, but a prisoner like the rest of the city, sentenced to an indefinite term of isolation amongst a web of tram wires as Volgas and Ladas rumbled past with callous indifference.

A short while later, the grouping of youths wandered past in a haze of cigarette smoke, and for a moment, Gustavs locked eyes with one of them. The boy gave him a curious look, then snickered and shook his head, before continuing on his way.

The Hotel Latvija was a modern, towering concrete block rising high above the city and casting its long shadow over the breadth of Kirov street. Inside, the lobby smelled of burnt coffee and shoe polish. Gustavs' reception was lukewarm, to say the least. For the woman behind the front desk, his mere presence seemed an interminable inconvenience. Her face was sour, her mood foul, and even her coiffure had an intimidating aura—dyed a frightening shade of burgundy and seemingly fashioned from steel wool. Gustavs didn't linger, and was promptly exiting the lift when he encountered another hotel staff member, seated at the end of the hall. A stout little woman, some indefinable age between thirty-five and sixty, she sat on a tiny wooden chair, chubby fingers fussing with a pair of knitting needles. Her plump face seemed tired, though not, in Gustavs' mind, for lack of sleep or over-exertion. Not tired, he thought. Perhaps, just worn. He gave her a nod and a smile as he opened the door to his room—neither was reciprocated—the hall monitor's eyes merely following him with practiced indifference until he passed beyond the threshold. Once inside he found his room comfortable if austere, the furniture simple, functional. He dropped his valise on the bed and walked over to the window, pushing the drapes aside and looking south: the Freedom Monument in the distance; a little closer, the golden onion domes of an Orthodox church sprouting skywards from the treeline. He recalled hearing that the house of worship had been turned into a museum. And just to the left of the hotel, a grandiose bronze statue of Lenin, hat in hand, pointing toward a bright, socialist future, or perhaps simply hailing a taxi.

Gustavs seated himself on the edge of the bed, removed his glasses and pinched the bridge of his nose, drifting ever deeper into that queer, semi-lucid dimension one entered when crossing time zones. The mild lunacy encountered in that chimeric realm between slumber and wakefulness as one traversed oceans and continents by air and sea, by car and rail.

He glanced at his watch. He'd made good time, in and of itself something of a miracle. If he rested now he would surely never wake in time for the meeting. And so he sat, bleary eyes fixated on his shoes while he went over the directions in his head, trying to settle himself during his first hours inside a police state.

The hotel itself was managed by Intourist, the leading—and only—Soviet travel authority, naturally a state-owned enterprise and, as such, little more than a supplementary tool of state surveillance. In all likelihood, the origins of Soviet tourism had manifested during discussions between high-level KGB functionaries; vodka-fuelled talks in reclusive dachas about how to further insinuate themselves into the private lives of their citizenry. Gustavs wondered how long it would take the *babushka* outside to unlock his room and rifle through his belongings after he'd left. He pictured her shorthand being transcribed onto a typewriter, an inaugural briefing on the lone salesman in room six-oh-three. Lotte seemed a step ahead, as always, and he was glad for her advice—his valise was mostly full of coffee, chocolate and blue jeans, thoughtful gifts for estranged relatives.

Restless and cheating sleep, his thoughts blindly followed a malignant trail of anxiety as it leeched its way throughout the crevices of his mind, finally settling upon the telephone that sat idly atop the nightstand. Some part of him already knew, but it was curiosity that gnawed at him now, an unrelenting itch. He rubbed the stubble beneath his chin for a long while before finally giving in to temptation, reaching for the telephone. He peered overtop at the black cord that disappeared into shadow behind the bed, then lifted the entire unit, examining its underside, turning it this way and that. Then, placing it carefully in his lap, he lifted the handset from its cradle, pinning down the dial with his thumb. He took a breath, steadying himself before slowly, soundlessly, twisting the mouthpiece and removing the cap.

A wave of nausea washed over him, fingertips suddenly cold and unsteady. Something from a childhood science project before him now, the alien inner workings of a common telephone. And yet, he was absolutely certain of what lay before him, neatly fastened and tucked out of sight. About the size of a small, silver coin, with a set of black and green wires that ran to a sleek metal tube, no longer than a fingernail. He tilted his wrist, revealing the cross-hatch grille of the microphone, tucked just inside the rim of the cylinder.

Time stood still for a moment. Gustavs wondered if they could hear him breathing. For some reason, he looked up and scanned the ceiling, as if he were capable of spotting some sort of covert surveillance device. Still, he had found this one. Something for him? No. Surely not. Just the room, then. Perhaps a room chosen for a particular type of guest. And in that case . . .

He willed the thoughts away for the moment, working methodically to rethread the receiver cap onto the mouthpiece, and replaced the handset. He exhaled, wiping his coat sleeve along the length of his damp brow. He checked his watch once more. He couldn't afford to be late, and couldn't bear to spend another moment inside the room.

TWENTY-ONE

Rising gradually from the sloping banks of the city canal, *Bastejkalns*—Bastion Hill—was a landmark of the city, as was the tranquil park of its namesake. Yet for all its serenity, the surrounding area held a far greater significance in the storied history of the capital. A demarcation line of a city within a city, a vestige of a bygone era. A time of medieval battlements and strongholds, when canals served as moats with fortified embankments, a time when Tsars laid siege to walls of stone, and Swedish kings traversed the river Daugava with armed flotillas.

As one moved south beyond the swaths of parkland, they entered a different age, the beating heart of the city known as *Vecrīga*—Old Rīga—where gabled rooftops and winding lanes had survived the carnage of the most recent war, the last in a long succession of brutal campaigns since its founding in 1201. *Vecrīga* remained, battered yet unbroken despite Hitler's air raids and Stalin's reprisals, the city forever caught between warring giants of the age, an invaluable chess piece in the great continental game. The old quarter endured, scarred and disfigured yet still standing as empires and kingdoms, duchies and dominions crumbled all around, goliaths reduced to brief passages in faded history texts, footnotes in dusty books neatly shelved in silent, darkened libraries.

And on that very morning, on the fringes of the famed neighbourhood, sat a lone woman on a park bench shaded by linden trees. She sat quietly reading her newspaper when a man approached with a hesitant stride, clutching a bouquet of white carnations. The woman looked up as Gustavs slowed, and he volunteered a half-smile as she gave him a quick once-over. He was suddenly less certain than a moment ago, given her stern demeanour, yet she wore the right shade of lipstick—a rich, vibrant crimson—and she was reading the latest edition of *Cīņa*, the Latvian Communist daily. She eyed him carefully as he stopped before her, glanced at the carnations, and then, almost imperceptibly, twitched an eyebrow. *Well?*

Gustavs cleared his throat. "I heard you prefer lilies, but they were all sold out."

An eternity passed. From the boulevard nearby, the impatient bleat of a car horn. At long last, the woman spoke: "It is sunflowers that are my favourite. Though it is not the season."

Gustavs took a seat next to her on the bench, unbuttoning his coat.

"Are you going to keep those?" the woman asked.

"Oh, of course," he replied, handing the bouquet across.

"Kiss my cheeks," she spoke again, this time through gritted teeth. Gustavs stiffly obliged.

Their pleasantries exchanged, the woman let out a laboured sigh—"God help us all"—turned her head and gave the most discreet of nods to two men smoking cigarettes a ways down the path. They immediately turned their backs and began to mosey off toward the canal, with Gustavs slightly uneasy that he had failed to notice them beforehand.

The woman said nothing more as she lit a cigarette, inhaling a deep lungful as if the smoke were the essence of life. She was quite young, Gustavs thought, with the short-cropped blonde hair of a pixie, a pert little nose and a strong chin. She wore a taupe overcoat with wide lapels, and running shoes with mismatched laces. A film director would have likely cast her as a secondary love interest, perhaps the elfin younger sister of the first lead. Gustavs, for his part, still felt like a man who'd never been given the script in the first place, only vaguely aware of his lines, to say nothing of his role.

The woman exhaled. "Gustav," she said.

"Yes."

"My name is Zāra." She looked him up and down once more. "Are you sure you're up to this?"

"Don't seem to have much of a choice, do I?"

"Isn't that inspiring . . ."

"I am, up for it. It's just, all of this, it's a bit new to me."

She flicked some ash into the wind, staring straight ahead. "Frankly, I don't really care. Do you think we receive training of some sort? It's new to everyone, and then it isn't. Because we cannot afford to be fools in our work, do you understand?"

He nodded uncertainly.

"This is no game to us, nor should it be for you."

Gustavs nodded once more, a child scolded into silence.

"Why are you here?" she asked.

"You needed my help," he said, somewhat defensive. "Lotte needed my help."

"And who is that?"

He hesitated. "Lotte . . ."

She conceded after a moment. "You know her."

Gustavs sighed. "Knew her."

"And just what is that supposed to mean?"

"She's dead."

This appeared to rattle the young woman for a moment, just the faintest tick in her jaw. She turned her head slowly to face him.

"Knew her."

"Yes."

"Since?"

"Since we were, well, children, more or less."

"An attractive woman." She took a draw of her cigarette. "Brunette, wavy bangs."

He waited, then shook his head.

She spoke slowly now, "What colour were her eyes?"

"The same as yours."

Zāra cursed under her breath, something Gustavs didn't catch. Her Latvian had a particular cadence to it, pitched and direct, and he found himself considering that she might be even younger than he had initially thought, possibly in her late teens.

"How," she said. Not a question, a demand.

"They shot her. On her back porch." The words sounded as alien to him as they did to her. Zāra cursed once again. This time he understood.

"You were there?"

"No."

"She said she trusted you."

"I know."

"Was she wrong?"

"I hope not."

"You better do more than hope in Rīga." Calmly, she brought the cigarette to her lips, took a measured draw, and settled herself. "She also told *me* that I should trust you."

Gustavs nodded.

"It's not a habit of mine."

"I can see that."

"Your smart remarks will not do you any favours here, tourist." She sighed. "At least your Latvian is decent. That's something, I suppose."

The entire charade was beginning to wear thin, and Gustavs was increasingly frustrated with his own anxiety and apprehension about the entire matter.

"Tell me what you need me to do," he said.

"She did brief you, did she not?"

"Yes."

"Dinner with the relatives."

"Yes."

She gave a slow nod of approval. "In order for this to work, you're going"—Zāra paused as a couple pushed a pram along the pathway, crested the hilltop and continued on—"in order for this to work, you're likely going to need to improvise, so it's best you prepare yourself mentally."

"I thought there was a plan?"

"Of course there is a plan, we always have a *plan*. Perhaps you failed to notice that we also happen to live under the constant watch of the goddamned Chekists. The best laid plans are usually nothing more than guidelines, and it's best you consider them as such. Better to prepare yourself for the inevitable."

"Which is?"

"Fucking catastrophe, usually."

Gustavs swallowed. "Terrific."

"I shouldn't need to tell you, you'll no longer have the sweet comforts of your democracy while you're here. If things go wrong, no one will be reading you your rights and offering you a telephone call. A telephone book perhaps, or a wire. But not much else."

She butted out her cigarette on the edge of the bench, then tucked it into her coat pocket.

"Tomorrow night, at six o'clock, you will be at the corner of Krāmu iela and Jauniela. You will meet a man there. He will take you to a nearby address where you will have dinner with your long-lost relatives."

"The Liepas."

"That's right. Do you remember their names?"

"I do."

"All of them?"

"Yes."

"They will provide you with the documents you need. Follow their instructions. Afterwards, you will return to your hotel, you will go to sleep, and you will have an uneventful journey home. It's that simple."

"Simple."

"There will be a man there, at the dinner. Līze's boyfriend, Dāvids. He is not to be trusted. Everyone is aware, so you don't have to worry. I'm only bringing you up to speed."

"Not to be trusted . . ."

"He is an informant."

"An informant?"

"Yes."

"I don't understand."

"You don't live here."

He considered this briefly, then said: "Actually, maybe I do understand . . ."

"Good. Because we can't afford for Lotte to have been wrong about you."

The comment made him uncomfortable. "And the documents?"

"We'll be in touch."

Gustavs nodded thoughtfully. "Easy."

"Easy. You are part of something much larger here, Gustav. We all have our role to play."

"Mm."

"Questions?"

Gustavs glanced around, timorously.

"Don't do that."

"Is this, usual for you, out in the open, like this?"

"No microphones in parks."

"But, surely we risk people seeing us. I don't exactly blend in as well as you."

Zāra permitted herself the hint of a smile, a glimpse of the schoolgirl behind the hardened spy. "Glad to see you're catching on."

Gustavs' brow was still furrowed with concern.

"We aren't entirely without our wits. The last time I was in this park I had chestnut hair down to my bottom. Today, I'm your long-lost love, tomorrow, nothing more than a memory. Not to worry."

"So that's what this is?"

"What could be more commonplace than a lover's spat in a park?"

"A spat . . ."

She nodded tersely. "I will leave first, and you, after a sufficient period of . . . grieving, will follow."

"How long should I grieve?"

"What kind of question is that for a lady?" she said, rising and tying her waistband. "An eternity, I suppose, but given the circumstances, ten minutes should be sufficient. Are you ready?"

"For?"

"All of this."

He did not take the question lightly, and after a moment, gave a single nod.

"Good."

Gustavs puffed his cheeks. "Will they follow me?"

"They might, but you likely won't see them. Anyhow, you're only headed back to your hotel, aren't you?"

"I suppose I am."

"Now, hand me my flowers." Gustavs obliged, and Zāra looked past him to a trio of matronly women ascending the hill on their afternoon walkabout. She inhaled deeply from the bouquet, then sighed. "Shame," she said.

"What?"

"Did you not know?" she said, eyes on the blooms. "White is the colour of mourning." She drew back her hand and swatted him with the bouquet, and once more for good measure, releasing a shower of crushed petals into the air and dropping the mangled stems in his lap. Later, Gustavs admitted to himself that, if nothing else, his reaction had certainly been convincingly genuine. One of the passing women audibly gasped, eyes wide with surprise, thrilled at having stumbled across the unfolding drama.

Gustavs sat, momentarily stunned as Zāra tugged angrily on her lapels, scoffed, and turned swiftly on her heel. The group of women had fallen silent, observing the young girl as she strode determinedly down the path before them. Then, almost as if rehearsed, they linked arms in solidarity as they passed, giving him a cool stare; Gustavs, the insensitive brute, the object of their collective scorn.

He remained seated on the bench for a long while afterwards, collecting his thoughts, petals scattered at his feet. An occasional breeze stirred the leaves in the treetops, revealing glimpses of a leaden sky that hung low over the city. The mood was rather appropriate for Gustavs; seated alone on a hilltop, shoulders slumped, the patron saint of the broken-hearted. Zāra would have been impressed. Eventually, he made his way back to the hotel where he collapsed onto the bed, not bothering to remove his coat or his shoes, and slept like the dead.

TWENTY-TWO

GUSTAVS AWOKE IN THE DARKNESS, STIRRED BY THE RUMBLE AND clang of a streetcar that passed somewhere in the night. Disoriented at first, he had the good sense to kick off his shoes and pull the bedcover over his head, drifting off once more into a deep slumber, and not waking again until just before midday. Seated on the edge of the bed, Gustavs felt rested, if not refreshed, which was at least something, he supposed.

He proceeded downstairs to the hotel café, where he realized that all he desired was a cup of strong black coffee. Despite a noticeable dearth of patrons, he was gently ushered away from a seat of his choosing by the red-haired woman—"oh, this one is reserved, but how about . . ."—and over to a smaller table within earshot of a man smoking a cigarette and reading an issue of *Sovetskaya Latvija*. The man wore an eager smile, tinted glasses and sported a bristling mustache, looking much like the same gentleman he'd spotted the day before while checking in.

Gustavs drank his coffee hurriedly, a man with a busy day ahead and, regrettably, no time to chat about his business in Rīga or waltz around other trappings. After several attempts to engage with Gustavs—" . . . And how are you finding the city?"—the man suggested, rather abruptly, that they have a drink later on, perhaps at the hotel nightclub. Gustavs, regrettably, could make no promises; it had been some time since he'd seen his relatives, surely the man would understand. Oh yes, he understood perfectly well, raising a hand in deference and smiling affably behind his shaded lenses. *Another time, perhaps.*

In preparation for the evening, Gustavs decided to take a walk south, skirting the perimeters of the old city, heading toward the famed *Centrāltirgus*—the Central Market. The air was cool, accompanied by a brisk autumn wind, and the city hummed at midday, bustling with locals going about their business.

Every now and again he passed uniformed officers, dressed from head to toe in their familiar pale green; somehow, they seemed to be everywhere. Most were quiet and unassuming, carrying briefcases on route to this meeting or that, wearing thick Karakul hats to ward off the cold. Others were of a different temperament— strutting about, imperious, looking down their noses at those who would dare to look them in the eye, of which there were very few indeed. On occasion, Gustavs would spot a gleaming black Volga with bug-eyed headlights—a gaudy riverboat on wheels, and when the light struck the tinted windows at an opportune angle, he could glimpse the podgy *apparatchik* slouched in the backseat.

The famed city market was housed in four repurposed Zeppelin hangars, enormous pavilions that had once offered up their specialties: fresh dairy products from that very morning, ripe produce, butchered meats and sea fare, while the surroundings had teemed with smaller-scale vendors—*vecmāmiņas*, long skirts and knotted kerchiefs, tending to crates of beets and radishes, perhaps a late harvest offering of wild strawberries. Bushels had overflowed with mounds of earth-crusted potatoes, while tables balanced stacks of purple and green cabbage heads with wilted leaves.

Today, the hangars were nearly empty, stripped bare, devoid of all abundance. Approaching the market, Gustavs' eyes fell upon a hunched woman, almost doubled over in a most unnatural position. She swept the vicinity of her stall with a broom made of nothing more than twigs and branches, bundled together by a frayed length of twine. And as he made his way through the dairy market, he watched as shoppers with empty plastic bottles stood patiently in line to receive their rationed share of milk—poured from a dented metal can with a funnel.

Having located the meat pavilion, he sidled up to a butcher's counter with a sad selection of anemic sausages and some skinned hares strung up by hooks. The butcher, a cantankerous man with rosacea, wore an apron spattered with blood and sinew and, taking note of Gustavs' accented Latvian, swiftly turned his back. Gustavs countered this opening gambit by clearing his throat and displaying a fold of American dollars, prompting a deep and appreciative grunt from the butcher. A moment later, a pork loin roughly the size of a brick was produced from somewhere behind the counter, and Gustavs paid a criminal sum for the pleasure.

As one climbed higher into Nordic Europe, passing the fifty-seventh parallel, the summers seemed endless and even in the most reclusive hours of the evening, the light dimmed but never fully faded. In winter, an everlasting twilight—the sun scarcely showing itself before retreating beyond the horizon.

And so it was that on an unremarkable Tuesday in October, dusk began to fall over the city, catching Gustavs somewhat off guard with its haste. Shadows lengthened from the rooftops, and the plummeting temperature ushered city dwellers back indoors, farmers back to their homesteads in the countryside. Gustavs himself had been hoping for a brief spell of shuteye in order to sharpen his faculties for the night ahead, but to no avail. Ever engaged in a private war with his subconscious, skittish nerves already heavily entrenched, they would not permit him any rest. Upon returning to the hotel, he lay awake on the pilly bedspread, staring at the ceiling, while outside, the pale, dwindling light bleached the cityscape, before finally relenting to the darkness.

Nightfall. Down the length of Lenin street, traversing the *Padomju Bulvāris*, Gustavs crossed the threshold into *Vecrīga*, dark and spectral. A quite different city. A city from another time, with narrowing pathways and listing brickwork, medieval lanes with cobbles worn smooth, courtyards overseen by sunken churches with steeples caked in soot. Certain streets were particularly neglected, punctuated by cracked windowpanes and swaths of embrittled concrete, graffiti sprayed erratically across paint that had begun to peel. Along his route he took note of a handsome arched doorway, weathered yet enduring, its fringes adorned with intricate stone carvings of blossoming daylilies. Beneath one of the blooms, scrawled in black paint: "Riga for Russians, Out with Latvian Fascists."

He waited for what seemed an age at the corner of Jauniela and Krāmu iela, a silent crossway where roofs of slanting clay tile all but eclipsed the moonlight. The hush was broken only once—the stumble of a couple of drunks, guffaws and impassioned slurs about the newest counter girl at the bakery. Their voices trailed off, distantly echoing against the stone, and an eerie mood settled over the street. No flashing, neon lights—those brash, blaring hallmarks of capitalism; no lighthearted jingles that floated merrily from a hotel lobby. Only a faint, crepuscular glow, coating the surroundings in obscurity, and the crackle and hiss of a radio broadcast drifting from an open window.

Just as Gustavs' subconscious began to mount another assault, he noticed some movement in an alcove to his right. A shadow peeled itself away from the wall, taking the shape of a man—a dark figure that materialized from brick and mortar and began to approach. Gustavs was rather uncomfortable with just how close the man had apparently been standing, and waiting.

"Good evening," said the figure.

Gustavs managed a tepid nod.

"I'm sorry for the wait. I had to make sure you weren't followed."

For a moment, Gustavs considered his response. " . . . Unless you're the one following me."

A smirk from the shadow? It was difficult to tell. "Yes," the man said, his tone revealing a smile, "unless I'm the one following you. Very good. Come."

"I wasn't given a name."

"Neither was I."

"Dāvid?"

The man had already begun to walk and now turned back, visibly grinning in the dim light, a broad jaw set above broad shoulders. "Come." He turned once more, and continued down the lane.

Gustavs hesitated. Well, what to do? *Don't trust anyone.* But who else would it be? He muttered a curse under his breath, and began to follow. As they proceeded down the cramped street, he noticed some movement in a dormer window on high, a curious someone in an attic who left the curtains ruffling, though he never saw their face.

The man lit a cigarette with a metallic lighter that snapped shut, and Gustavs followed the glow of the ember throughout the city. It soon became clear that their earlier meeting point was just that, and *only* that—he was soon utterly lost among the city's bowels, landmarks fading into irrelevance with each new turn, every serpentine passageway. A brief glimpse of a courtyard. A familiar stone gate. The same trellis with creeping ivy was passed, Gustavs could have sworn, no less than three times. The ascending walls encroached on the sliver of black sky above, further disorienting those already gone astray. At last, they turned inevitably down another side street into pitch darkness where the man slowed, turned into a nondescript doorway, and pushed open a wooden door that nearly swayed off its hinges. The foyer was warm and stuffy, the air heavy with the ammonia stench of urine.

Gustavs continued to follow the man up a flight of concrete steps, and could better observe him in the lamplight. He was sturdily built, with a wide back and bulging shoulders, his russet-coloured hair long and curling the length of his neck, draped over skin that was darkly tanned like leather. The sign of a *zemnieks*. When they reached the third floor, the man rapped a unique staccato beat on a door, entered, and motioned for Gustavs to follow.

"Gustav! Yes, hello! Come, come, here we are."

Gustavs wasn't certain who was speaking as he stepped forth into a cramped, smoky, busy apartment, bodies shuffling about in all directions. His eyes took in what they could: A couple of teen-aged girls stared at him from a worn sofa—sisters, most certainly, while his escort had already traversed the room and was arranging firewood in a small woodburning stove. A pair of children, a boy and girl no older than six or seven went tearing through the midst of it all, scolded by a stern woman from the kitchen. Next to her, a *vecmāmiņa* was preoccupied with a pot of soup and stirred its contents with care, pausing just long enough to flash Gustavs a warm, welcoming smile.

"At last, the man himself, how wonderful!" Gustavs spotted a middle-aged gentleman approaching from down the hall, skirting a table, pushing aside a chair, practically hurtling the children as he went. "Yes, yes!" he exclaimed, grabbing hold of Gustavs' hand and giving it several enthusiastic pumps. "Welcome, Gustav, I am Vītols, welcome to our home."

"Thank you for having me, I brought some, well—here," he said, fumbling with the roast in his market bag.

"Goodness me, look at this! *Oy*, Alfred"—the young boy stopped in his tracks, eyes wide—"look, it's almost as big as you!" The boy grinned, a bashful smile missing a set of front teeth, and sped off down the hall in pursuit of his sister.

"This is too kind, really, too kind," Vītols said, handing the gift to the stern woman, who tilted her head demurely. Gustavs removed the other items—chocolate, Nescafé, three pairs of blue jeans, handing them to his host. The woman pressed her lips together, nodding with sincerity.

"You really shouldn't have," said Vītols.

"It's nothing. I wouldn't dream to come emptyhanded."

The man steepled his fingers and dipped his head in a little bow. Then, "Gustav, this is my darling wife, Skaidrīte."

"Truly, this is very thoughtful," she said. "I hope you're hungry, my mama is making her pea soup, we have some smoked fish . . ."

"It sounds delicious."

"Yes, my mother-in-law, Otīlija."

Gustavs received another heartwarming smile.

"And of course, my daughters, Grieta and Ieva"—motioning to the couch—"and the little munchkins you've seen racing around, well, hah! Would you remember if I told you?"

Gustavs chuckled.

"Ah, not to worry. A great many of us, I know."

"You have a lovely family," he said, glancing around the apartment.

Cramped, but cozy, Gustavs thought. Antique furniture wherever there was room, great lumbering things with plentiful knicks and scratches; a parquet floor that had been worn smooth; a large bay window with curtains drawn, and by the stove, a formidable woodpile stacked with precision.

"Yes, it can be a bit busy," said Vītols, noting Gustavs' wandering eye, "but we are family, of course, and it suits us just as well. If we don't use up the space, you see, they move others in. For the good of the commune, you understand. And those that are assigned the new living quarters aren't always like-minded, if you follow my meaning." He proceeded to titter to himself, a strange little laugh.

Vītols was in his late sixties, Gustavs guessed, a tall and gangly figure beneath his button-down shirt and sweater vest. He had a head of thinning gray hair and a quirky Van Dyke goatee, equally as gray, and observed the world through clever jade eyes. His demeanour was chipper and cheerful in a very genuine sort of way, a man immune to life's great tragedies, and this carefree spirit was punctuated by a frequent and most eccentric little giggle, almost like an inherent tick.

"Are you going to have our guest stand in the doorway all night?" inquired Skaidrīte.

Vītols guffawed and pulled at Gustavs' arm, who resisted only slightly, motioning toward his boots.

"Oh, come now"—shooing this away—"we've had far worse on these floors than your boot heels. Why, just last month—was it? Yes, I believe so. Yes, I came home one afternoon, and do you know what I found? Hm? A shit! Can you believe it? Right here, in the middle of our living room."

"I'm sorry?"

"Oh yes, *exactly* what I said. A mean looking thing it was, coiled up on the floor in a neat little pile like, oh, like some kind of snake from—"

"For heaven's sake Vītol, will you please?" snapped Skaidrīte.

"I'm sorry love—yes, awful business."

Gustavs couldn't hide his incredulity, and was beginning to think he'd become the unwitting victim of some childish prank.

"But, who would . . ."

"Oh, our foreign residents, of course. A longstanding tactic espoused by the secret services, particularly back in the NKVD days. *Intimidation*, you know." Vītols placed his fists upon his hips, as if he were on the stage. "Here we stood, and here we shat! Though I must say, it seems to me they've become slightly less brutish in recent years, some of them, anyhow. The game has all become rather psychological. Still, whenever I'm reminded of it"— he pointed to a certain spot on the floor—"I begin to laugh! Not the intended reaction, I'm sure, but I can do no other than picture this strange man stooping, bare-assed, pants around his ankles in my living room!" He tittered once more, rocking on his heels.

Skaidrīte made a clicking noise with her tongue, a certain tone accompanied by a certain look, seemingly an innate talent of women and wives the world over. Vītols shut up like a clam.

"I'm sorry," Gustavs said, "that all sounds, well, just awful."

"Ah, never mind all that. Anyhow, shall we get to it, then, yes? Here, let me get your coat—Grieta? Will you take care of this for me, please." The younger of the two sisters approached from the couch, a sweet-looking girl, just barely a teen. She smiled, nodded, wrapped Gustavs' coat in her arms and disappeared down the hallway, the *zemnieks* rustling her hair as she passed.

"Now then," Vītols adopted the tone of a professor, "I understand you had a thorough chat with Zāra yesterday afternoon, is that right?"

"I believe so."

"Good. We don't have a great deal of time. Best we take care of things before Dāvids comes along. We can avoid any unnecessary complications."

Gustavs immediately looked to the hulking *zemnieks* who stood, arms crossed, leaning against the far wall. He stared back at Gustavs with a look of absolute indifference, before removing a glossy white onion from his coat pocket, and taking a crackling bite. He wiped his mouth with his forearm.

"Oh, Rihard you've already met, of course," Vītols added, sensing his guest's confusion. "A dear friend. Don't be intimidated by those biceps of his, they're only for the girls." He giggled once more, shoulders twitching. "We told Dāvids you'd be arriving for a late supper around nine, which means he'll believe it to be eight, so will likely show up around seven, just to be sure, in which case we have"—he tilted his wrist, glancing at his watch—"about forty-five minutes, I'd say."

Grieta reemerged from the hall, coat still in hand, and now carrying what appeared to be a miniature sewing kit, needles and spools and various threads. She sat down on the couch and produced a pocket knife which snapped open with a deft *click*.

"What is she doing?" Gustavs asked.

"Oh, not to worry, my Grietiņa is the best there is. A father is always proud, of course, but I say this without bias, if such a thing is possible."

"I don't understand."

Vītols lowered his voice to a whisper. "We have something for you, something to pass on once you've returned. You were informed, yes?"

Gustavs nodded, slowly. Little Grieta, with the help of her older sister now angling a lamp, went to work on the inner lining of his coat with surgical precision.

"The information has been encoded on a piece of fabric—that little roll on Ieva's lap there—which we stitch and sew into the garment itself. Seamless work, truly. No pun intended. No one will be able to tell, you likely wouldn't know yourself had we not shown you. But, that's a different matter. We have something else for you." He looked to his wife. "Darling, if you would be so kind . . ."

Skaidrīte whispered something to her mother, then turned on the radio—a scratchy symphony Gustavs didn't recognize.

"Rihard, if you please . . ." Vītols prompted, and the two men stepped to a nearby bookcase and began to remove rows upon rows, arranging volumes of texts, thick and thin, into wobbly columns on the floor. As they worked, Ieva rose from the couch and positioned herself against the front door.

Once the men had finished, they each grabbed hold of a ridge on either side—"On three . . ."—before lifting the bookcase and shuffling it aside.

"Carefully now," said Vītols, the room tense as the men worked in practiced silence, barely a creak from under their feet.

Beneath the case was a woven area rug, an orange and tan pattern of pagan symbols which Rihards folded aside, revealing a section of parquet flooring still glossy with its original sheen. Rihards handed a razor blade to Vītols, who then knelt with some difficulty and began to trace the inlaid patterns with his fingertips.

It was then that Gustavs noticed, for the first time, that the old man was missing two fingers on his right hand—his ring and pinky little more than mottled, pink bulbs.

Vītols gave a speculative scrape with his thumbnail, before deftly wedging the blade into an unseen cleft and levering a section of the floor. He lifted a most obscure section of wood, a puzzle piece of no discernible shape. "Yes, there we are . . ." he mumbled to himself, and began to fish around in the dark crevice beneath. He was in up to his elbow in the chasm before he finally removed a weathered leather dossier, bound by a string. He brushed it off and handed it to Rihards, who passed it to Gustavs.

The room underwent a revival. The two men restored the bookcase and its contents, Ieva returned to the couch, Skaidrīte continued mincing some green onion, and Vītols lightly dabbed his forehead with a checkered handkerchief.

"Right then, you have . . . thirty minutes I would say, to memorize this before Dāvids arrives."

"Memorize?" Gustavs glanced at the dossier, feeling its weight. "You must be joking."

"Thirty-five minutes, no more. Much as you can. This way," Vītols said, already stepping down the hall. "Focus only on the most pertinent details."

They moved past a closet-sized lavatory, a children's room and up a couple of steps into a claustrophobic office with a low ceiling. Inside there was a bureau, a large window, an enormous, overflowing bookcase, as well as pillars of books stacked high as the ceiling—piles on the desk, mounds on the floor, leather-bound volumes arranged along the windowsill. Gustavs stepped carefully for fear of knocking over a tower, and nearly did when Vītols stopped short to close the door.

Gustavs unwound the cord securing the dossier. "Thirty minutes, for all this . . ."

"Most will be irrelevant, but you never know. I'm eager to hear your thoughts. I can't let you take it with you."

"We can't sew some of it into the coat?" Gustavs asked, caught off guard by his own bravado.

Vītols reached into the dossier, an elfish smile as he crinkled the edges of some paper in his palm, breaking the silence in the stuffy room.

"Of course," Gustavs acknowledged.

"The fabric is thin and won't make a sound if they search you. Papers, well—only so many places you can hide documents like these, my good man. Unless you're going to show me a trick I haven't seen since Kolyma," he said with a snigger, appraising the size of the leather parcel. "A bit big for that, though, I would think." He gave a sly little wink. "Right, I'll leave you to it. You will have privacy here. I'll return in a few minutes."

The room was silent and still. The books, like barricades of revolution insulated the space from the outside world. Seating himself at the cluttered chestnut bureau, Gustavs adjusted a gooseneck lamp which caught a spectrum of dust particles in its beam. Then, he lifted a heavy flap and opened the file.

A portrait of a life: pictures, letters, keepsakes. Beneath some stray pages, he first removed a thin photo album made of pulpy cardboard. Inside, a black and white photograph sheathed by waxed paper that rustled at his fingertips. Two children, a boy and presumably his younger sister, dressed smartly for the occasion. The boy wore a dreamy sort of smile, the girl too young to understand. The picture was undated, and was the only picture in the album.

Then, letters. Sheets of tawny paper with elegant, if practically illegible cursive, declarations of love for "My dearest Yasha." Letters received? Unsent? Perhaps returned. Letters mailed to the front for a man disappeared. They were all signed with love by "G," and eventually, amongst the scroll, he deciphered references to *Köztársaság tér* and the *Államvédelmi Hatóság*. Magyar, if memory served. In regards to the first two words, he wasn't certain of their meaning—had known them once, of that he was sure. Though he recognized the second phrase, which, more often than not, was shortened to its acronym: AVH. Hungarian Secret Police.

Among the letters he uncovered some identity documents. A temporary passport, issued by the "Military Government for Germany, 1947." The photograph was torn out, the name scrawled in pen. He could make out the surname: Tereshenko. Below, the passport number, stamped in black ink: 62984. He put this to memory. Then, a second passport, more complete, this one of an older woman. A chiseled face, thin, heavily creased, a woman with dark, elemental eyes that were wary of the camera. No signature, only the smudged blue ink stain of a thumbprint. An illiterate woman, likely from a humble, peasant background.

Tereshenko, Valentīna Marija, born April 3rd, 1916, Dünaburg, Russian Empire. Dünaburg—German for Daugavpils, in Latvia's southeast. Gustavs rubbed his eyes and readjusted his glasses. *Pertinent facts only. No time.*

So then, someone who escaped. A family having fled the war, the advance of the Red Army. Displaced persons seeking safe haven.

Gustavs began to move at pace. An identity card—no, two cards, pale green, issued by the Control Commission for Germany, British Zone. Here he found the names. Tereshenko, Galina Petrova. Tereshenko, Anatoly Petrovich.

Bank notes, crumpled German reichsmarks from the war in

various denominations. One with a portrait of a German fräulein holding a stem of edelweiss, and just below, an address scribbled in red pen. A German address, somewhere in Föhrenwald.

Report cards. A clever child, all fives across the board. Galina's assessments.

More letters, much older, the paper almost translucent and ready to crumble at the touch. More legible, the penmanship, deliberate and refined. Treasured correspondence from a relative, a grandparent, perhaps. A governess? Written to "My darling Galochka," and signed with love: "Babka."

A photograph, a handsome officer, clean-shaven with piercing eyes, full lips. He turned it over—Yasha Khlebov, January, 1956. He considered the letters, and the term came back to him. *Köztársaság tér.* The famous square, the courtyard. He looked back to the picture. *Sent to quell the uprising in Budapest? Did you make it home?*

A final, thick envelope contained several sheets of similar letters, penned in indecipherable Cyrillic.

In the thick silence of the little library, Gustavs' train of thought was derailed by soft footfalls in the hallway, and he looked up to see Vītols stepping through the door, brandy snifters in hand.

"So," Vītols began, handing one of the glasses to Gustav, "what do you think? No, please, sit."

Gustavs sighed and leaned back in the chair, Vītols propping himself along the edge of the desk.

"I think . . . they're memories."

"Yes. Whose?"

Gustavs frowned. "Galina's, of course."

"Not Anatoly's?"

Gustavs stared blankly.

"Ah, you don't read Russian, of course. Forgive me. But, nevertheless—you are correct." He dipped his nose into his glass and breathed deeply. "And the woman?"

"The mother."

"Valentīna. A beautiful name, no?"

Gustavs nodded.

"And a beautiful woman. There was, something about her. An aura, you might say. And those eyes, goodness, it was as if she could gaze into your very soul."

"You knew her."

"A lifetime ago, back when I still had these"—he wiggled the red nubs on his right hand—"a young man, the prime of my life."

"You and her, you were . . ."

"Oh, no—hah! But how I dreamed! How we all did," he chuckled. "No, no . . . I met her only once. It was back in Kem that I first saw her—a transit point before they took us out to the islands. Out to Solovetsky."

"You were in Siberia?"

"Oh yes—Solovki is one of the oldest camps, I believe. They closed it at the start of the war if I'm not mistaken. Too close to the Finnish border, you see. But I was there, briefly, before they moved me to the ends of the earth in Magadan. Yes, yes. Frostbite," he said, examining his hand, impassive. "A small price to pay. But I had good boots, worth their weight in gold out there. We would stuff them with newspaper if we could find it, more often peat, tree bark, anything we could get our hands on."

The old man's eyes drifted once more to another time. "It was never the work, you know, it was just—Russia. Old Mother Russia. The elements, that's how she gets you." He shrugged. "Then again, I knew men who cut off their own hands not to lift an axe again.

We all respond differently, don't we? So, I've kept all my toes and I've kept my wits—most of them, anyhow, and that's surely something." He let out another curt giggle.

Vītols reached across, shuffled some pages around and found the passport. "Valentīna, yes." He stared at the photograph. "I saw her once more, a few days later, maybe a week, who knows for sure. She had already made inroads with the cook, clever girl. In Moscow, it was party officials whose favour one sought, but not out there. The cook, he was the one you wanted.

"The women . . . given the circumstances, they didn't resist, simply accepted the men as part of a bargain. And she had done well, bargaining for food. Not all were so fortunate. Not all got something in return." He sighed. "Reduced to animals, you see . . . Anyhow, we all knew the rumors. She had been the mistress of a high-ranking official in the security apparat, a certain Jēkabs Pēterss. Do you know of him?"

It took Gustavs a moment, but at last the name triggered a memory. "I do. Yes, that's right. He was instrumental in the Bolshevik takeover, was he not?"

"Head of the Cheka for a time as well, the mad dog."

"He was killed in the purges."

"That he was, Stalin's sweep of all Latvians. But, not before allegedly impregnating a certain young revolutionary, sentenced to a term of hard labour as an enemy of the people. Or, so the story goes. I can say this, she was a beauty, and she certainly didn't seem pregnant when I saw her. Rumors of the Gulag, we all thought, but as I said, who knows . . ."

"Well," Gustavs began, "*we* know."

Vītols smiled. "Mm, that we do. Thanks to Aleksandrs."

"Do you know where he is?"

"He is gone, Gustav."

"You're certain?"

"As certain as we can ever be; one does not often return from disappearances such as his. It must have been devastating for Lotte, but, for what my thoughts are worth, I believe the pair of them are dancing together now amongst the stars.

"He was a great asset, Aleksandrs. Arrogant, at times, but supremely effective. We had a publication, for a time, *Dzirkstele*, I might have"—his eyes darted around the bureau—"ah, here we are." He pulled a thin, sepia coloured booklet from beneath a pile of paper, handing it to Gustavs. The cover had an artist's rendering of a spark, hence *dzirkstele*, that burst into licks of flame, roaring upwards to the top of the page. It was the December edition of 1986.

"We would do it all ourselves, decide on the topics, collect the figures, arrange everything. It wasn't difficult to find a typewriter, only difficult to find time to use it for such a purpose. And with the walls being so thin . . ." Gustavs admired the cover page. "The artwork was done by my wife, in fact. Aleks would smuggle the edition out, either to Germany or Sweden, more often than not. We'd run a few hundred copies, then smuggle them back in for distribution."

"I've seen this before, at Lotte's, I think."

"She wrote a few pieces herself, yes. She was very proud of it."

Gustavs nodded.

"It was Aleksandrs that located these documents. He developed contacts like no one I'd ever met, could charm his way into any-one's kitchen. People naturally trusted him, gravitated toward him. And here, that's truly saying something. You see, we had Valentīna's passport for a long time, but it was he who followed his leads to an apartment on Elizabetes *iela* and found this treasure stowed away for, well, decades, most likely. Unfortunately, no photographs with the newer passport. With a bit of luck, you might have been able to identify them."

"What do you mean?"

"The Tereshenkos were in Germany, of course, the displaced person's camps set up by UNRRA. You've seen the documents," he said, motioning to the file. "A time of utter chaos. Thousands upon thousands of Balts, Poles, Jews, scattered among the British, American, French zones, and all seeking refuge somewhere. Thousands having fled the war and, depending on who you were, not entirely keen on returning home. In the late forties and fifties tens of thousands migrated everywhere—our brothers and sisters included—sponsored by foreign governments or lobby groups, destined for New York, Sydney, Toronto. Heaven help those in charge of the relocation efforts, and equally those tasked with weeding out fascist sympathizers, communists. Difficult, nigh on impossible to keep track of who went where and under which names. And with what sort of intentions. You begin to see where the cross-section is, Gustav." He took a sip of his brandy. "We believe the pair of them could very well be operating abroad as agents."

"Galina and . . . the brother."

"Yes. Anatoly. Despite what these documents might lead you to believe, we know for a fact that the siblings were never accepted or sponsored by anyone. Some time ago, we uncovered an application to emigrate to Toronto, in 1954. It was for a Sacha Malenkov—a man who looked remarkably like our young Anatoly—though the trail sputtered out. An application was made, at the very least, of that much we were certain. What happened afterwards, we discovered, was that Anatoly moved to Kaliningrad where he was educated under his assumed name."

"Malenkov."

Vītols nodded. "Eventually he moved back to Rīga and disappeared under our very noses, recruited by the NKVD. Few knew of him. We have falsified records that suggest immigration to London, though that proved a dead end as well. It was the same with Galina. For a time we believed that Yasha was a code name for her brother but, in the end, also a misinterpretation. A love interest, killed in Budapest, radicalizing her even further, if that were possible. We've uncovered many roads that lead to nowhere, however, in a roundabout way they do seem to point us in the right direction. We believe Galina could be working with him abroad, brother and sister, perhaps even posing as husband and wife."

"Do we know for how long?"

"Difficult to say. Moscow takes its disinformation campaigns very seriously. It invests a great deal of time and effort into these plans, these operatives. Not all agree with this subtle, yet effective approach—they have their own politics, of course, just as we do. In spite of all our efforts here, and those of our countrymen abroad, such as yourself, there is always a counterweight that comes from the East. And what better way than to infiltrate our communities, the very centers of resistance. They seek to rot the apple from its core. And if they can sow mistrust amongst ourselves, truly, they need little else. Lotte was very attuned to this, more than once she had reservations about the individuals granted exit visas for America, Canada. And she was often correct. The story is much the same for the Estonians, the Albanians, as you can imagine. All of our compatriots with similar movements."

Gustavs was silent for a time, deep in thought. The notion had first come to him while reading through the dossier, and now, much as he tried, he found himself repeatedly drawn to it. A creeping suspicion that seemed to slowly descend upon him from on high, conjured from thin air.

"What happened to the woman?"

"Valentīna? She died." He picked up the passport once more. "Tuberculosis. She succumbed a year after this was issued. A final gift from the camps. They mark you, you see, in their way. There seemed to be more death than life out there. Some of us were fortunate enough to leave, but you always take a little something with you." He cast an eye over his hand, forcing a pitiful smile. "A memento."

"So then, Malenkov or Tereshenko . . . or something else entirely."

"Yes, but thankfully, young man, we have a special contact. One that I'm most proud of, I should say. A sharp one, he is, in your very own hometown."

"In Toronto?"

"Well, he drifts about quite a bit, but yes. As I understand it, he's made significant inroads with certain departments within your government. To be frank I'm quite surprised at how many contacts he seems to have developed. A natural, apparently, much like Aleksandrs. He claims to have access to entire libraries of records—immigration documents, birth certificates, name changes, criminal histories. If you can confirm his suspicions—of which he has many, I'll admit, you may need to work to narrow it down—I believe we may be able to identify them."

"Identify them . . . in my community."

"Do you have any doubt?"

Gustavs sighed. "Lotte was certain."

"That she was. As am I. I've been at this game a long time. Long enough to trust my nose and know when the milk has spoiled.

It's true, there are many rules and best practices, but there is no accounting for the instinct. This you must be born with. Lotte had it, and she was certain about you."

"Certain about what?"

"There are other ways to pass this information, Gustav. But she insisted it be you. Simply put, she didn't trust anyone else to do it. And for *her* to say that . . ."

Gustavs took a drink. "And what about you? What do you think?"

"I don't need to trust you," he said with a grin. "I only need to trust her intuition. But you seem a decent sort." For a moment he chuckled at this, before his eyes began to wander, scanning across the rows upon rows of well-handled books. "And so it goes. Aleksandrs. Lotte. And I do believe your dear friend Imants. Yes, Gustav, the colours of our flag are appropriate enough. The blood has yet to dry." A muffled knock from the front door diverted their attention. "That will be Dāvids. Come now, let's have something to eat. Leave this to me," Vītols said, placing a hand over the dossier. "I'll be along in a moment."

Dinner was a delightful, if bizarre, otherworldly experience. The table spoke mostly in whispers, as if there were forever someone crouched in the hall with an ear to the door. With mismatched cutlery and chipped dishware they ate Otīlija's pea soup with pork, smoked sprats in oil, and a hefty loaf of black bread slathered with rendered fat. For dessert, peppermint tea and a bowl of fruit compote made from dried apples, pears and a hint of rhubarb.

Dāvids was an entertainer of sorts, a chiseled young man with windswept auburn hair and a pungent aftershave that reminded

Gustavs of pine resin soaked in petrol. He had the character of a man who enjoyed being the center of attention but managed to strike a delicate balance; he was polite, included everyone in his stories, knew when not to overstep. He inquired rather casually about the family lineage, with Vītols spelling out the ancestry in some detail, and Gustavs able to play his role by chiming in about Lotte, who was cast, as earlier agreed, as his second cousin.

Gustavs struggled to ground himself in the dizzying theatre, a house of mirrors where friends and loved ones could seal your fate with only a whisper. He sat, bewildered by the conflict that must have warred amongst those emotions; betrayal as a fact of life, or, perhaps for some, simply a game within a larger game. Vītols had an uncanny sense of timing, and an eerie ability to know exactly what Gustavs seemed to be thinking. Every now and again the old man flashed him a look, a shrewd flick of the eyebrows. *And here you see the silly games we must play.*

At one point the phone rang and a shadow seemed to sweep across the room, as if a phantom had taken a seat at the table. Vītols answered the telephone with a formal greeting, which apparently went unreciprocated. He spoke again, waited for several moments, then slowly replaced the receiver. To Gustavs, he said: "Not to worry. It happens, from time to time." When he sat back down, Skaidrīte patted his hand.

Rihards was the first to leave, and after a glass of schnapps, Dāvids and Ieva also departed to meet some friends, leaving Gustavs to bid his farewells to the remaining Liepas. The evening had been surprisingly tender, and a part of him felt as if they truly were his extended family. He even received a great squeeze around his thigh from little Marta, who thanked him sincerely for the chocolate, a bit of which remained smeared in the creases of her little mouth.

Vītols walked him down the stairs in silence, and from the foyer the dank stench of urine rose once more to greet them. Instead of moving toward the door, Vītols rounded the banister and turned in the opposite direction. "Come, this way."

He led Gustavs through a corridor, and outside into yet another dark alley, where the old man pointed toward a main artery in the near distance. "Always best to leave by a different door. Make a right at the end there"—he pointed—"and keep heading north. You'll find your bearings in no time."

Gustavs nodded.

"You'll be alright," Vītols said. Then, tapping his temple like a telegraph sounder, "Keep your wits about you, keep all you can in here. Our man will contact you once you return."

"How will I know him?"

"He will find you, there will be no doubt. Trust those instincts of yours. You'll also pass on the document from your coat, of course."

Gustavs combed his fingers nervously through his hair, reality beginning to dawn.

"Remember, you are no one. *Believe* that you are no one. And in that way, you give them no reason to search you. I would be more concerned about your time here in the city than at the border. If you can make it as far as Tallinn, you need not worry."

"That's reassuring."

"That is our reality, my good man."

"And if they do search me?"

"Well . . . I suppose we're all off to the Lubyanka then, aren't we?"

Gustavs puffed out his cheeks.

"Oh come now, it isn't all that bad. The tallest building in Moscow, the Lubyanka, did you know? From its basement you can see Siberia." He giggled once more at his own little jest, though

Gustavs found it difficult to share in the sentiment.

Vītols took him by the shoulders, gripping him firmly. "You'll be alright. Lotte had faith in you. As do I. God grant you speed, Gustav, and may He bless a free and independent Latvia." Then, Vītols caught him off guard, planting two firm, prickly kisses on either cheek, and smacked his shoulders once more.

Gustavs said nothing as he watched the old man retreat through the doorway, leaving him alone in the silent, darkened alley.

TWENTY-THREE

THE STREETS WERE QUIET, AND GUSTAVS MOVED CAREFULLY, AN unnatural gait as his mind wheeled. He reminded himself to move swiftly yet cautiously, ensuring to draw no attention. What resulted was a rigid half-trot down the street, arms stiffly at his sides, and the unnerving sense that the entire world was watching. At the very least, Eastern Europe was watching, as if a spotlight was illuminating his silhouette along the brick façades. He could feel the foreign piece of fabric practically smoldering in the lining of his coat, and the eyes of inquisitive strangers peering down from windowsills at the strangely dressed man and his brisk shuffle.

Silence. Only the sound of his footsteps now. Further down the street, some rustling to his right; a pair of stray cats nibbling at a small mound of discarded fishbones. Then, from up ahead, masculine voices drifted through the still air, some guttural chortling and Gustavs nearly gave himself away—a brief stutter-step as two officers suddenly rounded the corner and started toward him. The panic was immediate; his chest seized and the sensation flowed outwards from there, pins and needles and a warm rush of blood to the head. He reached up to loosen his collar, realizing it wasn't buttoned. *Put your hand down.*

The two men were still in uniform—thick pale coats with

epaulets, black leather boots—though clearly off duty. Even in Russian, Gustavs could recognize the drunkard's familiar drawl, accompanied by emphatic gesturing. Then, an even more frightening thought. Perhaps only an act. Some theatre to lull him into complacency. After all, the timing left slight margins for coincidence; he had hardly been walking for more than five minutes. Where they expecting someone? *No witnesses.*

It was too late to cross the street, and far too obvious. Turning back was certainly out of the question. Were they trained to notice mannerisms like that? Of course they were. Still, perhaps his reaction would be just what they expected—eyes downcast, bowed shoulders, a subservience which they had come to expect. To demand.

The two men seemed to lose their sense of humour as they approached, the joke having worn thin. Now, only twenty feet away, they mumbled softly to one another, and in the process succeeded in raising Gustavs' anxiety to near apoplexy. He forced his right hand against his side to mute the trembling, and with his left fumbled with his glasses, his pocket, the buttons of his coat. *Stop moving your hands.*

Ten feet away. Gustavs kept his eyes on the smooth stones before him, holding his breath.

Five feet. The militiamen were silent, and Gustavs exhaled, closed his eyes and gave in to his fate. He felt the quickening thump of his heartbeat. Heavy boots on cobblestone. Three men in the night, no one speaking a word.

As the officers passed, the man closest swung his shoulder out wide, knocking Gustavs firmly off balance, so much so that he stumbled backward and steadied himself against a parked van. The second man broke into a chuckle, though the culprit craned his neck and sneered. Gustavs kept his head down and said nothing.

He kept moving, the heavy weight of dread slowly draining away, relief flooding over him like an anaesthetic. *Get a grip*. He began taking long, steady breaths, countering the shallow inhalations; was soothed by a pulse that no longer threatened to burst from his chest.

Regaining his focus, he found himself momentarily disoriented, glancing back at an obscure side street. Was that where Vītols had pointed? He'd been so preoccupied with his impending arrest that he'd lost his bearings. He paused, turned to look back, decided to keep walking. Up ahead, the street came to an end at a wide intersection where a taxi went rumbling past beneath the streetlights. Gustavs kept on, reprimanding himself for his lack of attention.

A woman, seemingly materializing from nowhere, suddenly passed him from behind, walking at pace before slipping through a doorway up ahead. He followed through the wake of her perfume, slightly unsettled that he had never heard her footsteps.

Gustavs steadied his nerves and focused on his breathing once more. He began to take comfort in the morbid contemplation that the anxiety alone would likely carry him off long before any Chekist policeman could do him harm. The thought of having a heart attack and disappointing his would-be interrogators prompted an ironic snort.

As he neared the intersection, he scanned the decorative façades for street signs, and was caught off guard by a homeless man urinating in an alcove, humming a forlorn tune. The man finished, wiped his hands on his coat and placed a bent cigarette between his lips, before noticing Gustavs approaching. He then inquired about a light, miming the action deferentially with his hands. Keeping his distance, Gustavs shrugged in apology, and the man responded with a courtly, drunken flourish, almost as if to bow, and began humming once more. Gustavs wondered if there was anyone sober in this part of the city.

And then the humming stopped.

Gustavs felt the sudden darkness much as he saw it, heard it, smelt it—a shroud of cloth descending violently over his face, coarse fabric chafing his skin. Before his hands could reach upwards, the cloth tightened around his throat and he was yanked backwards, off balance.

Panic. His open mouth made a garbled sound as he grasped at his throat to no avail; the homeless man was strong, his movements swift and precise. Gustavs clawed at the hood, then howled as a boot drove into his knee, crippling him to the ground. He choked and gasped in the dark void. Suddenly, a blaze of light pierced the fabric, illuminating the darkness. Tires squealed across the road, an engine accelerating before finally coming to a halt, rumbling nearby. Gustavs reached for the hood again and felt the drawstring dig into the flesh beneath his jaw. A door slammed. Footsteps. He managed to cry out for help, though the bag only tightened, causing him to cough and hack into the musty cloth. He gasped for air, taking the rough fibres into his mouth.

"Dvai, dvai!" shouted a voice, and suddenly he was up on his feet, lifted by an iron grip that twisted his arm behind his back. The pain flared like a current of electricity through his shoulder, wrenching him upwards from the ground. Someone clasped his other arm. Two of them now, on either side. Gustavs writhed, struggling in vain, and like a marionette he bounded forward to their will.

His body was locked in a vice, but his mind was sharp, at attention, the adrenaline stimulating his wits. *The door, the car.* Gustavs kicked out a leg and it swung clumsily through the air, but did enough to send the three of them momentarily off balance. One of the men cursed and reaffirmed his grip; Gustavs howled, feeling as though his shoulder was separating from its socket. They lurched him forward and, still wriggling, he tried once more. This time his leg swung out and landed on something hard, his boot planted firmly against the frame of the vehicle, and he launched himself backward with all his might. For a moment he was airborne, the world dark and weightless, and then he struck the hard ground, scrambling blindly across the cold stone. He tore the sack from his head, momentarily blinded by the headlights as they flooded his vision. His right leg nearly gave out as he rose to his feet. He could hardly focus, glasses askew, but he spotted the blur of a man moving for him at the last moment. There was no time to think; he flinched, instinctive, ducking his head out of the way as a shirt-sleeve whipped past his ear, connecting with soft flesh behind him. Curses rang out, and Gustavs stumbled to one side.

Turning to run, he was rooted to the spot; someone had him by the collar once more. Adrenaline surged and panic had made him rabid—he spun and drove his knee upward into the man's genitals. The man cried out in agony before crumpling to the ground like a sack of bones. Gustavs kicked out once more, but the homeless man was upon him in an instant, appearing from a blind spot and sinking a fist into his belly, a steel piston that plunged deep into his abdomen. Gustavs heaved, collapsing to one knee, sucking the air for breath that would not come. Stars glimmered and danced along the periphery of his vision. The homeless man towered above him and snorted, more inconvenienced than angered by the altercation.

Thoughts vanished, for in the next moment Gustavs was lifted into the air by a crane, suspended by collar and waistline and heaved into the side of the automobile. He struggled feebly on the ground, still gasping for breath. The man continued to mutter insults, appalled by the audacity of it all. Gustavs was lifted once more and sent skidding across the hood, hurtling over the side and rolling into the middle of the street. He managed to break his landing with the side of his head, and immediately felt for blood. A dull tone swelled in his ears, a muffled frequency that held a singular note.

Glasses. No glasses. He swept his palms across the cobbles, desperately fanning his arms left and right. Bootsteps rounded the front of the vehicle, accompanied by the same guttural cursing. *Come on, come on.* He whipped his hands blindly about until his fingertips caught the edge of the frame, snatched up his glasses, scrambled to his feet, and ran.

Gustavs cut through the wind, legs pumping, his surroundings nothing more than a darkened blur. He tore down the middle of a nameless street in a nameless direction. Irrelevant, all of it. *Just run.* Only the sound of boots flying across the cobbles and strained, wheezing breaths. He didn't dare look back. He sprinted until his feet stung and his lungs ached, only the wind in his ears. There may have been footsteps behind, might have been stale breath on the back of his neck, but he didn't feel anything yet. Every step as important as the last. *Just keep moving.*

Up ahead, twin beams of light glowed upon a wall, then flared directly before him and he threw up a palm to shield his eyes. The glare was accompanied by the growl of another engine and the whinging of old suspension over the uneven road. His feet stuttered to a near halt, his knee almost giving way yet again as he stumbled before veering off in the opposite direction, darting down a narrow alley where the vehicle could not follow.

His chest was tight, throat dry, forehead slick with a lacquer of sweat. The lane was silent but for the echo of heavy footfalls resonating against the brick corridor. And then, suddenly, a new sound. A scream in the night, a feverish pitch—the voice of a woman. She shouted, once more and then again; he could hardly discern the words over the sound of his panting, the blood pumping in his ears. The words floated down over his shoulder from a distance, hysterical yet strangely familiar. Latvian words. Against his better judgment he slowed, only for a moment, and glanced back. At the mouth of the alley a car was idling, the back door flung open with Zāra, leaning halfway out, mouth twisted in furor.

"Get in you goddamned fool! Now!"

It took him a moment, the world shifting on its axis.

"Yes, by all means just stand there—will you fucking move!"

Gustavs snapped to attention and began racing back to the vehicle, a hardened limp in his stride now, his right knee volcanic and inflamed.

"Come on! Move!"

From a distance, his tunnel vision could see Zāra looking through the rear windshield as she waved him frantically onward. It was barely a run any longer, despite his efforts; only a hobble now, lurching toward the open car door. Only a few paces more.

"Hurry!"

Gustavs dove headfirst into the backseat, toppling over Zāra, awkwardly wedging himself along the floor. Zāra shouted something at the driver and struggled to grab the door handle. The engine revved and stalled, and Zāra shrieked as a body appeared from nowhere, crashing into the frame of the open door. Gustavs looked up at his nemesis, the hulking beast posing as a vagrant, face beet-red and contorted with rage. Zāra scrambled deeper into the vehicle but the man grabbed her legs, dragging her halfway out before raining his fists down upon her. She screamed as the man swung in a frenzy, spitting curses at the lot of them until the car rumbled to life once again, jerking forwards and beginning to roll down the street. The man was partway inside the car and the sudden movement was jarring; eyes wild and legs dangling beyond the door, he wrapped an arm around the passenger headrest and resumed the assault with his free hand.

The vehicle began to move at speed, with Zāra and Gustavs slowly gaining the upper hand. Zāra kicked out wildly at the man, her heels striking his barrel-chest and occasionally catching his chin, while Gustavs, still wedged along the floor, swung his fist upwards, connecting with anything that wasn't Zāra. The car bucked as it veered up onto the curb, and there was a moment of alarm in the vagrant's eyes as he slipped a few inches, his legs still caroming outside along the road. As Gustavs struggled to twist himself off of the floor, his hand grazed an empty bottle that had rolled beneath the seat. He grabbed hold and swung it at the man who swatted this aside, the bottle glancing off his meaty shoulder. Gustavs tried again, though the car swerved and the threesome tumbled awkwardly against one another, the bottle bouncing harmlessly off the seat cushion and out the door.

As they struggled to gain their bearings, the car vaulted up and over the curb again, the vagrant tumbling a good ways out. He grabbed a large mittful of Zāra's hair and dragged her toward him as she screamed, though she swiftly returned the sentiment, clawing at his face and digging her thumbs into his eyes. The engine roared alongside the cacophony in the backseat; curses and grunts rang out amidst the struggle, sweat and spittle filled the air.

Gustavs' eye caught something glinting faintly along the floor, a steel flask that had been wedged between the seats. He reached down, grabbed hold, and in a moment of lunacy, lunged forward at the vagrant, swinging wildly. Gustavs' weight pinned Zāra against the seat and forced their assailant off balance, scrambling for a handhold. He brought the flask down upon the man's head, then swung it again and connected fiercely with the ridge of his brow. The man roared and brought up a hand in defence, but Gustavs was relentless. He struck again, and again, swelling with conviction and wailing on him with all his might, both hands raining steel.

Suddenly the car shifted and Gustavs was thrown off balance, but he forced himself upright and continued his barrage. A fresh contusion split open along the man's hairline, streaming a river of bright red down the side of his face. The man's grip slipped once more as Zāra had also recovered and was kicking at the thick fingers that still clutched the upholstery. At last, the man's face became strained, no longer enraged but almost desperate, his teeth clenched and streaked with blood. Zāra stomped once more, Gustavs brought the flask down with both hands, and the man tumbled from the open door, his arms flailing before being swallowed up by the darkness of the street. They immediately looked through the rear windshield, watching a caliginous mass roll across the ground before finally settling into a still heap.

The driver slammed on the brakes and Zāra pulled the door shut. In the backseat, they stared at one another: Gustavs, glasses askew, breathing heavily; Zāra, short blonde hair in a swirl, her red lipstick somehow unblemished. The driver turned around to face them, and only then did Gustavs realize it was Rihards. The unflappable chauffeur opened his mouth to speak, then paused, furrowing his brow. A set of headlights burst through the rear windshield, illuminating his face, causing him to squint.

"Shit," said Rihards. "Who's that?"

Gustavs looked back. "The other one," he said, still panting.

"There's another one?" said Zāra.

Rihards sighed, facing front and putting the car back into gear. "There's always another one," he grumbled, and slammed his foot onto the gas pedal. The wheels spun violently, and they tore around the corner and down a main street.

"Are you hurt?" Zāra asked, a look of concern. "Let me see your face."

"I'm fine," Gustavs replied, removing his glasses.

"Good." She clasped a hand around his neck, and kissed him hard, lipstick smearing across his mouth. Gustavs sat, stunned. Then she grabbed him by the collar and tore his shirt, a button springing loose and fluttering through the air.

"Hey!"

"Drink this," she said, producing the flask—the bright steel smeared with wet blood—and tilted it liberally against his mouth, vodka streaming down his chin.

"What the hell"—he writhed, pushing her hand away. "What are you doing?"

Zāra took a measured drink, looked back at the headlights closing in, and replaced the cap. "Now listen, and listen well. Your night didn't go as planned—in fact, it went much better. While visiting with your relatives, everyone drinking and being merry, Vītols' youngest daughter couldn't take her eyes off you. And you, being the weak and lonely man you are, couldn't resist her advances. You shared a moment of forbidden, and somewhat incestuous, passion before you were caught in the act, Vītols chasing you out of his home with a dust pan."

Gustavs stared blankly.

"This is what you will tell the doorman upon your return to the hotel. He's a big man, and a pervert. You'll recognize him, he's there every evening. Once we lose this one"—she tilted her head to the trailing vehicle—"we'll drop you off around the corner. Give him details. As many as you can. Describe the daughter as if she were me."

Gustavs struggled to keep up, but the chips began to fall slowly into place.

"Are you with me?"

Gustavs thought about it, absentmindedly wiping at the vodka soaking his torn shirt. "I think so. How do you know he's a pervert?"

"How do I know men are perverts or that this man is a pervert?"

Gustavs brought his fingers to his mouth, the lipstick smeared across his face. He looked at Zāra, who stared coolly back.

"What—did you think I was that impressed?"

Rihards jerked the wheel to the left, narrowly avoiding a parked Moskvitch, then calmly spun it back before shooting out onto the open motorway. He moved swiftly through the gears as they sped along the river embankment while behind them, the headlights followed suit, never far behind. Zāra climbed over the console into the passenger seat.

"The farm?"

"Not much choice, now," replied Rihards. "Gustav, there's only the one?"

"I . . . yes, I think so."

"You think so?"

Zāra turned to face him, and Gustavs nodded. "It was only two of them. How long until there's more?"

Rihards glanced in the rear-view mirror. "This one will want to take us himself."

"Are you sure?" asked Zāra.

"No . . . but it's what I would do." Rihards spun the wheel again and they soared onto *Akmens Tilts*, the stone bridge that passed over the Daugava, leading off into the Western fringes of the city and beyond into the countryside. Gustavs watched the streetlamps flicker past, blurs of amber light in the window, a thick mist rising from the sweeping river beneath. Behind them, the headlights swung round, and followed.

"Does he know how many of us in the car?" Rihards asked, accelerating.

Gustavs thought about it, then shook his head. "I don't think so."

Rihards looked to Zāra, "Could just be you."

She nodded slowly, considering this. "He would have been too far to see anything else."

"Well, that settles it then . . ." Rihards said.

Now the vehicle truly began to fly, and Gustavs found himself digging his fingers into the seat cushion. The car whipped along the road, and he pinched his eyes shut as Rihards swerved around a broken-down wagon. The suburbs had given way to farmland in a matter of moments, a dark landscape of shorn wheat fields and freshly cultivated earth. Away from the city, the stars flickered majestically in the night sky.

"Ready?" Rihards asked.

Zāra stared straight ahead, and nodded.

Gustavs never saw the approaching curve. Rihards swung the car heavily to the right, tires kicking up clouds of dust as they spun onto an unpaved road. He killed the lights, and they plunged headlong into darkness, the twin beams from behind yet to follow. Zāra climbed overtop of Rihards, taking the wheel as the big man shifted to his right, keeping one leg on the floor.

"Got it?"

"Got it."

Gustavs felt the pedal lift for only a moment, before Zāra slammed it back down with aplomb. She looked over at Rihards, who kissed her firmly on the forehead, hesitated only a moment, before throwing open the passenger door and leaping from the vehicle.

Gustavs gasped and snapped his head around just as the head-lights reappeared behind them, bathing the car in a yellow glow. When he looked frontward once more, he saw the stretch of dirt road coming to an abrupt end. It petered out into an abandoned farmstead—a barn with a sagging roof, a mound of timber, the rusted shell of an automobile, overgrown with weeds.

Zāra stood on the brakes, turning the wheel with both hands, the car skidding across the loose ground much as Gustavs slid across the backseat into the side paneling.

"What are you doing?" he cried out.

"Do what I say," she said, the car rocking to a halt in a churning cloud of dust. "Get out of the car."

TWENTY-FOUR

The air was still and smelled faintly of manure. Field crickets trilled in the darkness. At the near horizon, obscure as it was, the forest leaves were changing colour, though Gustavs was certain he wouldn't live to admire them in the daylight. He felt strangely at ease, as if his mind had exhausted itself of all worry, of all fear; unwittingly maneuvered throughout the night, closer and closer to inevitability by forces far greater than himself.

He stood, squinting and averting his eyes from the piercing headlights that now shone, stationary, only a few feet away; a haze of dust drifting steadily closer from the sudden halt of the onrushing vehicle. Zāra was beside him—statuesque, arms raised high. The yellow beams cast an unwelcome spotlight on the pair of them amidst fields of umber and forests of shadow, while Gustavs contemplated the ironic comforts of futility.

The man emerged from the car in a rage, bellowing something in Russian, a tirade of guttural Slavic. They could hardly see him—only the flash and strobe of a silhouette as he stepped in front of the car, an ominous contour and the unmistakable shape of metal in his hand.

It was deeply poetic, Gustavs thought, that it would be here. That after everything, this would be the place. The blood of how many thousands had soaked the earth beneath his feet? Why not his own? Here, in *Vidzeme*. As good a place as any. Better.

The man shouted once more, incensed, his voice rising in pitch, and he lifted the pistol as he moved in their direction. Gustavs couldn't make out the barrel in the darkness, but tensed at the silhouette's every motion—the shift in his shoulders, his arm raised, flexed. He exhaled and forced his eyes shut, the headlights now a soothing, celestial glow. Heaven on earth; the lights beckoned him. The moment was endless, and he waited to be summoned by seraphim. He waited, at ease with the tremors that continued to spread throughout his limbs, and thought of Anna. What would she say, up there in the vast, night sky? *Silly boy*, she would tease. *How did you ever manage this?*

A gunshot split the air. Gustavs flinched, Zāra screamed. Next to him, the muffled sound of a body slumping into the dirt. Gustavs kept his eyes closed, glimpsing constellations. He clenched his teeth, grinding his molars together, awaiting his turn. *Get on with it. Goddamn you, just get on with it.*

Then, another scream, a different intonation this time—a shriek of frustration. A curse, in fact. Gustavs, still trembling, allowed himself to peer out, a pinched expression knotting his face. Zāra remained beside him, upright, hands on her hips, steadying her breathing.

"Jesus, Rihard . . ." she exclaimed.

"Are you hit?"

She exhaled, then shook her head.

Gustavs opened his eyes wider, and through the glare spotted Rihards, his muscular frame blotting out the headlights like an eclipse. In his left hand, he held what appeared to be a long, tapered spade. The man with the gun lay motionless on the ground, and Rihards ducked down to retrieve the weapon a few feet away.

Then Zāra was facing him. She had him by the shoulders. "Gustav. Gustav, listen to me." Now she held his chin. "Look at me. Listen to my voice. Are you hit?" She shook him for good measure. "Gustav?"

"He'll be alright in a minute," Rihards called in response.

Zāra gave him a quick pat down, ran her hands up the inside of his coat. She locked eyes with him and nodded. "You're alright. Now breathe. Just breathe."

His heart rate began to steady, reality descending as he watched Zāra march up to Rihards and strike him on the chest. "Unbelievable!" she cried out.

Rihards shrugged. "I couldn't find the shovel."

"Couldn't *find*?"

"I miscounted"—he half-turned and motioned sheepishly down the road—"I miscounted the posts."

"You . . . " She didn't finish, but smacked his chest once more for good measure, then sighed and hung her head. "You're an oaf, you know that. A big, dumb, loveable oaf."

"Alright, alright." Rihards held the Makarov in his hand, removed and examined the magazine, shoved it back into the frame and tucked the pistol by his lower back. "Forgive me?"

Gustavs observed this exchange as the tremors slowly dissipated, allowing him to finally depart his purgatory and rejoin the living. Gradually, he made his way over to the body where Rihards and Zāra were on their haunches, rifling through the man's pockets.

Gustavs picked up the spade and cleared his throat. "Where should we . . ." He gazed out into the rolling fields, his voice wavering. "I can start digging . . ."

Rihards and Zāra exchanged a look.

"He's not fucking dead," Rihards said. Then, to Zāra, "Where did you find this guy?"

Zāra smiled at Gustavs, watching the relief sweep over his face. "He's only taking a rest Gustav, not to worry. His hair might be a little out of place in the morning, but he'll live. We're not murderers."

"Right," he said.

"But, you can give Rihards a hand here . . ."

Rihards had already bound the man's wrists and feet with a length of rope, and was presently removing a cloth from his pocket to use as a gag. "Grab his feet," he said, and the two men hoisted the body just as Zāra started up the car. She pulled forward and slowly drove off toward the barn in the distance.

"We're taking this one," Rihards said, inclining his head toward the black Zhiguli. "Less likely to be stopped in this boat."

Once they had maneuvered the body into the trunk, Rihards stuffed the gag into the man's mouth, tied it off and slammed the lid. The three of them piled into their new vehicle—a dark, leather interior scented with American cigarettes and cheap cologne—and Rihards revved the engine before wheeling around and down the road, back toward the city.

"There's no question it was Dāvids," Zāra was saying, "but these two, it's not so clear. We have the Chekists to contend with, of course, but"—she looked to Rihards—"there would have been more of them, no?"

Rihards shrugged. "Hard to say."

"They're a clever bunch, the new Chekists. Well-educated, most of them with great aspirations in the Party. In the old days, back when my parents were active, they were mostly thugs like these two. But now, things are changing."

"Many of them prefer not to get their hands dirty," Rihards added.

"I'll admit, for a minute there . . ." Zāra left the thought unspoken. "But they don't seem like the type. Regardless, the KGB rely a great deal on their informants—Intourist guides, street toughs, lower-level operatives. These types don't shy away from earning an extra ruble or two and often, because of that, their information can be suspect. Usually out of greed, other times out of fear. Often it all gets muddied going up the chain of command, far as we can tell. Conflated. Embellished. Sometimes we get the sense they're victims of their own networks; too much information, and no one to sift through all the noise." Zāra tilted her neck to the side with a slight grimace, massaging behind her ear. "There are also vigilantes, you can call them. Gangs that will happily turn over their own mothers for a reward. It's difficult to keep track of it all."

Gustavs nodded along. "What will happen to Dāvids?"

"He hasn't outlived his usefulness just yet. Ieva keeps a close eye on him. Apparently he was already quite suspicious of you. Just generally or something more, we're not certain. She's a clever one, our Ieva. He likes to use her telephone, believes it's secure. She's just a pretty young thing, after all—what would she know? Apparently, there's been escalating talk about the forbidden zone on the coast."

"In Kurzeme? The border."

"Yes, but not just our border, of course, the Soviet Union's border." Zāra twisted in her seat to face him, drawing a map in her palm with a finger. "From Kolkas Rags down past Liepāja, for about three miles inland, it's a military zone. Closed off to outsiders. They're absolutely paranoid about this entire area."

"And Dāvids thinks I'm, what, part of some . . . operation?"

"To say that Dāvids *thinks* might already be giving him too much credit. Still, if there were any witnesses tonight, it works well in our favour. It would make perfect sense as a decoy—you driving west away from Rīga, toward the sea."

The city skyline came into view, church spires rising black against an indigo sky as they traversed the bridge. The fog had thickened, rising up from the Daugava and spilling over the embankment onto the streets.

"Won't they come for the Liepas?" Gustavs asked.

"As I said, Dāvids hasn't completely outlived his purpose. They will come for Vītols, yes, but he's not new to this. He will tell them all about Dāvids, about how it was *his* idea to bring you, a foreign operative, into his home. He will tell them about his outrage, and how he drove the pair of you from his house after discovering the truth. That Dāvids has been a double agent the entire time. And he will have everyone at the dinner as witnesses."

"You mean his family"—Gustavs shook his head—"they won't believe him."

"No, they won't. But they may change their minds when they find one of their own hogtied in his trunk." Zāra's eyes twinkled for a moment, and Gustavs realized it was the first time he'd ever seen her look pleased. She turned back around, facing the front.

"Believe me, this isn't how any of us envisioned tonight. As I said, our plans often work best with contingencies. By the time they—Rihard . . . Rihard!"

The crash of metal was deafening and Gustavs was thrown against the front seat. The sudden thunder was accompanied by the sound of shattered glass tinkling across the asphalt; the silence thereafter broken only by the low hiss of a tea kettle. Dazed, Gustavs untangled himself and climbed back into his seat, wincing as he rubbed the back of his neck, tender to the touch. Zāra and

Rihards composed themselves—he, rolling his head on his shoulders, then looking to Zāra, brushing her hair aside as she nodded. Before them lay the wreck of a gleaming black GAZ-13 Chaika, its chrome grill twisted inwards beneath a buckled hood, plumes of steam billowing upwards into the sky.

"Shit," mouthed Zāra.

The three of them sat perfectly still, squinting through smoke and fog as someone slammed the horn and raged inside the vehicle.

"What do we do?" asked Gustavs.

"Nothing yet," replied Zāra.

"That doesn't look like a taxi . . ."

"It isn't," said Rihards.

The driver side door flew open and a man emerged in a fury. The uniform blazed with starred epaulets and collar flashes, while a succession of medals gleamed, dangling from coloured ribbon along his left breast. He was an older man with a standard military hair cut—closely shorn and fully grey—while his cheeks were as red as a May Day banner.

"That's no chauffeur," Rihards said.

Zāra shook her head.

"Wait, look," said Gustavs, pointing. "The passenger."

They leaned forward and peered into the havoc, spotting a woman with waves of vanilla blonde hair and a shimmering necklace. She was coughing, waving away the fumes before her.

Rihards flung open the door. "No, no!" Zāra cried out in vain, grasping at his shirt sleeve. The officer, meanwhile, was convulsive in the night air—pointing and shouting in equal measure—eventually stomping imperiously toward their vehicle. Rihards calmly walked over to meet him, while Gustavs and Zāra looked on in horror.

The officer—though in all likelihood, some sort of colonel—berated Rihards, gesticulating wildly, thrusting outstretched hands toward the wreckage. Rihards approached timidly—open palms and supplicant nods—and hardly broke stride before drawing back his hand and smacking the officer across the mouth. The woman screamed from the Chaika as the officer stumbled against the hood of the car, gazing up at the towering *zemnieks* with a look of bewilderment.

Rihards grabbed hold of the man, frogmarching him around the vehicle as the woman emerged on the other side, a gentle breeze stirring her hair, a sheer ivory slip clinging to her buxom figure. Rihards took him by the scruff of the collar and drove his head against the roof of the car. Unsatisfied, he slammed it forwards once more, blood spurting from the officer's mouth onto his immaculate uniform. The woman shrieked in the middle of the road, hands drawn up to her mouth.

Gustavs and Zāra sat without a word, looking on in disbelief. The officer's legs buckled as he was suddenly yanked backwards, Rihards still clutching his collar and dragging him, stumbling to the edge of the embankment. The man continued to sputter, voicing his opposition in panicked grunts but seemingly unable to conjure any words. He was still in a daze when Rihards reached a powerful arm down beneath his legs, hoisting him up into the air.

"Oh my God . . ." whispered Zāra.

Rihards took two purposeful steps, gathering momentum before pitching the man over the side of the railing. The tangle of limbs vanished from sight, followed by a moment of suspended silence before a voice rang out and was swallowed up by a distant splash.

The woman screamed, first out of shock and then, doubled over, out of desperate intent. Rihards quieted her with an outstretched arm, pointing at her menacingly from across the way, his features chiseled out of stone. "Moonlight swim?"

Eyes wide, the woman clutched her pearls and took a moment before shaking her head, shivering in the middle of the empty street. Rihards paused, only just, ensuring that she understood, then marched swiftly back to the car, slumping into the driver's seat. He stared straight ahead, and sighed contentedly. "What a night."

"Will you drive already!" Zāra shouted. "Drive!"

Rihards reversed the Zhiguli from the wreckage, a piece of chrome clattering onto the road, the tires squealing as they roared forward and down the center of a wide lane. Gustavs swiveled in his seat to look back through the windshield. The woman was in hysterics, though he could no longer hear her over the sound of the engine. She paced on the spot, tousled blonde curls and chiffon negligée, while behind her, the Chaika trailed plumes of smoke. Rihards swung left down a side street, and she disappeared from view.

TWENTY-FIVE

Idling beneath the linden trees of a small courtyard, Rihards switched off the engine, plunging the vehicle and its surroundings into silence. For a time, the engine continued to rattle and wheeze from the evening's exertions.

In the passenger seat, Zāra turned to face Gustavs. "It should go without saying, but—you're on the first train out in the morning. *This* morning."

Gustavs nodded his agreement.

"For this to have any chance of working, you need to be gone. Which won't paint you in the best light, but it's necessary, you understand. You won't be able to return. Vītols will say that he witnessed Dāvids helping you get out. That when they grabbed you, it was Dāvids who drove the getaway car, and helped you escape."

"They saw my face," Gustavs said.

"They never saw mine," said Rihards. "Neither of them. All they know is there was a driver."

"For now," continued Zāra, "Dāvids likely still believes you're somewhere on route to the coast. It should give you enough time to board the first train back to Tallinn, and the first ferry out."

"They saw my face," Gustavs repeated.

"This one," Zāra motioned with her chin to the trunk, "he did, certainly. But he's not going anywhere until you're gone. The other man . . . tell me what happened, exactly."

Gustavs sifted through his memory, cobbling the images together. "It happened so fast. Everything is a blur. I can't say for certain."

"The man we fought, he was the one who grabbed you."

"Yes."

"And this one here was the driver," Rihards said. "When he arrived, you were, what—still walking? Or did they already have the bag over your head?"

Gustavs took his time, then spoke ruefully: "I took it off . . ."

"There's no guarantees, Gustav, you knew that," said Zāra. "But I don't mind the odds. The man who grabbed you, in the dark, he might have seen you for a moment, if that, before you got away, correct?"

"Yes."

"If the situation were reversed, do you think you could identify him?"

Gustavs thought about it, then shook his head.

"Well, there you are."

"Best not to dwell on it," Rihards added. "Good odds are the best certainties we have."

"I'm more worried about Vītols," Gustavs said. "And the Liepas."

Rihards shifted in his seat. "Listen, your sentiments are appreciated, so don't take this the wrong way—the information you've been given is quite valuable. Trust me. Even I don't know what it is, and that says a lot. Still, I'd be risking your neck long before I would put anyone from that family in danger, you understand? You're alright, Gustav, but you're not exactly my first priority. If you ask me, anyone can wear that damn coat of yours."

"Strangely, that's actually quite comforting."

"You might have noticed, Dāvids also—"

Rihards was cut off by a thumping sound echoing from the trunk. The three of them went quiet, all turning to stare at the boot of the vehicle. Another thump, followed by muffled rustling.

Rihards' brows flicked upwards and he sighed irritably. The thumping continued as he stepped out of the vehicle, rounded the back, and opened the trunk, obscuring the view from inside. Suddenly there was a rather loud, cracking sound, followed by a heavy thud. The rustling stopped. Rihards carefully closed the lid and returned to his seat, wiping his knuckles with an oily rag.

"As I was saying, you might have noticed that Dāvids wears some diabolical aftershave. He had it on tonight at dinner."

Gustavs was still looking at the rag. "I did, yes."

"A gift from Ieva, soon as we found out that he was less than reliable."

Gustavs looked puzzled.

"This one here," Rihards poked a thumb at the trunk, "we'll take back to the farm, knock him around a little bit. Nothing too serious. But not before I douse myself in that aftershave. He'll be blindfolded, of course, like you were, so, less senses to work with. There'll be no mistaking that scent in a barn full of pig shit"— Rihards frowned—"well, maybe not . . ."

Gustavs nodded his understanding.

"That, and when he turns up in Dāvids' car, there's only so much evidence even the Chekists can ignore."

Gustavs sighed. "So, what happens now?"

"Now you walk straight back to your hotel," said Zāra, "and make sure that brute at the front door knows what a great evening you had." She reached back and wiped the corner of his mouth with her thumb. He pulled away, taking a deep breath.

"Alright." Gustavs smiled meekly, then opened the door, stepping out into the night.

"Hey," Zāra called out, rolling down her window.

Gustavs turned to look back.

"You did well." Next to her, Rihards leaned forward and winked, a surprising bit of warmth from the stern *zemnieks*.

Gustavs wasn't feeling particularly appreciative, and then noted that he didn't really *feel* like anything at all. He said nothing, merely turned and winced at the throbbing pain in his knee. He stepped gingerly out of the darkness, and struggled to mask his limp as he traversed the courtyard.

It wasn't a long walk back to the hotel, though the streets were better lit than in *Vecrīga*, and the occasional passing vehicle calmed his nerves. At least, that's what he told himself. He channeled his anxiety into the transformation: the uncertain shuffle, the heavy lids, a slow blink to accentuate the self-satisfied smirk that he pasted onto his face. He spotted the doorman from across the street, standing idly in the glow of the hotel entrance. The man was immense, wearing a baggy, black suit, and had a head the size of a harvest pumpkin. Gustavs crossed—a casual, lilting stride—no longer the nervous academy director, but a savvy business entrepreneur, fresh and unashamed from his most recent misdeeds.

"*Dobryy vecher*," Gustavs slurred, the Russian passable with an almost theatrical nonchalance. The smirk spread the width of his face.

The doorman reciprocated with the slightest of nods, massive hands like pork hocks folded in front.

"I apologize, my Russian, is not so . . . *khorosho*," he said, chuckling at his own little jest. "Your language, it's so very difficult for me, but, your women . . . well," he blew out his cheeks, "my hat is off to you, my good sir." Gustavs found himself bowing much the same way as the homeless man had done earlier. He rolled his eyes—the smitten drunkard—and slowly, made as if to keep walking. *Enough? Another breadcrumb?*

The giant seemed to take note of the man before him, a thick fold of skin creasing between his small eyes. He pulled his shoulders back and shifted his weight. "You have good night, yes?"

"Good?"—Gustavs waved this away—"Good? Hah! I'm telling you, this girl . . . I feel like a new man. Reborn!" Gustavs smacked his chest for good measure.

The giant grinned, the conversation taking a pleasantly unexpected turn.

"You know she, well," he chuckled, shook his head. *Oh no, I can't even say it.*

"Russian girl, is best you know. Yes?"

Gustavs mimed an hourglass with his hands, palms smoothing the air. "Russian," he lowered his voice to a whisper, "and *crazy*." He laughed, and the giant followed suit, thick lips spreading to reveal two uneven rows of nubby teeth.

"Where you find girl like this?" the giant asked.

"My God"—he let out another sigh, shaking his head—"the father, he's going to kill me, you know."

The giant crossed his arms in front of his chest. "Daughter?"

"His youngest. She couldn't keep her hands off me! What can I do? I am only a man, only flesh and blood!"

The giant chuckled at this, his figure relaxing, enjoying the company of his new guest.

Gustavs was on the stage now, the spotlight demanding his theatre. He thought of Zāra. "She was petite, you know. Small. But such energy. And you know what we say, of course, 'good things come in small packages,' isn't that right?"

This was lost on the giant, a puzzled gaze as the maxim went sailing overtop of his massive skull. Gustavs quickly recovered. "So much energy, this one. Insatiable, she was. Couldn't get enough. More. More. And you know what?"

The giant was eager. "*Chto* . . ."

"She told me she's the quiet one in her group of friends, can you believe it?" Gustavs guffawed, dramatically wiping the lipstick from his mouth. He glanced at the red smear on his palm, then, wide-eyed, showed it to the doorman. Their eyebrows pitched in unison, the pair chuckling again.

The giant grinned and leaned in. "Perhaps, your girl, she has friend?"

Gustavs' turn to lean in, two old friends conspiring. "I can certainly ask," he said with a wink. The giant rumbled with laughter. Gustavs started toward the door, then said, "I'm going to see her again Thursday night."

"*Thoors-day.*"

"*Da.* I'll tell her to bring a girlfriend."

"I like big girls. I am big man, small girl is no good for me," the giant replied, confidently hiking up his pants.

Gustavs smiled broadly. "*Do svidaniya.*"

The giant gave an approving nod to his new friend, and directed his attention back to the street.

Stepping forward into the hotel lobby, the muted sounds of ABBA resonated from the nightclub doors. Gustavs could hardly have been more pleased with himself. For the briefest of moments, the fear had subsided, only to be replaced with near immediacy by way of a familiar figure—the ever-present mustachioed gentleman from the café. It seemed as if he were a permanent fixture of the hotel, much as the tinted sunglasses were a permanent feature of his face, even well after dark.

"Good evening!" the man exclaimed, a voice bursting with surprise. *My, such a coincidence! Can you believe it?*

"Oh yes, yes hello, how are you?"

The lobby. The café. Here, now, at this hour. Gustavs stole a quick glance at the newspaper in his hands, curious to see if it was the same edition from the morning.

"Wonderful! How is your family? They are well?"

A good memory, this one. "Yes, thank you, very well."

"But the night is young, I think, no?" The man grinned from behind his jaune lenses, and Gustavs began to accept that there would be no getting away from him this time. Another alibi wouldn't hurt, and so, slowly he retreated back into his heavily soused persona.

"Of course, I was just thinking so . . ."

"Aha! Let us have drink then, yes? Some wodka, good for your soul," he said, clapping Gustavs on the back. *Old friends, reunited.* "The nightclub, is good one, what do you think?" Here followed a most uncomfortable little dance manoeuvre—head bobbing, thumbs jabbing at the air as he gnawed his lower lip.

"If they have vodka, it must be a good nightclub," Gustavs replied.

What hilarity! The man tossed his head back and guffawed. "Come, come, let me show you how we live here in Riga! I am Arseny."

"Gustavs."

"Ah—you are Gustavs, and you are *welcome*." Another hearty laugh from his enthusiastic friend, and Gustavs was ushered through a set of doors into the blaring rhythms of Swedish disco.

Why Arseny had chosen a *diskotek*, as he called it, was unclear; the two men could barely hear one another over the speakers. The clientele was undeniably suspect, and Gustavs wondered how many of the women were honeytraps, dancing provocatively with KGB stooges and all manner of unsavoury characters. The dance crowd swung and gyrated eccentrically to thrusting basslines and synthesizers, while Arseny plied him with drink. The pair drained their glasses with an accompaniment of dill pickles and black bread. It wasn't long before Gustavs no longer had to imitate the mumbles of a drunkard, the vodka flushing his cheeks and warming him from within. It also helped to dull the whispers of his subconscious, forever warning him, spurring him onwards. *Run. Why on earth are you still sitting here? Run.*

Arseny was relentless, and possessed all the subtlety of a KV-1 tank. He shouted his casual inquiries over the booming loudspeakers, increasingly frustrated with his foreign guest who insisted, just as ardently, on forever guiding the conversation back to women and booze. Gustavs was wary about getting too drunk, but soon became just as concerned about the bar tab, wondering if it was a "favour" to later be leveraged against him.

Their waitress—a slim girl with a dated bouffant hairstyle— was quick to refill their glasses, and an aspiring starlet herself. She tilted the bottle with a strange slack-jawed expression—Gustavs presumed the intent to be provocative—as if the splash of vodka were somehow erotic. Glasses refreshed, she would giggle breathlessly at the pair of them, mouth still open, as if cresting toward orgasm. *What a pair of naughty boys you are!*

"You like? Good service, yes?" commented Arseny as he smoked his cigarette with flair, swinging his arm to and fro like a windmill, trying, rather unsuccessfully, to blow smoke rings. And then, the most casual of shrugs, and another harmless question for his guest: Would he be returning to the Soviet Union for future business? Perhaps some of his associates might be traveling? And what about his family, surely they would be keen on returning home one day soon?

Tipsy and increasingly lightheaded, Gustavs experienced a brief moment of panic when he considered what else might have been in his drink, though Arseny was clearly imbibing from the same bottle. He could feel the man probing around, burrowing like a rodent, sniffing out the perfect little crevasse to grant him access.

How best to approach this foreigner—was he weak? Lonely? A woman, potentially. The man was certainly interested in those, what with the faint smudge of lipstick staining his chin. But no, not tonight. A need already satisfied. Perhaps, angry? A bitter man. Overlooked in the workplace, unappreciated—they fail to acknowledge his contributions, fail to recognize him for all he does. A sense of purpose, then, a shot to the ego coupled with the sweet tonic of revenge. Or was he merely misguided—a deluded patriot, just another descendant of bourgeois nationalists. Blackmail, then. Forever effective. A hand to be forced.

The music slowed and a Russian love song cleared the dance floor but for the couples that embraced one another, sweaty, leaning into themselves. Gustavs also fell into the melancholia of the hopeless romantic, ignoring Arseny now as he longed for a nameless love. With a shirtsleeve he wiped the vodka from his chin, then stuffed the majority of a pickle into his mouth, coughing as he choked on the vinegar. This misery went on for a time, and the routine seemed to work on Arseny, who grew visibly weary, clearly annoyed that he had waited all day for such a promising opportunity. Gustavs, for his part, couldn't make heads or tails of the man, whether the entire charade was screening for recruitment, or simply a siphoning of information. He forced away thoughts that it had anything to do with *Vecrīga,* or the farm, or with Bonnie and Clyde, wherever they were in the commandeered Zhiguli.

At last, Gustavs slumped further down into his seat, humming along to the slow melody, lulled into a shallow slumber by alcohol and heartache and a drunkard's regret. Arseny didn't press for much longer, eventually rising to shake him by the shoulder.

"*Na Zdrovie!*" Gustavs blurted out, jolted back to life.

"I think it is enough for tonight, my friend," Arseny replied.

Gustavs waved his hand about with a frown, then reached for his glass, spilling it over his fingers. "*Na Zdrovie . . .*"

"*Da, da,*" Arseny said, patting him once more, and left.

Gustavs remained in his seat for a time, the music picking up once more, and when it did, the room began to spin. He rose unsteadily, which was no act at all, and started for the doors. He meandered through the lobby and, once upstairs, stumbled past the *babushka.* The same one? Who knew. She scowled, whoever she was, a woman the shape of a potato wrapped in a drab kerchief. And for the second time in as many nights, Gustavs slumped onto the bed with coat and shoes, and embraced the darkness.

Outside, the night air was cool, the temperature dropping rapidly in the late hour. Just a few feet beyond the hotel entrance, the doorman noted his breath had begun to steam before him, and soon found himself buttoning his coat. Tugging at a loose thread, his attention was drawn to the staccato sound of bootheels approaching from the walkway to his left. A young woman, alone and looking rather timid, stopped just short of the entrance and stared up at the towering complex. The doorman observed her slight figure, her innocent eyes and hesitation, the chestnut hair, freshly combed and tumbling down to her lower back. A lost little lamb.

"Good evening, young lady," he spoke in Russian. "A little late to be out, no?"

"Oh . . . well, no—it's just," the woman searched for the words, flustered. "Did . . . a man come by, recently? I mean, erm, a businessman, he was."

"Many businessmen at this hotel, my dear."

She smiled, embarrassed. "Of course. But, this one"—gazing dreamily up at the hotel—"he was from *Canada*," she emphasized the word. "With dark hair, and glasses . . . a very handsome man." She shied away, tucking her chin into her collar.

"Ahh," said the doorman knowingly, "I believe I do remember such a man. Handsome, indeed." As the woman blushed, he let his imagination peek beneath her heavy coat, and there it wandered awhile. *Lucky man*, he thought to himself. Had he paid closer attention, he might have noticed the shock of blonde hair that had come free beneath her dark bangs.

The woman chewed her lip for a moment, gazing upwards, then sighed. "No, no I shouldn't . . ."

"Shouldn't what, my dear?"

"Could you please, I mean, if you would be so kind . . . If you see him, tell him that Natalya was here. Could you do that?"

"Natalya, such a beautiful name for an angel such as yourself."

The ingenue flushed once more, a modest giggle. She glanced

up at the hotel once more, then took a couple of steps back before turning on her heel.

"You're welcome," the doorman said, probing.

"Thank you!" she called back, her voice carried off by the rush of a passing taxi. The doorman puffed out his chest once again, folding his hands before him. A grin tugged at his thick lips. "Thursday," he whispered to himself. "Thursday."

Gustavs slept fitfully. He managed a few minutes, here and there, woken by sudden bouts of fear and trepidation, drenched in sweat. At one point, roused by nausea on this occasion, he tugged at his cool, damp shirt, pulling it over his head before finally succumbing to rest for perhaps an hour, maybe less. And as he wrestled with capricious slumber, beyond the open drapes crept the first signs of dawn; the odd chirp of a spritely wagtail, the sky brightening into a deep shade of Prussian blue.

In the silent paranoia of his hotel room Gustavs waited, and waited still. And yet, nothing happened. There was no knock at the door, no ring of the telephone. His suitcase sat, idle, neatly packed at the foot of the bed. The fear remained, of course, saturating his mind, building gradually to some unforeseen crescendo just beyond the horizon where he would surely encounter his fate. Shadowy figures taunting him now, allowing, *encouraging* his mind to explore every grim possibility.

One summer afternoon, when Gustavs was only a child, he had observed their kitten Minka capture a small field mouse in the backyard. Time moved differently then, but Gustavs remembered the day clearly, sitting for what seemed like hours as Minka toyed with her captive—stomping its wriggling tail, gnawing its ears, tossing her prey into the sky—only to bat it out of the air with a nimble paw. At times, Minka would relent, the mouse given respite and allowed to lie, disheveled, limbs twitching in the matted grass. Sometimes it would feign death, laying completely still. And then, it would slowly gather itself, beady black eyes sensing opportunity, freedom just beyond the long grass beneath the hedges. It would shuffle an inch, and then another, limping toward the fence line in desperation, only to be trounced from above once again.

And seated on the edge of the bed, Gustavs, for all his want, could not be rid of that memory.

Amassing all the courage of which he was capable and, spurred on more by impatience than bravura, Gustavs finally ventured outside with a granular squint, a pair of taxis already parked out front. His driver stared with puffy eyes in the rear view mirror and said, "Central Station?," to which Gustavs, dry mouthed, simply nodded.

The foreign streets drifted past in the window, a Russian talk show murmured from the speakers. It was only when Gustavs glimpsed the train station that he noted, with the same prickly unease, that still nothing had occurred. Once inside, he purchased a ticket on the return passage to Tallinn, and stood off to one side of the platform, clammy hands wringing the suitcase handle like a wet rag.

Here, there was no one beyond suspicion. He eyed the young mother in the knit sweater, pushing her pram. She must have felt his gaze, glancing up, guarded eyes enveloped in blue eyeshadow. He turned his attention to a pair of men, slick as car salesmen with greasy hair and threadbare suits. Another gentleman with a combover and carrying a doctor's bag, minding his own business a bit too much. Deep in thought. Why did he never look up? A teenaged girl with fiery red braids looked over and smiled at him, a miniature bouquet of daisies in her hand. *Goddamn them all, wolves in sheep's clothing.*

Surely they had only let him get this far to observe his movements, to see where else he might lead them. And to *whom*. A last-minute dead drop. A brush pass within the crowd. Watching from afar, biding their time. All the time in the world. They could make him wait as it pleased them, the psychology as potent as anything. One's imagination the true oppressor now. Aleksandrs, snatched out of nowhere. And last night—how did they know? Dāvids. And how did *he* know? They were omnipotent. And they had him. Here, not only a prisoner in their police state, but reduced to imprisonment within his own mind.

Suddenly the air was stagnant, suffocating, and Gustavs struggled to draw breath. He gasped at the thin air until the breaths came faster, and faster still, his chest seizing without relief. He backed himself against the wall, clutching a palm to his breast. It thumped like a piston. Tunnel vision, the dark vignette closing in from all sides like a black hole, a vortex swiftly enclosing. Still he gasped. His legs gave way, soft and malleable, as he slid down the wall to the cold concrete.

A woman before him now, the mother with the blue eyeshadow. A worried look on her face. She called out to someone. *No. No attention, please.* She opened his coat, pinned his hand against his chest. What a silly face she was making. Her lips contorted, a concentrated grimace as she forced the air through her nose, shoulders rising and falling, breathing heavily. Deep breaths. *Deep breaths.* Gustavs followed suit, inhaling through his nostrils. Longer breaths. Slower breaths. The woman was nodding. Gustavs swallowed, felt the wet on his cheeks, his forehead. Her expression shifted, changed. A question puckering her brow. After a moment, he began to nod.

A strong arm reached beneath his armpit, and she helped him to his feet. As Gustavs gathered himself, he noted a few onlookers, curious more than concerned, wondering if he were about to drop dead on the spot. *An anecdote for a dinner party.* Eventually they lost interest, and Gustavs, wiping the damp from his face, resolved that he would not die here at the train station after all. Acknowledged that Death had not called upon him just yet—perhaps only waved from afar, a subtle reminder. Nothing more than a gentle prick with his scythe.

The event was so draining that Gustavs could only lean against a post while awaiting the train and contemplate the inevitable intervention, playing out every possible scenario until his ruminations became certainty. And still, *and still* . . . nothing happened. Not aboard the train, not in Tallinn. Not at Baltic Station, disembarking with the crowd, nor waiting in line for a taxi, shoulders tensing with every commuter that brushed his coat. Not at the border, at exit control, not aboard the gangplank of the ferry where the mist of saltwater tasted sublime. By the time he arrived in Helsinki, he was so thoroughly exhausted that he almost missed his flight. He was suddenly jolted awake by a flight attendant who, with her stern expression and chestnut bun reminded him of Renata, standing over him, gently shook his shoulder. "Sir? The flight is now boarding."

Gustavs cleared his throat and nodded, dumbly, as if he had just then been dropped from the sky and into an airport terminal. Somewhere, midway over the Atlantic, the plane encountered a rough patch of turbulence, and an unfortunate woman in an aisle seat ended up with hot tea in her lap. The ensuing commotion woke a great many passengers aboard, with the exception of one particular vodka merchant a few rows back—eyes closed, mouth agape—for whom the disturbance went entirely, and blissfully, unnoticed.

In Rīga, the elegant façade of the *Stūru Māja* was basked in a certain light, reflecting a soft, red dawn. Inside, there was a gentle double-knock on an office door, and a young man in an immaculately pressed uniform poked his head into the room. He held a teacup and saucer in hand. "Comrade Chairman?"

"Mm," hummed Zharkov, still facing the window. The young man obliged, promptly crossing the room, handing Zharkov his tea and retreating just as swiftly, closing the door behind him. Best to make oneself scarce, the young man thought, at times like these.

Tendrils of steam curled into the air as Zharkov idly stirred his cup, the scent of strong, black tea mingling with sweet notes of melted, blackcurrant jam. Too much work to be done. Too many fleas to smoke out into the open. It had been a month, now, since the protests at the Freedom Monument, and word had it that the Letts would be at it again soon. When was it—the 18th, they had said. Yes, the 18th. The briefings claiming that it would likely be more of the same. Crowds cheering and chanting, defying officer orders in the bloody streets. Chaos. Singing songs and laying flowers to glorify a past of, what—fascist rule? Of subjugation, pinned beneath the stiff boot of capitalism?

Ingrates! Ingrates with their revisionist history. And the same with those gutless worms in Moscow, passing themselves off as Communists. How dare they wear such insignia, how dare they stand before our colours. And without shame! Those ready to abandon, to disregard the blood and sweat of patriots who fought to build socialism! *International* socialism, as Marx had intended, and yet they lack the wherewithal to ensure order within their own state. Zharkov turned with a sigh, facing the portraits on the wall. "If you could only see what we have become . . ."

They had arrested hundreds the last time, militia stationed at every intersection, blockades set up and still they came and laid their wreaths, sang their pagan hymns. Open defiance of the regime and still, not enough? Not enough to warrant reprimand? Hostile agents in our very midst and still, we cower. For fear that, what—that film actor in Washington might powder himself in more rouge and spout further bigotry. The devil with all of them!

Zharkov took a sip of tea, strong with a hint of sweet. He felt adrift, lost in a barren sea, the ice having suddenly vanished beneath his feet. Vadim had his orders, and there was no doubting his loyalty, but how many dependable men could even be found? Truly, from the Baltic to the Bering—a handful, if that.

And now, this. On top of everything, as if sewing the fields with salt. Not that he particularly liked the man, his station be damned. A hardline reputation, but a soft middle. A lack of bite, a lack of gall. An orator, well versed in delivering impassioned speeches in dining halls—as if this were a novelty—but not much else. Still, pneumonia, they feared. And at his age . . . Pulled from his vehicle and tossed into the Dvina like some common vagrant. *In my very own city!* An unparalleled level of civil disobedience.

They were out of control, the lot of them, simply that. And far worse, there would be no denying it. For that is exactly what the reports would say, the murmurs back to Moscow: *"Zharkov may no longer be up to the task . . . Zharkov has unclenched his iron fist . . . Age has dulled Comrade Zharkov's revolutionary spirit . . ."*

He gritted his teeth. Who would dare—who would dare,

indeed! When it was he who remained as the sole vanguard on this Western coast, the watcher at the gates. While miles away, nothing more than contradictions amongst the lot of them, unwilling to do what needed to be done. Without the stomach for it, without the will. He would be damned if he succumbed to these political games, this pandering to the international community. The blood of the old guard ran thicker still. There was no retreat in Voronezh, and he would give no quarter now.

Let them come. Let them demonstrate once more. The leaders of this . . . this Helsinki group will be rounded up, and we will see what happens to the serpent when its head is cut. Their placards will burn. They will sing not for freedom, but for mercy beneath the shadow of our raised truncheons. We will lock the entire city away if we must, for the 18th shall be a day of reckoning.

TWENTY-SIX

A STORM HAD DELAYED THEIR ARRIVAL IN TORONTO, AND DURING the final descent Gustavs gazed out through the darkening sky at the world below, a haze of bright, shimmering cityscape, rivulets streaming down the porthole window.

Passing through customs, Gustavs noted that he wasn't entirely relieved to be home. The city felt foreign now, almost unfamiliar, had become something else entirely—menacing, rather than comforting—now that he was privy to certain realities. A city full of secrets that one desperately wished to know. Secrets that came with a cost. On arrival, he half expected a uniformed greeting party, De Rossi at the helm with a smug wisecrack, ready to take him in for questioning over Lotte.

He moved through the terminal slowly—his knee stiff and inflamed, swollen like a head of cabbage—absorbed by his own ruminations, revisiting history ever since he had first been handed that dossier. Whether his suspicions proved fact or fiction, there was still no trusting anyone. Not anymore. He needed answers, and knew where to begin, but feared walking the path. Feared where it might lead. The truth seemed as dreadful as the plague of uncertainty.

Outside, the rain was steady, the city shrouded in grey and Gustavs stood amongst a huddled crowd just inside the doors, working out where he had parked. He noted with relief that there were no idling Crown Vics, no strobing flashes of red.

A man materialized to his left—crisply dressed, bespectacled, with a boyish flush of colour to his cheeks. He held two coffees in his hands, and Gustavs recognized him immediately.

"Mr. Ziedins, welcome home," said Detective Horowitz.

Gustavs immediately looked past the young officer for his partner, then glanced around the vicinity. "Just you . . ."

"Just me."

Unconvinced, Gustavs scanned his surroundings once more. "Not an arrest, then."

"No."

"Good."

"I thought we—"

Gustavs stepped out into the rain, walking a few paces before he was halted by a snaking queue of passengers with dripping umbrellas. Horowitz followed, sidling up beside him, shoulders hunched.

"If we thought you had anything to do with Ms. Lazdina's death"—he raised his voice over the clatter of rainfall on the pavement—"I wouldn't be standing here with coffee."

Gustavs gave him a cool stare. "Where's your pit bull?"

"My car's just over there, come on and I'll tell you."

Gustavs didn't move, and Horowitz wrinkled his nose and grimaced, staring up into the shower. Raindrops beaded across his neatly pomaded hair.

"Detective De Rossi is currently on a leave of absence. Come, you can sit in the front. I just want to talk."

Horowitz turned on the engine, letting it idle, then switched off the jazz station that had fizzed to life. Gustavs removed his glasses to wipe the foggy lenses. "You wanted to talk," he said.

"Yes," Horowitz replied, smoothing his hair. "First of all, let me extend my sincerest condolences." He looked to his passenger who stared straight ahead, raising a coffee cup to his lips.

"Ms. Lazdina's passing was, well, it goes without saying, I suppose. More to the point, the events surrounding her death are currently being investigated—an open murder investigation, but you already knew that, of course . . ."

"Are you fishing? Because this coffee is terrible and we can do this with my lawyer." Gustavs noted his own callous tone. With everything that had transpired, the detective's presence, which at one time had caused considerable anxiety, had been reduced to a petty inconvenience.

Horowitz cleared his throat, his lips tightening into a thin, impatient line. "I'm not here about any of that. I'm here"—he shrugged his shoulders, as if conflicted—"well, I'm here to warn you."

"Why?"

"Don't you mean, 'about what'?"

"No."

"You know, maybe Angelo was right about you, why does it seem—"

Gustavs threw open the car door and Horowitz grabbed him by the sleeve.

"Alright, alright. Listen, I'm trying to help you. We've been onto something the past little while, and—will you shut the damn door, already?—I believe you have a right to know about it."

Gustavs waited a long moment before obliging.

Horowitz exhaled. "I'll get to the point, then."

"I wish you would."

"People these days seem to forget that we have a duty to serve *and* to protect. And I take my duties very seriously. My partner and

I, over the course of our investigation the past several months, have come to the conclusion that you're actually a fairly decent fellow, if an unlucky one, and just happen to be caught up in a hurricane of shit."

Gustavs took another sip of watery black coffee.

"My partner, regrettably, doesn't *completely* share this opinion. I thought he might have been coming around, but, as I said, he's currently on leave."

"Harassment or insubordination?"

Horowitz sighed. "There are some things you should know—things that, officially, I shouldn't tell you, but that doesn't always sit well with me. The *official* way. My integrity is not for sale, however, interpretations of duty can differ." Horowitz swiveled in his seat. "We do our best to get it right, but we're not perfect. Far from it. And I feel as though I have a personal obligation to let you know, man to man. We all have a code, principles we must live by, or we risk losing ourselves, would you agree?"

Gustavs conceded with a nod.

"This case has been sprawling for some time now, and we've been working closely, well, *I've* been working closely with our intelligence bureau. Angelo has his own views on sharing information," he added acerbically. "Regardless, the point is that, now that the case may have some real legs, a new team from Ottawa will likely be taking over any day now. The entire investigation will be pulled from our hands. CSIS will be stepping in."

Horowitz took a breath. "Charlotte Lazdina was killed, gunned down in her home by someone we believe to be a Soviet agent." The detective paused once more, seeking a reaction, but finding none. "I can't provide any more details—I don't *know* many more details, and this, of course, is what takes it out of my hands. Truth is, we were already following an older tip—somebody who might have infiltrated your community, or some such nonsense. It always sounded far fetched, it wasn't our usual portfolio—we're homicide, after all—so we didn't pay too much attention. At least, I didn't."

"But not your partner."

"That's right. Despite my appearance, Mr. Ziedins, I'm not as green as you, or my partner, may think. I was transferred and intentionally paired up with Angelo because, for one thing, he's pathologically incapable of maintaining a relationship of any sort, with any partner, but also, because he needed watching over. It was part of an assignment.

"There were rumblings, in certain circles—I'll spare you the service's politics—that Angelo wasn't exactly a straight shooter. The way he handled cases, even evidence. He rubbed a lot of people the wrong way. Big surprise, I know. Angelo is many things—a drinker, a vulgarian, twice divorced and not exactly in contention for any 'father of the year' accolades, either. He also happens to be natural-born police; he has an almost unparalleled instinct for this sort of work. There's only so much they can teach you about being a detective. He may be a bit rough around the edges, but I have to say, once that bloodhound catches a scent, there's no stopping him. And that's what you want. Someone who can get the job done. You see, it was Ms. Lazdina who tipped us off, initially . . ."

"She told me."

"Then you're aware that she and Angelo were romantically involved."

Gustavs looked up, and Horowitz nodded confirmation.

"Angelo . . . well, how else to put it, he was head over heels for the girl."

Gustavs considered this for a time, certain fragments of the picture shifting now, blurred peripheries coming into focus. The revelation was unexpected, but not surprising. De Rossi was not the first to fall under Lotte's spell, and her convictions knew no bounds.

"That's how he knew," Gustavs said, "why he always seemed to be a step ahead."

"At first, I figured he'd only be chasing his tail for a while. I waited for the butterflies to settle. He's my partner, but he's rather dysfunctional when it comes to just about anything other than police work."

"She fed him everything. All her suspicions."

"Which is what made it so confusing. She was incredibly charming, I don't have to tell you, but as I said—Angelo's a natural. Initially he may have tugged on a string or two simply as a courtesy, but he never would have disappeared so far down the rabbit hole without something to chase."

Gustavs tensed in his seat, felt a churning unease rising from deep within, as if his subconscious had raced ahead of him, hinting at what was to come. The same sickening doubt. It had been there in Rīga, in the quiet moments—in the silence of Vītols' office, in the stillness of his hotel room. And now it surfaced with a vengeance, a nebulous creation from the back of his mind, whispering secrets, whispering a name.

"He was onto something, Gustav. Someone. And when she was killed, he lost all sense of perspective. A bloodhound, I said before, well . . . it's as if he's snapped the leash. There's no need to get any further into it, but, Angelo has been suspended indefinitely, pending an internal investigation."

"He was onto someone . . ." *We think there's someone in the community, Gustav. An outsider.*

"Yes. He was." Horowitz's demeanour shifted with the gravity of the conversation. "Now, I want you to listen to what I have to say. What happened to Ms. Lazdina—"

"Lotte."

"What happened to Lotte . . . if we had acted sooner, if I had, paid closer attention, perhaps . . ." He trailed off, his posture shrinking in his seat. "We make mistakes, we're only human, but, we needed to act faster. We needed to act, period. And that's what I'm doing now. So I'll ask you again, please, just take a moment to listen."

Outside, the steady rain drummed the roof of the car. The windows had fogged with condensation, and the heavy scent of wet asphalt hung in the air. Gustavs sat still, his mind elsewhere. *We think it may have something to do with Imants . . . we think he may have been poisoned.*

"You've known her for some time now, only, by a different name."

"No . . ."

"Please Gustav, don't think, just listen. Listen without judgment, and then consider everything. Can you do that?"

He shook his head, pulse rising.

"I'm sorry. Truly, I am. I know this can't be easy to hear. Tatyana . . . her real name, is Mila Karimova."

"Stop talking."

"She changed her name, of course. We have records. I wouldn't speak a word of this if we weren't certain."

Gustavs stared out the window into the bleak grey, remaining still for a long time.

"I'm sorry, Gustav."

" . . . She defected."

"A perfectly reasonable explanation, wouldn't you say? A young Russian girl, an accent that couldn't be hidden?"

"She didn't want to be found." Gustavs looked to Horowitz, looked into his eyes, searching.

"Spies . . . usually don't."

Gustavs was shaking his head, hands trembling now. He put down the coffee and began wringing his hands together to quell the tremors. *A love interest, killed in Budapest, radicalizing her even further, if that were possible.*

"I know it's a lot, all at once."

"So where's your evidence?" Gustavs snapped, glaring at the detective. "Well? Or am I supposed to just take your word for it?" He battled his emotions, uncertain whether to resist or relent, the floor having suddenly crumbled and fallen out from under him. Had he always known? Only paranoid whispers, or something more?

"My evidence. My evidence is Lotte in our morgue, and the 9.27 millimetre bullet the coroner removed, fired at close range by a Makarov PM. Who do you think uses such a pistol, Gustav? It was an execution. A statement. My evidence is the beautiful Russian woman that appears seemingly from thin air, right around the time we first met at a funeral. A woman who came to this country under false pretenses, and wouldn't give you her real name. Tell me you knew her real name? Do you even know where she was the night Lotte was killed? Because we don't. I've even heard rumblings that they're going to be exhuming the remains of Imants Barons when the case is formally transferred. Do you have any idea what's involved in greenlighting something like that?" Horowitz tempered his voice, conscious once more of his tone. "Tell me this doesn't track with you. Tell me I'm off the mark."

Gustavs looked to the detective.

"I'm only homicide, and the implications here clearly go way above my paygrade, but if the suits from Ottawa are willing to go to these lengths, I can only imagine what they have on file, what they're putting together. Gustav, put your emotions aside for the moment, please. I'm no authority on espionage, but this is not how standard intelligence gathering works. People are *dying*, Gustav."

"So why tell me—you think I'd believe you, just like that? You think I'm in some kind of danger?"

"I think . . . I *wish*, I wish to God I could have warned Lotte when I had the chance."

Gustavs removed his glasses and rubbed his eyes.

"Just consider this, alright? An open mind is all I ask. Your first meeting with Karimova, do you remember?"

"Jesus Christ . . ."

"Think, Gustav."

He forced the breath from his lungs, shook his head. "No. It's impossible. It was me, I spoke to her first. It wasn't arranged."

"Are you sure?"

"I'm sure, goddammit. Alright?"

Suddenly, Gustavs felt a chill. A flush of dread spreading throughout his limbs. Not their first meeting—no, their first real conversation, after the recital. Kazakhstan. But not born there, her parents were in a camp, she had said. A camp, out in the east.

"Gustav?"

The dossier. What was her name? Pregnant, in the camp. In Solov . . . Solovskaya . . . *I met her only once. It was back in Kem that I first saw her—a transit point before they took us out to the islands . . .*

"Are you alright?"

"Solovetsky! Where is Solovetsky?" he demanded.

Horowitz was taken aback.

Gustavs' head whirred, separating fact from fiction, splicing together memory, insinuation. Born in the camps, with her parents? The woman—Valentīna! Had Vītols confirmed it? Already pregnant in Solovestky, or only rumours?

"No, it can't be her . . ." he mumbled.

Horowitz was saying something, but the sounds melded with the patter of rainfall. The husband. Christ, her husband. Never around, always out of town on business. The sudden separation, the divorce. *Agents working abroad, posing as brother and sister, husband and wife . . .*

Horowitz placed a hand on his shoulder, startling Gustavs momentarily. "Only you will know for certain. And Angelo, if you can get a hold of him. Gustav, tell me . . . do you know where she might be?"

His expression hardened. "You don't know?"

"I called in a favor before coming to see you. She's not home, not tonight, anyhow."

"This is—I don't believe this. If you're so sure, then why not arrest her?"

"There will likely be a warrant any day now. Nothing is for certain, Gustav. But as I said, I thought you should know. To serve and *protect*. We can't prove anything, but it's coming. And if we can get ahead of it, and that includes you, then all the better. Before she passed, Lotte told us—told Angelo, that she believed you would be considered a high priority target. For recruitment or otherwise, she didn't say."

"Lotte believed a lot of things," he scoffed.

"And like you, I also dismissed them at first. I won't make that mistake a second time. She said that, while you may deny it, many in your community consider you to be influential—or certainly have the potential to be. Which means this opinion is shared by all who have access to your community, those who may have infiltrated it, as she put it . . ."

Gustavs leant forward, holding his head in his hands.

"Who would be intimately familiar with your routine, your habits?"

"It's not her, it can't be . . ."

"Who would stand to gain?"

"Wait . . ."

"Who would—"

"Shut up—what day is it?"

The detective's brow twitched behind his steel-framed glasses.

"Day! What day is—"

"Thursday."

Gustavs became very still. Of course they couldn't find her. Tatyana wasn't home. She was at *his* home. With Omīte.

He threw open the car door, the downpour battering the pavement. A car honked as it passed, the driver gesturing angrily in the window.

"Where are you going?" shouted Horowitz. "Do you know where she is?"

"Where's De Rossi?" Gustavs shouted back, already outside.

The detective fished around in his pocket and held out a card. "He'll answer the second number, just keep calling. See if you can put your differences aside and put your heads together."

"Where is he?"

Horowitz shook his head, unable to hear over the roar of a passing bus.

"De Rossi," Gustavs raised his voice, "where can I find him?"

"I don't know. Working another angle, last I spoke to him. We didn't see eye to eye on this."

"Angle? What angle?" The rain streamed down Gustavs' face, blurring his vision, the wet beginning to soak through his coat.

"I believe she's your secretary."

"What?" Gustavs cupped his ear.

"Your secretary. Renata. Renata Zielinski."

TWENTY-SEVEN

SHEETS OF RAIN SWEPT DOWN FROM THE NIGHT SKY, TREETOPS rattled and swayed in the heavy winds. Streams rose from the gullies and rivers flooded. The city was practically deserted, its inhabitants bundled away inside, waiting out the storm, while the roads, slick with rainfall reflected the yellow glow of streetlamps.

Gustavs fumbled at the steering wheel, spinning it like a windmill before reaffirming his grip, the old automobile whingeing as it swayed to one side, rounding a corner. Wipers lashed the windshield at pace, struggling to contend with the relentless downpour. He sped through a light—more red than amber—and the car hydroplaned for a brief instant across a stretch of puddle before the balding tires regained traction. For an instant, Gustavs' thoughts cleared, and as the hazy lights of the intersection faded in the rearview, he recalled that it was a stormy autumn night just like this one, that had taken his wife.

Nobody on the roads, and nearly home now, though no closer to making sense of any of it. All the names, the conspiracies, the people he thought he knew, and the faces that claimed otherwise. Somehow he found himself trusting the words of a dead journalist and a degenerate cop more than anyone, though trust was a generous term. Peering through the windshield, his mind spun a film reel, images flashing: the weathered dossier and Galina's correspondence. Omīte's warnings of intimate betrayal. Tatyana's comments—edited, cut, dissected for new meaning. The click-clacking of Renata's typewriter. The film reel played, spliced and rewound, over and again, Gustavs desperately piecing together the truth that lay somewhere amongst the cluttered scenes.

Renata. It was *her* brother-in-law who couldn't take Kasia to ballet that afternoon. She knew he would offer to help, was familiar enough with his schedule to know he had nothing further that day. She *made* the schedule. On the surface, a chance meeting with Tatyana, an innocent encounter. And yet, as the film unfolded, Renata appeared less as an actress in the scenes, and more the director, the catalyst behind everything. Not a chance meeting at all—orchestrated, planned, executed with precision. Had he ever met Renata's brother-in-law? A Christmas party, a dinner? Maybe. He couldn't recall. His subconscious sifted for a name, a face, but they eluded him.

Nonsense. Impossible. Anna had known Renata for years, the pair joined at the hip in reviving the academy. He wasn't certain how they'd first met, but those could hardly be considered reasonable grounds. Who could remember such things? One evening, over dinner, a new name on Anna's lips, as innocent as that. Gustavs was introduced soon thereafter. Renata *Zielinski*. Polish. A Polish surname, anyhow, though Gustavs had learned to place less faith in names, venturing ever further into this world of shadows.

There was a sudden flash of lightning, the wipers rising and falling in sync, before the crack and rumble of distant thunder. Gustavs could hear Vītols' voice, a distant echo: *"Heaven help those charged with relocation efforts, tasked with weeding out sympathizers, communists . . ."* The postwar camps in Germany had been overrun—exiles of all nationalities, of all loyalties, filtering through the rubble and chaos of a continent in disarray, licking fresh wounds. A surname meant nothing. Renata could have been anybody.

He understood them better now, the Liepiņš family—keeping Dāvids close by once they had uncovered his true colours. Gustavs had fled Rīga as fast as he was able, desperate to be free of it all— the duplicity, the surveillance. It wasn't only the suffocating yoke of the omnipotent state, but its minions that silently crept into the privates recesses of life, slithered into the beds of loved ones, waited in the darkness for you to stumble into their webbing. The more Gustavs seemed to understand this world, the more he came to accept that he was not free of it, even now, an ocean away.

He skirted a stop sign and turned up the street, nearly home, before squinting ahead at a stationary car askew on the road. It was difficult to tell through the dark haze; a black vehicle, its hood protruding into the lane, a parking effort gone awry. Or, not yet complete—the dome light still on. The street was vacant and still but for the steady drumming of the rain. There was no one in the driver's seat, at least not apparently, nor was there a soul anywhere nearby. Gustavs realized the vehicle was parked only a few car lengths down from his house.

Rolling to a stop by the curb, he struggled to make sense of the scene. From the angle, he could see the driver side door was slightly ajar, though shadow obscured something just beneath, an object left on the road. Gustavs leaned forward and peered out, through night and rain and wipers that splashed at speed. Impossible to discern anything. As he stared, the sky opened once more, and the downpour resumed with renewed conviction.

Gustavs turned off the ignition and braced himself before stepping out into the storm, drenched from head to toe in mere moments. Thoroughly soaked, he did not hurry, but made his way cautiously toward the house. A burst of lightning flickered in the sky, illuminating the earth just long enough to stop Gustavs in his tracks. With a clearer view of the automobile, beneath the driver's side door, once obscured by the darkness, was a pair of boots. He could make out the contours now, and realized there was a person slumped in the driver's seat, out of view, legs splayed out onto the asphalt. Gustavs edged closer, stepping through puddles to the black Crown Vic, a body sagging halfway out into the street. Black shoelaces swam in a puddle like drowned worms.

He opened the door, cursed under his breath. His glasses were more hindrance than help in the deluge, and he took them off, better to observe the man. De Rossi's eyes were closed, his torso recumbent across the seat and center console, but Gustavs' attention was drawn to the dark smears that marred his abdomen, the crimson that leached into his white button-down. The detective's hands were stained with blood all the way to his elbows, clearly having tried to stem the bleeding from his wounds.

Gustavs gave an involuntary shudder, the rain suddenly much colder, his breathing shallow and unsteady. The detective was dead, Gustavs had no illusions, though he couldn't quite comprehend his own certainty. Still, he leaned over the man, carefully pressing two fingers against cool, stubbled flesh, feeling for a pulse that wasn't there. He noted a revolver that lay by the brake pedal, likely having slipped from De Rossi's hand, though the gunshots were not self-inflicted. Another peculiar certainty. The driver's seat, the steering wheel, the interior was streaked with wet blotches of red. De Rossi had struggled to staunch the bleeding, panicked and alone. Who knew for how long?

Someone knew. Gustavs turned, the rain streaming down his

face, and looked toward the house, observing its blurry outline, noting its silence. Not a soul. He turned back to the car, replaced his glasses, and hesitated. Then he took a breath, crouched down, and reached for the revolver. He held the pistol gingerly, intimidated by its weight, the metal like ice in his uncertain fingertips. Turning it over, he fiddled with the weapon until his thumb found the release and the cylinder swung outward. No bullets. Completely empty.

No—not empty. Spent.

Gustavs cursed again. Gathering himself, he finally tucked the revolver into his coat pocket and started back across the street. He felt the familiar surge of adrenaline, his body tense with each step, hands clenched at his sides. Approaching the house, he could see the lights were mostly off, from inside only the glow of a single lampshade in the living room.

He stopped. Something in the driveway, a presence, by the side door. Gustavs held his breath. *An apparition? Seeing ghosts now . . .*

No. Nothing imagined here. A mound, a dark heap with distinct features. Limbs. Gustavs clawed his fingers through his hair, mouthing expletives while scanning his surroundings, pacing from a distance. No one around. No one crazy enough to be out in the storm. And now, two bodies. Two bodies within fifty yards of his home. Staring at the black mass, he realized that he was shivering, the icy rain soaking his very bones.

The mound didn't move. Gustavs reached into his pocket and pulled out the revolver, hands trembling from the adrenaline and the cold. Holding the firearm unsteadily, he approached the body—a man's body, dressed entirely in black, crippled on the ground in the shape of a broken crucifix. After a moment, Gustavs lowered the revolver, certain now of why it was empty. Several bullets had torn through the corpse—through the shoulder and thigh, evidenced by peaks of tattered fabric; a section of the man's jaw and earlobe had been blown clear off, leaving flaps of bloody flesh like molded plasticene. The man's eyes were open, staring into the sky as droplets fell onto a frozen, ponderous expression. Gustavs didn't recognize the face. A face with a prominent, sloping forehead descending to a thick, singular brow. His mouth hung agape, a look of faint curiosity, as if about to pose a question.

Gustavs limped up the steps to the back door and turned the knob carefully, a familiar groan as it opened. He resisted the sudden urge to call out for Omīte; she would have removed her hearing aids by now. He shut the door and waited, allowing his eyes to adjust, before stepping softly down the hall toward the kitchen. Holding the revolver before him, he paused briefly to glance into the sunroom, and again down the staircase to the basement, finding only darkness. The old parquet floor creaked beneath his feet with every step, no matter how carefully he tread. And as he rounded the corner, in the ambient light that shone from the living room, he saw her.

Even in the semi-darkness he recognized her figure immediately. Familiar, yet estranged. She sat at the kitchen table—hands folded neatly in her lap, thighs together, feet planted firmly on the floor. Pale brown eyes stared up at him without emotion, another riddle upon her face. She was both beautiful, and terrifying.

Gustavs lowered the revolver, struggling with his words. "I don't even know what to call you . . ."

Tatyana didn't reply. A look of conflict in her eyes.

"What have you done?"

"Gustav . . ." she began.

From the living room to his left, a figure materialized in the doorway. It emerged from the shadows like a specter, taking the form of a woman, haunting the room with its presence.

"Good evening, Gustav," said Dagnija, the Makarov in her hand pointed at his chest. "It's been a little while, hasn't it, dear? Now, be a good boy, put that thing away will you? On the table, if you please."

Gustavs didn't move, couldn't look away. Dagnija's blonde hair was tangled and matted from the storm, matching her sopping mink coat that dribbled rainwater on the floor—a dead animal, drowned in a creek. Thick blotches of mascara were smeared beneath her eyes, cold and calculating as they gazed at him, her head tilted unnervingly askew. No longer the Dagnija he had always known, but a ghoul, having just then clawed her way from the depths of a well and emerged, soaking wet, in his kitchen.

"Come now," Dagnija said, indicating the table with her chin.

Gustavs held the revolver by his side, empty, and in no position to bluff. He placed it carefully on the table.

"Dagnija . . ."

"Oh, such a look of surprise," she said, combing the hair back from her face. "Though I will admit, I'm not at my best . . ."

Gustavs looked to Tatyana, her eyes still pleading, the same helpless dread that he couldn't quite grasp a moment before. The context different now, the expression exact. What was there to say?

"Now will you look at these little lovebirds. You know, I never would have bet on you to fall for a Russian girl, Gustav. Well, aside from me, that is."

Gustavs looked back to her, standing in the center of the kitchen now, the Makarov still fixated on him.

"Oh come now, such a look. We both know I could always get your heart pumping with the slightest touch"—she moved toward him, grazing his arm with a chipped, red fingernail—"now, sit down."

Dagnija stepped to the side, and Gustavs kept his eyes on her, seating himself next to Tatyana who clasped his hand with relief.

"What is this Dagnija?" he said.

"This? Well, you should know by now, I would think. You've certainly been digging around long enough, haven't you?"

"You're right. I have been digging."

"And what have you found, my dear?"

"Enough . . . Galina."

Her lips formed a mirthless smile. "My, my, what a busy little bee you've become."

He shook his head. "I don't understand, you're . . . you've been part of our community—"

"Oh save it, Gustav, for god's sake. Your only saving grace was the fact that you at least kept your mouth shut most of the time. Insufferable, the lot of you. With those tedious folk songs and your bourgeois nationalism—this is about *revolution*, Gustav. About the wheels of justice that have been in motion for seventy years! We all have our role to play in restoring order to this world."

"Justice, like the two men outside? That's not justice, Dagnija, that's murder."

"Murder *is* justice, you child." Dagnija scoffed and began to pace. "And to think I believed you would serve a purpose. Such naïvety! Such a small, sheltered world view. Still"—her tone softened—"I suppose it could have worked . . . don't you think? I would have had you wrapped around my little finger."

"So you won't even deny it. Imants too? Your own husband."

"Imants had one foot in the grave for years," she snapped, her voice cold. "I only helped him along with the other. And that's what your kind will never understand, the sacrifices that need to be made for the cause. That sentimentality is nothing more than a distraction. He had outlived his purpose. Mostly a drunkard, by the end, a gin-soaked puppet that tired years ago."

"You used him for his position. All of his critics . . ."

"I'll give him what little credit he deserves, he didn't soften in his later years, as so many of you thought. Quite the opposite, in fact, with his policies. However, *behind every successful man*—you know how the saying goes. I've had his ear for a long time."

"Still, it was always you they wanted. And naturally, they were right. You would have been perfect. *We* would have been perfect. Not another decrepit old windbag, set in his ways, but a young man, full of youth and vigor. Tragically unattached, the lonely widower. Humble. Easy to mold. We would have made such a wonderful couple, you and I. We could have steered the direction of the LNAK for decades . . ."

Gustavs was grimacing, though it went unnoticed. Dagnija continued to pace.

"But so naïve, hah! What must a girl do to get your attention? I'll admit that Anna was a terrible inconvenience—you would mourn for a period, naturally. It did stall things for a time . . ."

Gustavs tensed though Tatyana held him fast, clutching his arm.

"And still, for years you were blind to my advances. Practically throwing myself at you, how many times? I thought perhaps if I slept with Tomass it might catch your attention, rekindle that old rivalry between friends." She sighed. "I got it half right, I suppose." She lowered the pistol and paused to stroke the ruby petals of an amaryllis, the first in a long row of potted plants at the edge of the sunroom.

"Though I suppose you already had your eyes on this frail little thing, hm?" She jerked the pistol upwards and Tatyana flinched, looking away.

"What are you thinking, Dagnija—look outside. Look at the trail of bodies now. You think you can just manipulate people whenever you—"

Dagnija laughed, a malicious tone in her voice. "But of course I do, dear Gustav! Of course I do. We've been doing it for *years*. Make no mistake, all your political campaigns, the Christmas donations, the pathetic editorials in the Toronto Star. Do you really think they have any bearing on what goes on in the real world? Do you not realize that we are everywhere, have always been *everywhere*.

"And yet, not all that glitters, I suppose . . . the blade cuts both ways and Moscow has also been infiltrated in recent years, but it is to be expected. Old wood rots, infestation is an inevitability. A natural cycle. The party requires another purge. A return to the days when there were men strong enough to make swift decisions. Great leaders, *strong* leaders. Now we pander to intellectuals such as Gorbachev and look, the Kremlin—riddled with disease and overrun by class traitors. Jews. Trotskyites conspiring and plotting like roaches beneath your feet."

Dagnija was swept up in the momentum of her own speech, and Gustavs' eyes darted around the vicinity, searching for an opportunity. The living room was nearest, though the pair of them would struggle to make it in time. Dagnija stood blocking the path to the sunroom, as well as the staircase down to the basement. She still held the pistol, and there was too much ground to cover. He needed a distraction.

" . . . Rootless cosmopolitans, the lot of them. We will deal with them as we did in the old days."

"So that's it then, mass murder. Do you hear yourself? You're deranged."

Dagnija wheeled. "Deranged? How could any of you understand? When you gnaw like termites at the foundation of our union." She shrugged, matter-of-factly. "For that is your role, of course. You know no better. A maggot does not question why it devours the rotten fruit. It was Marx himself that said socialism couldn't survive surrounded by capitalist enemies. The solution has always been a very simple one—to be rid of them." She turned to face Gustavs and Tatyana once more. "It is the natural way of things. The inevitability of our social order, my dears. And sometimes, inevitability just needs a little push."

Outside, lightning flared across the sky, a clap of thunder following a moment later.

"This community took you in as one of our own . . ."

"Oh spare me your nostalgia, Gustav. This is bigger than you and your dwindling little crowd of exiles. Your merry band of idealists." She scoffed once more, "Liberty and freedom to what end? As a guise to exploit those who would shed blood to build a greater future, a better tomorrow."

Gustavs wondered how much time they had left. Had no one heard the gunshots outside? Masked by the storm. The sands of the hourglass were running out.

"I suppose you get it from your father, then," he said. "At least you come by it honestly. Your insanity, that is."

Dagnija met his eyes.

"Pēterss, was it?"

Dagnija snapped her head back and laughed. "I *did* underestimate you, Gustav. Truly, I must admit I'm rather surprised by your resourcefulness. Mm, to a degree, anyhow. He was not my father. If you had been a little more clever you could have lived to correct your source on that one. Although"—she drummed her fingertips against her lips—"Lotte, wasn't it? Your source? Ah yes, of course it was. Well, not much point in correcting her now, is there? Our very own Šarlote Lazdiņa, now there was a spoiled little whore if I ever did meet one . . ."

Gustavs stirred in his seat and Dagnija's eyes widened at the invitation.

"Hit a nerve, have I? Yes, darling Lotte. Such a shame, she too could have proved quite useful. But as always, these deeply rooted ideals . . . just like the rest of you. She was wrong, of course, about my father. My mother was quite good friends with Jēkabs Pēterss before he was executed. As was my father. A true communist, he died far too soon."

"Shame."

Dagnija didn't bite. "Not to worry. Tell me, are you a fatalist, Gustav?"

"Dagnija, listen to me. Please, listen. There's a dead policeman outside, in the middle of the street. Another dead man in the driveway. Whatever your plan was . . . it won't work. The police are surely on their way already."

Her brows twitched upwards. "Well, I should certainly hope so. I'm counting on them. You see"—she pressed a palm to her chest—"I'm only a victim, like yourselves. Poor Vadim out there was only sent along because Moscow didn't think I had the stomach for what needed to be done. Patience is a virtue and old men seem to struggle with it. Vadim has been working with Tatyana here all along. Or, should I say—Mila. A pair of Russian spies, the defector and the assassin. Tragically, she managed to kill you before I was able to wrestle the gun away and finish her off myself. I shall have to play the role, mind"—she brushed her coat sleeve—"it will be a shame to put a hole in this beautiful fur. But, as I said, you have never understood the sacrifice that is needed. And after all is done, there will be no one left for the police to talk to, except me."

Thunder rumbled in the distance, the slightest tremor in the walls.

"And you really think anyone is going to believe that, with the number of bodies piling up around you?"

"But of course I do, Gustav. Why wouldn't I? I'm just a damsel in distress and they, as you well know, are only police. Though I do suppose the Italian one had his moments . . . and look where that got him."

Tatyana spat something in Russian and Dagnija stormed forward, swatting her across the face with the Makarov. Gustavs shouted but Dagnija towered over him, the barrel now pressed firmly against his forehead, the metal cold and hard.

"One for you as well, darling?" Dagnija shouted, her voice shrill.

Gustavs moved slowly, lifting his hands from his thighs. He cast a sideways glance to Tatyana, an inflamed red welt already forming beneath her eye, a thin thread of blood. She steeled herself and glared at their assailant.

Dagnija exhaled. "Sadly, that was rhetorical, my dear. As you surely know, this is the last station for you." She stepped back, out of reach. Somewhere in the night, the low drone of a police siren carried through the storm. "Ah, there we are," she said.

Gustavs sensed the rising tension, the clock ticking. If he lunged, he might miss. Then again, what other choice did he have?

"And Omīte?"

"Come now, Gustav. Do you take me for a monster?" With her thumb she pulled back the hammer, the steel grinding and snapping into place. "Your aunt will pass peacefully in her bed. I'll see to that. Not the worst way to go, at her age . . ."

Movement in the hall, behind Dagnija. Gustavs' eyes followed without thinking, an instinctive reaction. For a long and dreadful moment, he thought he had given it all away, Dagnija's expression shifting, tracking, suddenly aware.

The room erupted as Dagnija wailed and spun round, the pistol flaring as it fired a spastic round into the ceiling. In the next moment another gunshot rang out and Gustavs' world was blinding, his knee bursting into a viscous mess of cartilage and bone. He seized, grabbing Tatyana and pulling her to the floor as the searing pain overwhelmed his senses. Glancing upward, he spotted Omīte just as she lost her grip upon Dagnija, shaken free and floating like a feather to the floor, moaning as she landed.

Dagnija whirled and spasmed, wailing like a banshee, flower vases crashing to the floor as her arms swatted the air. As she stumbled to one side, Gustavs glimpsed the cracked, wooden handle of Omīte's paring knife, the old blade buried firmly into the wet fur. Dagnija cried out, arms frantically grasping behind her, thrashing in vain. Another deafening gunshot split the air, shattering the kitchen window; a damp gust of wind blowing in from the storm.

Gustavs tried to rise and crumpled in agony, while Tatyana dove toward Omīte, lying huddled on the floor. Tatyana grasped Omīte beneath her arms, pulling her to one side, while Gustavs gritted his teeth and heaved himself forward, eyes fixated on Dagnija. The wind abruptly changed direction, rainfall spraying in from the open window. Red lights flickered in the distance, accompanied by the crescendo of police sirens.

And then, amongst the chaos—silence, a halting intake of breath. Gustavs noted the strange look of horror, the banshee's eyes wild but suddenly frantic. She let out another panicked gasp. Her arms began to flutter, unsteady on her feet. She had flailed to the very edge of the parquetry, her heel having slipped beneath the top nose of the staircase.

The world moved in frames, in brief stills. Dagnija's torso pendulated in the air, her coat billowing open. Another gunshot shattered a light fixture above, though Gustavs hardly flinched this time. Her hand fumbled at the row of flower vases, grasping at anything, at everything, before at last she finally fell, swallowed up by the dark chasm that had opened beneath her. Her scream was distant, muffled by the wind as she plummeted down the staircase, her voice silenced by a sickening thud and the tinkling smash of glass.

Gustavs crawled, levering himself with his elbows, his knee trailing a smear of blood as he made for the landing. Tatyana cradled Omīte against the far wall. The silence from the basement was unnerving. He peered over the ledge, looking down uncertainly, peering into the darkness where shards of broken glass faintly glimmered. Dagnija lay motionless at the bottom of the stairs, her body buckled in a most unnatural position on the tiled floor. The knife remained, all but buried into the folds of mink fur, while rose petals and dahlias lay scattered about her twisted figure.

TWENTY-EIGHT

THE EARLY MORNING AIR WAS FRIGID, THOUGH THERE WAS HARDLY a breeze, which, given the nature of Canadian winters, was enough for most to count their blessings. A light dusting of snow lingered, picturesque, along barren tree branches and virgin pathways. In the distance, chimneys and smokestacks billowed thick whorls of smoke into the still air.

Gustavs treasured his morning walks, even with the cane, finding great comfort in the serenity of the waking day. He left when it was scarcely light, and relished winter's silent majesty as the sun rose, gleaming and golden. He did, however, still curse the rubber ferrule of his new walking staff—no match for the slick ice—and, after his first humbling defeat, leaving him with a ghastly periwinkle bruise on his left hip, promptly replaced it with a tip of serrated metal. It would take some getting used to, the irrevocable limp.

As he proceeded along his usual route, a path as familiar as his own reflection, he noted a fellow early-riser seated on a bench facing the frozen pond. A man with a coat, not unlike his own— long, beige, with a thick, fur collar—and wearing a Homburg hat, also beige, with a chestnut ribbon band. The man sat, gazing across the vast stretch of ice, a fellow naturalist taking in the sights and sounds of a crisp, gleaming dawn.

"Rather brisk today," said the man, as Gustavs passed.

"Yes," he replied, slowing, but never halting his stride. "It certainly is."

Gustavs continued on, content with the morning's exchange. Perhaps the man was new to the neighborhood, unaware of the decorum. *Only smiles and courteous nods of greeting at this hour, thank you.*

"Deceptive, a sunrise like this," said the man again, still facing the pond. "Beautiful, and yet . . . clear skies, you know, no cloud cover. Makes for a very cold day indeed."

The snow no longer crunched beneath Gustavs' feet. Silence in the icy air.

"But it's the wind. That's the real enemy. Relentless. *Omnipotent.*" He emphasized the last word, sounding out the letters, a faint, indiscernible accent. The man turned slightly, smiling at Gustavs. "People underestimate the value of a good, warm coat. It can make all the difference, you know. Especially on a day like today."

Gustavs observed the man, this amicable stranger who then turned back to the pond and folded his hands overtop of a briefcase in his lap. Gustavs waited. In the distance, high above a forest of skeletal tree branches, a hawk circled in the sky. Gustavs waited still, then glanced around the barren park, and eventually stepped off the path and approached the bench. The man did not acknowledge him, and simply continued to stare forward, across the frozen water.

"It's strange, you know—it occurs to me that people these days, they underestimate value, the *purpose* of a thing such as a coat. Fashion has all but replaced the practically of one's clothing, haven't you noticed? Naturally, one has to look presentable, who doesn't like to dress with a bit of panache? But, what good will such cheap . . . *polyester* do for you? You'll turn into an ice cream! One needs proper fur, wool, sheepskin." The man sighed, a fog of warm breath. "Perhaps I'm only getting old."

The man shifted his attention to Gustavs, looking up at him. The man had a plain sort of face, unremarkable, with kind, knowing eyes. "Mr. Ziediņš," he said, and touched the brim of his hat.

Gustavs sat down.

"Tell me, does he still have that silly little beard?"

For some reason, Gustavs was compelled to look around once more, finding nothing but snow and silence.

"I was with him the very night he decided to try it out. We counselled him against it, best as we could, but the man was adamant. A wispy little thing it was at the time, we were only young men back then—boys, in fact—fueled by beer and that infectious optimism of youth. Impervious! But, as fate would have it, that was the very night he met Skaidrīte. Hah! Can you believe it? We were stunned. Who was this young woman? She must have been mad!" The man smiled to himself. "How wrong we were. And after that night, well, of course, there was no reasoning with him. What argument could be made? The beard had worked, and that was that."

Gustavs nodded, not exactly reluctant, but patient, and the man sensed as much.

"We were in Kolyma together, Vītols and I. He befriended me, he was almost . . . unnaturally kind. Unnatural, for such a place. When you're in the camps you learn the value of so many simple things—a coat, first and foremost. We all did. I've always been rather slight but, at that age, skinny as a bulrush I was. But"—he raised a single finger in a gloved hand—"I had a good coat. I knew that much.

"Vītols had already been there for some time and took me under his wing. They would prey on you, you see, the newcomers—we were the most vulnerable. Sheep from cattle cars dropped into a den of wolves. I'll never forget, there was this one fellow, a Tatar, a big hulking bastard he was. I could swear he had me in his sights before I even stepped off the train. Many of them, waiting for men like me. It was a logging camp and that very first day, sure enough, out in the forest, he came for me. For the coat." The man looked to Gustavs. "Vītols caved his head in with a rock. Didn't kill him, mind, just left him, well—what Trotsky might refer to as, *reeducated*." A sly little grin at this irony.

"But it was the wind, as I said. Not the snow, nor the ice, but the *wind*. It would cut you straight through to the bone. Like a scythe through fresh wheat, freezing your very marrow. I couldn't feel my hands after a while, could hardly grip my axe. So Vītols gave me his gloves. Told me, 'When you harden yourself, you pass this along to the next man.' It wasn't the gloves, he meant. It was the humanity, I realized, after a while. We survived by keeping our humanity in that place."

He removed the black leather glove from his hand and wiggled his fingers, observing them. "I don't do what I do for him. One must believe. Believe in the cause. But there is no question, that I owe him a debt, even if he may see things from another perspective. Different streams may run together, after all. Side by side." He replaced his glove.

"And now, Mr. Ziediņš"—the man removed a small pocketknife from somewhere within his coat, laying it on the bench—"if you would be so kind."

Gustavs took a breath, still processing the sudden detour to his leisurely morning routine.

"I believe, the left side, just below the pocket seam," the man said, smiling cordially.

"It's all just a game to you, isn't it . . ." Gustavs said.

"A game?" The man looked at him, forcing a tragic smile. "A game. Do you wish me to recite some tired cliché about, what, chess pieces and sacrificial pawns?" He looked skywards, contemplative. "If life were so simple. No. No, a game is something you choose to play. But this"—he sighed—"I believe this little . . . *drama* of ours, it chooses you. You'll forgive my philosopher's inclination, it's always been my nature." He nodded, as if coming to terms with his own sentiment. "For better or worse, it chooses us."

Gustavs weighed this for a time, watching the hawk drift on the currents high above, arcing figure-eights in the sky.

"So . . . that's it, then."

"If you were hoping for a tidy conclusion to all of this, I'm sorry to disappoint you. There are no bows or ribbons. All your burning questions neatly placed in a box, bound with string. Conclusions are a luxury few of us are ever afforded."

The man looked off across the pond, and, after a while, Gustavs picked up the knife, and began to work the blade into the lining of his coat. It didn't take long, the material giving way, and he removed a thin square of fabric, handing it across. The man pocketed it immediately, and tugged the brim of his hat.

"What happens now?" Gustavs asked.

"Well, I suppose if we continue on with our analogy . . . intermission."

"I need to know that my family will be safe."

"No one can provide you with such a guarantee, Mr. Ziediņš."

"So what can you give me?"

The man folded his hands in his lap, and considered the question.

"The knowledge that you played your role admirably. It's not something to be taken lightly. And it is not something that I say often."

"They're going to exhume Imants. The police have nothing but questions for me these days. The same questions, asked by different badges every time. But they won't tell me anything."

"Ricin, is our guess."

"Ricin?"

"Yes. A type of poison made from castor beans—a preferred method of the *apparat*. You may recall the Bulgarian dissident Georgi Markov, assassinated in London. When was it now"—his eyes squinted—"in '78, I believe."

Gustavs nodded. "The umbrella, they . . . injected him."

"Yes. Administered in small enough doses it can take hours or days to appear, usually with quite innocuous symptoms. Nausea, vomiting, diarrhea. Symptoms which, if they continued for long enough, would prompt you to make an appointment with—"

"A doctor."

"Correct. And if not of your own accord, then certainly at the insistence of your wife. A skilled agent could easily convince a man he were truly ill, and, if so inclined, could increase the dosage over time. Internal hemorrhaging is quite common, as is hematemesis—in layman's terms, the vomiting of blood. Sadly, not uncommon with severe alcoholics. I doubt Galina had intended on causing such a fiasco at your soirée, but these things are hardly an exact science."

Gustavs sat quietly, gripping the handle of his cane. "And this doctor?"

The man pursed his downturned lips in regret. "Your guess would be as good as mine. Our drama is one of shadows and apparitions. More often than not, they fade away when thrust upon the stage." He leaned in slightly, "We are not so keen on the spotlight."

Up on high, the hawk tucked its wings and plummeted, sweeping down and snatching at something unseen in the tall brush of the woodlot, before arcing upwards and away into the sky.

"Well then," said the man, rising to his feet. Once more, he touched the brim of his hat, and this time added a slight bow. "Mr. Ziediņš."

The snow crunched beneath the weight of his footsteps, as he made back toward the path.

"What is it?" Gustavs called out.

The man stopped, turned.

"In the coat."

The man smiled. "You never opened it," he said, voice carrying in the still morning.

"I thought about it." Gustavs sighed to himself. "More nights than not. I came close, a couple of times, but . . ."

"And why didn't you?"

Slowly, he shook his head. "I don't know."

"It's not for everyone. All of this."

Gustavs nodded.

A breeze stirred the air, releasing a brief flurry of snowflakes that drifted down from the treetops.

"Names," the man said. "Only names."

It took Gustavs a moment. "Like Galina." Then, a rather uncomfortable thought. "There are others?"

The man said nothing, a vision of beige, considering his words.

"Perhaps. Perhaps not . . . only time will tell. But there are always names."

AUTHOR'S NOTE

WHILE THIS STORY IS A WORK OF FICTION, IT IS FIRMLY ROOTED IN the historical context of the period. During the 1970's in particular, a great deal of mistrust developed within the Eastern European diaspora, in large part as a response to the levels of surveillance, propaganda and psychological warfare employed by the Soviet security services. Expatriates increasingly traveled to their native countries, often bringing many essential commodities to assist relatives and friends, although at times such activity prompted speculation and rumors of "ulterior motives" for visiting the Eastern bloc. The LNAK, amongst other Baltic organizations, were very active during this period in facilitating and empowering independence movements, however the extent of secretive, underground factions and "covert" efforts to undermine Soviet hegemony have been embellished for the purposes of this novel.

By the late 1980's the Soviet Union was in rapid decline, with regional campaigns for self-determination increasingly gathering momentum. In April of 1988, the impact of workers' strikes in Poland reverberated throughout the USSR, further inspiring budding liberation movements such as the Latvian Popular Front (*Latvijas Tautas Fronte*) and the Latvian National Independence Movement (*Latvijas Nacionālās Neatkarības Kustība*).

August 23rd, 1989 marked the fiftieth anniversary of the Molotov-Ribbentrop Pact, a treaty between Moscow and Berlin that included a secret clause dividing Europe into "spheres of influence," and served as a prelude to the occupation of various sovereign nations. To condemn this infamous alliance, citizens of Estonia, Latvia and Lithuania joined hands and formed a human chain connecting Tallinn, Riga and Vilnius, a column that stretched over 373 miles across the breadth of the Baltic states, an event known thereafter as *The Baltic Way*. Sources estimate that up to two million citizens gathered to stand in solidarity against Soviet rule.

Further instances of Latvian, and indeed Baltic, resistance, largely took the form of peaceful demonstrations, notably in the singing of patriotic folk songs, which had in recent decades served as substitutes for outlawed national anthems. While in Czechoslovakia the nonviolent protests of November, 1989 were dubbed the *Velvet Revolution*, the Baltic States would soon become known for their choral hymns and rock ballads, during their own *Singing Revolution*.

On May 4th, 1990, taking advantage of increasingly liberal Soviet reforms, a newly elected Latvian parliament declared its independence from the USSR, condemning the protocols of the Molotov-Ribbentrop Pact, and the subsequent occupation of 1940. Such perceived dissent was vehemently opposed by hardline factions and, reluctant to accept the departure of various republics from the Union, Moscow attempted to restore the status quo by subversion, as well as by force. In January of 1991, barricades were erected throughout Riga as the capital braced for clashes between pro-Soviet elements and demonstrators, a two-week period of unrest which resulted in the deaths of several policemen and civilians.

By August, Moscow was experiencing its own domestic calls for reform, with an attempted coup further precipitating the dissolution of the empire. On August 21st, 1991, Latvia upheld the declarations of the previous May and, after 51 years of occupation, officially proclaimed its independence.

ACKNOWLEDGMENTS

A GREAT MANY THANKS TO EVERYONE WHO HAD A HAND IN inspiring this story and helping bring it to life. There are certain authors and historians whose research I poured over, as well as friends and acquaintances who simply answered a poignant question or two, but in the end, it all comes together to play a significant role.

A special thanks to the Toronto Latvian community. Looking back, I feel this story was almost an homage of sorts to our wonderful *sabiedrība*, and being raised in its midst undoubtedly shaped the person I am today.

Thank you to all my English teachers and Latvian school teachers, especially the ones who encouraged my writing despite my concerted effort to ignore any and all advice. Perhaps there's a measure of comfort in the fact that it only took a couple of decades for your words to start sinking in.

There were a number of people who were gracious enough with their time to have a chat with me and discuss all manner of topics, and to them I am especially thankful. In no particular order, sincere thanks to Inga and Ilmārs Latkovskis, Viesturs Zariņš, Andrew Līdums, Klāvs and Aija Zichmanis, Inese Dreifelde, Elena Kozlovsky, Chelsea Chamberlain, and Rita Laima.

Thank you to my grandparents, Zigrīda and Alfons, for far more than I'm able to articulate. Ceru, ka jums patiks mans mazais stāsts. Thank you to my parents, Dina and John, for always being my first readers, editors and critics. And thank you to my wife, Erica, for supporting me without question and encouraging me through all the long hours spent bringing my stories to life.

Thanks so much to all of you. Liels paldies jums visiem.

Matejs Kalns was raised in the Latvian community of Toronto, Canada. He holds degrees in History from the University of Ottawa, and Human Security & Peacebuilding from Royal Roads University. He has worked in the fields of education and human rights for over ten years.

www.matejskalns.com

CPSIA information can be obtained
at www.ICGtesting.com
Printed in the USA
LVHW041941240323
742498LV00002B/75